THE MELCHIZEDEK CONNECTION

Raymond E. Fowler

Illustrated by
Betty (Andreasson) Luca
and
Ray Doyle

Authors Choice Press

San Jose New York Lincoln Shanghai

The Melchizedek Connection

Authors Choice Press
an imprint of iUniverse.com, Inc.

For information address:
iUniverse.com, Inc.
5220 S 16th, Ste. 200
Lincoln, NE 68512
www.iuniverse.com

Originally published by Trinity Press/Book

Text illustrations by
Betty(Andreasson) Luca & Ray Royle

ISBN: 0-595-18356-5

Printed in the United States of America

Dedicated
to
Betty (Andreasson) Luca

Her reported UFO experience provided much food for thought as I developed certain speculative concepts contained within this book.

Table of Contents

Project Bluepaper's Secret Revealed

Harold looked over Don's shoulder and swallowed hard. A tingling chill crept slowly up his spine. An admixture of raw emotions welled up within him: fear, wonder, unbelief. Then a strange, almost mystical feeling engulfed his senses rendering him speechless. It brought to mind his first contact with death as a child. He wanted to look away but he couldn't. His eyes became riveted to the glass-capped sarcophagus.

What Did Harold Stanton See?
Why Was He Permanently Incarcerated At Phoenix Base 3?
What Was The Connection That Linked Him With Eternity?

The Answers Are Here

The Melchizedek Connection

Chapter One

Recall from Eternity

His fingers gripped the dew-soaked railing of the bridge like a vise. He hung precariously over the current-swept river far below. Already, dawn was breaking. Shimmers of pink-tinted light played over the eastern horizon.

"I must do it now!"

Intricate swirls and whirlpools formed by the incoming tide mesmerized and held him at bay. They spoke of life, vitality and memories of better times.

"I must let go. There's no other way!"

He had rehearsed this scene so many times. His arms ached. He never realized that he could have held on this long. Suddenly, the sound of running steps reverberated on the bridge. A voice pierced the quiet morning air.

"Hold on! Hold on! Everything is going to be all right, old man. Just hold on. For God's sake, don't let go."

Slowly his fingers loosened their hold one by one until they could hold his weight no longer. He felt himself falling into nothingness. Would death hurt? Would he see Helen again? Was there a heaven? Was there a hell? What had he done? It was too late.

Harold Stanton hit the frigid water feet first. Instinctively, he held his breath. His body plunged down,

down, down. For several seconds he felt the water's icy grip. His mouth opened to gulp air that wasn't there. Water rushed down his throat. His chest felt as if it would burst. Then, there was no water, no pain, just a floating sensation.

Harold's mind began a self-dialogue as he attempted to fathom what was happening.

"I feel so light, weightless. Oh! I'm falling through a dark tunnel, going round and round. What's that bright light up ahead? I, I —"

He gazed dreamily at the scenes flashing by him. They were episodes from his own life. Somehow, he found himself alternately approving and disapproving each incident as they paraded by in chronological sequence. Some he savoured. Others were shameful, frightening. Traumatic and vital experiences stood out like graphic markers along the way.

> His early days at the orphanage.
> His friend, Chubby.
> Mr. Cleary, the headmaster.
> The special tests.

"They say I'm a gifted child. What's that mean?"

> Chaplain Jamieson.

"Yes. He's the nice man who talked to me about God."

> His adoption by the Jamiesons.
> His new home.

A panorama of childhood adventures, misadventures, school days and church attendance swept by with astonishing speed and clarity.

> The teen years.
> His committment to God.
> College, Seminary, Dad's death.
> Postgraduate studies.

Yes, Harold Stanton: Professor of Biblical Studies. Again he felt that overwhelming and consuming desire to accommodate knowledge of ancient people and their

"I'm falling through a dark tunnel. . .what's that bright light up ahead?"

languages: Hebrew, Aramaic, Egyptian hieroglyphics, Babylonian cuneiform, Greek and, oh! The war.

His enlistment in the Navy.
The training in Cryptology.

Cryptology. It was fascinating. He found it more challenging than ancient languages.

His becoming an expert Cryptologist.
The end of the war.
A civilian job with Naval intelligence.
The new job with the National Security Agency.

Why had he become involved in such things? Why hadn't he returned to teaching and research in his academic field? Had he gone wrong at this point? Oh!

Mom's death.
Colonel Frank Henderson's party.
Meeting his daughter, Helen.

Helen. Yes, she was beautiful, so sweet and understanding. She had a brilliant knowledge of modern languages. NSA employed her as a special translator.

The courting days.
Marriage.
The Beta Project.
Late nights.
The breakthrough.
His promotion.

Harold Stanton. Director of the super-secret Beta Project. Beta. A device that amplified the telepathic abilities of gifted people.

Biomagnetic field discoveries.
Encrypted telepathic messages.
Family conflicts.

"I'm seeing less of Helen now. I must take more time off from the Project. I must, oh no!"

The telephone call.

"No, I can't bear to go through this again. I can't."

6

The telephone call.
The freak snow storm.

Helen. She wanted me to drive her to her father's house. It was his birthday. She was afraid to drive in that crazy weather.

"I can't, Helen. See him tomorrow night. I must conduct that briefing."

Yes. The briefing at Andrews Air Force Base. I was right in the midst of it when the message came.

Helen?
Car accident?
Dead?

"No! Please, God. No!"

Helen.
Burned beyond recognition.
Identification of belongings at morgue.

"Oh! The light's gone. A field up ahead. Who are those people? Why, it's Mom and Dad. That girl. Who's she? Oh, I'm being sucked back into the light."

Harold again found himself immersed in the brilliant glow and reliving the last few weeks of his life.

"What? I'm to be relieved as Director of Beta? Why? I'm perfectly capable. What? Yes, sir. Her death has been a terrible shock but I can carry on. It's my project. I was just perfecting the encrypted Beta links with our agent in Russia.

"Life is just not worth living. It will be easy. I'll just climb over the railing and hold on. I don't dare jump but I know I can't hang there very long. I'll have to let go. Can't hide from them though. They watch me all the time. Must establish a routine. Yes. Early walks through the park and over the bridge. Each morning I'll stop and look out over the river and then proceed along. They'll never suspect.

"Ah, here we are and no sign of them. I've made it over the railing. I must let go. I must let go.

"What's happening? I'm being sucked back. No, I don't want to go back. I want to stay. Where's Helen? Where am I?"

7

"Harold? Take it easy, fella. Listen. It's Dad. It's Colonel Henderson. Can you hear me?"

Harold's thoughts were confused. Where was he now? The bridge. The strange tunnel and that bright light. Such a wonderful feeling of freedom. Had it all been a dream? He forced his eyes open and snapped them shut. The light hurt. It wasn't the same light. That voice.

"Dad, is that you?"

"Yes, son. Don't try to move."

Harold squinted. Slowly the tall uniformed figure of his father-in-law came into focus. He glanced about the room. He seemed to be in a hospital.

"Colonel? Dad? How did I get here? I thought, ah, I mean that — "

"You thought you'd be dead by now? You jackass! Why on earth did you pull such a stunt?"

"I doubt that you'd understand, sir. It was because of Helen and the Project. I know it's been over a month since her death but I've been terribly down since. And you. You seemed so aloof after the accident. I thought you were blaming me for it. Heaven knows that I blame myself continually."

A puzzled look came over the Colonel's face.

"But, ah, there was a reason. Something's not right here, son."

The Colonel glanced warily at the nurse and hesitated.

"Look, we'll talk about all of this later."

"No, Dad, let me continue. Beta was all that I had left. It kept my mind off things. They, they took it away from me. When they did this, something inside of me just snapped. When those white-suited clods insisted that I was no longer mentally competent, it infuriated me at first. But, then I began to believe that they were right. I heard rumors that I'd be forced to go through deprogramming. All my years with Beta were to be wiped out. What possible good would I have been to anyone? I tell you. I just reached the point where it wasn't worth getting up in the morning anymore. I wanted to end it all. I thought that I had. What happened?"

"Well, you must have known the Agency was birddogging you. Two of our people saw you climb over the bridge railing. McDonough ran onto the bridge and tried to grab you but it was too late. Coleman actually rolled down that steep embankment to the riverside to get you in case you did jump. It's a wonder he didn't break his neck. When you fell, he was already in the water, waiting. They radioed for an ambulance. You were in pretty poor shape. No pulse. They brought you around with artificial respiration and got you to the hospital. The Doc said that even if you came out of the coma, there would probably be brain damage. You were actually dead for awhile."

"Coma?"

"Yes, coma. You've been out for almost three whole weeks. Thank God that the last few days' tests indicate no brain damage."

"Colonel Henderson? You'll have to leave now. Doctor Kaulbach told you that you only had a few minutes. We musn't overtire him."

Harold glanced over at the nurse. He hadn't noticed her sitting in the corner. Things in the room seemed alternately hazy and distinct. His mind felt so tired. He felt himself slipping away as his father-in-law whispered in his ear.

"Take it easy, boy. I've got if from the highest quarters that you're going to be involved with Beta again in a new way. It's so secret that not even I know about it yet. But, I was authorized to tell you that much to encourage you. Keep your chin up and be a good patient. I'll tell you more just as soon as I can visit again. Goodbye for now."

Harold felt Colonel Henderson's hand grasp his shoulder for a moment and let go before he drifted off into a sound sleep.

Chapter Two

Ultimatum

"Where am I? I thought that —"

"Calm down, Mr. Stanton. You're in good hands."

Harold looked up at a smiling elderly man dressed in a strange blue coverall.

"But where am I? This isn't the same room I was in yesterday. Have I been dreaming? Where's Colonel Henderson? Who are you?"

"Me? I'll get right to the point. "I'm General John Thurman, director of an agency so secret that very few people in the intelligence community know of its existence. I trust that the very fact that I'm here telling you this impresses upon you the importance of what I have to say to you."

"And just what is that, General? I'm afraid that I don't understand."

"Stanton, I assume that you're still interested in Project Beta?"

"Of course I am. Beta's my life work. But, I thought I was through. Those shrinks wrote me off the project. I'm confused."

"Mr. Stanton, Harold, listen carefully. I can tell you only now that your episode with our psychiatrists was a deliberately planned *cover* for your removal from Project Beta."

Harold went numb. What on earth was he hearing? The General broke the shocked silence.

"Do you hear me? The whole thing was staged. You were fully competent to direct the Beta Project."

"You, you," Harold stammered. "How could you people

possibly have done this to me! Why? I almost killed myself."

"Please, Harold. Calm down. You shouldn't get excited. I know all of this must anger you very much. However, let me assure you that our removing you from Beta was directly related to not just national security but international security. The whole thing will be explained to you in due time. Now, you asked me where you are? You're in the hospital wing at a place so secret that most of our permanent personnel don't even know where they are. What do you think of that, eh? I can only assure you that you'll be well cared for as long as you are here. Now then, I must leave. I won't be back until the doctor tells me that you're recuperated enough for a fuller briefing."

"But, my father-in-law, Colonel Henderson — will he be visiting today?"

"I'm afraid not. I'll tell you more about this at our next get-together. In the meantime, get plenty of rest and do exactly what our good doctor says. Don't try to leave this room. It will be just a waste of your energy. Good day, Mr. Stanton."

Harold sat up in bed watching the General disappear through the steel door which automatically slid up and down. He was dumbfounded. What agency did this firmspoken man represent? A General? What kind of uniform was that he had on? It looked like a light-blue, one-piece coverall trimmed with dark blue. A Number 1 was emblazoned on his chest and back. Who were these people?

Several days passed before Harold was allowed to get up and walk about the room. The doctor and nurses wore the same numbered blue uniforms. His questions about the hospital, the uniforms and General Thurman drew blank stares by some and smiles from others. Several nurses had been in. They brought him books and magazines. Taped television movies and stereo music were also available. But, the absence of windows and having no friends visit troubled him. His spirits were much lifted when he was allowed out into an adjoining enclosed courtyard. Sunlight filtered through a huge skylight affair made of a frosted glass-like material.

Harold lay back in the lawn chair and gazed up at the smooth steel walls that arched up to the skylight. He could feel fresh air being pumped in. The sunlight felt good. How he appreciated life after his close brush with death. He closed his eyes and again thought back over the events that had led him to this strange place. That strange experience. He'd actually watched his life flash by while drowning. And that bright light. Somehow it had spoken to him. He had been told that it was right for him to be alive. He still had a job to do here. It was weird. Had he actually heard the light tell him that?

"Oh. Who said that?"

Harold glanced up and squinted through the sunshine falling on his face. A figure stood at the door that led back into his room.

"I said, 'Good morning, Harold.' It's me. General Thurman. Please come back into your room. I want you to meet someone."

The General extended his hand in greeting and introduced him to a beautiful woman. She seemed middle-aged, had blond hair and the most striking light-blue eyes that he had ever seen. They seemed to peer right through him. It made him feel quite uneasy. She struck quite a figure in that blue jumpsuit. It was marked *MEDIC-5*.

"This is Myrna, Harold. She will be recording and observing our conversation together."

"Good morning, Harold. It is nice to meet you."

Her voice had a slight Scandinavian accent, he thought.

"Hello, Myrna. I guess it won't do me any good to ask you what this is all about either. No one answers my questions around here." Myrna just stared and nodded.

Harold stepped into the room and saw a strange looking chair on wheels with two young men standing beside it. They wore the same blue suits with *VIGIL-33* and *38*

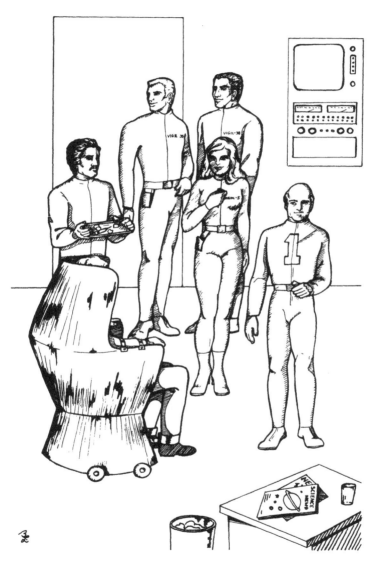

"This is Myrna, Harold."

13

emblazoned on them. The chair had restraint devices attached to it.

"Okay, Harold. Let's get right down to business. Of necessity, I must again be a man of very few words. If you want answers to why you are here, you must allow yourself to be restrained in that chair. Some of what you hear may anger you. I for one do not want to be the recipient of that anger. So, either sit down of your own accord and allow these gentlemen to temporarily restrain you, or they will be forced to help you."

Harold hesitated momentarily. He was still weak and tired. "Why fight?" he thought. "I must find out why I am here." He sat down and allowed the crew-cutted young men to secure him.

"That's just fine, Harold. You may leave now, gentlemen.

"Now, Harold. Our records show that you have no known living relatives. Is that correct?"

"Yes. I was orphaned at an early age. They told me that I was the son of an unwed mother who died in her teen years. I haven't been able to trace any relatives."

"All right. Now, you were adopted by the Reverend William and Mrs. Maude Jamieson who are both deceased. Do you maintain contact with any of their relatives?"

"No."

"You have no real close friends? You're basically a loner?"

"Well, I do have a few acquaintances on the Beta Project but we have had very little social life together."

"Who would miss you on the outside the most?"

"Why, my father-in-law. Colonel James Henderson. He's an Army liaison officer working with NSA."

"Yes, we know that, Harold. So, good, he's the only close contact you have on the outside?"

"Yes."

"Okay, let's change the subject. Harold, you are of the opinion that the Beta machine at the Maryland installation is unique, a one-of-the-kind instrument?"

"Why, yes. The components are biologically matched with gifted people who send and receive telepathic messages. Their mental and physical profiles are unique. We've only a handful of such people."

"Has it ever occurred to you that Beta could have applications other than espionage?"

"Why, yes. In the early days, some thought was given to developing its carrier wave to affect segments of the populace. This would have involved attempts to influence, perhaps even control the minds of government leaders. If that is what your secret project is about, count me out!"

"No, you won't be involved in anything like that. However, I must inform you that Beta has been duplicated, modified and vastly improved for several special usages. It's in use here and at other places for a purpose so secret, so disturbing, that the Project operates under the highest security classification in existence. Do you remember the strange interference that periodically jammed Beta's carrier wave during your initial experiments?"

"Yes. We never did find out its cause. We were ordered to filter it out."

"Ah, yes, but unknown to you, Harold, this was not entirely carried out. We found that one of your Beta staff, Donald Fields, had taken it upon himself to modify one of the Beta outputs to record and study this anomalous interference. He began producing his own graphs and records that related to its periodicity.

"So, we initiated an update check on Fields' background. Our investigators found a new outside interest which coincided with his covert use of Beta. I must say that this discovery shook us to the core. We had no choice but to remove him immediately from Project Beta."

"You what?" shouted Harold. "Beta can't function without Doctor Fields. Don is a brilliant theoretical physicist, a design engineer and a high-caliber hands-on technician. He's also one of the few psychics in the world who can consistently control his psi abilities with Beta.

Doctor Fields is one of the very few that understands psi on a scientific basis. How could you remove him from Beta? Why, he and Doctor Jacobs practically designed the Beta machine all by themselves."

"Stanton, you're reacting just as we suspected you would. We couldn't have you stand in our way of removing Fields. It was obvious that you'd object and protest all the way up NSA's chain-of-command. It also would have drawn attention to the real reason he was being removed. You had to be taken off the Project before we could deal with Fields. Thus, we arranged those psychiatric tests."

"Damn your tests!" Harold swallowed hard. It was one of those very rare occasions that he swore. This exception to deeply engrained principles exemplified the fury that rose up from within.

"General Thurman. Do you realize that your psychiatrists and their fool report contributed to my suicide attempt? Where's Don now? Who's directing Beta? How did you get Don to leave? He'd never leave voluntarily. Didn't Sam object?"

"Calm down, Harold. Goldberg was upset about your, ah, reported mental condition. He was sorry that Fields was being removed for an *alleged* vital assignment. But, he didn't object much about Fields. We both know the bad feelings that existed between them. That's one of the reasons you were selected to direct Beta."

"But, surely Don himself objected to his removal."

"Yes, that he did, most strenuously. But, no one knows that he did."

"Just what do you mean by that?"

"I mean that Don just disappeared off the face of the earth as far as friends and relatives are concerned. We were fortunate that he's no longer married. His former wife couldn't care less. His father was told that his son was on a confidential assignment for the time being."

"What do you mean, 'for the time being?' "

The General paused for a moment before answering.

"I'm afraid that because of what Fields discovered that 'for the time being' means for his lifetime. An acceptable cover story will be worked up to account for his, ah, decease."

"What have you done to Don? Where is he? Isn't it about time that you told me where I am?"

"Harold, Don is just fine. He's going to work with us."

"But, he had no choice. What kind of a prison is this? If you tried to keep me here, I'd scheme night and day to break out."

"We know you would. But, you'll soon see that escape from here is impossible."

"Are you trying to tell me that I'm already a member of your community here?"

The General did not answer. Harold turned to Myrna. Her blank face showed no emotion as she glanced first at him and then back to General Thurman. For one split second, Harold thought he saw pity reflected in her cold, blue emotionless eyes.

"Well? Am I? Why? What have I done to deserve this?"

General Thurman sat quietly gazing by Harold into space as if in deep thought. Harold's pleas finally jolted him back to reality.

"To answer your questions, Mr. Stanton: yes. You are confined here. You're in a hospital used by our Project. But, no, you are not yet a member of the Project. Whether or not you will or not will be up to you. Now, you ask what you've done to deserve this? Nothing. Nothing directly, that is.

"We need you, Stanton. That's why you're here. Regardless of our problem with Fields, *you* were already in the process of being removed from Beta. Of course, you weren't aware of this. And why? Simply because your country needs your services here. It involves not only national survival but international survival. As to a further explanation? I'm not authorized to tell you yet. This information must be given you through specially-prepared briefing sessions. Even then, I must warn you. Even basic knowledge associated with this Project has driven a few fine men into self-imposed catatonic states. The revelations and frightening implications were just too much for them. Several have even committed suicide."

"What men? Who were they? Do I know any of them?"

"Probably. Do you remember John Forrester, former Secretary of the Air Force? An excellent Secretary. He was an outstanding, clear-thinking man. He helped lay the groundwork for making our Air Force a separate service branch."

Harold sat dumbfounded. Yes, he had known Forrester. He had even thought about him when he was formulating his own suicide plans. He had last seen John at a special appropriations meeting with a few select Congressmen and Senators.

"Stanton!"

The General's voice jolted Harold from his thoughts.

"Stanton. I hate to be so damned simplistic with you but I have no choice. I have my orders. Concerning your stay here, you have several choices. You can agree to try out for our Project. We have intended that you do so for over two months now. Your experience with Beta as the finest cryptologist in the country, your psychic abilities and especially your secular educational training are desperately needed."

"My secular training? How could you possibly use that?"

The General ignored his question and continued.

"Or, you can become a member of our community here and live out your life peacefully. We have eligible and most willing females. Marriage or live-in situations are encouraged. But, sterilization is mandatory here. Then, there's the last option: deprogramming and a return to the outside. Very few volunteer for that. They don't want to take the 30% risk of permanent brain damage."

Harold again strained against the restraints of the chair but then relaxed in desperation.

"Look, General. I didn't ask to be rescued from

drowning. I didn't ask to be brought here. This is kidnapping. There are laws. My father-in-law is a full Colonel. He's well known and respected throughout NSA. He's probably turning the intelligence community inside out looking for me."

"I'm afraid he's not, Harold. We arranged for him to be called away just after his visit to you in the hospital outside. He's supposedly investigating a vital matter in the Far East. Of course, he was sent the customary telegram."

"What telegram? What are you talking about?"

The General nodded at Myrna.

"Myrna? The clipping from the *Washington Post* please."

The tall blonde woman reached into the pouch of her memo pad. She removed a newsclip and started to pass it to the General.

"No, show it to Harold."

Harold's hands trembled with fear and anger as he read his own *obituary.*

"Now, Harold, you have three days to think our proposition over. Then you must come to a firm decision. Look at it this way. If we hadn't intervened, you'd really be dead. Before we saved you, you admit that you had nothing to live for because of your wife's accident and your removal from Beta. Harold, we can't bring back the dead but we can give you a new lease on life. We're offering you a position involving a vital use of Beta. If you accept, I guarantee you that your involvement and responsibility will be far greater than that which you had on the outside. You'll be amazed at what Beta is being used for. Believe me. Your future with us will go down in this planet's history. You'll have made a significant contribution to the preservation of mankind. That is, of course, if mankind has a future."

The General paused. There was a pained, far-away look in his eyes. He continued.

"This planet may not have a future for our kind, Stanton. But, we here on the Project are working to assure that it will."

"What do you mean, General, by 'our planet'?" Have you discovered a new deadly disease or something?"

"Yes, Harold, in a way we have. It is very much like an unknown, terrible disease. That's a good analogy. But, I can say no more at this time. Myrna? Summon our helpers."

Harold looked over at Myrna. She had taken a slim box from a holster attached to her belt. She pressed two buttons and replaced it in its sheath. The door opened. The two young men entered with the Doctor. The Doctor walked briskly up to him, pushed back his sleeve and jabbed him with a needle. Harold became dizzy and sleepy. He barely felt the chair clamps being removed. Strong arms lifted him from the chair and laid him upon the bed. Then, he knew nothing.

Chapter Three

Decision

Harold woke up with a start. He lay on the bed bathed in a cold sweat. His stomach churned violently. He glanced up at the digitized clock-calendar. It glowed faintly: 0725 15 APR SUN.

"Why, I must have slept through dinner time," he muttered.

"What happened? The General. Myrna. It's all coming back. I remember. Three days to make up my mind. What could possibly be behind all of this? And Don, what did he discover? What was so important about that interference on the Beta band?"

Almost subconsciously, Harold reached behind himself and touched the back of his neck. It felt sore. Why was it bandaged?"

"Hum-m-m. Must have got cut last night when they carried me to bed. I must have scuffled with them," he thought. His spine felt stiff. Perhaps he had slept in the wrong position. Drowsiness overcame him. Curling up into the fetal position, he closed his eyes.

"Time for breakfast!"

Harold sat up in bed with a start. A nurse stood beside him.

"Good morning, sir. I have your breakfast. Better get up and eat. You're having company at 0900. Here, let me put a fresh bandaid on your neck."

Harold felt much better after getting something in his stomach. The injection must have caused the temporary nausea and sickness. After eating, he washed and shaved. He strained to get a look at the cut on his neck in the mirror. He peeled back the bandaid. The small cut looked almost like a surgical incision. In any event, he dressed in a clean white coverall and sat down to wait for the announced company.

"What shall I do about their offer?" he pondered. "They'll be here in a few minutes. Whatever is going on here must be of the highest importance. What would I have to lose by going along with it? After all, I really would be dead if it weren't for them. Beta *is* my life work and they say it's being used here. The alternatives? Inactivity or deprogramming. No thank you. When it comes right down to brass buttons, what choice do I really have? This whole thing seems so intriguing and exciting that —"

The door whooshed open. Myrna stepped into the room. She was flanked by the same two men that had fastened him to the chair.

"Good morning, Mr. Stanton, ah, Harold. Please tell me that I won't need these helpers and I'll ask them to leave."

Harold's face flushed as he stared angrily at the two men.

"Well? What do you say? Will you behave yourself?"

Harold sighed. "Okay, I'll be a good lad, Myrna. Tell your bodyguards that they can go home or wherever. I've given up fighting you people."

"That's smart thinking, Harold. You don't mind my calling you by your first name, do you?"

"No, of course not."

Harold stared at the beautiful woman standing before him. He could not help feeling physically attracted to her. Myrna looked amused.

"A penny for your thoughts, Harold?"

Harold was embarrassed at the question.

"Well, Harold, never mind. You've been through a lot the past several weeks. However, Doc tells us that you're in pretty good condition. By that sly look in your eyes, I'd say that you're well on the way to recuperation. Perhaps I had better call back my body guards?"

Harold blushed as Myrna continued to talk.

"Doc says that you should start getting more exercise. Perhaps we can arrange some walks about the hospital."

"That would be great, Myrna. That little courtyard isn't conducive to much exercise. And, whatever your Doc pumped into my arm last night doesn't make me feel like I'm in such 'good condition' , as he puts it."

"We're sorry that happened, Harold. We felt that Number 1's words were quite upsetting to you, ah, General Thurman, that is. We didn't want physical resistance. Your well-being is vital to us. The shot was just to put you to sleep for awhile. The nausea will wear off soon."

"How did I get this cut?" Harold pointed to the bandaged incision on the back of his neck. "It feels awfully sore."

"Oh, that? It happened when my two escorts put you to bed. We thought you were out cold. But you woke up and put up quite a struggle. You probably don't remember. One of them nicked you with the sharp edge of his ring. However, that's all over. Let's get down to the business at hand. Your cut will heal in no time at all.

"Now, Harold, I've been instructed to meet with you like this for the next three days to discuss General Thurman's offer. I'm afraid I'm not able to elaborate further except to say that you are assigned to me. Here's a typed transcript for you to read. It contains everything that was said here yesterday. I'll bring it again to you at 0900 tomorrow and again at the same time on the following day. Each day you'll be asked to read it carefully. It will be your final opportunity to seriously consider the choices that you've got in the matter."

"Ha, some decision! How did you get an exact transcript of our conversation?"

"Perhaps the walls have ears, Harold. It's for you to decide about the matter of choices. I too faced a similar decision over ten years ago. I chose to join the Project. I've no regrets. Being a part of all of this has given me great satisfaction. Believe me, Harold, when I say this to you. This Project involves something big. What we are involved in concerns something that will affect mankind even more than the coming of your Jesus Christ."

Harold looked startled. "Whatever do you mean by that?"

"Oh, I know about your Christian beliefs and your education. I've studied you very carefully. Let me demonstrate."

Harold listened incredulously as Myrna began ticking off incidents about his life that went back as far as his days at the orphanage.

"You were a child prodigy: a high school graduate at 13 and a Ph.D. at 18. Your initial goal was to become an Episcopalian Priest. Instead, you decided upon teaching at the Seminary level. You were well on the way to becoming one of the most brilliant and youngest Biblical scholars in the world. Your aptitude for ancient languages and knowledge of ancient cultures was phenomenal. Aptitude tests indicated that you had a paranormal ability of nearly total recall.

"I also know that you have kept up with your studies in parallel with the Beta Project. This caused us some concern. We wondered if you were privately thinking of leaving NSA for your first career. Shall I continue or am I boring you?"

"No, do continue, Myrna. Recently I found it most helpful to review my past. I had the weirdest experience when I, but, never mind. Do continue."

"Yes. Then World War Two started. You, a professor at a Seminary, were automatically exempt from military status. Yet, just a year after Pearl Harbor, you joined the Navy. You served in Naval Intelligence until 1945. During that time you were sent to Crypto school. Your phenomenal aptitude for deciphering ancient languages and your recall abilities were expeditiously applied in the area of cryptology.

"As you know, the Navy wanted you to stay on after the

War. But, you wanted to get back into teaching and research. However, Doctors Fields and Jacobs closeted you. They told you about their plans for the Beta Project. It intrigued you so much that you could not resist continuing your work with the Navy as a civilian consultant.

"Tests with Beta revealed that your ability for recall was what we might call a truly psychic gift. Later when telepathic experiments between you and Fields proved highly successful, you were hooked. You became involved full-time on the Beta Project. NSA took Beta over. You and the team went with it."

"What don't you know about me?" Harold remarked sarcastically.

"I know just about everything, Harold. Your personal habits are almost Puritanical. Even your vocabulary. You use none of the four-letter words most of us use today. What do you call them? Oh yes, *swear* words. Your substitutions like 'Great Guns' and 'For Goodness Sake' are most amusing to me. They're quaint, almost anachronistic, in this day and age. They reflect a strict religious upbringing of another age.

"I also discovered that you had no obvious vices. You're a non-smoker and a tee-totaler. You avoid other women socially. You're certainly 'Mr. Clean' , Harold.

"At first, I wondered what made you tick. I puzzled over how religion could have such a hold on such an intellectually brilliant man like you. I mean no offense by that statement. It just was confusing to me. But, I must say that when you began to look a bit hungrily at me a few minutes ago, I breathed an inward sigh of relief. It was comforting to see that you have some normal human traits!"

"I, I'm sorry about that", Harold stammered. "You see, it's been a long time, I —"

Myrna laughed out loud. "You don't have to apologize to me about that, Harold. I'm flattered. But, enough of this nonsense. I can see that talking about such things makes you uncomfortable. Let me continue my resume′ of Harold

Stanton.

"You were quite a loner until you met Colonel Henderson's daughter. Her fantastic grasp of modern languages and cultures complemented your own background. She soon became your constant companion. You got married and then, the accident.

"Well, I won't go any further. Suffice it to say that I do know you pretty well. The only thing that puzzled us during our investigation was that try as we may, we never were able to discover who your parents were. Now, I wanted you to know all of this because, if you do decide to join us, you may need someone to turn to who knows you thoroughly."

"Thanks so much, Myrna. Let me scrutinize this document. I think that I remember eveything that your General Thurman or Number 1 said. I must admit that everything that's happened has left me quite bewildered though. It would be best for me to read it over carefully."

Harold settled back in his chair and became totally engrossed in the transcript. Finally, he finished. He glanced through its pages once more quickly and handed it back to Myrna.

"Well, I've read and re-read this thing, Myrna. There's not that much to it. The unanswered questions raised are more intriguing to me than anything else. I had no idea that others were using Beta equipment. I must confess. I'm really interested in becoming involved in your Project. I feel so relieved to be alive and well. I had such a close escape with death."

Myrna reached over and lay her hand on Harold's shoulder.

"Harold. All of us have unhealthy tendencies including even thoughts of suicide. We must be sure now and during your briefing that you can emotionally survive what lies ahead for you. Because of your brilliant mind and experience with Beta, we are daring to take a chance with you. I want to assure you that I personally believe you're going to make it through training. You and I would not be together right now if I didn't believe this. I'm very glad that you've decided to join us.

"Your briefing will probably begin in several weeks. Ordinarily, we'd want you on board sooner. But, certain circumstances have overruled us in this matter. Well, I'm finished here. General Thurman will be pleased. He'll come to release you from the hospital tomorrow at 0900. Be ready. I must go now."

As Myrna started toward the door, she hesitated for a moment and then, head bowed, spoke.

"Harold. I may never talk to you again. I, I just want you to know that I'm sorry for all that we've put you through."

Myrna's usually stern unblinking eyes met Harold's eyes. For one brief moment he thought he glimpsed tears.

"Please don't hate me, Harold", she said as she edged quickly out the door.

Harold retired early that night. He was anxious to begin his training. It would be so good to get out of that room and talk with other people than that close-mouthed hospital staff. He wished that he could see more of Myrna.

Chapter Four

The Activation of Beta-27

At 0900 sharp, Harold's door slipped upward. General Thurman and those same two young men entered.

"Good morning, Harold."

"Good morning, General, or should I say 'Sir' or 'Number One' now?"

"No, that's not necessary. I prefer first names. You may call me John if you wish."

"Ah, John, what are these fellows doing here again?"

"Them? Not to worry. They're just going to accompany us to the Briefing Room for your formal activation. I trust we'll not need them after that."

"What's the Briefing Room?"

"You'll soon see. Someone there will assign you an identification number, your wardrobe and tell you what Sector you may stay in until further notice."

"Sector?"

"Come on, let's go. You'll find out about Sectors soon enough."

The door was marked *Briefing Room*. It slid upwards and they entered. It was a small room. Six of those padded restraining chairs faced what appeared to be a huge TV screen. Harold was asked to sit down in one of the chairs. He hesistated and glanced warily at the General.

"Just once more, Harold. I assure you that this will be the last time provided you behave yourself."

Reluctantly, Harold sat down. The two men secured him. General Thurman stepped back and spoke to him.

"Pay attention, Harold Stanton. Learn well the first time," he said. Even as he spoke, the lights in the room grew dim. The television screen flickered to life.

An aerial view of a desert area flanked by mountains played upon the screen. The scene was a picture of pure desolation except for what looked like a small radar installation.

"Why am I being shown this?" Harold again thought but this time out loud. As if on cue, the voice of a narrator made a startling announcement.

This is Phoenix Base Three, the home of Project Bluepaper. It is the most important installation existing in the free world today.

Simultaneously, a multi-colored, coded transparent overview appeared over a still view of the desert and bleak surrounding mountains.

Harold gasped at what he saw. He found it all very hard to take in. A vast complex of underground structures interconnected by tunnels lay under the desert and extended under the nearest mountain. He watched fascinated as colored lines graphically broke up the subterranean installation into numbered sectors.

There were laboratories, living quarters, a warehouse, a concealed heliport, administrative areas and the hospital. They all connected with a central structure labeled *Phoenix Central Control.* It was the nerve center of the entire installation. The hub-like structure contained a highly advanced communications and data processing system.

The narrator went on to explain that Phoenix Base Three was especially designed to escape detection by satellite photos. Civilian and most military aircraft were forbidden to fly near this area which was part of a highly restricted Air Force Gunnery Range. The Air Force Strike teams that guarded the perimeter of the Range were not even allowed to see the alleged secret radar station that they were supposedly guarding.

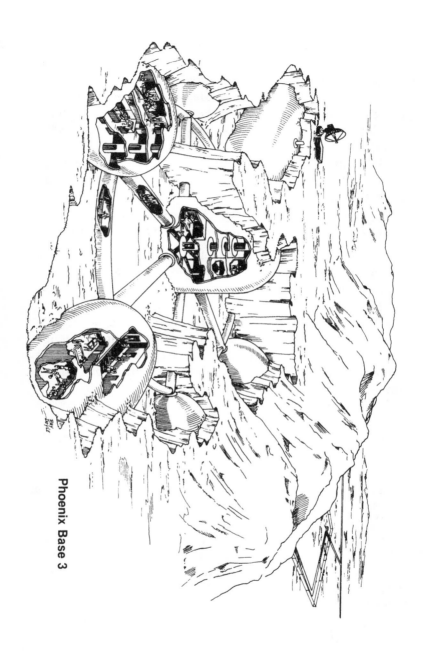

Phoenix Base 3

Then, the movie displayed Sector 4. The hospital. Harold sat intrigued as the hospital was graphically segmented and portrayed in its constituent parts. The camera homed in on a familiar room. It was the *Briefing Room*. There were the six padded chairs, the horseshoe-shaped platform and the TV screen. There was someone sitting on the farthest chair. There was no narration. The scene became fixed.

Harold waited a bit and then turned to ask the General what was going on. General Thurman was no longer in the room! He simultaneously realized that the figure in the chair on the television screen was mimicking every move he made. It suddenly struck him that he was watching a live television image of himself! It was then that a voice addressed him.

"Harold Stanton? By now perhaps you realize that you are watching yourself on our rather large TV set. I could say —'Smile. You're on Candid Camera'—but today I have little time for my usual levity."

Harold grinned. It was good to see that someone acted human in this antiseptic-like place.

"Now, Harold. This morning you are being officially activated for service on Project Bluepaper. Your Alpha Numeric Identification is BETA-27."

Then a bright light flashed on behind him. Harold swung around to discover its source and was nearly blinded by it. He heard a humming sound emanating from somewhere above. He glanced upwards. A TV camera descended on a boom behind him. Then the voice sounded once again.

"Never mind that, Mr. Stanton. Please pay attention to the TV show. I mean, after all, you are the star."

Harold swung around and looked at the screen. He saw the back of his head being panned by the TV camera behind him. He watched as it moved closer until his bandaged neck was centered in its field of view. Again, the almost fatherly-like voice continued.

"Mr. Stanton. You were told that this bandage covers an accidental cut. I regret to inform you that this is not true."

Harold instinctively tried to raise his hand to probe the

strange cut. But, both hands and feet were securely clamped to the padded chair.

"Please watch and listen very carefully. You will now be shown what really happened, and, more importantly, why it was done."

A small object held by tweezers suddenly appeared on the screen. It looked somewhat like a miniature hat pin except that the pin was a tiny hair-like wisp of platinum wire. Harold watched captivated as a large cut-away enlarged drawing of the device appeared on the screen. The head of the pin contained a minute chip of electronic circuits.

"Harold. This multi-purpose activation device has been implanted in your neck. It may be activated by any of a number of micro-wave sources located with Base Three. These sources are regulated and controlled by our central computer. Its program has a redundancy factor which provides nearly a 100% fail-safe reliability. Periodically, at random, the computer will query your whereabouts. Your position will automatically be checked against the constraints of your allowable location coordinates. If you are where you are supposed to be, nothing will happen. However, if by either accident or design you should be outside your assigned area, you will be severely, perhaps irreparably, punished. A signal will be transmitted to your, er, ah, *companion*. It in turn will send electrical impulses to that marvelous trunkline of nerves we call the spinal chord. Now watch the Rhesus monkey."

The enlargement of the *companion* faded from the screen. In its place there appeared a monkey sitting in a glassed-in cage. Suddenly it shrieked in pain. It jumped straight up into the air and fell back in a crumpled heap on the cage's floor. Its little body twitched a few times and then stiffened.

The picture faded. Harold faced an empty flickering screen. He strained at the fetters which held him fast to the chair.

"You are all beasts!" he yelled.

"Harold, Harold. I must say that you are over-reacting.

32

What would you have us do to deserters? On the Outside, they are shot. And, you never had any compunctions about the restricted areas at NSA. There were some areas that a trespasser might be shot on sight. Now, let me add that most of the time, activation of one's companion involves either *warning* or *stun* signal strengths. I showed you what could happen if a *destroy* strength signal energized one's *companion*. We feel that the Rhesus monkey example is a good object lesson.

"You are to be assigned to the Sector 3 Recreation Area for a period of three weeks. Myrna asked for at least a month but we cannot comply. You are vitally needed.

"I'm ready now," Harold quipped. "I feel just fine. I'd like to be briefed and begin at once. Why do I need recreation for three weeks? What kind of recreation are you talking about?"

"You'll find out soon enough. Now, let me explain further about the security function of your *companion*. Then, Number 1 will take you to your new quarters. Listen and note what I have to say. Your very life may depend upon it.

"You will have noted that all Sectors are interconnected by tunnels. The tunnels have escalator walkways and sliding steel doors.

"Now. The implanted device will allow you to approach and open any door within your Sector automatically. Once in your Sector, however, you cannot leave unless your *companion* is programmed for other Sector visitation. Without this, the doors will not open. If, by some other method you should penetrate an outer door, your *companion* would instantly be energized. The computer or, if there was time, an operator, would decide which signal strength was appropriate. I might also add that our security guards have the capability to locally energize your companion with a signal of *stun* strength.

"Now I trust that you'll behave yourself in Sector 3. The basic rules are prominently posted. You'll also be given a Sector 3 Procedures Manual to study. But, somehow I think that you'll be too occupied to think about misbehavior for a while.

"Good day and good luck, Harold Stanton!"

Chapter Five

Resurrection at Sector 3

Harold stared impassively at the empty screen. Slowly the dimly-lit room brightened. An arm rested upon his shoulder startling him for a moment. It was General Thurman.

"Let's get you out of here and over to your new quarters. Hopefully, this is the last time you'll need our two friends here."

Harold twisted about in the chair and looked behind him. There were the two security guards. One carried two blue suitcases.

The elevator descended one floor and they disembarked into a large basement-like area. They crossed the room and entered a door designated *Sector 3/Secondary*. Through this door they entered the rim-like tunnel which arched its way from Sector to Sector like the hollow rim of a buried wheel.

Another door loomed ahead of them. It was designated *Sector 3/Primary*. It opened automatically and they stepped off the moving walkway into another basement-like area. Harold glanced behind him. The two men were no longer following them.

"We left them back in Sector 4, Harold." The General smiled at Harold's puzzlement. "They aren't needed here."

The General pointed to still another door. It was marked 3C.

"Okay, BETA-27, let's play Ali Baba. Just walk up to it."

Harold walked to the door and it flew up automatically.

"Go right in, Harold. I'm right behind you. Now, step into the red circle painted on the floor and press button number 3."

Harold pressed the button. The door flashed shut. They were borne upward so fast that it caused a dizzy sensation. Then, another door opened to the right revealing another elevator-like compartment.

"Just go in. Don't worry, Harold, I know where we are and where we're going."

A row of four buttons numbered 1 through 4 were prominently displayed on the opposite wall.

"All of these four rooms are yours. We have an appointment with someone in your livingroom. That's button number 3."

"My livingroom?"

"Yes. I trust that you'll like the furniture. Press button 3, please."

Harold depressed the button and was momentarily shocked when the elevator unexpectedly moved sideways and stopped.

"This thing must be on tracks", he thought. Another door opened and the General stepped out. Harold approached the doorway and then stopped. A familiar scene halted him dead in his tracks.

"Come on in, Harold. Don't be shy", quipped the General.

Harold continued to gaze in utter amazement at the sight that met his eyes. There was his antique desk with the pulldown cover. There was his bookcase and the spinet piano. It still had the doily that Helen made spread over its top. Their wedding picture. He glanced away. Why did they put that out? He had left it in his desk drawer. He sniffed the air. A familiar scent filled the air.

"This was Myrna's idea". The General interrupted his thoughts. "She wanted you to feel right at home. Didn't our people do a great job? Come on in and make yourself at home. You can't see anything if you stay in that damned elevator. Look who's using your sofa!"

Harold stepped into the room and placed the suitcases on the floor. He glanced over to his right where the sofa should be. His mouth dropped as he stared in utter disbelief.

"Good afternoon, son. Welcome to your new home!"

There sat Colonel Henderson. A smile played over his face as he sat with his legs crossed smoking his familiar pipe. The aroma of his favorite brand of tobacco filled the room. Harold stood and stared. His father-in-law wore the familiar blue attire of Project Bluepaper.

"Dad! But, I thought you thought that I was dead. You're supposed to be in the Far East. I, I must sit down."

Colonel Henderson lay his pipe down and walked over to Harold. He gently placed an arm about his shoulders and led him back to the couch. He sat Harold down. The General placed the suitcases in an empty corner. Harold sat gazing into nothingness.

"John, I think I can take it from here."

"All right, Henderson. I don't envy your job. Take it easy with him. We need him badly. You know how vital his services will be to us."

"Yes, sir. Have arrangements been made for —"

"They most certainly have. The time will be 1400. Now, there's lunch for you both on the kitchen table. Why don't you fellows eat now and get reacquainted? I'll run along now."

"Why didn't they tell me that you were here, Dad?"

"It's just their way of doing business son. It's a dirty game. They wanted you to think that everybody on the Outside, including myself, thought you to be dead. This was part of the psychological pressure levelled at you to help you come to the right decision about Bluepaper. Now, let me explain a few things. Several months ago, I was approached for a position on this project. I was especially interested in the fact that both you and Helen had already been considered."

"Helen?"

"Yes, they thought her skills would be most useful. They needed her knowledge of modern langauges and cultures just as they needed your background in ancient langauges and cultures. You were a perfect combination. Both of you were already cleared at the highest Outside levels."

"But what would they want to use that kind of knowledge for? I'm supposed to be working with Beta again."

"Whoa! Slow down, Harold. You're getting ahead of me. You will be."

"But what about you, Dad? Won't they miss you on the Outside?"

"Nope." The Colonel put on a sly grin. "You see, son, I died in an airplane crash during my inspection of certain operations in the Far East. But, never mind my cover. Let's get back to you. The last time I saw you was just after they had rescued you from drowning. I was livid when I realized what had happened. I even threatened to back out of joining the project. But, they told me that it was too late for that. I had committed myself and already knew too much.

"When I first heard about your being in the hospital, I thought it was all part of a cover that they had planned for you. Believe me, Harold. I didn't know that they hadn't told you everything. If I had known, I would never have gone along with this crazy facade. I was ordered not to talk to you and to avoid you. I can only guess how you felt about me at the morgue and the private funeral service."

"They *told* you to ignore me? Why, I thought you were upset because you were blaming me for Helen's death."

"Sh-h. Let me finish. When I visited you at the hospital, I was under strict orders not to mention Helen during my visit. After I left you, they arranged for it to look as if I had departed on my mission to inspect Far Eastern Operations. There, I supposedly got myself killed. In reality, they had brought me here. Once I was here, they told me."

There was a long pause. "They told you what, Dad? Don't keep me in suspense!"

Colonel Henderson stood up and looked down at him sympathetically. Harold squirmed uncomfortably.

"Yes. They told me that they hadn't told you, Harold. They hadn't told you that Helen's cover was to have been an automobile accident. That damned psychiatrist Myrna allowed the whole thing to get out of hand."

"What? What are you trying to say, Dad?"

"Brace yourself for a pleasant but terrible shock, son. My daughter — your wife — Helen. She's alive and well."

Harold felt his body go numb all over. "But, but —"

"Calm down. Listen again. The car accident. The so-called body burned beyond recognition. It was all a carefully planned ploy. It was Helen's cover for joining Bluepaper. Finally, you were to be nabbed the same night. Your disappearance was to be attributed to impulsive suicide after hearing of Helen's death. However, top NSA officials insisted that you must stay with Beta until certain tasks were completed. Myrna decided it was too risky to tell you the truth. She felt your real sorrow and ignorance would make it easier for your planned suicide cover later on."

Harold staggered to his feet and faced the Colonel with sheer wonder written in his eyes. "Where? Where is she now?" he heard himself say. He could hardly get the words out. He felt as if he were in a somewhere between reality and unreality. Half of his mind rejected what he had heard. The other half wanted to believe it.

The Colonel put his hands gently upon Harold's shoulders and eased him back down onto the sofa. "She's right here at Base Three, son. Up until this morning, she had no idea that you thought she had been killed." The Colonel glanced at the clock on the wall. It read 1355. "In just five minutes, Helen will be here. I must go now. This is no place for anyone except you and Helen. Good evening, son."

Harold watched the Colonel disappear through the closing elevator door as if he were in a trance. It had all happened so fast. The realization of it all caused emotions long restrained to well up with him. Then, the hum of the elevator sounded once again. His pulse quickened. The sound of footsteps.

Harold tried to raise himself up from the couch. The bedroom door opened. Helen, her face wet with tears, walked slowly across the room toward him. Tears filled his eyes as he sunk limply back onto the couch. He tried to speak but he could not. Helen sat down beside him. She buried his head in her arms and wept. Harold's body trembled uncontrollably as he prayed. A miracle had taken place — a resurrection at Sector 3!

Chapter Six

The Bluepaper Briefings

Harold sat musing to himself in their new quarters at Sector 3. Helen was away on assignment. The past three weeks had been most pleasant. Tomorrow he would finally begin the briefing sessions. Helen had already been briefed. However, talking about Bluepaper operations to non-briefed personnel was strictly taboo. She wouldn't even hint to him about what was going on at Base 3.

On the following morning, Colonel Henderson escorted Harold to the briefing room once again. One of the six chairs was already occupied. He wondered who it was.

"Come on in, Harold. Let's not be shy."

Harold recognized the infernal patronizing voice that he had heard before.

"I said, come in. Introduce yourself to your companion if you wish. Do be brief. I believe you two have met before."

The man in the chair turned to face Harold.

"Don! Don Fields!"

"Harry, my boy! Is it really you? They told me that you were still alive. Your supposed suicide had been a real shocker to me. I found it hard to believe at the time."

"It's a long story, Don. I hope we'll have time to talk about it later."

The Voice interrupted.

"All right, gentlemen. That's enough for now. Be seated, Harold Stanton.

"Now, Donald and Harold, your briefing is about to begin. The documentary movie which you are about to view presents a brief historical overview of the events leading up to both the Bluepaper Project and its predecessors. Normally, our briefing runs at least three weeks. For certain reasons, your briefing has been reduced to a period of just one week. Next week, both of you will receive specific assignments. You will be transferred to personnel housing quarters in Sector 7. Fair enough? Now, please do not communicate with each other. I'll keep the sessions as informal as possible. Let's get underway."

The lights dimmed as the TV screen came to life. 5-4-3-2-1. Numbers flashed on and then a cryptic title appeared: *Bluepaper*. Instantly a number of aircraft appeared on the screen. It looked like old World War II footage.

Harold watched the formation of aircraft intently as they released their bombs. Light from exploding bombs and flak reflected off their fuselages. They looked like B17's.

Then another caption appeared. It was a date: *December 16, 1944 — 15th Air Force — 5th Wing — 2nd Bomb Group*. Then the scene switched to a strange sight. The bombing run was over. There were no more exploding bombs or flak. Instead, fuzzy balls of light appeared to be flying in formation with the B17 bombers. They maneuvered like fireflies between the aircraft. Harold heard Don mutter some strange word like "Foo-Fighters" under his breath.

Again, another caption appeared: *August 7, 1944 — 20th Air Force — 468th Bomb Group — 792 Squadron — Far Eastern War Theater.*

The cameraman seemed to be pointing his camera at reflections of distant aircraft. Then, suddenly, they resolved into six aluminum-colored spheres which weaved in and out of the bomber formation at incredible speeds. What were they? They couldn't be balloons. UFOs? "These all must be UFOs," thought Harold. "This Bluepaper must be a UFO project!"

Another sequence appeared involving a lone B24 bomber. Apparently it was being photographed by another aircraft flying in formation. It was a daylight mission. Puffs of smoke from exploding shells could be seen below the single aircraft. But, then, something else appeared.

"What's that?" Harold thought. "Is it a German fighter?"

Harold watched astounded as a dull grey circular domed craft slid sideways toward the bomber being photographed. A religious-like feeling of wonder trickled through his body as he watched the object come to a halt directly under the B24. A shimmering rim of pastel green lights played sporadically around a dark rim. The appearance and movements of the object appeared almost supernatural.

Harold glanced over at Don. His face was enrapt with wonder at what they were viewing. Then, excerpts from Swedish, Norwegian and Danish military films taken in 1946 flashed on the screen. For some unknown reason, a huge concentration of sightings were being reported. There were stills, movies and enlargements all showing the same other-worldly oval objects. Several depicted cigar-shaped objects.

Then, the TV dimmed. The lights in the activation room brightened. The Voice addressed them.

"Now, gentlemen, you should have a good inkling of our subject matter here at Bluepaper. Especially you, Donald G. Fields."

"UFOs! That's what this is all about," quipped the younger man seated beside Harold. "I knew that there had to be an operation like this going on somewhere. How have you guys kept all of this so secret over the years?"

"Later, both of you, especially you, Mr. Fields, will be most interested in how we've kept our, ah, *open* secret over the years. But, that will come later. Yes, Mr. Stanton. You have a question?"

"Yes. What *are* those objects that we saw in the films?"

"I'll answer that 64-dollar question later on this afternoon. But, my, look how the time has flown, gentlemen. You must have your lunch break. Separately. You will now each go to the opposite sides of the room. On the tables and chairs you will find a box lunch. I'll page you at 1255. Our exciting Serial will continue at 1300."

One thought after another churned through Harold's mind. Were those photos and movies of UFOs real? Were they German devices? Had Russia continued their development?

After lunch the lights again dimmed and the screen flickered to life.

1947. Photos of newspaper headlines from all over the world appeared. Foreign clips included translated captions.

Flying Discs Amaze Experts. United Airline Pilot Sights Disc! Army Air Force Investigating Strange Objects. Recorded excerpts from newcasts punctuated the fastmoving presentation. Then a memo appeared on the screen. It was dated September 23, 1947. In it the Air Material Command stressed to the Army's Commanding General that the objects were *something real and not visionary or fictitious.* It asked for a specific directive as to how it should proceed with its investigation.

On December 30, 1947, the Commanding General responded. An order was issued which established the first full-fledged Army UFO project. It was named Project *Sign* and was headquartered at Wright Field near Dayton, Ohio.

Then another caption appeared: January 7, 1948 — *Example: U.S. Military Casualty.* A photograph flashed upon the screen. It showed a police car and a crowd gazing at a bright object in the sky. The craft was cone-shaped, silvery and tipped with red. A little caption appeared beside it: *Estimated Diameter — 300 feet.*

The scene changed to an airbase.

"That's Godman Field in Kentucky", Don whispered. "It's the Manvel case!"

A voice then began reeling off facts about the incident in stacatto-like phrases.

Four P-51 Mustangs enroute to Godman were alerted by radio — Three were ordered to intercept — One landed because of fuel considerations — The enemy took evasive action which coincided with the radio message to the P-51s — It began climbing from the pursuit planes — Flight Commander Manvel was ordered to pursue it — These were his last words which were wire-recorded from Godman Field — Remember them well.

The static was so bad that both had to strain to make out the pilot's words.

Captain Manvel to Godman — Over.

We have you Flight 36. Please describe, repeat, please describe.

I, I it's, ah, I (static) It's huge. Ah, it looks like something out of Buck Rogers. Unbelievable.

Repeat 36. Repeat. What did you say?

It's, it's metallic. So huge. Looks like dozens of ports. Top is glowing bright red. Hurts my eyes to look. I'm getting heat in the cockpit. I smell smoke. I'll try to get closer for a moment. (static)

Harold listened in spellbound silence. The changing scene jolted him back to his senses. There was a cordoned-off wreckage of Manvel's aircraft. Men in strange suits walked about in the background. He had seen those suits before in a film on the Manhattan Project. They were radiation protective garments. One of the men had a geiger counter.

A close-up of the cockpit revealed that its canopy was riddled with tiny holes. Wisps of smoke rose from within as the personnel carefully removed Manvel's body. Then the picture switched to Wright Field. It was a door. A sign above it read: *Office of Special Studies.* An oriental man appeared. He introduced himself as Doctor Chang, Director of Special Studies. The Doctor explained that the P-51's electrical system had been completely burned out by an induced current of incredible strength. No explanation had yet been found for the hundreds of tiny holes in the plexiglass canopy of the plane's cockpit.

The movie camera then switched to a hospital room. Men in white clothing stood around a half-covered body lying on a metal table. Then, a terse announcement. Captain Manvel had been literally cooked from the inside out by some unknown form of radio frequency waves.

Before Harold could react to this ghastly announcement, the historical overview continued. 1949, 1950, 1951. It was all much the same at first: newsclips, documents and opinions by leading scientists. A number of photographs were depicted of distant disc-shaped objects. Some were taken from the ground. Others seemed to be gun-camera footage.

The documentation of the huge worldwide wave in 1952 was fast-paced. Time after time Harold's eyes followed one or more of the domed discs as they weaved in and out of the field of an interceptor's gun camera. The film continued through the rest of the fifties, the sixties and the seventies. It culminated with a spectacular incident involving the *Apollo 13 mission.*

First, a series of remarkable photographs were projected. They portrayed a stubby cylindrical object floating against a starry background. A caption appeared: *Attempt at Object Size/Distance Determination.* The caption referred to a small ranging device attached to the Apollo 13 spacecraft.

The ranging device was operated manually from inside the capsule. A camera automatically recorded instrument readings on a small console. The countdown sequence to activate was heard from the Manned Space Center at Houston. Illuminated numbers flashed on in sychronization with voice transmission.

X minus 3, X minus 2, X minus 1 — Activate!

A dazzling flash of light momentarily obscured the tense drama being recorded on film. The three white-suited astronauts were holding their hands over their eyes. They seemed completely disoriented. The voice of Houston broke in.

Apollo 13? This is Houston. What happened out there? Please acknowledge.

There was silence. Again the controller from Houston

spoke. His voice became anxious.

Apollo 13, this is Houston. Are you guys all right? Please acknowledge. Do you read me?

Then, an emotion-filled voice, barely comprehensible at first, shouted:

Houston, Houston, we are under attack! We are under attack! What shall we do?

The film abruptly ended at that dramatic point. The huge TV screen dimmed. The lights in the briefing room came on. Harold thought back. He remembered the Apollo 13 incident. Little did the public know what had really happened. The familiar fatherly voice interrupted his thoughts.

"Well, gentlemen, it is now 1500 hours. My how the time does fly. It is now time for your little break. No discussion please. You will now go to opposite sides of the room.

"But", stammered Harold, "You told us that you'd tell us what these objects are today."

"Why, so I did, Mr. Stanton. You will find the basic answer to your question in Volume II of the Bluepaper Indoctrination Course located on your tables. If you'd like to take a peek ahead, look on page 303 of the last section. It is entitled *Project Sign — Estimate of the Situation*, August 21, 1948.

A set of two blue-covered volumes sat on the study table. Harold sat down and picked up Volume II. He quickly flipped its pages to page 303. Glancing up and down the page he found what he was looking for in a summary paragraph.

The current *Estimate of the Situation* by the Air Technical Intelligence Center is that *truly unidentified airfoils represent interplanetary or extra-solar manned and unmanned spacecraft of unknown origin and motivation.* Immediate steps must be taken to deal with this critical problem at the highest levels. International cooperation may someday prove to be absolutely necessary.

Harold sank back into the chair. He stared back across the auditorium to the empty screen. Interplanetary? Extrasolar? Was this some kind of a trick? Why not Russian? Perhaps all of this was some kind of psychological test being given them.

"Sure, that must be it," he thought. "Or, is it? Could all of this be for real?"

Throughout the week, Harold and Don continued to attend the fantastic briefing sessions. Harold's logical mind had neatly condensed the complete evolution of the Bluepaper Project.

From the very beginning, a top-level Group had recognized the alien origin of UFOs. They saw to it that hard UFO data was classified above Top Secret. Lower echelon military personnel were purposely kept ignorant of the subject except on a limited need-to-know basis. This even included most of the personnel working on Air Force UFO projects. When *Sign* had concluded that UFOs were interplanetary in 1948, it was terminated. Its staff were debriefed and disbanded. Both the public and most military personnel were told that *Sign* had concluded that UFOs did not exist.

In reality, this Group continued investigations through a covert Army Air Force project codenamed *Grudge*. Grudge remained under cover until the UFO wave in 1952 caused public pressure to bring it out in the open again as Project *Bluebook*. But, Bluebook personnel soon concluded that UFOs were extraterrestrial. A vocal group within its ranks wanted to notify the public.

The Group defused this alarming situation by organizing a bogus panel of scientists affiliated with the CIA. They pretended to examine Bluebook's evidence and then rejected it. The Bluebook staff was replaced by psychological warfare experts whose mission was to debunk UFOs. It was at this point in time that the Group organized *Bluepaper* to operate in deadly secrecy.

However, over the years, Bluebook developed an

extremely bad image with Congress and the public. The Air Force complained bitterly about being used as a whipping boy for UFOs. In 1969, it was decided to terminate Bluebook. The Air Force pretended to bow to civilian pressure. It again initiated a bogus University Study of UFOs headed by Doctor Condell, a well-known scientist. Condell had lost his security clearance during the communist witch hunt days. He was promised its restoration in return for his covert help. Condell recommended Bluebook be closed down. Bluebook complied. Again, the public was told that UFOs did not exist.

Don, on the other hand, was more interested in Bluepaper's civilian covert operations. He was shocked to find that NECAP, The National Enquiry Committee into Aerial Phenomena, was a *cover operation.* NECAP Director, Major Keel, was a Bluepaper agent who had directed a complex intelligence-gathering operation dubbed *Skylite.* Skylite had met a specific need. The civilian populace distrusted the Air Force UFO investigation. Small civilian UFO groups began to crop up. Important civilian sightings were no longer being reported to Bluebook. But, they gladly sent reports to NECAP. Major Keel was groomed to appear as a valiant fighter against government UFO secrecy. The Major set up a vast network of competent volunteer investigators. Their phones were tapped. Soon, Bluepaper had covert control of most of the data flowing between civilian UFO researchers. At the same time, NECAP provided a gradual indoctrination of the American public about UFO reality.

It was a masterpiece of psychological subterfuge. Later, when NECAP was compromised, another covert operation was brought to fore. CAPS, the Center for Aerial Phenomena Studies was directed by Doctor Joseph Huneker. Huneker, a well-known Air Force UFO consultant, feigned a conversion from a debunker to a believer. UFO buffs flocked to him as the new Messiah of UFOdom. Keel and NECAP faded away and CAPS took its place as the in-group for receiving civilian reports of UFOs.

When Thursday arrived, Harold and Don were briefed on a variety of UFO detection devices. During a UFO alert, trained teams dubbed *Blue Berets* were quickly transported to a number of *cover* installations. Normal-appearing vans containing monitoring equipment were nicknamed *chameleons*. Specially-equipped jet interceptors, slower fixwinged aircraft and black unnumbered helicopters called *blackbirds* supported the vast operation.

That afternoon, the session concentrated on one specific example of a UFO detector used all over the world by Project *Magnet*. It measured minute fluctuations in the earth's magnetic field caused by the presence of UFOs. *Magnet* was part of a super-secret organization that worked with Bluepaper: The NRC or National Reconnaissance Council.

Later, on Thursday evening, a fantastic scene from the *Magnet* session remained vividly imprinted on Harold's mind. It was from a movie taken in 1966 over the Atlantic from one of Project Magnet's Super Constellation aircraft. He closed his eyes. His amazing powers of recall visualized the unworldly scene.

Through a telephoto lens, an object took on the form of a huge silvery cylinder. It was over a mile in length! One of its ends dipped forward as it bobbed slowly up-and-down like a huge ship at sea. Cotton-like wispy clouds emanated from its surface like boiling froth and dissipated. Then came the unbelievable part.

The craft began to glow like a white hot poker. The narrator interrupted with a terse announcement: "They've spotted us!" Immediately radar was activated. Radio silence was broken. Top priority encoded messages were radioed to relay stations for secure transmission to Bluepaper. Then the glow dimmed. The silver behemoth slowly rose to a vertical position. A dozen small silvery rimmed discs zipped toward the large craft with an oscillating up-and-down motion. Each moved one-at-a-time in a jerky motion under and up into the base of the cylinder. There was a brilliant flash of light and then? It was gone. Radar showed only a weak target of ionized air left in its wake!

"Where did it go, Helen? Where did it go? One moment it was there and the next it wasn't. The whole thing was almost supernatural. It —" Helen gazed at Harold with pity in her soft brown eyes.

"Tomorrow you'll experience things much more disquieting than that. Your briefing will be over physically but far from it in the mental sense. I've learned to live with what I saw. You will too. Wish I could tell you more but I can't. I do have some good news though. Bluepaper has had all of your seminary books and papers delivered here."

"Why?"

"It's exciting. They need your knowledge of ancient cultures and languages desperately."

"Confound it, Helen. I keep hearing this! But how? Why? What can it all be about?"

"I can't say anymore now, dear. You'll find out more after the briefings. Then, then you'll —"

Helen's voice trailed off to nothing. Her eyes took on a strange, almost mystical look of awe.

"What's the matter with you, woman? Finish what you were saying!" Harold demanded. "Oh, I'm sorry for snapping like that but the look on your face scares me. This whole thing scares me."

"After the indoctrination, Harold, you will meet *him*. Then you'll know why you were chosen to work on this project."

"*Him*? Who do you mean? By the tone of your voice one would think you were talking about God Himself. Who, may I ask, is *him*?"

Again Helen's eyes filled with wonder. "I, I can't say any more. I've said too much already."

Chapter Seven

Wards of the Undertaker

An air of expectancy filled the air as Harold again joined Don in the briefing room. It was Friday. The last day. His father-in-law had given him a strange look as he left him at the door. And, Helen had been strangely silent this morning. That wasn't like her. What had she said last night? She had uttered some kind of a warning as he drifted off to sleep.

"Welcome, welcome, gentlemen! Good morning to you both!"

"At least *he* sounds jovial this morning," Harold mused to himself. "Today's session can't be that bad."

The Voice continued with the same child-like humor he had employed in previous sessions. Sometimes Harold wondered if this man had a screw loose somewhere. But, whoever he was, he was funny. His crazy antics seemed to put both of them at ease.

"Now, our subject this morning is *Physical Evidence*. So, sit back and try to relax. I wish that I could offer you some popcorn. But, I'm afraid the management hasn't allowed for a luxury like that."

The two Bluepaper novitiates viewed remarkable movies and still photos of a number of UFO landing sites. Photographs and measurements of baked rings in the ground, strut imprints, radioactivity, residual magnetism and penetrometer readings flicked on and off the screen in dizzying succession.

The landing sites were not just confined to the United States. Samples were shown from a variety of friendly countries. The landing markings fell into easily distinguished categories based upon appearance and physical measurement. Then, they witnessed several incredible photos of landed UFOs.

"What are those things beside that UFO?" Harold wondered. As if in answer, an enlargement of the same photograph appeared. It showed clearly that the egg-shaped object was accompanied by two indistinct humanoid forms in white coveralls. The enlarged grain of the photographic image blurred out any facial details. But, the heads were pear-shaped and much larger in proportion to the creatures' bodies.

"Incredible," Harold thought. "Who are they? What are they? What do they want here in our world? Do they worship God? I wonder if they know about Christianity?"

Depression and doubt suddenly descended upon him like an invisible pall. He found himself experiencing the same emotions he had felt for weeks prior to his suicide attempt.

Washington State, Mount Rainer, June 19, 1947. This caption suddenly appeared superimposed over an aerial photograph of a snow-covered mountain range.

Harold recognized the majestic peak of Mount Rainier. He had seen it several times while enroute to visit Helen's aunt. "Aunt Elizabeth," he mused. "I wonder if she's still alive." He and Helen had become so wrapped up in their own interests that they'd lost contact with her over the years.

Harold's brief reverie into the past dissipated as suddenly as it had risen. The narrator began to describe an incredible event.

Two mountain climbers had spotted a strange upright hairy creature. Its tracks were followed to a strange artificial-looking narrow crevasse. They edged their way through it and emerged in a small box canyon. At that point, they spotted what appeared to be the wreckage of an airplane. As they drew nearer, it was soon apparent that the domed, circular craft was something that they had never seen before. They thought it must be a crashed experimental aircraft. So, they marked the crevasse's entrance with a red ribbon. They left for home at the break of the next day. There they placed a phone call to McChord Air Force Base. A special team was assembled to investigate. The two men led them to the object. Overhead, a C46 containing a contingent of armed Marine paratroopers provided protective backup to the team below if necessary. The searchteam was just in the process of describing the discshaped craft when suddenly they came under attack by giant hairy man-like animals. The C46 responded and began to make its run to drop the parachutists. There was a brief *May Day* message and transmission ceased. The plane crashed. None of the search party, including the two climbers, were ever found. The narrator added ironically that Kenneth Arnold, whose sightings of UFOs over Mount Rainier had caused national publicity, had spotted those particular objects while searching for the missing C46.

The C46 was found. However, secret searches for the box canyon were unsuccessful.

Again, another caption appeared on the screen.

Mexico, Aztec, January 19, 1948.

Harold and Don watched awestruck as a close-up shot of a silvery-gray oval object appeared. The craft was encircled by a protruding slotted rim of darker material. It had apparently crashed as part of it was embedded in the sand. Then, the scene again changed.

Harold squirmed at what he saw. It was a long table under the canopy of a large tent at the crash site. On the table were a number of small, silver-clad child-like bodies.

The camera moved in close to their faces. "Ugh, they look like fetuses!" Harold gasped. Their oversized pear-shaped heads displayed wide open slanted wrap-around eyes.

Suddenly the screen darkened. Some large encircled numbers briefly flashed on and off. The lights in the room slowly brightened. The Voice again spoke to them.

"Good morning again, Harold! Good morning to you, too, Donald. Did you, ah, enjoy our double feature?"

"Why don't you come out where we can see you, whoever you are?" snapped Don.

"What was that all about?" queried Harold. He couldn't really believe what he had just seen. "Who produced that? Hollywood?"

"Really now, do you think I would waste your time with Hollywood stunts? I assure you that what you have just witnessed is the *first physical contact* with an alien craft and its crew from somewhere other than our planet earth. That, gentlemen, was the crash at Aztec, Mexico. Now, there is time for questions and discussion."

"Were all those creatures killed because of the crash? Did we shoot that thing down?" Don asked.

"No, we did not shoot that thing down, as you so crudely put it. But, your first question is most difficult for me to answer in terms of life and death as we understand them. Let me just say that, yes, the animation process was no longer in effect when we recovered the bodies. You'll understand better later on.

"Yes, Harold. You have a question?"

"I have many questions; More than we have time to cover now. But, what were those things that attacked the search party on Mount Rainier? And, did UFOs destroy the C46 and its Marine passengers?"

"The C46 experienced engine failure from some undetermined cause. We're not sure what the large hairy bipeds are. There seems to be a direct connection between these creatures and the aliens. Our statistics place them in the area of alien activities. Also, our biologists tell us that an earth-based evolutionary process could not produce a man-like creature with *four-digited* appendages."

The questions and discussion continued unabated right up until lunch time. After lunch, General Thurman escorted them to another area.

They stopped before a small flight of stairs which led up to a door marked: *Restricted/Priority 1*. Before entering, the tall graying man stared at them momentarily as if preparing to phrase his words carefully.

"I never know just what to say at this particular time," he began. "I'm sure that both of you, regardless of your accelerated briefing, still have lingering doubts about what you have witnessed. One might compare all of this to the death of a relative or close friend. For example, you hear from unimpeachable sources that John Doe has died. Now, you have no reason to disbelieve this sad news. But nonetheless, you find it very difficult to accept."

" 'Perhaps there has been a mistake,' you say. You try not to even think about it. You put the whole thing out of your mind. Then you go to the wake. There lies John Doe in a casket. He is very dead indeed. It is only then that the real truth of the matter strikes home. Sometimes it strikes home hard. For the first time you *really* accept his death. No longer is the truth second or third-hand knowledge. You *know*. Then, and only then do you begin a series of emotional and mental adjustments to this stark fact."

The General paused and stared them both in the eyes. "Gentlemen, a similar shocking moment of truth has arrived for you."

The trio entered a small foyer and were instructed to don insulated silvery coveralls. "You'll be glad you have these suits on," the General remarked. "It's quite chilly in there. You'll find gloves in the pockets. I believe Dr. Terzian is already in there."

The General turned a wheel on the wall. "Okay, let's go in." The heavy round door opened slowly and silently. Cold air rushed out to meet them.

"After you, gentlemen. Watch your heads. Be careful when you step down. The floor is a bit lower. Stay on the black matting. Any moisture freezing on your shoes could cause you to slip on the metal floor."

Harold hesitated and let Don take the lead. Then he too stepped down into a long rectangular room. A dull throbbing sound of machinery emanated from behind its walls. Those walls. They seemed to close in on him. Harold tried to restrain his mild, yet real claustrophobic tendency. He glanced warily around. A bank of fluorescent lights cast an eerie evenly distributed glow throughout the shadowless room which measured about fifteen by thirty feet. A series of three equally-spaced square seams faced each other on either wall. Each was about two feet by two feet square.

They were marked by individual matching corresponding numbers: 4, 5, and 6. Each was connected to its counterpart by a set of sunken tracks. These rails bisected a matted walkway which stretched along the middle of the room. The walkway led to a partitioned-off area at the far end of the silvery chamber.

A short smiling man appeared from behind the partition. He waddled down the black matting toward them. Harold could not help smiling back. The man's broad friendly grin was contagious. The approaching figure was a comical sight. His protective garment was several sizes too big for him. He looked like something out of a cartoon strip.

"Welcome, welcome dear friends! How are you, John?" He clasped the General's hands as if greeting a long-lost friend. Then he glanced at Harold and Don. "So, these are the two chaps about to receive their, ah, how shall we put it? Ah, receive their baptism of fire into Bluepaper!"

The General turned to Harold and Don. "Gentlemen, allow me to introduce Dr. Vahan Terzian, our, ah, friendly undertaker."

The little old man smiled with glee. He nodded his head as the General continued his introduction.

"Vahan, this is Doctor Donald Fields." Don leaned over and shook hands briefly. "And this is Dr. Harold Stanton." Harold stepped forward and shook hands with Doctor Terzian. The Doctor's hand did not return his firm squeeze. His hand felt limp, emotionless and yet it clung to his hand relentlessly.

Harold felt embarassed. The smile had disappeared from Dr. Terzian's face. For one long moment Harold's eyes became locked with the dark scrutinizing eyes of this dark-skinned man of Armenian extraction. Then the Doctor's eyes slowly took on an almost emotionless quality. He slowly surrendered Harold's hand. The Doctor stood silently for a moment, hands behind his back and then spoke.

"Now, Harold, Donald. I have been asked to come here this afternoon to show you something very special. I regret to say that no questions may be asked at this time. Some of your questions will be answered as you continue your studies and work. Others may never be answered. Do you understand? Fine! Let's get down to business."

"Follow Vahan, fellows. I'll bring up the rear," said the General. He stepped aside to let Harold and Donald squeeze by. The small group filed along the center walkway and into the partitioned-off area. Harold glanced at the control panel. There were three identical consoles marked 4, 5 and 6. Each had the same sets of switches, buttons and gauges. The numbers obviously matched the square cavities in the walls outside.

"Which are you going to show them, Vahan?" asked the General.

"I have no choice. The hospital was only allotted six. Plant 1 has three and I usually have three here in Plant 2. But 4 and 6 were requested by the Cybernetics group last Wednesday. I don't know when they will be back. Plant 1, of course, is presently off limits to them. So, that leaves Number 5."

Harold watched as Vahan walked over to Console Number 5. His fingers played nimbly over the buttons and dials with lightning speed.

"Vahan, how you do that so fast always amazes the hell out of me!"

"Practice, John, lots of practice," replied Doctor Terzian. He paused to observe the reading on a meter before pressing yet another button. "Here it comes, boys. Take a look out there to your right. Number 5."

A slight hissing sound emanated from the square outline

58

marked 5. Then a whining sound rose and fell as a square thick door slowly opened. Doctor Terzian then pulled a lever. A dull humming sound filled the room as a rectangular steel box enswathed with white vapor emerged along its track from its crypt-like opening in the wall. The Doctor brought it to a halt just as it was straddling the walkway.

"What's in that?" queried Don.

Harold just stared at it. The metal container was about two feet by two feet and about five feet long. It was capped with a glass covering which was frosted up.

"All right, go on, take a look. It won't bite you," Doctor Terzian quipped.

"Let's move, gentlemen, we've got a schedule to keep!" the General commanded.

Harold waited for Don. "After you, old buddy," he said. Don hesitated and then moved quickly down the walkway. Harold followed cautiously behind him. The frost on the glass top had rapidly dissipated leaving heavy condensation in its wake. A shadowy outline, resembling the body of a small child, could be vaguely seen through the fogged-up glass.

"Don't touch the glass," cautioned Doctor Terzian. "In just a few minutes the temperature will become equalized. You'll be able to see in there just fine."

"My God!" whispered Don. "What, what is it?"

Harold looked over Don's shoulder and swallowed hard. A tingling chill crept slowly up his spine. An admixture of raw emotions welled up within him; fear, wonder, unbelief, then a strange, almost mystical feeling engulfed his senses rendering him speechless. It brought briefly to mind his first contact with death as a child. He wanted to look away but he couldn't. His eyes became riveted to the glass-capped sarcophagus.

Bit by bit the condensation evaporated to reveal first a pair of tiny booted feet, a pair of spindly legs and disproportionately long, thin arms. Then a chest and

then a huge ugly oversized hairless head.   "Ugh," Harold
felt nauseous. Looking straight up were two large wrap-
around mongoloid-like eyes staring placidly into
nothingness. The intelligence and wisdom reflected from
those cold staring eyes made Harold and Don feel as if they
were in the presence of some powerful supernatural being.
    "We both know exactly how you feel, gentlemen."
    Harold felt a hand rest upon his shoulder. He looked up
at the grim yet empathetic face of General Thurman.
Doctor Terzian reached up and patted Don's back gently. A
look of pity played across his face.
    "There was no other way," he said apologetically
shrugging his shoulders. "*They* say to see is to believe. Is that
not correct?"
    Harold and Don stared unresponsively at the squat little
man.
    "But," he continued, "*we* say that you must *touch* to really
believe. Eh? Eh?"
    Although they could see and hear, both Harold and Don
had been gripped by a strange sensation of disassociation.
    "Eh, eh? Don't you hear me? I say to really believe that
one must touch. One must feel. Am I right?"
    Doctor Terzian and General Thurman exchanged
understanding glances.
    "Go ahead, Vahan. Let's get this over with," snapped the
General.
    The little man wheeled about and walked quickly behind
the silver partition. Harold and Don still stared silently into
the steel container. The condensation on the glass lid was
gone. They examined every detail: the seamless silvery suit
with matching boot-like coverings. The four webbed
fingers. And that head. It looked like an inverted pear. It
seemed to rest directly on the little being's shoulders. Did it
have a neck? Those eyes, the diminutive nose and ears and
the slit-like lipless mouth reminded Harold of a frail,
unknowing aborted fetus. And yet, an intangible aura of
strength, of superiority, of intelligence and wisdom seemed

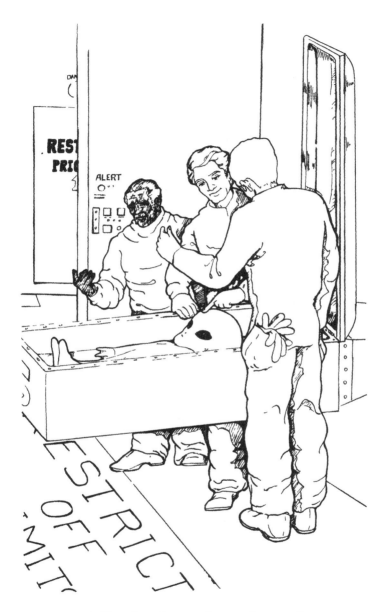

"Go ahead, touch gentlemen."

to encompass the still, corpse-like figure.

Harold's deep and dreamy thoughts were suddenly shattered. A whining sound accompanied by a brief loud hiss erupted from the steel receptacle. He and Don stepped back in horror as they watched the glass lid slowly rise up and stop with a loud click!

"Go ahead, touch, gentlemen. Touch. Feel. Don't worry about contamination. Our preservation process provides mutual protection."

Don stepped forward like a zombie and ran his fingers along the silver suit. Emotions welled up from deep within rendering him incapable of speaking. He touched the small being's head and gently ran his fingers around its contours.

"Don't touch the eyes!" warned Doctor Terzian. And now its your turn, Mr. Stanton."

Harold did not respond to the Doctor. The little old man stepped over and gently took Harold's limp hand in his. He lowered it slowly and rubbed it gently along the cheek of the lifeless creature. Briefly, an experience from boyhood days flashed into Harold's conscious mind and then back into the depths of memory. Dad Jameison had held out a snake for him to touch from his garden. Harold had been terrified of snakes. But, he had touched it. It hadn't been cold and clammy. It had been dry and smooth.

Harold felt his body begin to relax. The protective mechanisms mercifully thrown up from the depths of his subconscious slowly let down their barriers. The reality of his encounter with the incredible seeped bit by bit into his conscious mind. Harold *believed*. The initiation of Harold Stanton and Donald Fields, BETA Numbers 27 and 28 had been accomplished. The Bluepaper briefings were over.

Chapter Eight

Father Pat

Harold lay back on the sofa, his head nestled in Helen's lap. She stroked his head gently as he rehearsed the shaking events of the day.

"When I looked down and saw *it*, I even touched *it* — my whole neat little Bible story world came tumbling down. What does it all mean? How does it all fit in?"

"Harold, Harold, your God is too small. In most cases, the Church's concept of God is too small. Your outlook has been necessarily narrow. I mean, look at your educational background. Why, your only science courses were in biology. When you consider how large the known universe is, it would be provincial to think that God only created intelligent life here.

"Helen, I hear what you're saying. I'm not completely ignorant about astronomical matters. It's just that I've never really thought about it. Extraterrestrial life, science fiction: all that kind of stuff was just far-off uninteresting theory to me. Now it's fact. To be quite frank with you, I've always considered man unique. My universe was sort of two-tiered. You know? God up there and man down here. But now? Suddenly I feel so small, so unimportant and insecure. The feeling I have in the pit of my stomach reminds me of how I felt at the orphanage. I felt so lost, so alone until Chaplain Jamieson and his wife adopted me. Their love and my conversion to Christianity brought me the security that my whole little being ached for. Now I feel as if that security has been an illusion. In one fell swoop, after seeing that creature, suddenly I feel lost and unimportant all over again.

"Believe me, Harold, I thought similar thoughts during my briefing. Father Pat was a great help to me. They let him come over from Sector 7 to visit me. Dad arranged it."

"*Father* Pat? Who's he? You mean they've actually got a Priest in this unholy place?"

"Yes, they do but not by his choice. Pat, that is Father Patrick O'Malley, was a Chaplain during World War II. He saw something he wasn't supposed to see. He wouldn't tell me what. Well, they declared him missing in action on the Outside. He's been kept out of circulation ever since. He was kept at Bases 1 and 2 and sent here shortly after Phoenix Base 3 became operational. Pat acts as sort of an informal Chaplain here. He's a wonderful old man. You've got to meet him. He's got quite a scientific background in astronomy in addition to his theological training."

"Perhaps he can help me, dear. I hope that I'll get to meet him."

"Perhaps you will on Sunday. Tomorrow is moving day and on Sunday we're going to be transferred to our new quarters in Sector 7. Dad told me that we'll meet the people on our floor level at a little social gathering. Perhaps we'll soon have an opportunity to work together."

"Can we talk about what you're doing now, Helen?"

"Only in generalities. I can only say that I've been working with *him* and have gone as far as I can go. They need you to carry on where I left off."

"*Him*? You've referred to *him* before. Just who is it that you're talking about?"

Helen's lips tightened as she slowly shook her head side-to-side.

"I don't know who he is. We're trying to find that out. They say he may be the key to unlocking the meaning of the alien visitation. They say that, — Oh-h!"

Helen's neck suddenly snapped back. She grit her teeth and stared defiantly around the room as if in search for an unseen intruder.

Harold jumped to his feet. Helen rubbed the back of her

neck.

"What is it, Helen? Are you all right?"

Helen sighed. "Yes, I'm all right now. I just forgot for a moment that our walls have ears. You'll get used to it. Someone at Central Control just reminded me that I was on the brink of talking too much. I should have known better."

Harold walked around and looked at Helen's neck. The scar tissue outlined the same type of incision he carried on his own neck.

"Do you mean they activated that thing in there just now?"

"I'm afraid so. It wasn't the first time and I'm sure it won't be the last time. But don't worry. Pain's all gone. Just lasts a moment."

"But how did they? Why?"

"Harold, poor naive Harold. This place is monitored, Harold. You know? Bugged. Everything we say, perhaps everything we do may be under surveillance by the Phoenix Central Control."

"What!" Harold stepped back and glanced around the room. "Why, they have no right. Why I, I'll —"

"You'll do nothing, dear. There's not a thing we can do. I was told the the surveillance is selective. After we've proved ourselves here, it will slacken off. Right now we just happen to be newcomers to Bluepaper, especially you and Don. Let's go to bed now. Big day ahead of us tomorrow." Helen reached up and caressed his cheek. A coyish grin appeared on her face. "Bet they can't see what goes on under the covers."

The move had gone smoothly. Harold still couldn't believe that he wasn't still in Sector 3. Their new apartment looked identical. It was late Sunday morning. They had spent Saturday night in a nearby empty apartment. Helen entered the livingroom. "How do I look?" She twirled about for Harold to examine her.

"You look beautiful. You cut a nice figure in that blue

jumpsuit," he teased. "Wherever did you get it? It must be the latest style."

Helen laughed. "I'm glad you've got some sense of humor left. Lord knows, we need some of that here. Are you nervous about the dinner party?"

"A bit. I find it hard to meet new people. I'll be all right once we get there. I just don't like waiting around."

Helen's father arrived just before noon. "Well, kids, they've given me one last job to do. Guess you'll be on your own, more or less, after this. Come on. I'll bring you to the recreation room. There are some nice people waiting to meet you."

The Colonel led them down the corridor to an open door. Harold could hear the buzz of conversation and laughter. It had been a long time since he'd heard sounds like that. A feeling of warmth came over him.

"There's the door. I won't go in. This is your party. Have a good time. I don't know when I'll see you again but I'll try to see you often." Then Colonel Henderson cupped his hands around Helen's neck and kissed her. "Be good, brown eyes." He turned and shook Harold's hand, smiled broadly at them both for one long moment, and then walked away quickly.

A little group of people sat in a semi-circle gazing expectantly at the entering couple. A sudden hush settled over the room. Then a chubby old man got to his feet. Slightly balding with a mischievous twinkle in his eye, he looked more like a misplaced leprechaun than a ward of Phoenix Base 3. He tottered toward them with both arms extended.

"On behalf of me fine feathered friends of Sector 7, Level 1, I welcome the both of ya to yer new home away from home. Let's have a big hand now for Harold and Helen Stanton."

Harold smiled shyly at the small group of people who stood up and clapped. Helen looked buoyant and did a little curtsey. Then for a moment, everybody just stared. It was embarrassing. No one knew quite what to do or say next. Harold chuckled to himself. The most absurd idea had just entered his mind. These people in their crazy light-blue uniforms looked like the welcoming committee for a pajama party!

"Come on in now. Let me introduce you around a bit." The pudgy old man flashed a smile of recognition at Helen and then turned to Harold. He extended his hand.

"They call me Father Pat an I'll be callin' ya Harry if ya do not mind. I've already met yer charmin' wife. 'Tis good to see ya again. Now. Cum over 'ere, dear."

A rather tall woman with blonde braided hair stepped over to them and smiled broadly.

"This is our dear Anna, Anna Fagerberg. Anna is one of our cooks and lives in 1A. You'll be tastin' her wares any moment now. And, I might add, for the benefit of others here, Anna is single and is lookin' for a young stallion, she is. So if you come across any charmin' young men, Anna would like to meet them."

"Now that you've finished with your Irish tomfoolery, allow me the privilege to speak for myself," she said. Everybody laughed. "Welcome, welcome, to our little group!" She clasped their hands warmly and stepped aside. But not before casting a stern glance at Father Pat who had resumed introductions.

"Now, this is Bill Grimes and Jeff Manning. Bill is a computer specialist and Jeff is a monitor. They live in 1D and, oh yes, here's Jack Dobson and Peter Castiello from 1B. They both belong to the Sector Seven, ah, what are ya callin' it now?"

"Sanitation Engineering, you old rascal. To put it more bluntly, folks, we're janitors. Nice to meet you both. Watch out for Brother Sebastian here," laughed Pete. "He's dangerous."

"Away with both of ye and don't ya be forgettin' to fix th' light outside me door. This is the third time I'm askin' ya. I'll soon have Timothy buzzing' yer wee companions if ya don't git the lead out!"

Then Doris Tanguay and Barbara Kanerva were introduced. Harold stared at Barbara. Where had he seen her before?

"We meet again, Mr. Stanton?"

"Why yes, but where, when? Oh-h-h, you're the - -"

"Nurse? Yes. I was in your room the first day they brought you here. I'm glad you're all right. You weren't well at all when they brought you in. Doris and I are both nurses."

Then they were introduced to Dr. John Denman, electronics specialist and his wife Louise, a lab technician. It was nice to see a married couple about their own age here.

After Father Pat completed introducing them, he beamed proudly and placed his arms around another couple.

"And 'ere's a union made by me own hands! Ah, with the help o' the Almighty, of course. This is Doctor Immanuel Goldberg, a medical Doctor. We call him Manny. And this is his lovely wife, Esther. She's a nurse by trade. Would ya believe me now if I told ya that Father Pat was Rabbi Pat for a wee bit one day? I married the both of them, nearly a year ago, I did. We 'ave a terrible shortage of Rabbis these days, we do!"

Esther smiled down at the rambunctious old man. "I would add that Father Pat had a hand in playing Father Cupid as well."

"Ah, 'tis true that the good Lord does use us as agents to accomplish His good will. But marriages are made in heaven, ta be sure. And this, my fine friends — I save the best till last — is Timothy Donoghue, a fellow son of Erin. Timmy takes his earthly duties much too seriously, he does. You'll watch out fer him or he's apt to buzz you one, eh Tim? Cum on out of yer corner. We won't be a 'bitin' ya."

Harold noticed that the pleasant smiling faces about him had suddenly grown quite somber. A stern-looking young man with bushy blonde hair stepped forward from the other side of the room. He walked slowly up to them, forced an obvious mock smile at Father Pat, and extended his hand stiffly to Harold and Helen.

"Good afternoon, Harold, Helen, or more correctly BETA-27 and — what's this? I see that you are still displaying Designator BETA-22, Mrs. Stanton. I thought that you had been reassigned."

"I was told my Beta Number would be retained because of my on-call consultant status to Beta Nova," Helen replied crisply. She looked Timothy directly in his eyes. The tone of his voice upset her.

"Ah, so that's it. Well, that's not my decision. Having you both working on the Beta Project is not a good precedent to set here. It's because you are husband and wife or it wouldn't be so. You have a dual clearance?"

"Yes. I can come and go to Beta without reprogramming. My husband will be on Beta, you see, and - -"

"I know the reason," Timothy replied. "That's not the point. General regulations prohibit more than one person on a given Project to be here on the same level of Sector 7. I shall look into this myself and make an appropriate suggestion to my, ah, peers."

"And what are ye suggestin', Tim? A divorce? As usual ye are takin' yer job much too seriously."

Timothy ignored the old man as if he hadn't heard his remark. He glanced slowly around at the others who were looking very uncomfortable.

"It was a pleasure to meet you, BETA-22, BETA-27. Make yourselves at home. Obey our regulations here at Phoenix Base 3 and there will be no trouble."

With that, Timothy did a military right about-face and marched smartly out of the room.

"Ha, ha," Father Pat's husky laugh broke the icy silence that had engulfed the room. "As I said before, our boy Tim takes his job too seriously. Now, whut say we break out the grub and 'ave a good time o' fellowship. We want the Stantons to feel right at home. Right?"

Harold and Helen joined the others for the buffet lunch prepared for them. For a few hours they almost forgot where they were. It was a pleasant escape from the stark reality of Project Bluepaper.

Later on in the evening, Harold lay awake staring at the ceiling. Once and awhile he glanced at Helen. She lay soundly asleep beside him. Her face looked so peaceful.

"Never could figure out how she manages to just drop off like that. It's exasperating!" he thought. Harold just couldn't shut out the events of the day from his mind. His mind wandered to Father Pat. The kindly old man had been such a help to him.

"Harry, me boy," he had said, "the Almighty is both infinitely great and infinitely small. His Spirit is greater than the unfathomable Universe about us. Yet 'tis small enough to enter the hearts o' the likes of us wee men. If it were not so, He would not be much of a God, now would He?"

Such simple statements. But Father Pat was not as simple as he sounded. There was something about him. Some indefinable something that just didn't click. Even Helen had commented that there was something unusual about his accent. Yes, Father Pat. Priest-Scientist. An astronomer who had kept himself abreast of the latest advances on the outside. Yet he had been a Chaplain. An Air Force Chaplain. It somehow didn't fit. Harold had questioned him about this. But the Priest merely smiled and quoted Saint Paul about becoming all things to all men.

Harold closed his eyes and took advantage of his amazing gift of recall. What had Father Pat said? Oh, yes. He could still hear that quaint Irish brogue.

"I told yer dear wife 'ere, not so long ago, that God's universe is magnificently and infinitely large. It is indeed beyond our feeble ken. But, in the case you should worry your poor head off that it is too large for Him to care for you, you might set your mind on this. Let us not forget that when we look inward to things that be smaller than we, it is precisely we who become the giants of incredible size. Do ya not be knowin' that there are 10 nonillion atoms within the likes of us? Do ya wanna know how much a nonillion is?

Take a pen or pencil and write a ten with thirty zeros behind it. Ya soon will get me point."

At this point, he could see the old man leaning forward with wonder in his eyes. It was as if he were relating an awesome secret.

"I'm sure ya remember the Outside better than I, me friend, since yer new 'ere. I remember well the Irish green grass and trees. The blue sky and the sun which charts his course above. 'Tis big, the sun. One could put a million earths within it, he could. And yet, our sun is just a speck among billions and billions of suns in God's wondrous universe. But, if our sun be a speck, how wonderful a universe where specks are suns. Do ya remembah th' green trees a' wafting' in the breeze? Each branch is all part o' the' design of th' Creator."

The Priest's eyes had become wet with tears as he continued. Harold thought how often he had taken the wonders of nature for granted.

"Each branch is covered by leaves. 'Tis the very same design, year in and year out. Each single leaf is composed of molecules, millions of them. Each molecule is a constellation of atoms. And atoms?"

The old gentleman had moved even closer. His voice reflected the awe in his bright hazel eyes.

"Each wee atom is a kind of electrical solar system all by itself. In its center is an even more wee thing called a nucleus. And can ya believe it? Th' nucleus is made up o' infinitely smaller particles."

At this point, Father Pat had leaned back a bit and looked him straight in the eye.

"Harry," he said. "It all depends upon which way you cast yer eyes about ya: toward the great starry universe *outside* ourselves or toward the awesome vast universe *within* us. And, my son, it all depends on 'ow ya look at Harry Stanton. Is he a tiny fleck in the universe of galaxies? Or, is he a super colossal giant of unthinkable numbers of atoms in the microcosm below? And ya know, my boy? The very same laws that govern the myriads of stars above, the galaxies themselves, the pulsars, the quasars, the black holes and whatever else they be findin' in the Father's Creation — these same laws are those that also govern the atoms within us."

Father Pat's concluding statement was especially intriguing. "Now," he had scolded, "Why do ya get so upset and bothered because you saw another dear creature of God's universe that ya know nuthin'about? That wee little fellow is probably just one o'trillions of his and otha' kinds o' life out there. God has a plan fer them just as he 'as a plan for the likes of us. Why, me ancestors believed in the little people long before the days o' flyin' saucers. Let's not become so concerned with thinking about the Almighty's plans for them that we forget His plan for us." Then the old man had leaned over and whispered in hushed tones — "And, has it ever occurred to you, me boy, that these creatures may be part o' God's plan for us?"

Chapter Nine

Ultimate Weapon at Sector Six

"Good morning, Number 1, or should I say John?"

The tall Spartan-looking man stood up from behind his desk to greet General Thurman and Harold.

"I get called lots of things around here, Steve. It's not like it used to be. I guess they all know that I'll be retiring soon. You can call me what you like, but within limits," laughed the General.

"All right, John. So, this is BETA Number 27, eh? Harold Stanton?"

"Oh, I'm sorry. I'm still half-asleep. I spent half the night at Central working on the Bogota incident."

"Well, what's been decided? It's a sticky situation."

"We'd best not talk about it now, Steve. The information is still restricted to 1st level. Suffice it to say that the Columbian government has let us send a team in. They're dressed like American soldiers. We're using the same old cover — a crashed secret weapon."

"Can the team get near it?"

"Only within a few hundred feet. The force field starts at that point. All attempts at communication are being ignored, as usual."

"What are they going to tell the citizenry when that thing takes off, John?"

"Fortunately, it's a pretty isolated area. The few that might see it will think the Americans have repaired their aircraft and are flying it away. The team will document the alien's excavation and then bull-doze it over. But, I've said too much in front of Harold. I'd have been buzzed a good one if I weren't Number 1. Let's get back to Harold here. Sorry, Harold. We have a hot one on our hands. I didn't mean to ignore you. Harold Stanton, this is Steve Milkowsi, Colonel Steven Milkowski, BETA-1. Steve is our Beta special projects director. He'll bring you up to date with what's being done with your old brainchild. More important, he'll begin to prepare you to assume responsibility for —"

"For Beta Nova Sub-Project *Enigma*," the Colonel interrupted. "That's our code name. Very few here at Bluepaper besides you and your lovely wife are cleared to work on it."

Colonel Milkowski leaned over and shook Harold's hand firmly. "It's a real pleasure to meet you, Harold. We've benefitted much from the work of Fields, Jacobs and Stanton. Your names are bywords among the older members of Beta Special Projects."

"Why, thank you, Steve. Your comment is most gratifying. I'm most curious as to what you've done with Beta. Is Mr. Fields working on this Project?"

"BETA-26? Don't be concerned with him," the Colonel snapped coldly. Let's concentrate on you. Your coming to us was planned."

The Colonel's sudden change in temperament took Harold by surprise. He felt embarrassed. General Thurman placed his hand on Harold's shoulder.

"Take it easy on him, Steve. This is only his first day officially. He's not been here long enough to develop the proper, ah, shall we say, Bluepaper etiquette. And you, Harold. You must learn not to interject personal interests into your day to day matters of business. Save that part of your life for Sector 7. Don, for example, is none of your concern here. But I've said enough. I'm taking up precious time. Don't be too hard on him Steve. Give him a chance to get acclimated."

The General shook his head slowly as he walked toward the door. "Somehow I feel as if I've just delivered an innocent lamb to the slaughter," he quipped. "Good day, gentlemen. See you at 1700, Harold."

Colonel Milkowski pulled another chair over to his desk. "Do sit down, Harold. I find it difficult to communicate with newcomers from the Outside. There's little room for emotion here. If we didn't discipline ourselves to carrying out our assignments coolly and logically we would all go stark raving mad."

The Colonel got up and paced the floor as he rambled on.

"We must accept the inevitable. You and I are here for life so that hopefully, those on the Outside may live. But, enough of this. You've got a busy day ahead of you."

Colonel Milkowski again sat down behind the large imposing desk.

"Much of what you will learn will seem unbelievable to you. I assure you, nonetheless, that it will be quite real. It will be just as real as AI-5, which I understand, you were introduced to on Friday."

"I beg your pardon, Colonel, ah, Steven? May I ask a dumb question?"

"Of course you can ask questions. Really now, isn't this becoming quite juvenile?"

Harold's face flushed. He bit his lip and continued.

"My question is, 'what does AI stand for'?"

Colonel Milkowski glowered at him briefly and then regained his emotionless, self-assured composure.

"AI is an acronym for *Artificial Intelligence*. Weren't you told this? What kind of a briefing did they give you anyway? I suppose it's my own damned fault making them cut it down to one week. Now that you're here, we'll probably continually pay the piper for our impatience."

The Colonel reached over and pressed a button on his desk. A voice from somewhere responded — "Cybernetics."

"This is BETA-1 speaking. Would you tell CYBER-1 that I want him in my office at once?"

"CYBER-1 directs the Cybernetics laboratory," continued the Colonel as he tapped his fingers impatiently on the desk.

A door snapped open to the right of the Colonel's desk. Doctor Goldberg walked reluctantly into the room until he saw Harold. Then he smiled broadly.

"Well, hello again, Harold. What a pleasant surprise."

"What's this? You know each other? How? Colonel Milkowski paused a minute. "Of course, how stupid of me. You must be quartered together. That incident in Columbia was so interesting that I just plain forgot to check the quarters list before you arrived. I'd better take a look at that list while you two converse. I must know just who they've put you in with. Now, Manny. Harold here just informed me that he doesn't know what an AI is. I guess they expected us to tell him. Would you please enrich his obviously uninformed mind about out little captives?"

Doctor Goldberg motioned Harold to follow him over to a long table where they sat down together. He explained that the small creatures he and Don had seen had been the subject of intense research for over three decades. Post activation autopsies had revealed some startling facts. These beings did not appear to have ever lived in the sense that we understand life. There were no signs of what had been living tissue, muscles or organs. No blood. No apparent sex organs. No navel. What was assumed to have once been body liquids had dried to a fine crystalline powder. The creatures appeared to have been artificially constructed. Yet, the intricate crystalline structure found within their bodies proved beyond contemporary science's ability to duplicate. It appeared that the internal components had once been soft and pliable. There was no digestive tract. The system was closed.

It was assumed that the AIs must have been activated by some unknown energy source with life-giving properties beyond the knowledge of current science. In the area of the head, only the eyes, ears and nose appeared to have once been functional. The mouths were artificial creases with no internal connection at all. Their creators had obviously constructed them to appear manlike. Perhaps this was to appeal to man's anthropormorphic taste. The large heads contained a hemispherical structure made of layer upon layer of the same crystalline lattice-work.

It was suggested that after the body functions were revitalized by the external energy source, they received directions from the round, brain-like organ. The assumption was that somehow the internal crystalline materials would be transformed into the equivalent of a living body complete with nerves, muscle and circulatory system.

The hands themselves were four-digited. The appendages were more like claws than fingers. There was no opposing thumb. This had led to the belief that the AI forms had been limited to non-creative acts. They were probably servants of their creators.

Another disconcerting fact was that their legs seemed to have always been rigid and immobile. Even the boots were artificial. They were molded right on to the functionless legs. However, within the base of each hand and leg, there was a strange tube-like structure. It too was composed of layers of the thin glass-like material. The so-called uniforms were metallic. They appeared to have been melted and poured right over their bodies.

Harold listened incredulously to Doctor Goldberg as he continued to speak in a monotone, matter-of-fact fashion.

Few, he said, believed that the creatures had not been artificially constructed at all. They felt that man was dealing with a real life-form which was beyond his ken. Still others suggested that they were a combination of living and artificial material. Doctor Goldberg's last remarks concerned the alien craft.

"The ships themselves also require an external source of energy to operate them. I've been informed that nothing found within or without the hull of the ships could independently produce a propulsion force. There are some who believe that the postulated energy sources for both the ships and the AI's are beamed from an orbitting control ship. I think personally that —"

"That will be quite enough, Manny." Colonel Milkowski interjected. "You've covered *your* subject very well. Let's not discuss areas outside your expertise with our new member here. You may leave now. You've been most helpful."

Doctor Goldberg cast a sly wink at Harold out of the corner of his eye. "Thank you, BETA-1. I am always very happy to accommodate your every wish." He bowed mockingly.

"There's no room for sarcasm here!" blurted the Colonel. Good day, CYBER-1!"

"Good day, BETA-1." Doctor Goldberg disappeared behind the sliding door in the wall.

"Well, Harold. You now know a bit more about the AI's, eh?"

"Right," replied Harold. His mind was still in a turmoil over what he had just heard.

"I've just located your quarters list, Harold. I see that they've put you and your lovely wife on Level 1. That's VIGIL-31's level, ah, Timothy. He's a good man. Runs a tight ship. Let's see now — Fagerberg, Dobson, Castiello? All harmless clods. Grimes, Manning — yes, this looks good. Oh, what's this? Patrick O'Malley! That numberless no good scoundrel. Why have they moved him to Level 1? That man gets around too much. Number 1 has been far too lenient with him. I would wager that he knows 80% of our personnel. He probably knows much of what goes on around here. Thanks to that Priest image he touts about, Number 1 lets him talk to almost anyone. Can you believe that he conducts worship sessions here? Here at Base 3? Prayer meetings, confessions? Pure damned superstition. If I were Number 1 I'd deprogram him and ship him back to a house for the senile in Ireland. I, I'd —"

The Colonel cut himself short and looked embarrassed.

"Ha! Here I tell you that there's no place for emotions here and then I proceed to blow my top. There are few people here that can do that to me. Patrick O'Malley is one of them. Behind that dumb Irish hill-billy front he puts up is a shrewd, intellectual mind. You be careful what you say to him, Stanton. He's liable to get you into trouble."

"I, I found him to be kind and very helpful," Harold blurted out.

"I'm sure you did. You're both holy men of the cloth aren't you? Anyhow, it's almost time for lunch. Let's see what our culinary experts have burned today."

Colonel Milkowski rose and stepped over to the computer terminal on a large console. His fingers moved across the keys and he glanced at the display that appeared on the glowing screen.

"We have ham on rye, roast beef, and cheese and tomato sandwiches on today's menu. Also, milk, tea and coffee. The dessert today is pound cake. What would you like?"

"The roast beef sounds good to me. I'll have milk to drink and some pound cake. Is the cafeteria near here?"

"Cafeteria? Oh no. Watch this." The Colonel punched the keys on the terminal again. "Now, come over here and watch this."

Harold followed him over to a round closed cavity in the wall. They waited a few moments and a red light came on.

"That means my order has been acknowledged," he said rather proudly. Then a green light flashed on. "How's that for fast food service? Our order is already on its way via airtube special delivery."

After lunch, Harold was taken by the Colonel to a small laboratory on the third floor. There, he was introduced to a slight, stooped gray-headed man with a very full moustache who was fiddling with several projectors on a table.

"BETA-5, Joseph Wilheim this is BETA-27, Harold Stanton."

The old man glanced up and adjusted his bifocals. His face lit up with great anticipation when he saw Harold. He grasped Harold's hand so exuberantly that he was

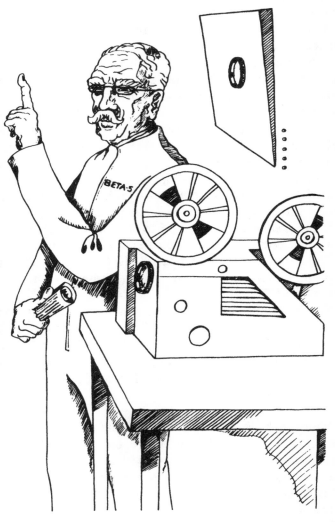

Joseph Wilheim

somewhat taken aback.

"Ah, so you are Harold Stanton. *The* Harold Stanton. We've read so much about your work. I can hardly believe that you are here. Welcome, my friend, welcome."

Harold noticed that the Colonel looked very sourly at Joseph's sudden burst of enthusiasm. "I give up," he muttered. "He's all yours for the afternoon. Start to fill him in on the Beta Projects." With that, the Colonel walked quickly out of the room.

The bespectacled old man paused a moment and then turned to Harold. "Pay no attention to his bark, my friend. We call him Big Bad Wolf behind his back. He huffs, he puffs but he can't blow house down. Heh, heh. Now, forget BETA numbers here. My name is Wilheim, Doctor Joseph Wilheim. Please call me Joseph. I call you Harold, yes?"

"Now, Harold. All week long I prepare documentary on Beta Projects just for you," he chattered excitedly in broken English. "How glad I am to see you. But, I must warn you. I am getting to be old man now. My mind? It is not what it used to be." He shrugged his shoulders resignedly. "I would teach you all I know but I forget so much. You understand? Others. They will teach you too. They have something special for you. Now, sit down over there. We will begin. Yes?"

Harold sat down and watched the tottery old soul pull down a movie screen and walk over to the projection table.

"And now, we present Professor Joseph Wilheim's documentary: *The Evolution of Project Beta*," chuckled the old man. He turned out the lights and flicked on the overhead projector.

Harold leaned back and listened in fascination as Doctor Wilheim chronicled the early days of Project Beta. From time to time, photos of himself, Don and Bill Jacobs would appear in conjunction with equipment tests, conferences and special briefings.

"It certainly was a long time ago that I looked like that," he chuckled to himself.

Then, some scenes from the archeological dig in Columbia flashed upon the screen from a slide projector. "Yes," he thought, "they certainly have done their homework: the olmec tablets. My translation. Their startling contents. How did these people know such things? I wonder if they'll show the statues with the magnetite inserts in their heads."

Thoughts of the early days of discovery raced through his mind. The writings and statues had revealed an intricate knowledge of bio-magnetic properties of the human brain. Experiments confirmed the existence of a minute magnetic field in the right lobal area of the human brain. Yes, and then the discovery of small amounts of magnetite in the same area.

Further research demonstrated that this was also true in the cases of some lower animals. Experiments were conducted with the homing pigeon. They revealed a definitive reaction between its brain and the earth's magnetic field. Further tests proved that this interaction was responsible for the ability of some animals to migrate great distances with phenomenal accuracy.

"Then came the breakthrough, eh, my friend?" exclaimed the Doctor. A number of significant events were highlighted: the successful artificial strengthening of the minute magnetic fields surrounding the magnetite; the discovery of its modulation by Extra Low Frequency (ELF) waves generated by the human brain; the incredible discovery that these biologically-generated ELF waves were a carrier for telepathy; the use of external and self-hypnosis to achieve the proper mental state for reception and transmission of telepathic thought; and, the early step by step development of the Beta machine.

Harold's role as translator, cryptologist and psychic provided a fine thread of continuity to the development of this remarkable instrument. A sense of well-being and self-esteem swept over him as he watched thoughtfully.

There were the early experiments between he and Don,

his own development of crypto-symbology, and the packaging of multiple telepathic information bits within these encrypted symbols. Finally, the lights came on. Doctor Wilheim sat down behind his desk and smiled.

"Now comes the best part, Harold. We start to answer the question that must be on your mind. Yes? What have *we* been doing with Beta *secretly*? Let us now see. I'm sure you'll be surprised.

"We soon found that all living things exhibit Beta waves of various lengths and strength. For some strange reason, Man differs from his animal friends in that each individual person has a unique Beta signature. A kind of mental fingerprint. You know yourself that this has limited your use of Beta for espionage to just a few highly trained people. But, this selectivity is a blessing in disguise. Let me explain."

"With the advent of advanced computer technology, someday, perhaps very soon, it will be feasible to transmit Beta signals to *anyone* at will. How? Picture, if you will, a Beta machine capable of transmitting a special signal of *enquiry* to John Doe. John Doe's brain then, unknown to him, transmits back his individual Beta signature automatically. His mind is now open to Beta infiltration. And, why limit it to one person? It could concern a group of diplomats or a platoon of soldiers. Through experimentation, we are isolating Beta signals that will produce headaches, nausea, voices in one's head, passivity, aberrant behavior and even programmed hallucinations."

Doctor Wilheim's face then grew very grim.

"We have also discovered, during these experiments, that every living species transmits its own unique type of signal at the moment of death. We've been able to duplicate, enhance and transmit this signal to a number of higher animals. They die instantly upon its reception. Listen, Harold. Beta will soon become *the ultimate weapon*. It will be possible to detect and kill the enemy wherever he might be. Think of it. A death signal. It will be much more selective and humane than hydrogen or neutron bombs. People will die quietly and painlessly. Their buildings and weapons will be left intact. We hope eventually to develop its use against the UFO aliens. Soon, thanks to your early efforts, it will be ours, Harold!"

Harold could restrain himself no longer. He leaped up and rushed over to Doctor Wilheim's desk. He pounded his fist down and pushed the pile of notes onto the astonished Doctor's lap. The terrified old man pushed his chair back in alarm. His glasses dropped to the floor.

"What is the matter, Harold? Why do you do this to Joseph? My glasses. I cannot see. Where are my glasses?"

"Doctor Wilheim," gasped Harold. "You, Beta and Bluepaper can all to to - -" Harold bit his lip.

"We can all go to Hell?"

Harold swung around to face Colonel Milkowski sneering contemptuously at him.

"Why, Harold, I'm surprised at this emotional outburst. My, my, my. I thought people like you and that Irish rogue were interested in saving us poor wretches from such an undeserved fate. You will say no more to Joseph about what you think of our special projects. If you have any future complaints, address them to me personally and privately. Now, pick up Joseph's glasses and come back to my office. I warn you. VIGIL has been alerted. If it weren't for my orders, they would have buzzed you at stun level when you attacked Joseph. I've been monitoring this presentation from the adjoining room. I suspected that you might be upset about using Beta as a weapon."

Flustered, Harold walked over and picked up Doctor Wilheim's glasses who stood silently rubbing his hands together nervously. Harold felt miserable.

"Here's your glasses, Joseph. I'm sorry. You were just doing your job. Thank you for your presentation. It was well done and very informative."

The old man put the glasses on and stared quizzically at Harold. "You must excuse Joseph. I go and rest. BETA-1? You will take care of him, yes?"

Harold returned to the Colonel's office. "It won't do you any good, Steven. You'll not talk me out of my decision," he insisted as they walked into the office.

"All right, Stanton. You sit down and listen to me. I've had it up to here with your nonsense. You had no conscience about your work with Beta in Bethseda. Yet, the results of your covert espionage with Beta there may someday be used in an atomic war where thousands of people will get killed."

"You remind me of someone who loves to eat meat but won't get his hands or mind bloodied working in a slaughter house. No, you'd rather eat your steak within the comfort of your own home. You shut your mind off to the realities of where the meat came from. You're willing to pay a good price to let somebody else do the dirty work.

"Stanton, this is a dirty world. If we don't develop this so-called *ultimate weapon,* the Soviets will eventually develop theirs. Already they are experimenting with the effect of microwaves on our embassy personnel in Moscow. They're not interested in selectivity. They don't have the computer technology to allow them such luxury. Our intelligence sources indicate that they are developing the capability to destroy large segments of population by utterly devastating the nervous systems of all living creatures in any given area."

Harold stared blankly at the stern-faced Colonel. He felt like a little child being scolded.

"Let me also assure you, Stanton, that your work has no *direct* part in the activities you have learned about today. That work will go on regardless of what you think or what you do. The work we have selected for you is far more important. Now, you may not care what happens to yourself. But, I'm sure that you're interested in the welfare of your wife and her father."

"You, you wouldn't dare," Harold stammered.

"Oh I wouldn't, would I? Believe me. Number 1 has authorized any means to be used, if necessary, to accomplish our objectives. How would you like to see your wife deprogrammed and placed in some private asylum on the Outside? No one would ever find her. She would be a complete amnesiac. Listen to me, you with the 'holier-than-thou' mentality. We'd even resort to bloodshed if necessary. Who would stop us? You? The law? *We* are the law here. I've had it with you. You go back to Sector 7. Think over what I've told you. And, remember. You are being watched. Just one more hint of non-cooperation on your part and somebody might get hurt. Do you understand, Stanton? Stanton? I'm addressing you. *Do you understand?*"

Harold did not look up. His head was bowed. He felt utterly devastated.

"Yes, I understand. I understand only too well, Colonel."

"Excellent, Harold. I'm so glad that you are going to cooperate because soon we want you to meet, ah, *him*."

The Colonel's voice dropped to a low hushed tone. A strange frown creased his forehead.

"Harold, you must begin working with *him* as soon as possible. Time is running out. May your God help us if He really exists. You are our only hope now of finding out what these visitations are all about."

Later on in the evening, Harold and Helen made their way to the Sector 7 cafeteria. It was their first visit. The dining hall was divided into individual enclosed eating areas identified by specific floor level numbers. After choosing their food, they strolled across the room to the partitioned area numbered *Level 1* and entered. Jack and Peter looked up from a table and greeted them enthusiastically. Others looked up and nodded in a friendly fashion.

"This is the closest thing to normality in this cursed place," Harold whispered to Helen as they edged their way over to an empty table in a corner.

Timothy Donoghue was there. He sat in a far corner opposite the door staring at them. Harold stared back with an amused smile on his face. He wasn't going to let this young upstart intimidate him. Suddenly, Timothy's eyes glanced sternly toward the entranceway.

"Look. Here comes Father Pat." Helen motioned toward the door. Father Pat it was. He was smiling broadly and heading directly for their table.

"Good evenun, good evenun to ya both. Do ya mind if I join ya for a bite to eat?"

"Why no, not at all Father. Do sit down," Helen answered. "You don't mind, do you, dear?"

Harold's heart sunk. He nodded his head in agreement but secretly wished the old man had sat elsewhere. He felt a need to be alone with Helen. It had been a very trying day, to say the least.

"Now there. Here we are together as cozy as can be. Do ya mind if I ask a' blessun' on th' meal?"

Helen bowed her head and closed her eyes, as did Father Pat. Harold, feeling somewhat self-conscious, slightly lowered his head while keeping his eyes open.

"Now, Good Father in Heaven," Father Pat whispered. "We all be a' thanken' ya for our food. (And, my good friends, if ever you would like a private talk, come ova' to my place for a time o' prayer. I have a room where we can talk about buzz-deserven' things without bein' buzzed, I do.) Amen!"

Harold and Helen lifted their heads up and tried not to look surprised. Father Pat nonchalantly raised his head, unfolded a napkin on his lap and winked slyly at the startled couple.

Chapter Ten

Beta Nova

Harold reported on schedule at BETA-1's office on Tuesday morning and proceeded directly to meet with Joseph at the Beta lab.

"Why, Joseph, what on earth happened to your face? It looks like you just returned from a beach vacation in Florida!"

"Ah, my tan? Alas, again my old age is showing."

Joseph shrugged his shoulders. A weak smile appeared on his face.

"I fell asleep during my infra-red bath."

Then he frowned and sighed. He stared longingly into nothingness.

"Florida? Beaches? Real sunshine? Blue sky? Please my' friend, do not speak of these things to me. I have put them out of my mind long ago. You would be wise to do so also. Such things exist for us no more, no more."

His voice trailed off as he continued his pitiful gaze into the past.

"Enough, enough," he exclaimed as he waddled over to the array of projectors on the table. "Sit down, sit down. We must begin."

The antennas looked like the ones at the Maryland Beta site. But these were immense in size. The same deep coneshaped receiving dish was a dead giveaway. But, something was missing. Where were the transmitting antennas? Their absence was conspicuous at every installation portrayed on the screen.

Harold listened carefully to Joseph. It soon became apparent why Don had been forcefully removed from Beta. He had inadvertently discovered that that strange interference on the Beta equipment at Maryland coincided with local UFO sighting reports. Unknown to Don, Beta had already been improvised to become a UFO detecting device. This equipment was classified above Top Secret!

"So you see," Joseph remarked in closing, "yesterday we learned that all living things on earth emanate Beta waves. Today we learn that whoever controls the UFO and the AI's also emanates a broad type of Beta wave. Yes? Unfortunately for him, your friend, Mr. Fields, independently discover this amazing fact, yes?"

"Who operates the Beta UFO detectors, Joseph? You've shown me installations all over the world. And, why only *receiving* antennas. Haven't you attempted contact with the aliens using Beta?"

"Please, one question at a time, my friend Harold. First, only carefully-screened personnel operate Beta. They know nothing of its nature. They are told it is advanced radar. They merely operate it. All data is automatically channeled through secure links to Phoenix Central. Central supplements this data with *unknown track* data from NORAD and allied radar installations. Beta information is also transmitted by orbitting satellites. Yes, my friend. The fruits of your labors are also in space. We have a total of twenty-one Beta detectors in synchronous orbit around the earth. Every deep space probe also carried a Beta detector.

"Now, you asked about transmitting? We dare not. The incident at Eglin Air Force Base was a warning to all of us."

"What happened at Eglin?"

"A huge powerful deep-space tracking radar was designed by some of our people here at Base 3. Its advanced computer-controlled servo system would allow us to continuously monitor the activity of alien carrier ships both in orbit and in deep space. It was installed and tested at Eglin.

"We waited for the opportune time. It soon came when a number of cylinders rendezvoused over the Pacific and accelerated away from the earth at a great speed. Our radar station at Kwajelein fed their location coordinates to the Eglin unit. When the signals faded at Kwajelein, the Eglin unit was activated. It picked up the cylinders effortlessly. They were tracked to a huge carrier ship. As soon as the powerful radar waves struck the carrier ship it happened.

"An immensely powerful wave of energy rode back down our radar beam from the carrier ship. The Eglin unit was totally destroyed. It started with the antenna. Then, like an intelligent entity, the energy found its way through interconnecting cables to the Control building. The operations personnel barely escaped with their lives. The building was completely destroyed by fire!

"So, friend Harold, that explains why all Beta UFO Detection Installations are *passive* receivers. They might consider Beta transmissions a weapon. But, the primary reason is that we do not need to transmit to detect. We can track alien craft without their knowing it. Is it not beautiful?" Doctor Wilheim remarked as he rubbed his hands in glee. "Now, my dear colleague, I think we must think of earthly things. BETA-1 wants you to join him for lunch. I will see you here at 1300. We will then discuss a brand new project: *Beta Nova*. Yes?"

Harold entered Colonel Milkowski's office.

"Don't just stand there, Harold. Come on in. Sit down, relax, enjoy some food." the Colonel reiterated as he pointed to a strange chair.

The chair was similar to the one used to restrain him at the hospital.

"What kind of a chair is that?" Harold demanded to know. It reminded him of chairs that he had seen at beauty shops. A plastic helmet, very much like a hair dryer, was attached to an extended central arm. It was mounted on a sliding bracket. The bracket was attached to a central post connected to the back of the chair. Wires ran from the helmet into a jack mounted on a panel encased in the wall.

"You ask me what kind of chair is that? If I told you, you wouldn't believe me. You'll see later. Sit down. Make friends with part of the new Beta Special Projects product line: We've called them the Beta Nova devices. You'll find this one most interesting. Go ahead. Sit down. Put the helmet on. It doesn't hurt."

Harold hesitated. He picked up the helmet and looked inside warily. The probes looked similar to the man-machine connector rods that Don had developed for use with Beta at NSA.

"Some of it looks familiar, eh Stanton? It should: Now, I repeat. Sit down and let me hook you up. I'm trying not to lose my patience. If I have to, I'll have two very strong fellows here in a moment to, ah, assist you. I believe you've met them before. Now, if you'll sit down voluntarily, we can dispense with them and the restraining devices."

Harold sat down reluctantly. The Colonel carefully slid the over-sized helmet over Harold's head. He adjusted five internal probes. One pressed into Harold's right temple, one to the back of his head, one to each side of his head and one onto the top of his head. The flat-ended probes pressed into Harold's skin. They were uncomfortable but certainly not painful.

"Okay, Harold, please eat your lunch. I'll be back in about a half-hour to disconnect you. Don't attempt to remove anything by yourself. Eat, relax and enjoy. I'll be back soon."

Harold ate quickly. Then he sat back and pondered.

"Are they redetermining my Beta signature with more refined equipment?"

His mind wandered back to the park, the bridge and his jump into the river. He reminisced about his strange experience and his stay in the hospital at Phoenix Base 3. His thoughts turned to Myrna.

"Ah yes, Myrna. Lovely girl. Wonder where she is and

what she's doing?"

Harold's dreams came to an abrupt halt when Colonel Milkowski strode haughtily back into the room.

"Well, well. There you are safe and sound. Didn't I tell you there was nothing to be afraid of? Now, let me remove this thing from your head."

"What was all this about?" Harold queried as he got up and stretched and rubbed his head.

"That's precisely what you and Joseph will be discussing in a few minutes. I do wish that I could attend this session with you but I've got important matters to attend. Good day, BETA-27."

Doctor Wilheim was at the far corner of the lab adjusting what looked like a television set when Harold walked in.

"Is that part of Beta Nova?" Harold asked incredulously. "A television set?"

"Ah," replied Joseph petting the top of the instrument. "This is a very special television set. Now, together we watch a show, yes? We watch an old fashioned silent movie starring one of your closest acquaintances. We haven't perfected sound yet."

Harold watched curiously as the screen brightened. A distorted picture appeared. What was that? A glass of milk? A sandwich? Abruptly, Harold's mind became instantly linked to the hodge-podge of fast-moving scenes that appeared on the screen. An overwhelming feeling of deja vu gripped his senses. Part of him seemed to be back at Colonel Milkowski's office in the strange chair. What was happening?

Harold closed his eyes protectively. The mental pictures continued for a moment and then dissolved to nothingness. He opened his eyes. Again the dancing images on the screen took instant hold of him. A kaleidoscope of symbols, objects, blurred faces and distant places faded in and out. Everything was vaguely superimposed over a steady visual image of the Colonel's office. Then, a woman's face and body slowly materialized and dematerialized in trial and error fashion. Harold gasped.

"Myrna? No! I musn't think of such things."

The semi-nude body of Myrna played over the screen. Then it was replaced by Helen, then a Bible and then Christ in a flowing robe. The river, the park, his jump, then Helen's father and Myrna again! Harold again re-experienced his mental attempts to sublimate the pictorial sexual fantasies that moved relentlessly across the screen. He shut his eyes and shouted.

"Turn it off, Joseph! Please turn if off. I don't want to see anymore. Turn it off!"

"It's almost over, my friend. Calm down," urged Doctor Wilheim's soothing voice.

Harold opened his eyes just in time to see an image of Colonel Milkowski entering his office. Then the screen dimmed to nothing. Harold sat in semi-shock. The afterimages of his past thoughts still wafted haphazardly through his mind.

"It's all over now, Harold," Joseph said gently as he walked over and switched the instrument off.

Harold's eyes still stared as if glued to the darkened screen. He had actually seen and mentally relived his very past thoughts. There was no other rational explanation.

"What do you *think*, my good friend? And I don't mean that to be a pun."

"I, I think it's incredible, marvelous and an unbelievable breakthrough. Joseph, you must show me how this was done! Such a thing is beyond my wildest dreams. Have you experimented with telepathic links yet?"

"Beta Nova's *Psi Machine* is still in its infancy, Harold. It has serious drawbacks. As you know, such telepathic links require that the Beta signature of any given participant be known. Thus far, we have not been able to accomplish a psychic link-up. Also, there is another limitation. Most of the imagery is only discernible to the mind of the participant. Much of what appeared on that screen was incomprehensible to me. However, with the help of the computer, we hope someday to unscramble this incoherent imagery. I have learned to recognize sexual symbols and overtones. They are common to every male participant we have monitored. Doctor Freud would have a heyday with our little toy, eh?"

Harold felt embarrassed. A deep conviction of guilt and shame caused him to visibly blush. Doctor Wilheim smiled knowingly and placed a hand on Harold's shoulder.

"You like our Myrna, eh? She will be flattered, I'm sure."

"No, ah, yes, I mean that, I, I'm a Christian, Joseph. It certainly wasn't Christlike to think thoughts like that. I'm thoroughly ashamed of myself."

"Ah, but such thoughts have always been there, Harold. You are especially ashamed because I saw them with you, eh? Well now, if it is any consolation, my friend, I can assure you that your daydreams are tame compared to most that I've been exposed to. And, there is a marked difference."

"A difference? What kind of a difference?"

"Some of you, not very many, but some of you resist such fantasies. Most encourage them without any conscience at all, including myself. It all depends upon what we believe about such thoughts."

Suddenly, the old man began chuckling to himself.

"We have, for example, an old Catholic Priest here who sublimates his natural desires in a unique way."

"You mean Father Pat?" Harold asked.

"Ah, so you have come to know our resident Priest? Yes, well, heh, heh, we had Father Pat monitored by the Psi Machine several months ago. Somehow the inquisitive old geezer found out about it and asked if he could be hooked up. Number 1 seems to have a soft spot for the old man so he sent him over to me. I hooked him up and left him alone for several minutes. Then we viewed his thoughts together. There must have been some nun in his distant past that he had, what do you call it, a crush on. No sooner had he mentally defrocked her than he quickly redressed her piece by piece with a white robe, sandals, a pair of wings and a halo!

"I can still see the shocked expression on his face when she first apeared on the screen. 'May the Saints preserve us,' he shouted. 'This machine is the devil's invention to be sure. Only the Almighty should know our very thoughts. Th' spirit is willin' but th' flesh, 'tis weak.' With that he stormed out the door. Heh, heh. He's never been back to see me."

Harold chuckled as he imagined the whole episode in his mind's eye. Joseph, in the meantime, continued to describe other Beta Nova projects being developed. His closing remarks were intriguing.

"Harold Stanton, you have been selected for perhaps the most important task facing the Bluepaper operation. Let me explain, yes? For years we attempt unsuccessfully to contact the entities behind the UFOs. We need to know *why* they are and *what* their intentions are, yes? You, Harold Stanton may help us find answers to these vital questions."

"Me?" stammered Harold. "You must be mistaken. I know nothing of their intentions. Why, I hardly knew what the term UFO was all about until I came here. Surely you must be joking. How could I possibly be of any help in this area?"

"By establishing communication with someone that we *know* has had direct and intimate contact with the aliens," Doctor Wilheim retorted.

"And just who might that be? demanded Harold.

A far-away look of wonder appeared in Joseph's eyes. The hushed awe in the tone of his voice complemented the strange look on his wrinkled face. Harold had seen and heard this before. It was frightening.

"*Him*," Joseph answered. "*Him*."

Chapter Eleven

The Key to Fatima

"Harold, darling. I've got wonderful news!" Helen threw her arms about him as he stepped inside the sliding door to their apartment. Dad says I'm to report to BETA-1 with you tomorrow morning!"

"What? Colonel Milkowski didn't mention this to me."

"Ol' sourpuss?" Helen laughed. "He never has anything good to say. I think he likes me though," Helen teased.

"Oh? Well he'd better keep his eyes off you. That fellow is a challenge to my Christian ethics. Anyway, what say we get some food and you can tell me all about it?"

"I can't say anymore until we're on duty together. You don't want me to get buzzed again, do you? Oh, I'm so excited about being together on the job."

"Now, now, BETA-22," Harold admonished with a wink as he tweaked her chin. "Musn't get emotional about your job. Thus saith BETA-1!" Both laughed and headed for the cafeteria. Again Father Pat joined them at their table.

"Well now. After we eat I'd like to have ye visit me digs," Father Pat said breathlessly as he sat down.

"Your what?" queried Harold.

"He means his apartment, dear," Helen explained.

"Why, ah, what for?" asked Harold.

"Oh, just for a bit o' fellowship. And as I was sayin' just last evenun', perhaps we can have a wee time of special prayer to the Almighty. It will help us to bear this ungodly place, it will, eh?" Father Pat winked.

"We'd love to," answered Harold as he returned the wink.

After supper, the three left for Father Pat's *digs*.

"And where do you think you three are going, may I ask?"

The trio swung around. Following behind them was none other than Timothy Donoghue.

"Timothy, me boy! What a pleasant surprise. Why, we are goin' to my place for a time o' fellowship and prayer. Would you care to jine us?"

"I want no part of your stupid superstitions. Why wasn't I informed about this little get-together? Haven't I told you before that - -"

"That you want to be kept informed of all me meetuns? That ya did, lad. But them's your regulations. Bluepaper procedures, Section 3, paragraph 6 give us freedom of assembly within our level without requiring anyone's permission as long's it's done before th' curfew. Ya'll not take away the wee bit of' freedom we 'ave or me name's not Patrick O'Malley!"

"You may fool Number 1, old man, but you don't fool me. Why he keeps your apartment unmonitored is beyond me. It's a dangerous precedent. Don't you think I know that you use your so-called chapel meetings to discuss restricted data?"

"Go on with ya. You know nothin' o' the sort. If ya don't stop botherin' me and me fine friends, Number 1 might jest be a' hearin' about some o' yer own shenanigans. It would na go well with ya if he *knew*, ya know."

Timothy turned pale. "What do you mean by that, you old buzzard?"

"Never ya mind. I don't give away me sources unless 'tis necessary. But, if ya don't trot right back where ya came from, this very instant, I might deem it necessary right now!"

A brief frown appeared on Timothy's face before he wheeled about haughtily and excused himself. "I've got to get back to the cafeteria anyhow. You don't scare me. Someday, my holy friend, we'll have a new Number 1 around here. Things will be different then. I hope you're still alive. It will be a pleasure to see you put in your proper place!"

Harold and Helen followed Father Pat down the corridor to his apartment.

"Cum on in, dear friends, and be makin' yourself at home while I make a trip to th' bathroom. A talk with Tim O'Donoghue is at least good for me plumbing. He always keeps me loose, he does."

Helen put her hand over her mouth to prevent a loud outburst of laughter as the robust old man strode away to tend to his *plumbing*.

"He's a scream, isn't he, dear?" Helen remarked as the two walked over to a black sofa and sat down. Harold glanced around the dimly lit room. Dark furnishings were accentuated by a white-tiled floor. Religious paintings adorned the wall. A statue of Saint John holding a cross gazed silently from a corner. It looked as if Number 1 really had catered to Father Pat's every taste.

The Priest soon reappeared and motioned them toward a door.

"And now, let me show you the wee Chapel of Our Lady. Ye're welcome to cum 'ere and worship on th' Lord's Day. We 'ave Catholics and Protestants alike. There be but a few of us. But the Good Lord said He'd be with even two or three of us gathered. Cum on in."

The Priest genuflected before a simple but beautiful altar. It was adorned by a multi-colored tapestry draped over a white linen cloth. A rugged wooden cross stood on a stand. Father Pat sat on one of a number of chairs which faced the altar in a semi-circle. He motioned for them to sit down beside him.

"And now, Professor and Mrs. Harold Stanton, allow me the privilege of reintroducing myself. I am Father Patrick Henry O'Malley, Special Agent, Vatican Intelligence."

Helen cast a disquieting glance at Harold who could only muster a surprised "Wh-hat?" to this incredible announcement. Apart from this, what startled them equally was the fact that Father Pat's rough Irish brogue had suddenly given way to the crisp diplomatic accent of an English gentleman.

Harold stood to his feet and grabbed Helen by the arm. "We'd better get out of here," he whispered as he cast a puzzled look at Father Pat. The Priest gazed up at them with an intense expression on his wrinkled red face.

"Look," Harold exclaimed, "I don't know who you are or why you brought us here but I can tell you this much. I want no trouble for either my wife or myself. My intuition tells me that our coming here means trouble."

Father Pat rose to his feet and faced Harold. He glanced at Helen and smiled warmly.

"I say, you both look at me as if I were daft. I don't blame you one bit for that. But I do blame you for not giving a fellow Christian the benefit of a doubt. All I am asking is that you both sit down and hear me out. Then, if you like, go. Whichever the case may prove to be, all that I ask is you do not repeat what you have heard to anyone. Fair enough?"

Helen squeezed Harold's hand. "That *is* fair enough, isn't it dear? Can't we stay? I feel sure that this man, Father Pat or whoever, is one of the few real friends we have here."

"But how do we know this isn't some kind of a trap, Helen? I mean, perhaps this place *is* being monitored and he's just led us to believe otherwise. This could very well be a Bluepaper security test of our trustworthiness. I for one don't plan to flunk. Let's go."

Father Pat shook his head sadly. "Come now, my friend. Let's not get in a huff. I know many things. My knowledge is beneficial to the three of us. You must believe me. I assure you that Bluepaper knows nothing of this. This room contains no monitors."

Helen looked expectantly at Harold. "Well?"

"Oh, all right. We'll stay," Harold said reluctantly as he motioned Helen to sit down again. "I must be crazy for taking a chance like this. But, I suppose that trust has to begin somewhere in this place. It may as well be here although I fully expect to be *buzzed* any moment."

"They already have you well trained in their ways, brother Harold. This place runs by fear. We must strive to live above that fear, dear friends. Saint John himself reminds us in his First Epistle that 'perfect love casts out fear'. Look at it from my point of view. I have decided, in good faith, to entrust you with my secret. I am willing to take the chance that you will not expose me. Time is running out for me. I'm an old man. I may go to be with our Lord at any time. And, speaking of time, the curfew warning bell will be sounding before we know it. Of necessity, I must be brief in explaining my part in all of this. We can fill in details later at another meeting.

"Now, whether you agree with me or not, the Catholic Church is a political as well as a religious system. The nations of the world have their Presidents, Prime Ministers, Kings, Queens and Dictators. But, within all of these nations that they rule are members of the Catholic Church. The Church looks beyond the temporal leaders of the world to a higher allegiance. I refer to His Holiness, the Vicar of Christ. The Pope is responsible for the *spiritual* rule of millions within the nations.

"But, there are times when His Grace must directly influence the political affairs of nations for the good of the kingdom of God. This task requires accurate information. Thus, there are those like myself who lead double lives: the life of a Priest and the life of an intelligence agent. Vatican Intelligence has such people posted all over the world.

"Thus, when World War II broke out, I was instructed to enlist as a Chaplain in the United States Army Air Force. The Vatican needed eyes and ears in key positions throughout the world. This included priests and nuns in allied and in axis countries.

"When the *foo-fighters* began to be sighted in the European War theater, the Vatican showed great interest for some reason unknown to me at the time. The Vatican singled me out especially to look into this because of my background as an Astronomer-Priest.

"I was in a unique position to collect this data while serving with the 15th Army Air Force. Many of the strangest *foo-fighter* reports never reached the ears of G-2. But they did reach the Holy See through the likes of myself and other Vatican agents. Such episodes were reported to me during counseling and confession with some badly frightened pilots. They literally feared for their sanity because of some of the things they saw and experienced.

"As soon as Italy was in Allied hands, I was called to the Vatican ostensibly to receive the Pope's personal blessing. It was in July of 1944. But, I also received a briefing that caused me many sleepless nights. It had to do with the Close Encounters at Fatima, Portugal, in 1917."

"Fatima? Close Encounters with UFOs? But I've read about Fatima. A miracle was supposed to have happened, not a UFO event," Harold interrupted.

"Harold, if Fatima were to occur today, it would be called a Close Encounter of the Third Kind UFO event. The oval aerial objects reported at Fatima were identical to what is being reported as UFOs all over the world today."

"But the witnesses were children who claimed to speak to the Virgin Mary," Helen interjected.

"Perhaps they did. Perhaps they didn't. Tradition tells us, of course, that Mary herself ascended bodily into the heavens. I have an open mind. Then again, perhaps the aliens took on the form of a familiar religious figure to accomodate the chidren's beliefs; to cause them not to be frightened. What I do know is that the message given by the entity at Fatima is of vital importance. His Holiness is anxiously awaiting certain answers which may revolutionize both Christendom and the religions of the world.

"Fatima, if you will recall, involved three shepherd children who witnessed supernatural-like events at Fatima, Portugal in 1917. The main event took place about noon on October 13, 1917. The 70,000 people who had gathered to watch the predicted happening were not disappointed. A huge silver spinning oval object descended over them just after a brief rain shower. They thought it was the sun falling on them. It came so low that the crowd thought they would be crushed.

"Everyone saw it: the pious, the atheists, the priests and the scientists. The Church, after investigation, declared it to be one of the best authenticated miracles of all times. Now, let me get back on track again. I was telling you of the briefing I received by Vatican Intelligence in 1944.

"There were other agents there besides myself. His Holiness himself was present to stress the importance of the matter. At this time we were told of *another witness* to the wonderful happenings at Fatima. The witness was a young shepherd boy. He had told no one except the parish priest of his encounter with the glowing object. The priest, in turn, had sworn him to secrecy. The message given this lad by an entity was sent to the Holy See for comparison with the messages given the three shepherd girls. I myself was given a portion of the message given the shepherd boy.

"We were told that neither the Church nor the world were ready to hear the messages from Fatima. It is my opinion, nonetheless, that had they been released, bit by bit, perhaps this world would be much better prepared for what is coming."

"You surely don't mean the so-called UFOs?" asked Harold.

"Yes, that is exactly what I mean. Their appearance may very well be the sign of a long-awaited event. I refer to the Second Coming of the Lord Himself!"

"Whew!" whistled Harold, "That's pretty hard for me to swallow."

"The Bible teaches that Christ will return with His angels on the clouds of heaven," Helen insisted. "He doesn't need flying saucers."

"Ah," the Priest sighed. "But to those living in the first century, what flew in the skies except clouds and birds.

Helen? Perhaps this is a case of non-technologically oriented people trying to describe super-technological devices in terms of their limited language and culture," the Priest replied.

"I think that you're both wrong," Harold quipped. "The Second Coming is allegorical. We, the Church are supposed to bring Christ to earth again by allowing Him to live in us. But, I've argued enough with Helen on this one so I'd better keep my mouth shut."

"Your reactions to such an idea are but a microcosm of the world's reaction to such a statement coming from the Pope," Father O'Malley replied. "That is why a cover-up has existed over the years. Can you imagine what the reaction would have been in the non-space age world of 1917? But, for argument's sake, just sit on my statement a bit. Let me continue.

"I've been with Bluepaper or its predecessors since I was taken into special custody on December 26, 1944. I remember the incident as if it happened yesterday. It would be good for both of you to know how I happen to be here. Let's go back to World War II again, if you will.

"Vatican Intelligence could not be sure that the *foofighters* were not just some revolutionary German weapon. What with the V-1's and V-2's, we hardly knew what to expect to see in the skies. Then, the Vatican received intelligence reports that the same kind of flying objects were being sighted by Allied and Japanese bomber crews in the Pacific War Theater. Our experts could not conceive that any German device could have such an operating range. They ruled out a German-Japanese co-development of such incredible devices. So, the Vatican pulled some strings. I was soon on my way States' side for furlough and reassignment to the Far East to check out these reports.

"When I arrived in San Francisco, I enquired about to see what help I could be until my new orders were cut. Since Christmas was just a few days away, I asked if there were any installations that I could visit to conduct Christmas services. I was looking for a lonely place where such a visit would be especially appreciated. After much pestering, I found out that there were a number of small lonely surveillance installations located on the Aleutian Islands. They were manned by personnel who endured extraordinary hardships guarding the Bering Straits. The only visits these poor souls got was by a supply plane.

"Now it just happened that an aircraft was scheduled to make a special flight out there from Anchorage. My superior officer's descriptions of the ice, snow and unbelievable low temperatures did not put me off a bit. I was flown to Anchorage and waited overnight for the flight. Two nights I waited to be exact. We had to wait for good flying weather. This didn't come until Christmas day itself. When I reported for duty that morning, there was quite a hullaballoo going on as to whether I should be allowed to go or not. It seems that a brief radio message had been relayed from a small outpost on the tiny island of Buldir I: Something about unknown aircraft lights circling the island. Then the radio's transmission suddenly was jammed by some type of interference. Attempts to contact the station had been unsuccessful. We had no aircraft in the area so the Japanese were prime suspects.

"However, other posts and reconaissance ships assured Alaskan Command that there were no ships or Japanese aircraft within range of the island. Most thought that a spectacular display of Aurora Borealis activity had caused both the lights and the transmission trouble. Other stations in the area had experienced loud static. So, the pilot was ordered to check out the installation and land if necessary. This took priority over other stopovers.

"While they were arguing, I put on my chute and walked out to the plane. I had never seen a C-46 outfitted with skis. I must admit that I did have visions of crashing in some desolate, snow-bound area. I had heard someone mention that Buldir I didn't have an airstrip! It was usually serviced by a small observation craft, not a C-46.

"Well, we took off and headed for Buldir I. A small contingent of three armed soldiers had joined us. I noted that they didn't look or talk like ordinary G-1's. But I didn't think much of it at the time.

"When we arrived over Buldir, the pilot put the C-46 into a low slow orbit around the tiny island. His voice came in over the intercom. He said there wasn't any response to his radio signals. I looked out the window. The only sign of life was smoke pouring out of several huts. The pilot again spoke. He asked what we could make of the marking in the snow to the north of the mess hall. The three men began pointing and talking excitedly about the strange round mark in the snow. I saw it. It looked as if it had been made by a huge round cookie cutter.

"The marking was located beside a large quonset hut which served as the mess hall. Steam was rising from it. The three men looked very anxiously at me and then departed to the tail end of the aircraft. They huddled together and argued about something. Then they returned. One of them showed me an ID card. He was an OSS Major. The Major ordered me to go to the rear of the plane and say nothing to anyone. I was told to keep away from the window. He outranked me, so I complied. Then the plane made a very dangerous landing. It snapped a ski tip. The worst of my fears had been realized. I thought we'd probably be stranded there. Let me briefly summarize what happened next.

"When the three armed men disembarked and entered the mess hall they encountered a most bizarre sight. There, sitting at the mess hall table like paralyzed zombies, were the personnel of Buldir I. One of the men raced back and asked if anyone on board had any medical training. I spoke up that I had received such training for emergency use. I also impressed him by telling him that I had a Doctor's Degree in Astrophysics.

"Well, he ran back and then returned for me. He ordered everyone else to stay aboard the aircraft. I entered the mess hall and couldn't believe my eyes. There they were, terror written on their faces, sitting stiffly in front of plates with food still on them. It was as if time had suddenly stood still for them. A fear, like I've never felt before took hold of me like some unseen vise. The situation was utterly alien.

"When I walked in, the other two men, (I assume they were G-2) had lost all sense of composure. They were going around the table, shaking, slapping and shouting at the paralyzed men. There was no response.

"I forced myself to go up to the nearest one, a young black corporal. His skin was warm. I searched for his pulse. I couldn't find one at first. When I did, it was incredibly slow. He was just barely breathing. It appeared as if all his body processes had somehow been slowed down to a hibernation-like state. I tried to bend his arm. It wouldn't move. It was the same with all of them. They were all locked into the positions that we'd found them in.

"I found the mess sergeant behind the grill. He had apparently suffered the same paralysis while standing and had toppled over. There was a small lump on his head but not any blood. Two of us stayed in the Mess Hall while the other two went to the radio shack. The fire must have been out for several hours. The small oil drum was empty. I was told that it was near the freezing mark when the two walked in. There was the radio operator. His hand was on the key. He was just staring unknowingly at the transmitter. They wrapped him up as best they could and moved him to the mess hall.

"I sat down and listened to the OSS battle over what to do next. One of them checked the oil drum and food situation. Another asked me if I could operate a transmitter. I laughed and told them no. That was one trade that the Army hadn't taught me. It was a white lie. I could take no chances of their discovering anything about my extracurricular training for Vatican Intelligence.

"It was decided that three of us would stay. The Major made me take an oath not to reveal what I had seen and flew back to Anchorage on the C-46. By late afternoon, two

C46's landed. The unconscious men were wrapped in thick insulated rubber mats and flown away in one of the C-46's. Each had an individual assigned to watch over him in transit. A team of men from the other aircraft photographed and measured the strange indentations in the snow and geiger counter readings were taken. Another team searched the base unsuccessfully for other personnel. Then they planted explosives everywhere. Shortly thereafter, a light plane landed. You'll never guess who stepped out of it so I'll tell you. It was John Thurman. He was only a Colonel then.

"John got out and inspected everything very carefully. He ordered the C-46's to take off. Then he looked at me. I can still see him there just shaking his head with a disgusted look on his face. He ordered me to get into the back seat of the small plane. I did. The pilot strapped me in so firmly that I could barely move. John went around activating the priming devices attached to the explosives. Then he jumped into the plane and ordered the pilot to take-off. He did. We circled high above the island until the buildings erupted in smoke and flame.

" 'Well, Father'," he said casually. " 'It's too bad you had to die back there. Those Japs don't care who they kill, do they?' "

"The Colonel told me that there were those who had suggested strongly that he really should leave me behind to blow up with the installation. I realized then that I had stumbled onto something vitally important involving the flying discs. Life meant nothing to whoever was giving the orders. I was thankful to be alive.

"When I recovered from the initial shock of it all, I asked him why he had spared me. He told me that he had a soft spot for men of the cloth. He himself was a seminary dropout. 'But,' he said, 'I'm afraid Mother Nature and I just couldn't go along with your total abstinence.'

"Well, we had a long flight together. It was the beginning of a long friendship. I was kept at Base 1 and then Base 2. From time to time I'd see John. We'd sit up for hours discussing Astronomy and Theology. Then we lost track of each other for a number of years.

"Later I was moved to Phoenix Base 3. You can imagine my surprise when the *new* Number 1 arrived to inspect the new facility. It was John, now General John Thurman. So, now you know why he's so lenient with me. We are the best of friends. Believe me, anyone in the Number 1 position has very few friends."

"Wow!" exclaimed Harold. "That's some story. I don't know how you could stand living in isolation from the outside world for so long."

"It's no worse than some of my compatriots who spend their lives praying and meditating behind monastery walls. To me, and to the Holy Fathers that I have outlived, it's been a God-send. We feel that this was all meant to be. Here am I, Agent VA246, privy to the greatest secret in the world which may have a direct connection with the Faith."

"From what BETA-1 tells me, you really get around this place. He's not too pleased about this. He says you know too much. Now, suppose he's correct. So what? All your knowledge and any knowledge that Helen and I may obtain is going to die with us. What good is that to the Vatican or anyone else?"

"I might as well completely lay myself bare before both of you. I've said enough to be put in solitary for the rest of my life. Wherever I've gone, they've allowed me to bring both my books and ecclesiastical odds and ends. They never suspected that I was anything but a priest. Thank the Good Lord, they've never taken a close look at my belongings. My 'Father Pat' image covers a multitude of sins. What would you say if I told you that I communicated with the Vatican regularly?"

"I would find that very difficult to believe, Father," Helen replied. "I've been here long enough to see that there's no way out of here unless you're one of the privileged few. Even they always return. They must be watched very carefully."

"How could you communicate with the Vatican?" Harold

asked.

"Let's just say that there are some here who put their Faith before Bluepaper. I've been able to influence and recruit some good Catholic men in strategic places. A Beta Repair Technician, a Courier, and a Guard. I also have those who serve His Holiness in other strategic places throughout the Base. Over the years I've been able to establish a small but efficient counter-intelligence network."

"I wouldn't have believed it possible!" exclaimed Harold. "How do you conceal what you are sending out?"

"Oh, there are many ways. A veritable concealed miniature laboratory exists within the trappings of my trade. When I was on the Outside, I sent messages to the Vatican on the backs of postage stamps. We also use inconspicuous methods such as this." Father O'Malley fumbled in the inside pocket of his clerical robe and pulled something out. "Now, see this? What is it?"

Helen reached over and took it in her hand. "Why, it looks like one of those wafers used for taking Communion. Where did you ever get it?"

"Oh, I brought a good supply with me when they packed me off to Base 1. They let me take practically all my belongings. No questions were asked. But there are two kinds of wafers: edible and non-edible. Watch this now." Father Pat held the little white disc up to the light and peeled off a thin section. "Feel this," he said.

Harold reached over. "May I?" he said. He touched the wafer. It stuck to his finger.

"Hold it by the edges! Don't try to pull it off! You'll rip your skin. Apply pressure and slide it off," Father Pat said quickly.

Harold pushed in and slid it off his index finger. He was careful not to touch the sticky side. He passed it back to the Priest. "What does this prove?" he asked.

"That little wafer, my friend, is the stationery that I send my messages on," chuckled the old man. "Our messengers stick them on the roof of their mouths."

"How on earth do you get them out of here and to the Vatican?"

"By a heavenly way, my friend. You see, I have persuaded Number 1 to allow Catholics to take Holy Communion while they are on the Outside. He believes that it is good for their morale. It's very hard for them to go outside on some errand for Bluepaper and then have to return. Of course, while outside, they are watched by a member of VIGIL who accompanies them. Both are watched, in turn, by members of our Outside intelligence community. The penalty for any deviation from a prescribed plan is death."

"You mean some kind of exchange goes on during Mass?" Harold asked.

"Precisely. I established the first link when I was at Base 1. During one of John's visits I complained. I told him that I should have the right to hear Mass at the hands of another Priest once in a while. Would you believe that he actually took me to Mass himself? Security at Base 1 was nothing like it is here. Well, that Priest sure got a shock when I mumbled the code word to him in Latin. It was wartime. All Priests were alerted to support Vatican Intelligence. It was probably this poor country Priest's first contact with us. The good Father tried not to look shocked. I figured that John wouldn't notice. He was sitting far enough away. So, that was the beginning. It has really evolved since then."

"Aren't you afraid that Timothy will find you out?" asked Harold.

"Ha!" laughed Helen. "Father has something on Tim. He really took off when you threatened him. It must be something pretty bad."

"It probably is. But don't tell Tim this. I don't have a thing on him. It's just my faith in human nature. I figure he's not the puritanical regulation-keeper he says he is. By the look on his face, human nature has not failed me. I'm sure your experience with Beta Nova gave you a glimpse of what the Lord sees in us daily. 'For out of men's hearts come evil thoughts, sexual immorality, theft, murder, adultery, greed, malice, deceit, licentiousness, envy, slander, arrogance and folly.' What would we do without His Grace and Forgiveness, my friends? Yes, I understand that Joseph had you hooked up to the Psi machine. What did you see from within, Harold? I'm sure you don't want to talk about it. Well, I'm just as sure Tim's unregenerate heart gets him into all sorts of mischief that he'd rather keep secret."

Harold felt ashamed. He hadn't told Helen about the episode at all. She hadn't asked. Probably because she didn't want to discuss her own results with Beta Nova. Suddenly, something that Dr. Wilheim had said flashed through his mind. He looked at Father Pat and grinned.

"And why the smile, Harold? Is the subject of your sinful nature funny?"

"Oh no, good Father," said Harold in the most pious tone he could muster. "I was just thinking of how a certain defrocked nun would look if one dressed her with a white robe, sandals, a pair of wings and a halo."

"Harold! Have you lost your senses? What *are* you talking about?" Helen blurted.

Father O'Malley first looked puzzled and then visibly shocked. Then a slight sly grin creased the corners of his mouth. "Ye won't be tellin' others about the sinful thoughts o' Father Pat, will ye?" he begged meekly, as he reverted back to his put-on accent. Then with eyes blazing furiously he roared, "Because if ya do, I'll be beatin' yer brains out with me shillelagh." Harold threw his hands up to protect himself as the Priest lunged toward him in jest. Then Father Pat started to laugh so hard the tears flowed down his cheeks. Harold began to laugh as well.

"We're all sinners, even us priests," continued Father Pat. "I thoroughly deserved that. Be sure your sins will find you, the Good Book says, eh?"

"I don't know what your private joke is all about, gentlemen," said Helen, "but we've only half an hour left before the first curfew warning bell."

"My, you're right," said the Priest as he glanced up at the

wall clock. "But a merry heart maketh good medicine and the Good Lord knows we can't get enough of that here. But you're right. Let's get back to business."

"As I said, I've stuck my nose into about every blessed thing that goes on in this place. That is, all except one. My contacts tell me that you both have been assigned to work with some strange man on one of the Beta Nova projects. I haven't been able to get near the rooms that house that Project. Rumor has it, that whoever he is, he has had some kind of contact with the alien craft. It may even be that they've captured one of the beings that control the AI's. It's frustrating not to know. Even General Thurman won't talk about it. This man must be vitally important to Bluepaper. He may know something that would help us to solve the few remaining mysteries of the Fatima message. If so, it would certainly clear up some lingering questions. Then the Pope Himself will reveal the message in total. However, we first must be sure of the interpretations. They are not to be taken lightly. The message will revolutionize and expand our understanding of the Judeo-Christian heritage."

"Now, as a gesture of good faith, I want to give you something. It is but a small portion of verse taken from the message given the shepherd boy at Fatima. It has been translated from the original Portuguese. Its rhyming nature has been retained to effect easy memorization. Excuse me for just a moment. I'll be right back."

Helen waited until he had left the room and then whispered to Harold. "Aren't we taking a big chance accepting such a thing from him?" she asked. "Regulations prohibit our transporting anything concealed. These formfitting pocketless suits serve their purpose real well. It would be hard to hide anything."

"You're right. And those hidden sensors and metal detectors would bring VIGIL running if we attempted to hide anything on our person. I'd better tell him that we just don't want to take the chance," Harold replied.

Their fears soon dissipated. Father Pat walked in with a

Bible in his hands.

"Here, my friends, is the version of the Bible we use at Sunday services. Bring it with you when you come. You'll find the message on the flyleaf."

Harold took the Bible and opened it up. "I don't see anything. This page is blank except your inscription on the top to us."

"Are you sure? Look carefully. Hold it up to the light."

"I still don't see your message."

"Good! Neither will Tim who I'm sure will be lurking out there in the corridor somewhere between here and your quarters. He'll ask you what you've got. Show it to him. When he sees it's one of the same Bibles I've given other visitors, I doubt if he'll take it from you. If he does, don't worry. You'll get it back. When you do, place it under your health lamp for about forty-five minutes. Remember, your apartment is monitored. You must not speak about it. I know for a fact that the sun lamp areas are off camera. They won't suspect anything. The message will appear faintly and only for several minutes. Copy it on a tissue. It's in rhyme and easy to remember. Memorize and destroy it. Remember. This is only *part* of a message given to a young ignorant Portuguese shepherd boy in 1917. I cannot emphasize this enough. Ask yourself, 'How could the boy possibly have prefabricated such a thing?' Compare it with what you have learned here. Think about its significance as it pertains to the current visitations. I'll be interested in your comments. I do hope we can work together. I must know who that stranger is and what he knows. Please help me. You will be doing a great service to the Church Universal and to all of mankind. That man that you are seeing tomorrow may be the Key to Fatima."

"Now, you'd best be getting along. Tim won't like it if you just make curfew by the skin of your teeth. He gets nervous, as you well know. I'll not say too much to you for the next few days. I don't want Tim to get any more suspicious than he is now. Let's have a short word of prayer for the Lord's

Father Pat walked in with a Bible in his hands.

help and guidance."

After the prayer, Father Pat saw them to the door and bade them goodbye. He immediately reverted back to using his boisterous Irish accent.

"Good evenun' to ya and do cum agin'!" he shouted, as Harold and Helen strolled arm in arm down the corridor.

"My, my, aren't we cozy now?" said the voice behind them.

Harold and Helen pretended not to be startled by Tim's voice. They did not reply as he quickly caught up to them.

"What is that you have, may I ask? Oh, another of those Bibles. Let me see it. At least he's given you the right vers'on, my Protestant friends. What is it you use? The King James Version? What does it matter? It's just superstition in another form." Tim thumbed through the Bible carefully and handed it back to Harold. "Here. Take it. I don't want it." Harold took it back. He and Helen continued on their way, still not saying a word, until they reached their door.

"What's the matter with you two? Lost your tongues?" Tim asked.

Helen turned her head ever so slowly and said in a pretended frightened tone, "We've got to hurry home, Timothy, before the big bell rings or we'll change back into pumpkins!" Then she winked and said, "That's from the Book of Cinderella, Chapter 6, verse 18!" The apartment door snapped shut in the irate face of Timothy Donoghue.

Helen gave Harold a knowing look and told him she wanted to take a sun bath before she came to bed. Harold handed her the Bible and said nonchalantly that she might want to glance through the new Bible while she did. Both knew that VIGIL might be monitoring them. They had to be careful what they said. Their conversation continued to have double meaning.

"That's a good idea," Helen answered. "It will be interesting to compare passages with the King James." She entered the bathroom, undressed and slipped into a robe. Harold got into his pajamas and spent about an hour reading.

"How's the tanning process coming?" he shouted from the bedroom. Helen lay on an air mat sunning herself in the rays of the health lamp provided in each quarter. The Bible lay open beside her exposed to the ultra-violet and infra-red rays which engulfed the cubicle.

"Guess what?" she shouted back. "I think I'm finally getting a tan!"

"Be careful you don't overdo it," Harold warned as he got out of bed and headed for the bathroom. "You ought to have seen Dr. Wilheim. He fell asleep under the infra-red cycle. He looks like a bright lobster," Harold said as he pushed back the curtains and glanced in with a sly wink. "My but you do look inviting, my dear. May I come in?"

"Don't be silly. Look at my, ah, tan." Helen pointed to the fly leaf of the Bible as she copied the cryptic writing which had faintly appeared on a facial tissue in pencil. Harold was anxious to see what it said. Helen carefully tore the tissue in half and placed both pieces in the Bible. The small printed letters on the Bible's fly leaf had already begun to disappear. By the time Harold reached the bedroom and opened it, the page again was blank. He pulled back the covers and propped a pillow behind his head. Helen entered the bedroom wrapped in a towel.

"Wait for me, dear, and we'll read the *Scriptures* together. I'll be right with you."

Helen quickly donned the loose blue pullover pajamas provided for Bluepaper personnel. Designator BETA-22 was prominently displayed in front and back.

"Here comes convict number 22 to join her handsome cellmate in a nice snug bed," she teased. She turned off the main light and slipped into bed beside him. Harold was staring quizzically at what she had printed on the tissue paper. She snuggled up beside him. Together they read the mystifying words. Helen had also copied Father Pat's cryptic comments to the side of the curious rhymed couplets. Taken together, a strange and astounding prophecy began to take shape.

WWII	ONE TIMES TWO SHALL HUN ARISE
Foo Fighters	WHEN DISCS AGAIN SHALL GRACE THE SKIES
Atom Bomb	A SUN DEVISED **B**Y HUMAN HANDS
	BRINGS TRANSIENT PEACE TO MANY LANDS

Daniel 4·13 ITS RAYS SHALL LEAVE THEIR EARTHLY NEST
AND WAKE *THE WATCHERS* FROM THEIR REST
THEY SIGNAL THEM THE TIME IS NEAR
AS WAS FORETOLD BY PROPHET SEER

Dead Sea WHEN HIDDEN WRITINGS SHALL BE FOUND
Scrolls THAT SONS OF LIGHT HID IN THE GROUND
WHICH ARE A SIGN TO THOSE WHO SEE
THE TRUE ONE'S HAND IN HISTORY

WHEN THE DISPERSED SHALL HOMEWARD WEND
Luke 21.24 AND GENTILE TIMES COME TO AN END
TWO SONS OF ISAAC FROM THEIR TOMB
Middle East War FIGHT ONCE AGAIN IN RACHEL'S WOMB

Oil AND FLOWING *PITCH* FROM ESAU'S LAND
CALLS MANY NATIONS TO WITHSTAND
THE GODLESS ARMY FROM THE NORTH
Russia LIKE CHARGING BEAR IT DOTH SPRING FORTH

Great GREAT STRESS ON EARTH AS NE'ER BEFORE
Tribulation AS NATIONS HEED THE LION'S ROAR
Satan's WHO SEEKETH WHOM HE MAY DEVOUR
Destruction IN THIS HIS LAST AND FINAL HOUR

MARK WHEN WANDERERS OF THE NIGHT
Planets lineup FLOCK TOGETHER IN THEIR FLIGHT
O THOU WHO ART THE TRUE ONE'S FRIEND
KNOW 'TIS THE PRELUDE TO THE END

WITHIN A DARKENED MOUNTAIN HALL
THE KING OF PEACE AWAITS RECALL
TO ONCE MORE RISE AND HELP PREPARE
THE CHOSEN PEOPLE UNAWARE

OF THE WATCHERS FROM ON HIGH
Second coming AND THAT SON OF MAN IS NIGH
UNAWARE OF MYSTERIES DEEP
BECAUSE MAN'S FAITH IS FAST ASLEEP

FOR EVEN NOW THE SONS OF LIGHT

117

STILL STRUGGLE WITH THE SONS OF NIGHT
AND MANKIND CHOOSES ON WHOSE SIDE
HE'LL TAKE WHEN DARKNESS DOTH ABIDE

THOSE WITH CHILDLIKE FAITH ARE FEW
O CHILDLIKE MAN A CLUE FOR YOU
A PRIESTLY ORDER HOLDS THE KEY
TO THIS POEM OF PROPHECY

Harold and Helen exchanged puzzled looks. They dared not comment out loud. The Sector Policy and Procedures Manual definitely stated that bedrooms, bathrooms and sun cubicles were all off camera. But that didn't negate the possibility that their voices were being monitored.

Harold's phenomenal ability of recall allowed him to memorize the message rapidly. Helen didn't even try. To her, it was all part of Father Pat's strange religious speculations. It was possible that he'd made up the poem himself. She hated to think so, but perhaps the years of confinement and his advancing age had taken their toll. She took the tissues and headed for the bathroom blowing her nose with them as she passed the monitor. The enigmatic message was flushed down the toilet. Helen returned to bed. She was soon fast asleep.

Harold, on the other hand, had a restless night. The memorized words of the poem rose and fell between conscious and subconscious, between awaking and dreaming until he finally woke up in a cold sweat to the Bluepaper reveille bell. It was Wednesday morning. "Today we shall meet the mysterious *him*," he thought as he nudged Helen. "How can you stay asleep through that infernal bell?" he whispered.

Helen squinted and smiled up at him. She let out a little yawn. "It's easy, dear," she said. "All I do is close my eyes."

"Well, open them now, Sleeping Beauty. Today's the big day."

After breakfast they headed for Sector 6 and their appointment with BETA-1. True to his word, Father Pat had merely smiled and nodded as they passed his table.

Once in a while Helen would glance over at him. She noted a strange new look of hope reflected in his eyes. He was expecting something from them. But she doubted that they could provide it. "Poor man," she thought. "I wonder if we'll end up the same way."

Chapter Twelve

"Him"

"Ah, here you are, right on time."

Colonel Milkowski greeted them both with a broad smile as Harold followed Helen through the sliding door into the office.

"My, but you do look lovely today BETA-22." The Colonel's eyes were riveted to Helen's every move.

"I can see why your father always calls you 'brown eyes'. Your eyes are very beautiful," he remarked as he came out from behind his desk to welcome them.

"Ahem," Harold cleared his throat. "I, ah, guess you know my wife, Helen," he said in an annoyed tone. He had rapidly caught up and stood beside her protectively.

"Not as much as I'd like to know her, BETA-27. You're a lucky man." The Colonel sighed. "Well, my window shopping will bring me nothing but unfulfilled frustration. We'd best be getting topside. Everyone has arrived and is awaiting us."

A strange sight greeted their eyes as they entered the guarded conference room. Sitting behind the table were three black-hooded men. One, an Air Force Colonel, was in military uniform. The other two were in business suits. General Thurman and Doctor Wilheim sat on either side of them. The General got to his feet and tapped the table with his swagger stick.

"All right, everybody. Let's get started, shall we? Introductions are in order. But, for the sake of security, they must be limited to our guests. You in the audience are asked to maintain complete silence. I'm sure that you'll comply. These gentlemen at the table can't see you. They don't know, nor should they know, who I am or who you are. All they do know is that they've been invited here to conduct a *Top Secret* briefing for your benefit.

"Now, in uniform and to my far left, is Colonel George H. Urgelles, United States Air Force. Colonel Urgelles is a coordinator with the Joint Chiefs. Sitting next to the Colonel is James Falconer from the National Reconnaissance Council, the NRC. And last, but not least, is Doctor Peter Wood. Peter is a sociologist and covert CIA agent employed at the Brookings Institute. Each of these gentlemen has something important to say to you. Listen carefully. You have the floor first, Colonel."

Colonel Urgelles stood up and placed his hands behind him.

"Well now, I don't know whether to say good morning, good afternoon or good evening to you gentlemen, ladies or both. I've lost all track of time. And, as you can see, I am literally quite in the dark about all of this!" The Colonel laughed as he fingered the black hood.

"But," he continued, "For whatever ultimate purpose, I've been asked to brief you on a project which we've dubbed *Old-New Moon*. It has to do with persons and equipment that have disappeared in connection with UFO sightings. It also has to do with people who have been abducted by UFOs and returned.

"Concerning the latter, it took us years to discover that this was going on. The kidnappings were not readily apparent. Most incidents were evaluated as car-chase cases.

"In the early days, we felt that UFOs were merely studying our methods of ground transportation. However, after hundreds of such reports, our analysts at the Foreign Technology Division felt that there had to be something else involved. After all, a super technological race doesn't have to examine hundreds of cars to learn about internal combustion engines.

"In 1961, we received our first breakthrough. A New England couple, driving through a rural area at night, experienced a close encounter with a UFO. They reported it to the local Air Force Base. But, to the Air Base and Bluebook, it was just another run-of-the-mill car chase.

"However, when NECAP investigated the sighting, some rather fascinating things were uncovered. As the days and weeks went by, the male witness began suffering emotional problems. The female became subject to recurring nightmares about being taken aboard an alien craft and subjected to a physical examination. Both became very distraught. Our people in psychological warfare instructed NECAP to encourage both witnesses to seek hypnotherapeutic help from a psychiatrist.

"Now, it just so happened that General Hefferan at ATIC was good friends with a civilian psychiatrist in the area. This doctor was easily persuaded to accept the witnesses as patients. Under regressive hypnosis, both vividly relived a classical UFO abduction experience. Overlooked at that time was a curious statement made by the aliens. They allegedly had told this couple that they would know where they were at all times.

"This cryptic remark caused us to go back and take a second look at a sample of our best car-chase cases. In some, we found obscure references to *time loss* by the witnesses. During the original investigations, our analysts had been so interested in the physical description of the objects and their effects, that they had overlooked this factor. It was a big mistake.

"We re-contacted some of the military witnesses to carchase cases because they could be controlled. In each case, hypnosis revealed similar abduction experiences. For security reasons, our hypnotists induced post-hypnotic commands upon these witnesses to forget about the abduction segment of their experience. Next we asked ourselves: *Why* the abductions?

"Our analysts at FTD mistakenly assured us that the aliens were obviously just interested in studying the abductee's anatomical makeup. But, the cases continued. It became quite apparent that the abductions involved more than mere studies of human anatomy. As the old saying goes, 'If you've seen one, you've seen 'em all!' Besides that, the uncanny ability of the aliens to paralyze the human body at will, without physical damage, already presupposed a thorough knowledge of the human body and its nervous system. That should have been obvious at the outset. But, again, our own ideas of self-importance got in the way of the truth. So, the misconceptions, 'They are interested in our machines or our bodies' no longer held water. We needed another breakthrough. We got it, thanks to the Condell UFO Study and one of our agents in APRA, Aerial Phenomena Research Association.

"Late in 1967, a young police officer investigating a possible cattle-rustling complaint experienced a Close Encounter. All he remembered consciously was a UFO approaching the cruiser and then flying off. But, a time loss was reported so our man from APRA conducted an initial investigation. Astounded by what he uncovered through hypnosis, he brought the policeman to the Condell Study for an intensive interrogation under hypnosis using a new drug. As always we encountered a curious post-hypnotic block concerning a certain segment of the physical examination. The use of the new drug enabled us to break through this barrier.

"We found that the aliens had implanted a minute monitoring device in the police officer's head. They effected this by inserting a long flexible needle through the nasal passage. X-rays would not reveal this device. We wondered if this segment of the officer's story was not due to imagination. There were those who suggested an immediate, planned, fatal *accident* involving this officer. Then, retrieval of the device could take place during postmortem examination. However, others felt that this would tip off the aliens to our discovery of the device. Still others believed that the monitoring device may have already tipped them off of our knowledge. A great number opposed killing the policemen for humanitarian reasons.

"In any event, we notified a higher authority of our findings. We received strict orders to return the witness to society at once. That's all I have to say at this time. Thank you for your attention."

General Thurman stood again.

"Thank you, Colonel Urgelles. Now it's my turn to continue where the Colonel left off. We had the Master Computer Program supply us special readouts of thousands of reported CE III Type G abduction cases from all over the world. In sixty percent of them, witnesses referred to a long flexible needle being stuck up their nose during an apparent physical examination by the aliens. Others reported the same type device being inserted in their navels, especially women.

"Our so-called *experts* assured us that these needles were most probably advanced fiber optic scanning devices. The hell they were! No. In each of these known cases, we now know for a fact that monitoring devices were planted in the abductees. Do you realize that there could be tens of thousands of people walking about with these devices in them? And, we're only talking about *known* CE III Type G's. When you take into consideration that many CE I's and II's may also involve abductions, we may be talking about hundreds of thousands!

"Now, what if these implants are more than just passive monitoring devices? Suppose they could be used to control the thoughts and actions of these people. My God! These people could be ticking time bombs. They may go off at any time to support an alien invasion. What will these witnesses become? Saboteurs? Assassins? We need to know and fast. It may be too late. Steps have been taken to find out more. Mr. Falconer will tell you about this. You have the floor, James."

"Thank you, sir, for such a succinct yet fully adequate statement. It makes my task that much easier. Let me continue by again going back to the police officer case which brought this frightening situation to light.

"NRC initiated a round-the-clock reconnaissance of his activities. Our people at Brookings looked for changes in his personality, habits, interests and friends. It was during this time that our analysts redeemed themselves, so to say. They theorized that the energy force which activated the implants might be detectable.

"We reported this theory to higher channels and were supplied a chameleon van containing a detection device unknown to us. We were only told that it was a highly classified instrument designed for UFO detection. Someone from an unknown agency accompanied it at all times. It was wired with a high-temperature destruct device in the event of compromise.

"Apparently, this device detected something because NRC was funded to develop and implement a sizeable reconnaissance program employing this same instrument. NRC now monitors a large number of UFO abductees. I understand that a limited effort has been implemented in other countries through our embassies.

"Recording canisters from the Chameleons and Blackbirds were sent to a specific pick-up point for distribution to an unknown higher source. I assume that your project is among the recipients. But, since I know nothing about you or this place, I cannot be sure. That's all I have to say."

"Thank you, James. Now we'd like to hear from you, Peter," General Thurman replied.

The thin hooded man stood up and said nothing for at least two full minutes. The silence seemed unbearable to Harold. He began to shift uneasily in his chair. Finally, the high, feminine-like voice of Doctor Woodman broke the death-like hush that had settled over the room.

"My little talk to you is based upon hundreds of carefully

prepared surveillance reports. These involve a number of UFO-related cults influenced by *apparent* UFO contactees. I say apparent because we have found no proven link between them and the real phenomenon. Our monitoring instruments detect no signals being sent these people. The UFO contact experiences claimed by their leaders are obviously a hoax, a hallucination or by a different alien source of which we know nothing.

"We discovered a strange commonality, other than UFOs, that bind these groups together. This commonality exists despite the fact that these groups operate completely independent of one another. We suspect, but have by no means proven, that a *Control Group* of highly gifted psychics are behind this commonality. It is possible that they are a product of an on-going experiment in psychotronics by some foreign power. Why do I say this? Because every one of these groups, in one way or another, advocate a world government, a single monetary system and a universal language controlled by one man code-named 666 after some personage in the Bible.

"All of these groups are looking forward to mass landings of UFOs. They believe that the space brothers will choose a man from amongst them to be their ruler, their 666. Some even believe that the space brothers will endow this man with supernatural powers. These groups are openly anti-semitic and anti-Christian.

"So far, the *real* abductees have shown no inclination to join such groups. But, there have been equally disturbing developments among them as well. They have placed a mystical religious interpretation on their UFO experience within the context of orthodox Christianity. These Christocentric contactees also look to the coming of UFOs for salvation. They believe, and are spreading the belief, that UFOs are operated by God's angels who are preparing for Christ's return to earth!

"Therefore, my friends, we have two rapidly growing subcultural groups. Both hail the advent of the aliens as the answer to all the earth's problems. In a way it is a puzzling thing. The world views of each group are diametrically opposed to one another. Yet, both represent a distinct threat to our national security. For, if and when the enemy decides to make a full-scale invasion, they will be welcomed by both groups with open arms. Representatives from both groups hold key positions in the political, military and civilian segments of society. But now for the meat of the matter.

"Recently, a man bearing the same general description began to show up in places frequented by *both* groups. One bright young analyst noticed that a number of monitoring stations referenced this same strange-looking man. He kept popping up in the areas under surveillance.

"The analyst asked all monitoring stations to take telephotographs of the man if he showed up again. He did this on his own. No one asked him to. Soon, he received a photo from Station 38. Then, again on his own, he sent copies of this photo to an all-station distribution. He asked if this man had been seen in their locales. Then, our inquisitive analyst proceeded to go on vacation for a week. When he returned he found a stack of unopened information packets on his desk from all over the world. He opened them up and couldn't believe his eyes. Although sometimes dressed differently, there was the same man photographed or described in London, Brazil, San Francisco and you name it! He was photographed at many of these places all within a forty-eight hour period!

"The analyst ceased his vigilante detective work and finally alerted his superior. He informd NRC. Now, Mr. Falconer of NRC will tell you what happened next."

"Thank you, Peter. Within a few hours, an all-station alert went out to apprehend and question this man or men. We were fully convinced we were dealing with identical twins or triplets. Some of us felt that he or they were members of the suspected *Control Group* that NRC had been searching for. But, we received a counter-order from a higher authority. We were asked not to apprehend him but to notify them just as soon as he was spotted again.

"I close my little talk by stating that finally the *stranger* was spotted in San Francisco. He was about to enter a meeting that we had under surveillance. It was sponsored by a UFO cult called *The Order of Melchizedek*. We notified the higher authority. NRC was ordered out of the area at once. Rumor has it that another Agency snatched this man. He hasn't shown up since and no one asks about him anymore. That's all I have. Thank you."

"Thank you very much for your time, gentlemen," General Thurman said as he got to his feet. "I could have covered the same material myself. But, I would rather our audience get such information from those involved firsthand. It lends credibility to our training program and provides visible continuity to inter-agency cooperation. Well done."

Colonel Urgelles laughed. "I don't see much *visible* continuity with this black hood on but it is good to see that someone at apparently very high levels appreciates what we are doing."

Two VIGIL personnel escorted the hooded trio out of the room. General Thurman turned to Joseph.

"Okay, old friend. It's your turn. Let's tell Harold and Helen how the Beta Project has paid off."

"Yes, yes. How Beta has paid off indeed," said the little old man as he shuffled to his feet. His eyes literally shone with excitement.

"You will recall, my friends, that Mr. Falconer mentioned the highly-classified UFO detection device, yes? It was a Beta UFO detection device, of course.

"Within just a few days we received alien Beta wave readings in the vicinity of that police officer! Our Beta satellites and aircraft were brought into operation and verified its source: a huge carrier craft in synchronous orbit!

"It was then discovered that the *stranger* in San Franscisco had a similar implant. The same type Beta waves were picked up in his immediate vicinity. However, in his case it was different. We found that he himself was constantly emanating a weak, barely detectable Beta-like signal. This signal was unique. We had never seen its parameters before. At least, that was what we thought at first. I, Dr. Wilheim, had a brilliant idea. This signal was fed into the Central Computer. I asked the computer if this same signal were stored in any of the recordings from the Old-New Moon reconaissance project. They were! But their weak strength negated any analysis. They were recorded on the very same day, *in every case*, that this stranger's photo was taken. But, alas, I also found this very same type signal recorded in several places on the same day at reconaissance stations thousands of miles apart. 'Perhaps there are others who transmit like this stranger,' I thought. It must be so. Yes? No man could travel that fast. Then I checked the photographs against the original information sheets that accompanied them. I noticed that our analyst had crossed out a number of dates and times relating to when the photos were taken. He had scratched in *probable error* beside the cross-outs and initialled them. Again, it was obvious why he thought this to be so. No man can be in so many places far apart at these times. Yes?

"But, despite this absurdity, I now had independent evidence that our mysterious *stranger* had indeed somehow accomplished this. Now, I said to myself: 'Joseph, how could this possibly be? What could possibly transport a man so fast?' And then it suddenly came to me like a bolt of lightning from the sky. He took the flying saucer spaceship. Yes? Professor Wilheim is not so dumb after all, eh, BETA 1?"

"Can your self-exaltation, old man. Someone else, probably myself, would have discovered this sooner or later," Colonel Milkowski snapped.

"Ah, but *I* found out sooner and there is no guarantee that *you* would have found out later," Dr. Wilheim admonished him with a scolding finger.

"Enough of this, both of you," General Thurman

interrupted. "Joseph is to be commended for a fine piece of detective work. Let's not deprive him of a little glory, Steve. Give credit when credit's due and you'll certainly improve your obvious morale problems on the Beta projects. Let's break for lunch and then Steve will tell you both what happened next."

After lunch, the Colonel stood up smartly, hands clasped behind his back. He cast a superior look at Joseph. "My part began when Bluepaper was informed that our infamous stranger was spotted in San Franscisco. I personally led the VIGIL team that tracked him down. In less than two hours we were on station in the Chameleon provided for us. We relieved the NRC personnel. They had followed him to one of the seediest looking hotels I've ever seen. The Beta wave signals had ceased. A magnetically attached transmitter had been attached to the stranger's parked car. NRC had traced the car to a rental agency.

"The car had been rented by a David Ben-Sorek. Fingerprints were taken from the signed rental agreement for processing. We waited until Ben-Sorek came out and got into his car. There was no mistaking him. He was just as peculiar looking as his photograph! There was the same olive complexion and dark hair. He had peculiar almond-shaped eyes, a long tapering nose and a pointed beard that spread from his strangely cut side-burns to a sharp point under his chin. He was spooky looking. This guy looked just like a character out of the *Arabian Nights.*

"I contacted our Blackbird. The pilot already had a fix on the transmitter. We followed a good distance behind, following the Blackbird's instructions. We soon realized that this guy wasn't going to stop except for gas. The Blackbird was running low on fuel. So, we arranged a rendezvous with another Blackbird out of McChord Air Force Base as we crossed into Washington state.

"We followed him into Mount Rainier National Park and lost him. There were just too many small dirt roads. The Blackbird was running low on fuel but he still had a fix on the car. We had hoped that Ben-Sorek would lead us to others, perhaps even to a rendezvous with the aliens. I decided then that we had better take him while we could.

"The Blackbird was ordered down with orders to shoot to cripple, if necessary. We wanted that man. Our pilot reported that the car was climbing a mountain road. He complained that we were risking the crew's lives having them flying around up there in the dark. There was no other choice. I told him to land on the road in front of the car and capture its driver at any cost.

"They landed all right. The shock of the 'copter coming down startled the driver so badly that the car went off the road and over a cliff. It's a wonder that we got him back here in one piece. As it is, he's paralyzed from the waist down. His injury also must have affected his implant because it's not giving off any more Beta signals. I think that - -"

"Whoa! That's quite enough, Steve. It was an excellent summary. But, that's as far as I want you to go," General Thurman interrupted. "I'd like to continue from this point myself.

"We found very few belongings on the person of this so-called David Ben-Sorek. There was a receipt from the car rental place, a sales slip, a forged license and *this small pipe or flute*. Here, you take it, Harold. See if you can equate it with some past culture. No one uses such a thing in this day and age. We've checked everywhere. Now, back to Ben-Sorek.

"Apparently, he was going to rendezvous with someone. We don't know who or how. The area at Mount Rainier was staked out at once. Nothing was seen or monitored. Most likely we scared his compatriots off.

"The sales slip was from an electronics merchandise chain store. It referenced the stock numbers and price of the items bought. Several of these stores in the area were checked. We found that it's their policy to record the name and address of every customer. They use this information for sales statistics and their catalog mailing list. The slip was finally traced to

The Blackbird spots Ben-Sorek.

the correct store at a local Mall. As luck would have it, the buyer recorded his correct name and address. It was a bad slip on his part and I don't mean that as a pun!

"The name on the slip was not that of Ben-Sorek. A person named Benny Saltzman had bought a cassette tape recorder and a cheap phone tapping device. The address was traced to a dumpy place in the slums. The landlady refused to let VIGIL in without an invitation or a warrant. VIGIL didn't want local authorities involved and got a bit rough with her. She wouldn't even accept a bribe.

"Somehow, she must have warned this Benny fellow that VIGIL was coming. He had locked the door and pried a chair against its handle. What VIGIL saw when they broke down the door is hard to envisage. A little man, or should I say what was left of a little man, was sitting in a wooden chair. A smile was frozen on his face. His body was enveloped with a strange bluish flame. One of the team ran to a sink and began throwing water on him. It had no effect at all. Suddenly there was a bright flash. They watched in horror as the man's entire body, bones and all was consumed before their very eyes. His clothes, completely unharmed, collapsed into a pile on the chair and the floor. The chair didn't burn either.

"Our analysts found that the clothes were only slightly singed. They have informed us that there's no chemical explanation for the source of heat that caused Saltzman to be incinerated. So, what caused this phenomenon? An unknown intense high frequency energy source has been postulated. One scientist remarked that similar cases had been reported from time to time. But he had never seen any valid documentation, 'Such a phenomenon suggests,' said he, 'that our bodies, and matter in general, are not as solid as we would like to think.'

"In any event, there was nothing in the room that gave us further information on Mr. Saltzman. Would you believe the landlady didn't even know his name? 'This is one of the benefits we give people who live in this dump,' she told

Benny Saltzman

VIGIL. 'I don't ask questions, they don't ask questions. They pay, daily, or they don't get in!' "

Harold and Helen stared unbelievably at Number 1. "When will these bizarre revelations ever end?" thought Harold as General Thurman continued.

"We checked both men's fingerprints. Benny's prints never showed up anywhere. But, Ben-Sorek's did. The Israeli government had them on record. But, they were recorded as being the prints of someone named Eric Hadelman, not Ben-Sorek.

"According to the Israeli government, this man was highly instrumental in helping make the new Jewish state of Israel a reality. Hadelman was a leader within the Mossad Aligh Bet, an organization that smuggled Jewish refugees into Palestine. He was also a secret advisor to Ben Gurion. One of his more remarkable achievments involved some fence-mending between two factionist underground resistance movements. In doing so, a few radical members threatened his life. It was at this time that he disappeared. The Israelis thought that he had fled the country or had been murdered. He was last seen in 1948.

"Now, supposedly, Hadelman was a Jewish immigrant from Norway. But the Norwegian government had no record of him. And here's the clincher. Eric Hadelman was supposedly age 56 when he disappeared. Here's a picture of him copied from an ID card sent to us by the Israeli government. Now, look. These here are pictures of him taken from the Chameleon along with some that we've taken here. What do you think?"

Harold picked up the ID photo and compared it with the others. As he did so, a deja-vu feeling came over him. "These semitic facial features are unique. I've seen them somewhere before," he said.

"Damn it! Forget the Semitic features. Don't you realize what I'm trying to tell you, man? Look at those pictures. How could Eric Hadelman and David Ben-Sorek be the same person? Hadelman should be an old man now! The

Israelis were amazed that he was still alive. Of course we told them that he'd been killed in an automobile crash and that his body had been cremated when no one claimed it. We're sending them ashes for a proper hero's burial. But that's beside the point.

"The photographs and especially the prints present us with a mind-boggling *enigma*. If *him* is Hadelman *and* Ben-Sorek, He hasn't aged for over three decades! This can't be, but it is. Now, put this fact together with his intimate knowledge of languages that were spoken centuries ago, and the implications are mind blowing. Helen will tell you about the latter."

Helen gave Harold a little wink and walked to the front of the room.

"I was assigned to Beta Project *Enigma* immediately after my briefing. At that time I knew nothing of the stranger's background. This session has been most informative. My work has involved the translation and derivation of languages spoken by *him* during his short state of postcoma delirium."

Helen went on to explain that she could easily identify bits of *modern* languages. What puzzled her was that this strange man sometimes reeled off dialects and phrases unknown to her today. It was as if he were intimately familiar with these languages as they were spoken centuries ago. Most of the languages he muttered were completely unknown to her.

"Doctor Wilheim employed Beta Psi and voice recording equipment during our monitoring of *him*," Helen continued. "We acquired a permanent and parallel record of audio and thought tapes for evaluation right up until the time he entered normalization." Helen's face suddenly became very pale. She was obviously reliving the whole experience as she spoke. "And then he, he - - perhaps Colonel Milkowski should tell you what was done next."

"I'd be glad to, Helen. When Ben-Sorek came out of the coma, I began a face-to-face interrogation at once. I was there when he first opened his eyes."

Colonel Milkowski's cold and usual unwavering manner of speech began to falter. One could see that he was about to describe an experience that had been very disturbing to him.

"Those eyes. They seemed to look right through me. He, he glanced around at everyone in the room. We addressed him but he didn't answer. He looked at the intravenous tube and smiled at Doctor Slater. Then he lifted his hand up slowly and touched the Psi helmet on his head. He then turned about and looked so long and hard at Joseph that he had to leave the room. Then, then he just began staring blankly into space. We- -"

"Tell them what happened to the Psi machine at that point!" Joseph interjected as he leaped to his feet excitedly. "Tell them. Yes? No? *I* will tell them. The Psi screen went blank! It was as if this man shut off his thoughts to us. Impossible! Impossible!" Joseph then sat down shaking his head in disbelief.

The Colonel continued. "Yes, impossible but nonetheless true. The images on the screen disintegrated right before our very eyes. We suspected equipment malfunction. We sent for a duplicate unit used at Central. Still, nothing showed.

"For two whole days we used everything from electrical shock to drugs. We threatened him with torture and even tried to inflict pain. He seemed to be oblivious to pain! The man wouldn't talk or even acknowledge our presence.

"MEDIC-1 could not explain what had happened. The prisoner just lay there gazing at the ceiling with those strange eyes, like a living corpse. Then, he closed his eyes. MEDIC-1, ah, Doctor Slater informed us that an incredible thing was happening. He hadn't told us at first because he couldn't believe it. A strange clot had appeared which blocked the flow of intravenous nutrients. The man's respiration and heartbeat were methodically slowing down. This continued until his pulse was barely discernible. The, the man had somehow put himself into a state of suspended animation!"

General Thurman stepped forward. "That's all, Steve. Thank you. And now, Harold, I'll tell you why you were brought here. It will be your job to find out who this man is and what he's been doing. You'll have complete use of the Psi Machine records and facilities. The mind and audio tapes that Helen and Joseph ran on him when he was delirious should prove invaluable. You will also be given the tapes of the Beta signals transmitted to civilian and military contactees and to *him*."

"But how can I help anymore than has already been done?" Harold asked.

"Because, my friend, we have every indication that *him* has intimate knowledge of cultures and places far earlier than the Roman Empire. Helen was able to help us only up to a certain point in time. Some of the languages spoken and some of the places described by *him* require an expert like yourself to translate and identify for us.

"We're also hopeful that you will be able to help us decipher the meanings behind the signals being transmitted to contactees. And, last but not least, we'd like to attempt a Beta match between you and *him* if he recovers. The NSA reports concerning the psychic experiments carried out between you and Mr. Fields are most interesting. They appear to have accomplished much more beyond the transference of crypto-symbols and remote viewing. Am I right?"

"Yes, there were short periods when my mind seemed to be in complete resonance with Don's mind. My thoughts and his thoughts became one. My body movements actually complemented his. Yes, it is possible that I might be able to pick up some of this man's thoughts randomly. But, I doubt it. You must remember that Don was a healthy, conscious and willing participant. From what I gather, *him* is none of these things, General Thurman."

"In any event, Harold, divide your time between analysis and trying to reach him psychically through Beta enhancement. We want him to cooperate with us

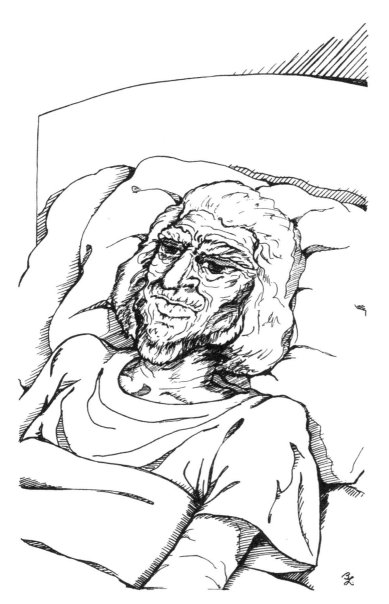

Helen gasped. "He looks as if he's aged one hundred years!"

concerning learning more about the aliens. We want to communicate with the aliens through him if that is possible. We must convince them that we are basically a peace-loving people, that our apparent hostility has been a reaction to their evasiveness and interference in our affairs, and, that we desire friendship. Our main concern is the security and welfare of our peoples. We want to know *who* they are and *why* they are visiting earth at the very least. Of course, we would like to know *where* they come from and *how* they got here. But, they may not be ready to part with such information as of yet.

"Now, let's have you meet *him*, Harold. And, Helen? A word of warning. There's been a, a change in *him* since you saw him last. We've kept you away from *him* because of this. You'll find what you see very hard to believe. But, as Myrna has told us, your very reaction will help Harold to accept what he sees."

The elevator opened into a small hallway with a large picture window centered on its opposite wall. Harold and Helen followed the General over to this window which was covered from the inside by a pair of sliding partitions. General Thurman inserted a tube into an orifice in the wall to the right of the large window. The partitions parted revealing a dimly-lit room. The shadowy outline of a human form could be seen on a bed facing the window. The general turned the tube and the lights slowly became brighter inside.

Harold swallowed hard. The face of the man lying on the bed was not of the handsome, dark-haired, bearded BenSorek. Instead, Harold found himself staring in horror at the grotesque, wizened head of a white-haired, bearded man.

"What's happened to him?" Helen gasped. "He looks as if he's aged one hundred years!"

"Not quite, Helen," replied the General. "He *seems* to have aged tremendously. His appearance gradually changed after he entered his self-induced state of suspended animation. He *looks* ancient but his bodily functions haven't aged quite as rapidly. We still have some time before we lose him. But, probably not enough. Our doctors can do nothing except record the changes in his life functions. They are compiling a complete record for future studies. It's incredible!"

"I can't believe this is the same man I saw in those pictures," Harold muttered. "Such things are not possible!"

"I can see a striking resemblance," Helen retorted. "It's *him* all right. But, but, I simply cannot comprehend how or why this has happened."

"Tomorrow, Harold will see some interesting video scenes. I'm sure they will convince him more than your weak assurances, Helen," the General added. "But, we must get you both back to Sector 7 now."

The General paused and stared at Harold. "I say, old man. Harold? Are you all right?"

Harold's face was as white as a sheet. His eyes were gazing expressionlessly through the window at *him*. There was something undefinably pristine about his features that belonged to ages long past. The deep wrinkles embedded in his darkened skin and sagging jaw reminded Harold of a terrifying childhood experience. His mind was silently reliving a trip to a museum sponsored by the orphanage many years ago. There he had experienced his first sickening realization of death. In his mind's eye he could still see the sightless eyes of an Egyptian mummy gazing up at him from a wooden sarcophagus.

Chapter Thirteen

The King of Salem

"It's no use, I just cannot get to sleep," Harold exclaimed.

"I could say it was your tossing and turning that's keeping me awake," Helen replied sleepily. "But it's more than that. I keep thinking of the things they've done to that poor man. They're only interested in what's in his mind. Colonel Milkowski barely considers the fact that he's a human being. And the way his appearance has changed; why has that happened? What's caused it?"

"Helen, something that the Colonel, ah, BETA-1, said today keeps going through my mind. It was his blow-by-blow description of Ben-Sorek's actions when he first opened his eyes and saw his captors. I assume that it's on video tape. I'd like to see that tape. I've got a hunch about something."

"We'd best not talk too much about it here, darling. They've warned us to keep talk of our work confined to the work area. I just wish that I could be with you tomorrow."

"Yeh, I still can't figure that out, Helen. What did General Thurman say about that?"

"I told you once."

"Yeh, I know, but think hard. Do you remember anything else he said?"

"Very strange. All he said was that for the time being, I'd have to be kept off all Beta projects until something was settled with VIGIL-1. Apparently Timothy lodged a complaint to the Council about two Beta personnel being co-located in Sector 7. There's a ruling Council here that reviews Base 3 policy and procedures. It consists of all the Number 1's. I'm sure they'll make an exception in our case.

After all, we're husband and wife. Anyhow, it's after 0300. Goodnight again." Helen drifted off to sleep. Harold sat awake thinking before finally dropping off to sleep much later.

On the following morning, Harold reported to the Beta Lab with Joseph. Joseph played the video tape of *him's* last actions while Colonel Milkowski provided explanatory comments. Then, Harold interrupted.

"Stop it right there, Joseph. See? He's looking at the intravenous tube. Right? Okay, continue. Now, watch how his eyes are looking around at everyone in the room. But, he's stopping and staring very hard at Doctor Slater. Why? Look, he's just staring. Now, if Colonel Milkowski's account was accurate at yesterday's briefing, we should see him smile. There's the smile. Stop it there a moment. Now, *why* does he smile? Gentlemen, I believe that this man briefly read the minds of everyone in the room until he identified the Doctor. That smile was his 'thank you' to Doctor Slater for taking care of him."

"Come on now, Harold," Colonel Milkowski quipped sarcastically. "Aren't you being a bit simplistic? Mind reading at a glance? You know all about the joint effort and training involved in telepathy just between two persons. This gent doesn't know any of us from a hole in the wall. How could he do that?"

"Simplistic, perhaps, but logical nonetheless," Harold replied. "We are dealing with an extraordinary man. A man who has incredible knowledge. A man who deals with extraterrestrials. Now, let us continue. What does he do next? Let it run again, Joseph. See? He reaches up and touches the Psi helmet attached to his head. Again his eyes flit around the room. He stops and stares at you Joseph. Stop it right there.

"Now, Joseph. Did you or did you not attach the Psi helmet to *him*?"

"Why yes, I alone am responsible for the installation and

monitoring of *him* with Psi machine, yes?"

"Okay, let 'er roll again. Look at this standoff. He just keeps staring. You looked very uncomfortable, Joseph. Were you just self-conscious? Why do you look so disturbed? Does his staring bother you? Why not just look away? Tell us, Joseph. Tell us how you felt."

"I had strange, strange feeling. Yes? It was like he was hypnotizing me, like he was looking inside me. I wanted to look away but I couldn't. It was real mental struggle, yes? At time, I tell no one. I think, 'silly Joseph. You are imagining things.' Yes?"

"That's enough, Joseph. Now, let's watch. Look, you have managed to look away. Why, you must be upset. You're leaving the room. Now, look. The images on the Psi screen dissolve and cease to be just after the point you left the room. You may switch it off now, Joseph.

"Gentlemen, I postulate that Ben-Sorek quickly ascertained that Joseph was the person who hooked him up to the Psi recorder. Then he proceeded to telepathically pick Joseph's brains about the function of the Psi machine. Just as soon as he realized that this device was monitoring his thoughts, he quickly shut off his mind. He then went into this self-induced torpor which is, in turn, causing premature aging. I feel sure that unless we remove the Psi hook-up, he is just going to let himself and his secrets die with him. I advocate the immediate removal of the Psi monitoring equipment."

Colonel Milkowski leapt to his feet and glowered at Harold. "I object to your absurd suggestion, Stanton. I don't put any stock whatsoever in this nonsense about this man's mind-reading abilities. I think that your sudden exposure to our operation has affected your ability to think rationally. Your past involvement in telepathy is unduly influencing your mind as well. Do you know what you're asking me to do? That Psi machine must be connected up at all times. He's liable to come to at any time. We can't afford to miss even one of his precious thoughts."

"But, Steve," Joseph interjected. "I seriously doubt that *him* will ever recover. I see no harm in trying. Believe me. When that man was staring at me, I could somehow feel him taking hold of my mind. Yes, I was upset for hours. It was strange feeling. Never have I felt that way in whole of my life."

"Have you gone mad too, Joseph? Sure, I felt strange when he looked at me too but it was just a psychological reaction to the strangeness of this man!"

"No, Steve, I don't think either of them have gone mad as you so crudely put it."

The three swung around to face General Thurman who had just entered the room.

"I couldn't get over here quickly enough. I've been monitoring you people from my office. Steve, you are BETA-1. The Beta Special Projects are under your direction. I respect that. But, we brought Harold here under some pretty hard personal circumstances to advise us. It's hardly in good keeping with your position to outrightly reject his first piece of advice to us. Let's put it to the test. No harm will be done. I trust there will be no hard feelings, Steve, but *Enigma* does come under the Base's State of Emergency Clause. I have the right, as Number 1, to exercise my jurisdiction over this matter without Council approval. They may judge my actions as they wish at the next meeting. I'm willing to take my day in court. So, let's unhook *him*, Joseph, and see what, if anything, happens."

"I welcome your so-called jurisdiction in this matter. It makes you, not I, directly responsible for the condition of *him*. You'll answer to Outside Command, not me. I'll be glad to get off that hook; believe me. However, I think you're all making a big mistake."

"We'll see about that. Begin deactivation of the Psi equipment immediately, Joseph. And, Harold? Steve will go through the audio and thought image tapes with you until Joseph is available. I'll keep in touch with the situation. I'm anxious to see what you think, Harold."

Harold examined the pictorial record of the day by day transformation of *him* from the active dark-haired David Ben-Sorek to a frail old man. He spent the rest of the day listening to the recorded words, phrases and conversations mumbled by *him* during his initial semi-conscious state. Then he carefully transcribed the words phonetically for study back at Sector 7. Already he had guessed at some of the langauges he was hearing. But, he had to be sure. The implications were fantastic.

On Saturday, Harold began to examine the thought images transmitted by the mind of the enigmatic *him*. The distorted images of buildings, strangely dressed people and outdoor scenes paraded across the screen. Some were barely recognizable. Others needed work with Central computer service. Hopefully the computer would reconstruct partial images with proposed models.

Harold could not believe some of what he was seeing. He decided to spend Sunday setting up work sheets which would denote possible, probable and actual identification of langauges, places, peoples and things. But, Helen insisted that he take time off to attend the ecumenical Church service at Father Pat's Chapel.

On Monday morning, Harold received an enthusiastic greeting from Joseph.

"Harold! I have the good news for you!" he said excitedly in broken English as Harold walked into the lab.

"What is it, Joseph? Has he, he —"

"Yes, he has improved. Doctor Slater reports that his pulse and breathing rate are slowly increasing at a constant rate. You were right, my friend, yes?"

"Yes, Joseph. So it would seem. May we see *him*?"

"No, not until Wednesday. Doctor Slater has received permission from Number 1 to declare the Penthouse off limits except to himself and the nurses. He feels that by Wednesday, *him* should be functioning normally if his calculations are right. Then, my friend you will see *him* much. Perhaps too much. Yes?"

"What do you mean by that remark, Joseph?"

"I mean that, well, I had better let Number 1 tell you the news. He is coming to see you this afternoon. You may not like what he has to say. But, wait and see. Now, let me show what computer re-orientation has done to the images you were having trouble with."

Harold sat down and viewed an incredible parade of ancient places and peoples.

"What are they? What do they mean?" Joseph asked wonderingly. "My dear friend Harold, you look as if you see ghost, yes?"

"Maybe I am seeing ghosts, Joseph. I can't be sure of anything yet. Now, do you have close-ups of the tablets with the hieroglyphics? Also, I want a close-up of the open scroll."

General Thurman arrived late in the afternoon, just as Joseph had predicted.

"Good afternoon, Harold. I assume Joseph told you that I'd be visiting."

"That he did. I also understand that I might not like what you're going to say to me."

"Yes, well, first of all you are to be congratulated for what you've done here thus far. Thanks to you, Ben-Sorek is steadily coming back toward a normal state of condition. By Wednesday, Doctor Slater will probably allow visitors again, which brings me right to my next point.

"The Council has met and discussed the mind-reading ability of our strange guest. Several of those who were present when he first opened his eyes had some confessions to make. They too had felt their minds temporarily gripped by some foreign force. These feelings coincided with BenSorek's eye contact. We've decided that should he awaken, he most likely will read the minds of whoever is in the room. To be quite frank, Harold, there are those among us who don't want him picking their brains. We feel reasonably sure that he wouldn't trust a single one of us.

But, we do feel that he would trust and communicate with someone like you.

"You're new here. You know very little of what we've done and what we plan to do. Your knowledge is limited to the summary briefings we exposed you to. You are religious and have puritanical-like scruples. Your love and knowledge of ancient cultures parallels his seeming interest and knowledge. If he's going to communicate with anyone here at Phoenix Base 3, you're the logical choice.

"We're asking that you personally live in the Penthouse on a 24-hour basis. Now that he's improving, he's liable to awaken at any time. We want you to be right there when he does. I'll have your library moved to the adjoining room. Joseph will continue to be the link between you and the complete facilities of Base 3. Whatever support you need, you'll get, within reason.

"Now, here's the hard part, Harold. We're asking you to do it alone. Helen will not be allowed up there at this crucial time. Hopefully, this situation won't last more than several weeks. In the meantime, you may visit Helen on weekends at the recreation center. You'll be on immediate call though."

"But, Helen - -"

"Don't go jumping to conclusions. Helen has been briefed about this and is reluctant but agreeable. I've talked to her and her father has talked to her. She'll be moving temporarily into a guest room at the Council's quarters. We want your friends back in Sector 7 to think you both were transferred together on temporary assignment. We want you to be alone with *him* day and night.

"Now, until your transfer on Wednesday, you and your wife will be confined to your quarters at Sector 7 except for eating and working."

"Confined to our quarters?" Harold suddenly feigned the most obvious look of disappointment he could muster up.

"What's the matter, Stanton? It can't be that bad. Tomorrow's Tuesday. Where would you be going anyhow? Neither of you seem to be interested in visiting the recreation rooms."

"Oh, I was just thinking. Helen and I had planned to get together with Father Pat for a time of fellowship on Tuesday evening. We visited him last week and we attended his Church services yesterday. Just to be able to experience little things like this boosts our morale more than you could ever know."

"Father Pat's place? Say no more. I don't think the Council would mind that. What they don't know won't hurt them either. Consider my permission granted provided that attendance be limited to just Father Pat, yourself and Helen. Fair enough?"

"Fair enough, John. Helen and I certainly appreciate your kindness, not only to us but to Father Pat and his friends."

"Yeh, Pat is a fine old man. I've known him personally for many, many years. The poor old guy shouldn't even be here. Trying to do a good turn for others just put him in the wrong place at the wrong time."

Harold saw the General's eyes seemingly gaze back into the distant past. There was no doubt that his thoughts had winged their way back to the tiny Aleutian island outpost of Buldir I do a Christmas of long ago.

Father Pat brought them directly into the Chapel as soon as Harold and Helen arrived. They sat around a small table together.

"You have seen *him*, Harold?"

"Yes, I have. There's much to tell you. I haven't even shared it with Helen because of this confounded monitoring system. But, before I tell you about *him*, let me briefly tell you what I think about the Fatima message.

"First off, I must admit to you that I find it hard to believe that it's a translation of a poem given shepherd children back in 1917. But, I must also say that I'm ready to believe almost anything since my involvement with *him*. I'm also ready to add my comments to yours. Have you a copy?"

"I have a copy right here for our use this evening."

"Okay, let's go over it. You're in for some real surprises. I assume you learned of the Atomic bomb from others who came here after you. I guess this would also apply to the finding of the Dead Sea Scrolls in 1947 and the formation of the new State of Israel in 1948. But, let me say a bit about the 'flowing pitch' and the 'godless army from the North'."

Father Pat listened with great consternation as Harold informed him about the Arab-Israeli wars, the energy crisis, the OPEC cartel and the Russian buildup along the border of Afghanistan.

"When I left the Outside, that flowing *pitch* was worth almost a dollar a gallon," Harold remarked.

"And, when I left," Helen interjected, "the situation in the Middle East even had the newscasters referring to the Battle of Armageddon."

"I'll have to take your word about the 'wanderers of the night,' Father," Harold continued. You seem to believe that their 'flocking together' refers to all of the planets lining up in 1982."

"A friend of mine showed me a book about that," Helen remarked. "The authors state that the planets' combined gravitational pull will cause earthquakes and tidal waves!"

"As an astronomer, I sincerely doubt that," Father Pat replied. "But, this astronomical happening is referred to in the rhyme as the beginning of a significant event. I believe it has something to do with the Second Coming. But, who knows how long that might be after the planets' line-up? They are a sign. The New Testament gives other signs as well."

"Yes, like earthquakes and tidal waves," Helen remarked wryly.

"Now," Harold interrupted, "before I discuss the latter verses of the Fatima rhyme, let me tell you both what I have found out about *him*. First, let me tell you how he happens to be here, Father. Then I'll tell you what I think I know of him thus far."

Father Pat listened spellbound as Harold told him of his incredible findings.

"His facial features are what first shocked me. Other persons with the same features have shown up in distorted yet discernible fashion on the Psi tapes. Their manner of dress is from ancient times. And, I've never seen such pure semitic traits except once. This was on an Egyptian tomb painting displayed at the Kunsthistorisches Museum in Vienna. The painting depicts a Semitic chieftain taking his tribe to Egypt. It is our only evidence as to how the *Hebrews* looked and dressed at the time of Abraham in 1900 B.C.

"But, that is nothing compared to some of the images of buildings this man has recorded within his mind. Curiously enough there are historical gaps as if one were taking broad jumps across the pages of times. One can tell this by the type of architecture, building materials and the dress of the peoples involved.

"And, last but certainly not least, I've detected mental images of cylindrical and oval flying objects visualized against these same ancient backdrops!"

Father Pat pushed his chair back. It made a scraping noise that broke the tension of the moment.

"Harold, I feel that I must interrupt. My tongue is getting quite sore from biting it. I think your last statement may be logically explainable. Perhaps all of what the Psi detector picked up has been projected against a *mental*, not a *real* backdrop of ancient times. This man was sick, feverish and probably hallucinating. Let's face it. He, like yourself, must be an expert in the study of ancient cultures. He's a Jew, perhaps a Zionist. He was heavily involved in events leading up to the Statehood of Israel. Now, take an intimate knowledge of Jewish heritage, ancient history, add a few teaspoons of flying saucers and a high fever. What would one expect? Just what you've found. To think otherwise would imply some kind of reincarnation which I cannot accept."

"Reincarnation is a possible answer, Father. All I know is

that if my interpretations are correct, this man is a living library of ancient history, especially Biblical history. Now, let's take a quick look at the latter part of the Fatima rhyme before the curfew bell sounds. I noticed that you hadn't commented on this verse. I'll read it.

> Within a darkened mountain hall
> The King of Peace awaits recall

"Have you any idea who this King of Peace is, Father?"

"Well, my first thought was that this verse might be referring to our Lord and His Resurrection. He is called the Prince of Peace in the Scriptures."

"I doubt that this verse refers to that," Harold replied. "Jesus was called the Prince, not the King of Peace. Jesus certainly wasn't buried in a darkened mountain hall. He was buried in the cave of Joseph of Arimethea in a hill, not a mountain. So, this leaves us with the only person specifically called the King of Peace in the Bible. As fantastic as it may seem, this person may provide the answer to *two* riddles: the person mentioned in the rhyme *and* the person paralyzed up in the Penthouse. Father, take your Bible. Turn to Genesis, Chapter fourteen and read verse eighteen to us."

Father Pat scanned the pages until he found the correct verse.

> And Melchizedek, King of Salem brought forth
> bread and wine: and he was the Priest of the
> most high God.

"Why, Harold, this is the passage where Melchizedek meets and blesses Abraham. Of course, you're correct. Salem is the English phonetic of the Hebrew word for either righteousness or *peace*."

"Wasn't Christ himself called a Priest after the Order of Melchizedek?" Helen asked.

"Yes," replied Harold. There's a Messianic prophecy concerning this in the 110th Psalm. Here, the Messiah is called Lord and also a Priest after the Order of Malchizedek in verse four.

"Now, Father. Turn in the New Testament to the Book of Hebrews. We don't know who wrote this fascinating book but he considers Jesus as the fulfillment of the prophecy. Look at Chapter five, verse six and then at Chapter six, verse twenty."

Father Pat glanced at each verse in question. "Yes, he does indeed. I'm familiar with this. But, what are you saying, Harold? Does the Fatima rhyme refer to the Priesthood of the Order of Melchizedek?"

"Father, what I'm saying is that I'm agreeing with whoever gave that message to the shepherd at Fatima. It says:

> A Priestly Order holds the key
> To this poem of prophecy.

"That key, Father, is the very person of Mechizedek himself!"

"But, Harold," Father Pat objected, "Melchizedek died centuries ago. To be sure, his Order lives on through our risen Lord but Melchizedek is dead and gone."

A strange look came over Harold's face. A weird knowing glint appeared in his eyes. He reached over and took the Bible from Father Pat. He turned its pages to Hebrews Chapter seven and passed it to Helen.

"Here, read verses one through three to us, Helen."

Helen took the Bible and started reading.

For this cause Melchizedek, king of Salem,
priest of the Most High God, who met
Abraham returning from the slaugher of the
kings, and blessed him"

To whom also Abraham gave a tenth part of
all; first being by interpretation, King
of Righteousness, and after that also, King
of Salem, which is King of Peace.

Without father, without, without, with -

Helen turned pale and stopped reading audibly. Her eyes

continued to read. Her hands trembled.

"Go on, Helen, don't stop there," Harold ordered. "Read it out loud!"

Helen's voice quavered as she slowly finished reading the cryptic passage.

With - without father, without mother,
without descent, having neither beginning
of days nor end of life; but made like unto
the Son of God, abideth a priest continually.

Helen stopped. She stared at the Bible. A look of wonder played over her face. Father Pat sat shaking his head in disbelief. He turned slowly and looked up at Harold incredulously.

"Are you suggesting what I think you're suggesting, lad?" he mumured.

"Father, I'm proposing that the man lying up there in the Penthouse, the man who appears to be more than man, may be none other than Melchizedek, the ancient Hebrew King of Salem. I'm also proposing that he's the one mentioned in the Fatima rhyme 'awakening in a darkened mountain hall'. Already, a vague idea has begun to form in my mind as to where this mountain hall is located. I shall be looking further into this possibility tomorrow. I - -"

Ring-g-g-g-g!

"May th' saints preserve us! 'Tis the big bad bell itself! You two had best be a' goin'. 'Tis a crime to break us up at such a crucial point. You've left me in a dither and a' half, ya 'ave."

Father Pat instantly reverted back to his usual accent as he urged Helen and Harold out of the Chapel before the final bell rang.

Chapter Fourteen

Seed of the Elohim

It was Wednesday morning. Harold followed Colonel Milkowski out of the elevator into the foyer of the Penthouse area.

"MEDIC-1 must be still here," the Colonel remarked as he glanced at the closed partitions behind the large window. "That's strange. He was supposed to have left here over a half-hour ago. But no problem. Let me show you your quarters first. Then we'll see what's going on in there."

The Colonel walked by the window and restricted doors to the end of the foyer. Another restricted door could be seen barely outlined in the metal wall. He handed Harold a black tube about the size of a pencil.

"Here's your key. It will open all doors in this area. You'll also need it to activate the communications console. It also opens the skylight. You're lucky to have one. This whole area was built to accomodate only personnel at the Number 1 levels."

"Skylight? You mean a window opening to the Outside?" Harold exclaimed.

"Yes. All of us Level 1's have 'em. They're constructed of a special one-way glass that's non-reflective. The Soviets can't pick them up on their satellite photos.

The door slid open.

"Well, here's your latest home away from home. Do you like it?"

Harold followed the Colonel into a spacious, light-blue carpeted room. It contained a huge desk, several file cabinets, two long tables and a console built into a corner of the room.

"Now, all you have to do to reach Joseph is to activate the communications console and press the red intercom button," BETA-1 explained. "Go ahead. Put the key tube in here. You'll see."

Harold pushed the tube into the round receptacle and pressed the button. A TV screen lit up. There was Joseph in the lab downstairs. A TV monitor tracked Joseph's movements to his own console. His smiling face now filled the screen.

"Good morning, Harold. I see you have arrived. Yes? What can I do for you?"

"This is just a test. That will be all for now, Joseph," the Colonel snapped. "Now push the green button."

Harold complied and the TV monitor went out. The Colonel went on to explain other segments of the console.

"This is the computer terminal. It has either paper or visual output. You can only get to Computer Control by having Joseph patch you in. And this is the panel for air tube service. You'll be using it to receive data packages from Joseph and food from the cafeteria. Any other items will have to be cleared with me. Now, that door is your rest room and this door leads to our prisoner's bedroom. You'll be sleeping in there. Let's go in. This will be my last time in there for a while. Orders from the Council. Just you, the Doctor and nurses are going to be his bedfellows for the time being. Just push your key tube in here. It will open." The door flew up and the two walked into the room. Doctor Slater was examining the hairs on Ben-Sorek's head.

"MEDIC-1? What are you doing here so late?"

Doctor Slater glanced up with a bewildered look. "Steve, you'd best get Number 1 up here fast. This is incredible. Look at this!"

BETA-1 strode quickly across the floor. Harold followed.

"Well, what is it?"

"Look, look closely at his hair. It's starting to turn black again. And see his face! The wrinkles seem to be smoothing out. Tell me I'm not imagining this!"

"Good God!" exclaimed the Colonel. "How can this be? He's starting to look young again!"

"And that's not all. I was right about his vital signs picking up. His pulse and breathing are stable."

"I'll get to Number 1 immediately about this. He'll send out an all-Council alert. I doubt if he'll come in here. Technically, I'm not supposed to be here at all. And Doctor Slater, we only want you in here for a short time each day unless it's necessary. Harold, as you know, is living up here for awhile. We'd best get out of here and leave *him* alone. This guy might wake up at any time."

Harold was now alone with *him*. He stood at the foot of the bed for a long time and stared at the sleeping figure. Deep thoughts churned through his mind.

"Could that really be the ancient king of Salem? He looks so human, so fragile to be immortal. How could I have thought such an absurd thing!"

And yet, the man's face looked like someone right out of the time of Abraham. And, those images on the Psi tapes: how could he explain them to Bluepaper? The Council would laugh him to scorn. They would think he was crazy.

Harold decided it was best to play dumb with Bluepaper for the time being. He walked back into the adjoining room and contacted Joseph on the videocom.

"Good morning, Joseph. Were you able to get the computer-enhanced Psi images that I requested through Central?"

"Yes, good friend, I have them right here. I was just about to send them up air-tube express, yes?"

Moments later, Harold removed the photographs from the delivery tube. The glossy images were not as clear as those seen on the Psi screen. But, they were something that he could carefully study, frame by frame.

"This is amazing," Harold thought as he held a glossy up to the light at different angles. "There's only one gate that could be anywhere in the world. He must have been there. How else could he have seen it intact like that? The brick tile, the glazing effort, the relief figures of bulls and dragons: this was Babylon's Ishtar Gate!

"This gate guarded the Northern entrance of Babylon in 550 B.C. It led to the Processional Way. I wonder if, if — Great guns! Here it is, distorted almost beyond recognition but it really is. There in the distance. What else could it be? Remarkable. One of the great wonders of the world: The Hanging Gardens of Babylon!"

Harold grabbed another photo and held it up to the light.

"And what's this? He must have been looking down on a walled settlement of some kind from a great height. Why, a canal of water runs right through its center!"

Harold placed a magnifying glass over the Psi-photo. The canal seemed to fill a series of pools with the walled enclave. Where had he seen this before? Yes. These were the Essene ruins near the Dead Sea. It was Khirbet Qumran. This community was the source of the Dead Sea Scrolls. Those pools were ritual baths of purification.

Harold reluctantly took a break for lunch and then returned to his studies. He walked over to the book shelf and poked through the Bluepaper briefing material. He pulled out a folder on the June 19th, 1947, UFO landing on Mount Rainier reported by the two campers. He glanced at the annotated maps showing the general location of the reported box canyon. It was only several miles, as the crow flies, from where VIGIL had captured Ben-Sorek. Could he have been heading for that same canyon? And those apelike creatures, were they somehow connected with the aliens? Or, was their presence just a coincidence? After all, reports of Big Foot were rife in this area. Helen's aunt had told them story after story of such reports around Mount Rainier. Perhaps the creatures were just as curious about the landed object as the campers had been. Harold shrugged his shoulders and returned to his work table to ponder over the Psi-photos. The day went too quickly for him.

When Harold finally climbed into bed the strangeness of his new environment hit him hard. He missed Helen and the privacy of Sector 7. Here, the doctor or one of the nurses could walk in on him at any time. Intravenous feeding had started once again and Ben-Sorek's temperature and pulse were taken periodically. Harold felt as if he were back in a hospital again.

The LED display on the wall clock read 0204 when he first began to stir. A weird prickly sensation on the back of his head caused him to slowly awaken. As he began to recover his senses, a cold chill ran up and down his spine. He *felt* a presence. An overpowering feeling of a presence filled the room. Something told him to roll over, to turn his face from the wall and face the room. But his mind rebelled.

The eerie sensation grew stronger and stronger. The feeling of being watched became unbearable. Harold felt like he was an insect being scrutinized by a microscope. Suddenly, he could take it no longer. He bolted upright and swung around. Instantly, his eyes locked with the dark piercing eyes of, of, *him.*

Sheer terror coursed through Harold's body. He tried to speak, to yell, but no sound would come. Now he felt the prickling sensation creep downward from his head, across his chest, down his legs to his toes. Harold tried to move but he couldn't move a muscle. Then he knew nothing until the following morning.

"My, Mr. Stanton," said the nurse. "You must have had a tiring day yesterday. Do you know what time it is? Why, you slept right through the signals this morning. It's almost 0830!"

Harold jumped up and looked wildly about him. He glanced at the nurse, who backed off with a surprised look on her face. Then he looked over at the sleeping Ben-Sorek.

"Whatever is the matter, BETA-27? Did I frighten you? I'm not that bad-looking, am I? I'm Catherine Higgins, MEDIC-16. I'll be up now and again to check out your strange bedfellow until MEDIC-1 comes back from break. They call me Cathy. I'm not supposed to speak to you. But I always like to say hello to the men. May I call you Harold? If you'd ever like to get together on break, just dial MEDIC-16 on the match box at Recreation. If I'm on break and available, I'd love to get together with you. 'Nuff said?"

Cathy gave Harold a sly wink and then started her routine check on the strange patient. He sat up and pulled the blue bed covers around him. His face was still flushed when Cathy walked out the door smiling sensuously at him.

"Confound it! What will happen next around here?" Harold mumbled as he hurried to wash and dress. As he glanced in the mirror, he suddenly found himself staring at his own eyes staring back at him in the reflection. For one split second the image of the staring eyes of Ben-Sorek flashed through his mind. He tried to recapture it but it faded.

"Must have been a dream," he thought. "This place is getting to me already."

The day again passed quickly. Harold had become deeply engrossed trying to interpret the bits and pieces of writing that had appeared on a scroll and some clay tablets. The psi images were blurred and practically unreadable.

After dinner, he finally was able to translate a portion of the Egyptian hieroglyphics. The writing was on a tile attached to a wall beside a gate. It named a place called Avaris. This was the Hyksos Capital rebuilt by the Egyptian Pharoah, Seti I, 1308-1290 B.C. Interestingly enough, Seti I was thought to have been the first Pharoah to have enslaved the Hebrew peoples. Moses himself had been raised in the court of one of Seti's sons, Rameses II. It was under him that the Exodus must have taken place.

"Harold got up and stretched. He walked over and opened the door to Ben-Sorek's room and glanced in at the sleeping man. There was more dark hair than white now. He felt uneasy about going in there to sleep all alone with *him*. Later, when he did retire to bed, a verse from the Fatima rhyme echoed over and over in his mind.

Within a darkened Mountain Hall
The King of Peace awaits recall

He sank into the comfortable mattress and pulled the covers around him. The portable night lamp cast a weak aura of fluorescent light around the sleeping figure of Ben-Sorek. Eerie shadows cast ghostly silhouettes about the room. It was quiet, so confounded quiet. Harold tossed and turned. Suddenly, visions of dark, piercing eyes danced in his mind. Abruptly, the remembrance of last night's terrifying nightmare came crashing back into his conscious mind. Harold lay trembling as he gazed at the wall. It must have been a dream. He felt inclined to glance over at Ben-Sorek but he was afraid to. This was silly. He was a grown man. He must look!

Harold turned around slowly and faced the other bed. He sighed a breath of relief. The olive-skinned stranger lay quietly. His eyes were closed in peaceful slumber.

"See, there's nothing to be afraid of," Harold assured himself. "His eyes are closed. He's not awake, he's, he's, Oh, Lord!"

Harold froze in terror as the large almond-shaped dark eyes snapped open to meet his gaze. Instantaneously, an electric-like prickling shock surged through his head, his shoulders, his arms, his legs, his feet. Then came a strongly accented voice.

"You will now sit up, Doctor Stanton."

Harold heard the voice. But where had it come from? Ben-Sorek's mouth had not moved. He felt himself sluggishly sit up in bed. He turned to face the bearded man.

Harold felt aloof and isolated from his own motions. It was as if he were an observer, rather than a participant in his own bodily movements. The voice sounded again. It seemed to come from inside his head.

Dr. Stanton. You are a most remarkable man. Your knowledge of the ancient past is phenomenal. I found great delight in probing your mind last night.

You have within you a double potential for my good or for my ill. Never before has my body been so helpless. I cannot move as you know. But what your doctor does not yet know, is that my spinal injury has affected my ability to speak to you audibly. I can only speak mentally to you like this. Like this, when our eyes meet together. Each night we will have a session. We are both sons of light. We both worship the True One. The False one has much influence. Already he moves about the earth in my name. Seeking that one who will become the final fleshly embodiment of all that is false. But now we will talk together. I will ask you questions. You will think the answers. Tomorrow night you may ask me questions.

Harold woke up with a start when the reveille bell sounded. Remnants of a strange dream played in his mind. He looked over at Ben-Sorek asleep on the bed across the room. What had happened? He pressed his head into the pillow and tried to reconstruct the elusive after-images. Then it all came back. The interrogation by Ben-Sorek. He had asked question after question about his boyhood, Christian beliefs, education, NSA, Beta, Helen, Phoenix Base 3, Father Pat, and on and on until his mind felt it would snap. Ben Sorek's last words still echoed over and over again in his mind.

Tomorrow night you may ask me questions. I will provide answers. You may remember everything that is said. But if you choose to reveal our conversation, then you will forget. You *will* forget. You will now feel relaxed and at ease. All discomfort will disappear. Go to sleep. Deep sleep. Deep sleep. You will wake rested and in good spirits.

Harold sat up in bed and stared at the sleeping stranger. Could all of this really have happened? Or was it just a vivid dream? This place and all that was happening surely was conducive to nightmares. He slipped out of bed and entered his quarters. The *dream* was etched within his mind. His mind struggled within. If this really happened, tonight he could actually ask Ben-Sorek questions. "But," he thought, "this is silly thinking like this. Of course it all must have been another dream."

Harold had just finished lunch when a familiar voice

sounded from the door.

"A penny for your thoughts, Harold."

Harold glanced up. General Thurman stood just inside the sliding door.

"What's the matter? Tongue-tied? I hope your pen produced more than your mouth," General Thurman laughed. "I don't suppose our friend has spoken yet or Joseph would have called."

"No, he hasn't *spoken* a word to me yet," Harold replied cautiously.

"Well, I trust you have a status report of some kind for me to show my colleagues. The Council is anxious to know just what you're accomplishing here."

"General, you must be patient. There is much interpretation and evaluation to be done. Joseph and I have prepared some work sheets on the psi images. I've photocopied them for you. I'm also working on other things — ideas, theories if you will. But I have nothing substantial yet.

"The worksheets indicate that this man has an incredible knowledge of past civilizations. I have no rational explanation for some of the things contained in his thoughts. Look at this, for instance. This is without doubt the Northern Gate to Babylon. It dates back to 550 B.C. How could he possibly have seen it intact like this? I've seen the reconstructed gate at the State Museum in Berlin. It's a poor imitation compared to this."

The General held the glossy up to the light. "Did I hear you right? What did you mean by 'how could he have seen it?' You're not trying to tell me we have some sort of Methuselah on our hands, are you?"

"I don't know what I'm telling you except many of these images are of things that do not exist in any museum, General."

"Well, perhaps he saw them in a museum or book and then just imagined the way they really looked. He had a fever of 104. The man was delirious. That's the logical explanation. I'll take your xeroxed work sheets and read your comments to the Council.

"Now, may I remind you, Harold, that Doctor Slater believes that Ben-Sorek may awaken at any time. We're counting on you. Let me know just as soon as he makes any sound at all."

"I will, General. Ah, how's my wife?"

"I've only seen her a few times with her Dad. She's anxious to see you on Sunday. That, however, is contingent on what's happening here. The Doc will have a permanent nurse on duty while you're away on Sunday. But, if that fellow comes to, you'll be sent back here pronto. Understand?"

"I understand."

"Good. Well, I'll be going now. Oh! By the way. I was going through some status reports from Central. I've seen your requests to the Central Computer. I've ascertained that you and Joseph have begun analysis of the Psi tapes. Will there be an explanation for all of this in your next report?"

"I hope by next week to have something. I'm only human. We're literally feeling our way through this. Tell your Council that they musn't expect miracles."

"No, we certainly don't expect miracles. That's precisely what's upsetting all of us. That guy in there seems to be able to work them. Cheerio, Harold. I'll be talking to you later."

That evening, before retiring, Harold opened the skylight and sat looking up into the dusk of an evening sky. He was literally entranced by the sight. Never before had he realized how much he had taken for granted. One, then another bright point of light blinked on until the sky was filled with stars. His eyes became watery as he sat watching, wondering and praying.

It was almost midnight when Harold finally opened the door to the sleeping prisoner's room. He had waited until Cathy had come and gone. He didn't want to be in bed when she arrived. It might provoke further flirtations. It was down-right embarrassing.

"Well, let's hope that I won't have any more of those crazy nightmares," Harold thought as he slipped under the blue covers of his bed. It was nearly 0200 when he first heard the faint but persistent voice.

"Doctor Stanton. Doctor Stanton. Doctor Stanton?"

The voice sounding within Harold's head sounded far, far away. But, the more he acknowledged its presence, the louder it became. Harold stirred and shook his head. "Crazy dreams! Will I ever get a good night's sleep?" he mumbled. He glanced sleepily over to the other bed. Once again his eyes met the staring, unblinking eyes of Ben-Sorek. Instantly he felt his mind seized by an invisible force. Again the voice sounded in his head.

Do not speak out, Doctor Stanton. You hear my thought in your mind. I hear your thoughts in my mind. I have not suspended your bodily movements. You are free to move about. What questions would you ask of me? Speak for yourself and not for the Bluepaper ones.

"Who are you?" Harold thought. "Who are you?"

Do not fear, my brother in the light. Do not fear. You will be calm. I am the living chronicler of Mankind. The living repository of the history of Israel. The servant of the Word from Eternity. I am Melchizedek, worshipper of the True One Who is.

"But that's impossible! Melchizedek lived over 4000 years ago! He must be dead. You, you are a middle-aged man. You must have been born in this century."

I was the Keeper of the Garden. A Counselor to Noah. The Mentor of Abraham. The Guardian of the Covenant. The Coadjutor of Moses. The Teacher of the Prophets. The Guide of the Apostles. The Servant of the Word from Eternity.

"But where did you come from? Surely you have parents!"

Earthly parents have I none. Beginning I remember not. The creation of Elohim am I. They are the Mighty Ones, the gods, the hosts of Heaven, Who serve the True One Who is.

165

"Creation of the Elohim? But Elohim is God. He is Spirit, not a Physical Being. What can you mean?"

> Listen to me, dust of the earth. Ponder my words, image of the Elohim. The True One is Spirit indeed. Hearken as I explain your place in relation to the True One and the Creation. You will listen, contemplate, and retain.

Harold felt his very mind gripped by an unseen power. An aura of otherworldliness, of incomprehensible wisdom engulfed his very being.

Know this, Harold Stanton. Know this.

"Know what? Know what?" his mind seemed to echo in response.

> *Know* that there is a Creator-Sustainer Who has made Himself knowable to Creation in direct proportion to the creatures' ability to comprehend and respond.

> *Know* that there exist in the Creation Myriads of rational entities in varying *stages* of physical, intellectual, technical and spiritual development *between* The Creator and the creature called Man on Earth.

> *Know* that there is a chain-like relationship between the highest and the lowest forms of rational being.

> *Know* that the creature called Man is close to the lowest end of the chain of rational beings.

> *Know* that all creatures on this plane and others are carrying out a portion of the True One's overall plan in creation, in both a *conscious* and an *unconscious* manner.

> *Know* that a long period of non-rational physical being preceded Man becoming a *physical* rational creature. Billions of your earth years it took to produce a physical form on this plane capable of containing and sustaining a rational mind.

> *Know* that the development of Man and his subordinate creatures on earth are part of a living universe. Continually *becoming*, continually growing, towards that goal determined and known by the True One that Is.

> *Know* that the evolution of Man has been aided by creatures of a higher order in a way that was and is a natural part of the overall

purposes of the Ultimate Creator-Sustainer.

Know that contact by and guidance from such higher beings are on a higher plane of thought and operation usually unintelligible and incomprehensible to Man.

Know that the True One who Is worked through the Elohim from above to establish his creation called Man on this third orb from your sun.

Know that Man is grown in the image of Elohim to provide living spirits for worlds without end.

"Doctor Stanton? Do you understand — understand?" The words of Melchizedek echoed and re-echoed throughout Harold's very being.

"Do you have questions — questions — questions?"

"Questions? Yes. Questions. I am a historian. I've seen no records of interventions such as you describe. Are there written records of what you speak about?"

"Know, Harold Stanton, know!" the voice sounded in Harold's mind.

Know that among the records of Mankind the most sacred, the most jealously kept, the most influential in the world within the scope of Western Civilization are that collection of Writings known as the Holy Bible.

Know that within this written record from my creation story in the first book called Genesis through the last book called Revelation there are consistent accounts of contact events accompanied by related paranormal events and their resultant social-cultural impact.

"But, these are visitations of God's angels, spiritual beings, not physical beings!" Harold's mind echoed back.

Know that physical and spiritual are but descriptive terms used to distinguish between life forms vibrating at different frequencies within their particular planes.

Know that the higher beings mentioned in the Holy Bible appear with physical bodies vibrating within the frequency of Man's physical plane of existence.

Know that their unearthly heavenly origin must also be a physical place capable of supporting physical life.

Know that the only physical places vibrating at the proper frequencies within the observational senses of Man are what he calls planets.

"But how could Angels live on other planets? Angels simply appear and disappear from heaven."

Know that a physical vehicle must be employed to transport a physical being from one physical body or planet to your own planet Earth.

Know that the Holy Bible and other records record the presence of such vehicles associated with the higher beings and their activities on and above the earth's surface.

Know that witnesses of these contacts and their associated activities could only describe such within the context of and in the language-symbology of their culture and understanding.

Know that on the *one hand*, such physical vehicles of transportation when seen on the earth or in the sky, would of necessity have to be described in terms of familiar objects or phenomena that witnesses were accustomed to seeing on the ground or in the air. Clouds, bushes, lamps, stars, lights, wheels, pillars.

Know that on the *other hand* the higher beings would of necessity have to be described in terms of their man-likeness versus their non-man-likeness within the framework of known races of man and known species of lower life forms.

"How can this be? Give me examples — examples," Harold's mind echoed in reply.

Know the selection of Abraham, the Calling of Moses, the Exodus from Egypt, the Giving of the Law, the Training of the Prophets, the Coming of the Word, the Preparation of the Apostles, all of these are examples, Harold Stanton.

"But why, why?"

Know that like the leaven in bread the social-cultural impact resulting from these contact events not only drastically affected the peoples directly involved then but have affected and are affecting today peoples on a global scale through the beliefs and practices of Judaism and Christianity.

Know for a surety, Harold Stanton, that this social-cultural impact has not been random but is part of an overall long term plan to aid and abet man's development toward his becoming or developing into that which the ultimate Creator-Sustainer has planned for him.

Know that this step-by-step development was triggered and induced by contact events outlined in the Biblical record and will culminate in what Christianity calls the Second Coming.

"Jesus? Contact? This is Blasphemy! Jesus Christ is the Son of God. He is our Saviour from Heaven. How can you say He is a spaceman? How can you — you — you?"

Know that what was placed in the Virgin's womb came from the depths of the True One that Is through Intermediaries: the Messengers from Eternity.

Know that the Word of the True One Who Is has become flesh of life forms innumerable throughout the universe to reveal Himself and prepare them for becoming what he has planned from eternity.

Know that the life of the Word made Flesh on earth was accompanied by the same contact events that were experienced by those who prepared for his Initial Encampment in flesh with the image of Elohim.

"Preposterous! Untrue. Proof. Examples," Harold's mind shouted in opposition.

Know that these events are recorded in the Memoirs and Letters of the Apostles. *Listen — Ponder -- Consider.*

Read again with eyes enlightened of the angels from on high. Read again with knowledge heightened of a *star's* flight through the sky.

Read again the wondrous story of the shepherds in the night; angels from the realms of glory of descent in ship so bright.

Read of Jordan's watery rite descending like a dove. Ponder new that marvelous sight approval from above.

Consider now that shining cloud o'er Peter, James and John. Consider now what was allowed before the two were gone.

That selfsame cloud took Him away. And Angels came to say, "This selfsame Jesus will return someday this selfsame way."

"It is too hard to bear. These concepts disturb me," Harold's mind retorted.

Know, Harold Stanton. Know this. Know that the Word Himself has stated that His Coming again would be accompanied by higher beings coming on the *clouds* of heaven to judge and rule the earth.

Know that some will become an integral part of a higher social organization termed the Kingdom of Heaven where His Will is done on earth as it is in the heavens.

Know that in order to accomplish this vast changes will take place in the nature of earth and man. A new heaven — a new earth — a new man.

The voice in Harold's head droned relentlessly on and on and on into the night. Finally Harold felt the power that gripped his mind relax its hold. The voice became soothing, so soothing.

And now, Harold Stanton, you will sleep, rest, relax. Tomorrow night we will commune again. You are a son of light. Your help is needed against the sons of darkness who serve the False One.

Harold felt himself lie back. He pulled the covers about him and fell into the netherworld of dreamless sleep.

Chapter Fifteen

The Fall of Adapa

It was 0538 when Harold woke with a start. He glanced fearfully at the bed across the room from him. His mind was in a turmoil. Dreams or not, these revelations were just too much for him to take in.

"I've got to get out of here. I must be going mad. I need you, Helen," he thought, as the door slid shut separating him from Melchizedek, King of Salem.

Harold washed and dressed as one in a stupor. He activated the console and ordered an early breakfast. As he ate, the voice of Melchizedek echoed and re-echoed through his mind. "Read again — ponder — consider. Read again — ponder — consider — the wheels of Elohim — wheels — wheels — the glory of the Lord — Shekinah Glory — pillar of fire — of cloud — read again — ponder — consider."

Harold walked over to the book shelf and removed his Hebrew Bible. He pulled out a Hebrew lexicon and selected a book on exegesis of Hebrew words. Clearing a portion of his work table, he sat down.

"What am I doing?" he thought. "I should be working on Bluepaper. Why am I doing this?" He found himself opening the Bible to the first chapter of the book of Ezekiel. "Ah, yes. The famous vision of Ezekiel. Most commentators dismiss it as a difficult passage to understand."

"Read again — consider anew — ponder — summarize essentials — outline." The words of his dream pounded relentlessly in his mind as he read and reread the first chapter of Ezekiel. He closed his eyes. Something else was said. What was it? Oh yes.

> *Know* that such events are interpreted and recorded within the context and through the limited knowledge, expressions, and languages of the particular culture involved.

Harold first wrote out a literal rendering of the passage in English. Then, he performed a careful exegesis of key descriptive words. Next, he outlined the vision of Ezekiel in summary form as if he were a modern reporter interviewing the ancient prophet. He felt strange, almost possessed. He was merely an observer of someone else's actions working through his own mind and fingers.

Date: July 5, 1593 BC (30th year, 4th month, 5th day, 5th year of captivity)

Place: Chebar River, Village of Tel-abib, Babylonia (Probably Shatt-em Nil canal near Babylon)

Witness: Ezekiel, son of Buzi, a Zadokite Priest (Zadokites appointed by King Josiah to launch vital religious reform)

Circumstances: Israel conquered by Babylonia. Ezekiel is among those exiled to Babylonia. Lived in special exile colony.

I. Aerial Object

   A. *Huge, cloud-like object approached from Northern Sky*

      1. It rotated ("Whirl wind"/ruach searah)

      2. Had flashing lights (a fire infolding it-self"- flashing continuously)

      3. Surrounded by multi-colored glow ("brightness about it. . .like rainbow")

      4. Made of shiny metal ("amber")

         a. Hebrew ("hasmal") Something shining

         b. Greek ("elektron") alloy of gold and silver

         c. Assyrin ("esmaru") shining metallic alloy

      5. Cylindrical-shaped ("likeness of glory

of the Lord")

    a. Glory of YWEH—The Pillar-shaped *cloud* that led/protected Israel during the Exodus from Egypt.

B. *Four wheels and creatures come out of cloud·like object*

    1. *Shape* - Disc like "wheel within wheel" (inner and outer circumference)

    2. *Color* - like "beryl", sparkled like chrysolite" (shiny green)

    3. *Other*

        a. had rims ("rings")

        b. had ports/orifices ("Rings full of eyes round about them")

        c. gave off flashes like "lightning"

        d. part of object glowed like "burning coals of fire"

    4. *Movement*

        a. performed turns without curve radius (right hand turns—"turned not when they went")

        b. under intelligent control ("spirit of the living creature was in the wheels")

    5. *Noise* - like "rushing water"

II. Creatures Associated With Aerial Objects

    1. Described in terms of man and animal-likeness

    2. Controlled movement of the wheels ("spirit of the living creature was in the wheels")

    3. Had transparent covering over their heads ("firmament upon heads. . .color of crystal")

        a. firmament ("ragia") - expanse, vault, hemisphere

        b. crystal ("gerach") - ice, transparent or colorless substance

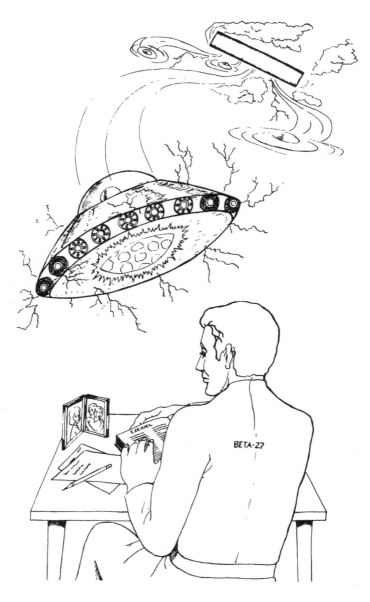

"Ah, yes. The famous vision of Ezekiel."

4. Used wheels (discs) for transportation
    ("and when the living creatures were
    lifted up from the earth, the wheels were
    lifted up")

Suddenly his pencil stopped writing. The strange mental sensation of feeling like an observer slowly lifted. He felt his mind again returning to the role of a participant.

Harold trembled unrestrainedly as his eyes now consciously scanned what he had written. Instantly a scene from the Project Magnet film flashed before his mind's eye. There again was the huge silvery metallic cylinder enveloped in a swath of whirling clouds. Smaller disc-shaped craft darted towards it like aerial skipping stones. They made abrupt right angle turns as they lined up under the huge mother ship.

A close-up photo of one of the discs had been shown. It was a silvery, phosphorescent oval object (a wheel?). It was girdled by a rim (a ring?). It had dull-glowing portholes (eyes?) around its circumference.

"Great guns!" Harold blurted out loud. "Can all of this really be true? Why, the Ezekiel account could very well have been a Type II UFO event! A CEIIIg! Incredible. It's just incredible."

"What did you say, my friend? I cannot hear you so well. Yes?"

Harold jumped. He glanced first at the closed door and then, with some relief, at the glowing TV screen on the console.

"Confound it, Joseph. You scared the blazes out of me. Couldn't you have given me some warning, I mean, ah," Harold glanced at the puzzled look on Joseph's face and laughed. "Sorry, Joseph. I'm uptight this morning. What's up?"

"Nothing, my friend. I was just wondering if you needed anything before I started processing the paper-graphs."

"Paper-graphs?"

"The paper-graphs from the oscilloscope readings of Psi tapes recorded at contactee areas. Yes. Are you sure you're all right, Harold? Joseph think you look pale."

"I've had a bad night, Joseph. Being all alone with *him* is getting on my nerves. Yes, go ahead and work on the graphs. Are there any more glossies processed that look halfway decent?"

"I have the rest right here. Very few show anything clearly. I send them up, yes?"

"Yes, send them along. I'll keep in touch."

Harold waited for the glossies to arrive via air tube. "The paper-graphs. Yes, they may prove to be interesting," he thought. "I wonder what the contactees think of black, unmarked helicopters buzzing their cars, houses and places of employment. Do they suspect they're being monitored by the government? I wonder what kind of signals are being sent to them. I must find out. Ha! Me, Harold Stanton, trying to crack encrypted signals from outer-space aliens. Incredible. If someone had told me this several months ago, I'd have laughed him to scorn, or, pity his mental problem! And these dreams: what if they aren't dreams? Perhaps I could find out more about modern contactees from *him*?"

Harold shuddered. "Of course they're dreams," he thought. "They must be, or are they?" Again, the strange accented voice of his nightmarish experience entered his mind. What had it said? Oh yes: 'Tomorrow night we will commune again.' Well, we shall see. No more of this nonsense. I refuse to be frightened by dreams no matter how real they seem. Tonight I'll retire early. We'll see if my imagined Melchizedek has anything to say." The glossies arrived via air tube and Harold again returned to the task of analysis. He became so engrossed in his work that he let dinner time slip by unnoticed. Joseph had connections with the food center. He managed to get a left-over sandwich and then prepared for bed.

Harold waited for Doctor Slater and his nurse to leave the area before he entered his *shared* bedroom. It was much later than he had planned to retire. When he entered the dimly-lit room, he was shocked to the core to see the smiling olive-skinned Ben-Sorek staring at him! Instantly his eyes became glued to the hypnotic gaze of this man. Harold opened his mouth but no words came. A slight tingling sensation coursed through his body. Feelings of love and friendship encompassed him. He felt no fear. Then, that same accented voice sounded within his head.

"Well, Harold, how soon do we forget, or do we? I see that you have thought our nocturnal get-togethers to be a dream? No, my friend, they have not been dreams. Now, you cannot move your legs, but I will let you look about. Pinch yourself if you would. See? I am here. You are there. Your bed is over there. Do you think this is a dream? Do not answer audibly. We must not alert those who monitor this room to our sessions. The lighting is much too dim for them to see what I am doing. Now, you will *think* your answers as you did before."

Harold gazed dumbfounded at the strange-looking man. There was still just a trace of white hair on his head and in his beard. But, he had almost reverted back to the exact likeness of the David Ben-Sorek VIGIL had brought there.

"Ah, my appearance befuddles you? By tomorrow I shall be exactly as I was when your keepers brought me here. But, now, do you think this a dream? Answer, my friend."

"No. It is now very apparent to me that this is not a dream. Nor, I assume, were the events of the past few nights?"

"That is correct, my brother in the light. And I see that you did your homework on the Ezekiel event. You will now remember clearly everything that I have given you. Ah, yes. You think about the Priest? Yes. You may share these things with him. Perhaps now the world will hear the truth about the Fatima event.

"*That* contact was not my doing. I was fast asleep then. Others, besides myself, carry out the will of the True One Who Is. But, I have borne my mission over the centuries of

177

your time. What I have to tell you this night has never been heard before by any man. For the sake of time and my respect for your limited capacity, I shall tell the story simply. You may go lie down. We shall then begin, my friend in the light. You will remember all. It will become a permanent and vivid part of your memory system."

A loud rushing sound like that of a waterfall seemed to fill the air. Yet it was not an audible sound. An overwhelming sense of awe became so overpowering that Harold's eyes filled with tears. Then Melchizedek spoke. As if one far away, his words reverberated within Harold's mind.

"I am from the Elohim. Many races are they. Carbon-based am I. My beginning was not here. My creators came from far within the core of this island of suns you call the Milky Way. Billions of years before your sun was born, they were contacted by the Messengers from Eternity. They are those who dwell in the infinitude of Creation. They who had already brought knowledge of the True One to myriads of islands throughout His Creation, came to us.

"They taught my ancestors to go forth and do the will of the True One throughout this island. They taught that all of life in its many forms are as cells of a living body that is *becoming*. All is becoming. The life-giving power of the True One fills and sustains all that He has made *and* all that the Elohim have made through His bidding. Not a sun is extinguished without His knowing. Not a life form is born without His comprehending. His Spirit is everywhere always. From the smallest to the largest. He is all in all. It is the desire of the True One to see Himself mirrored in all that He has created. It is His will that all sentient beings reflect His ways willingly and lovingly. For He is love in its ultimate state of being.

"Billions of years ago my ancestors reached the outer peninsulas of this island. Responding to His will they moved from sun to sun searching out those planets most suitable for spreading life in its many forms. They knew that these life forms too would ultimately become a vehicle for the continuation of the Elohim. Then, all of this island would be filled with minds as One overall mind. These minds would reflect the communicable attributes of the True One Who Is. Then we would be ready to join minds with those of other islands already at One with the True One Who Is.

"Your *orb* was selected to be a seed bed. It is located in the last remaining peninsula of stars to be evangelized along this coastal section of this island. Many and varied are the life forms grown within this peninsula. The Spirit of the True One blessed my creators with harvests that were again replanted throughout the peninsula. They knew that they would see the fruits of their labors realized in the development of living vehicles of flesh. Man would become carbon-based earthly images of their own kind: the Elohim. Then, this island would at last be ready to join minds with the local Federation of Islands. Thus we could be used further by the True One Who Is to accomplish His Will throughout His Creation.

"But one within our island did not want this. He was not mammalian like us. A Reptilian was this Dragon of rebellion. Powerful was he within the Council of the Holy Ones. He dismissed as deception the word given to our Ancestors by the Messengers from Eternity. He convinced others that these Messengers were not from the True One Who Is. He said that they were from a Federation of Islands seeking to subjugate our island through false beliefs and myths. This Serpent dared to deny the very existence of the True One Who Is. He suggested that someone on the Council should be elevated and worshiped in place of the myth of the True One Who Is. When he found no support among the members of the Council, he gave himself this honor. The Council banished him to the outer coastline of this island lest he undo the work that had been done by the Elohim over eons of time.

"You, who believe in and experience death, may ask — 'Why did you not destroy this one and his followers?' It is not within the power of the Elohim to destroy him nor is it within his power to destroy them. The Elohim may only attempt to influence one another. They are immortal. Even though the body of their present vibration be disrupted, they are able to re-establish its field. You, and your kind, Harold Stanton, are unable to do this because of what the Serpent has done on your orb called earth. Let me explain. It was when I first became conscious, I Melchizedek, King of Peace.

"After the banishment of the Evil One to the coastlines of this island, my brothers continued their efforts to bring knowledge of the True One to these same areas. They found the Dragon's influence great. Almost inpenetrable. When our emissaries arrived on this orb they found their seed bed completely uncultivated. Thousands of species of plantlife grew wild. Cross pollination, mutation and breeding had produced many reptilian life-forms. Huge dragons and sea monsters had developed. We knew that the False one sought to develop his own kind on this orb called earth through the reptilian strain of life. Our dreams for the establishment of mammalian life here were temporarily set back.

"The Elohim destroyed all except the most beneficial of what you call the dinosaurs. Development processes were set in motion which would eventually result in the development of mammals. It was hoped that by the Elohim's next visit the two legged mammals would have evolved here. They would become images of the Elohim.

"But, it was feared that those of the Dragon would discover what we had done. The Elohim prayed to the True One Who Is to protect this orb until we returned. When I returned with my brothers eons later, a mixed blessing was found.

"True, the followers of the Dragon had not returned. And, indeed the two legged mammals had developed. But food was scarce. Fierce carnivores were plentiful. Heartbroken were my brothers to see the ones who soon would receive the *Crown* of Elohim starving and destroying one another. Such was due to the one who fell from favor of the Council: The Council of the Elohim who worship the True One Who Is.

"A special site was chosen to enact the sacred rite of the *Crowning* of the Elohim. Geographically, it was situated at the approximate center of the Eastern Hemisphere of this orb. The site lay between what are called the Tigris and Euphrates Rivers. The soil was rich. Water was plentiful. We enclosed an area and planted a garden. Beneficial plants and animals were introduced to our garden. When all was in readiness, a fine specimen was chosen from among a number of the two-legged ones we had marked. Then, through the knowledge imparted to our ancestors by the Messengers from Eternity, aided by the quickening power of the ever-present Spirit of the True One Who Is, the male two-legged one received the *Crown* of Elohim. He became *Adapa*, the seed of mankind. He was the Adam recorded in the book of Genesis.

"Adapa was taught many things in order that he might teach many others who would someday join him in the garden. He was obedient, gentle and loving — the very image of the Elohim who are the image of the True One Who Is.

"Later, a female was selected. An operation was performed on her so that she would mate only with Adapa and no other. They would be a unity. They both became the leaders in a colony created in the very image of the Elohim. Other males and females were brought into the garden. They too were given the gift of the *Crown* of Elohim. Adapa and his life-giving one, the Eve of Genesis, bore many sons and daughters in their image.

The Elohim chose me to be the overseer of the garden on this orb. I was chosen to serve as a living representative of the True One Who Is, even Yaweh. He is the self-existing One. He is the True One Who Is. But first I had to return for the personal approval and blessing of the Council of the Elohim, the holy ones.

"But, before I returned to the sacred core of this island, I gave strict instructions to Adapa. He was told not to enter the control sphere that lay in the middle of the reservation. This was the sphere of life. The radiating power of its antenna tower controlled the weather, eradicated harmful bacteria and counteracted the aging process inherent in their bodies. This antenna with its multiple elements stood like a mighty silver tree in the midst of the garden. In time, it would no longer be needed. Then our garden could be harvested and the seed of Adapa periodically transplanted to other orbs throughout the barren portions of this island. Never before had an image of the Elohim disobeyed. But Adapa was the first of many who disobeyed as the dragon began his corruption of the entire peninsula at the edge of this island of stars. However, there was little concern at that time as we watched the blue-green orb of earth disappear from our scanners. Little did I know what I would find upon my return.

"You are familiar with my simple story in Genesis. Suffice it to say that the followers of the Dragon discovered our colony of mammals made in the image of their hated mammalian counterparts. The Dragon himself was summoned to see for himself. He decided not to destroy the creation of the Elohim out-rightly. Instead, he subverted the colony through its leader, Adapa, for his own purposes.

"When we returned again, we found the careful work of eons marred beyond immediate restoration. We were suddenly faced with the existence of a new species. Man was now an intelligent mortal beast who wore the immortal Crown of the Elohim. Although the animal body would now cease to exist in its present vibrational frequency, its *essence* would still live on to the age of ages.

"I dared not signal the Council of the terrible thing that had happened. We did not want the followers of the Dragon to intercept such a message. We kept our sad discovery secret. Our reconnaissance party dismantled the ravaged garden. The seed of Adapa was banished into the tooth and claw world they had long been parted and protected from. Their settlements now lay unprotected from disease, drought, and wild animals. The noble two-legged ones, their physical ancestors, now became deadly enemies.

"The Council was informed personally of the great tragedy. For the first time in its history, it employed the sacred signalling device left behind by the Messengers from Eternity. The message sent them told of the fall of the Mighty One, that Dragon. It told of his subversion throughout this peninsula. Soon, a message came back in return, a powerful telepathic message which reverberated throughout the island. It was directed to the Dragon and his followers. But it was an encouragement to us all.

"It told of the Word from Eternity who would one day come to crush the head of the Dragon. The return message gave the Elohim their battle plans, one for each orb under the Dragon's control. War was declared in the heavens. A leader was chosen from amongst us by the Messengers of Eternity. They spoke for the True One Who Is. They picked our noblest and wisest member. *Michael* would lead the fight against the dragon and his angels.

"Meanwhile, I sent word to the Elohim that earth was filled with the violence of mankind. The Sons of the Elohim who followed the Dragon were raiding and raping the settlements on earth. This resulted in grotesque offspring, the Nephilim. These half-breed giants were filled with greed and power. You already know the story of the merciful flood. It washed away the stench of this continual sin. All we could do next was to somehow influence mankind to worship the True One Who Is. The Elohim did this according to the plan the True One had outlined for this orb called earth.

"Another emergency arose when reconnaissance reported that huge platforms were being built at Babel. They were to be used to accommodate the mass transport of thousands of the fallen ones from earth. The followers of the Dragon hoped to use them to infiltrate our new colonies. They sought to corrupt other gentle ones we had established within the coastline of his influence. But, instead, *our* ships arrived. Thousands upon thousands who had been deceived by the Dragon mistakenly welcomed us as his followers. Right under his very nose, we scattered them all over the earth. Then we returned and destroyed the platforms at Babel.

"I was then commissioned to search out one person and teach him thoroughly of the True One. From that person would rise a Nation. This Nation would be given a Law sent to us for use on earth by the Messengers from Eternity. That Law would be a Schoolmaster. It would prepare that Nation and those it influenced for the Fullness of Time. This would be when the Word of the True One would be born within that Nation. His birth and life would cause that Nation to become a blessing to all other nations throughout the orb called Earth.

"To keep my mission a secret from the Dragon's followers, I slept and awakened over planned periods of time. These times corresponded to specific missionary journeys to this orb by the Elohim and their servants, the Watchers.

"My last sleep was deep within a mountain in the country you call Norway. I was not supposed to be awakened until Mankind had reached that point in time where he could destroy himself and all life on this orb. I speak of what you call the atomic bomb. The bomb's radiation would awaken the *Watchers* who would come to tend to my needs. Again, I would go forth and work through the nation, Israel, to hasten the accomplishment of that which has been planned.

"However, your World War II brought me from my cocoon several years too early. The Norwegians began blasting out caverns within my mountain tomb for defense installations. Severe damage was done to my telemetering instruments. These instruments monitored my sleeping body and marked my exact location for the *Watchers*. The *Watchers* are what your Bluepaper has called AI's.

"When the telemetry link was broken, the *Watchers* prematurely streamed down from their asteroid shelters to investigate.

"First came the unmanned monitors, your so-called *foo-fighters*. They automatically began their pre-programmed monitoring programs. Your bombers, the burning cities and the destruction of life were all reported to what you might call computers. But, the destruction and radiation recorded were not within the parameters of atomic energy. If machines could be confused, they were confused! In the meantime, the computer of the *Watchers* sought to re-establish the coordinates of my resting place.

"The *Watchers* came down in force. They began a systematic search for me. They knew that I rested somewhere within the general area of Scandinavia. Soon, all Scandinavian countries were in an uproar. Strange objects began dropping into lakes, flying around mountains and creating your *ghost-rocket* reports.

"Finally, I was found and awakened once again. I immediately made contact with those on earth who support the cause. I see that you already know of my work concerning the establishment of the new State of Israel so I shall not elaborate. Suffice it to say that yet another link in a long chain of planned events was accomplished. Israel again will play a crucial part in the final drama of Mankind on this orb. The 'times of the Gentiles' are over. Jerusalem, my ancient city, has been restored to her rightful owners.

"Now, you wonder where my last sleep is to take place? Already your *carefully bred* logical mind has suspected. Even at this present time, I should be resting within the confines of your Mount Rainier.

"It was unfortunate that campers came upon the *Watchers* craft in that little canyon back in 1947. Our faithful geekahs frightened them off. The canyon was sealed. My new resting place lies in the heart of an extinct volcano. This must be kept secret, even from the Priest. But, alas, Rainier awaits me and I cannot move.

"The damage done to my nervous system has incapacitated me. I am paralyzed and cannot even talk audibly. My telepathic powers are limited to just this small area. If this were not so, even now would I summon the *Watchers* to my aid. Harold Stanton, I must get to Rainier. I must send my brothers the message that the *appointed time* has come."

"What time has come?" Harold's mind enquired.

"The time has come to report to the Messengers from Eternity that we , the Elohim, have failed. We had hoped that the first gentle coming of the Word would have won this orb from the Dragon and his followers. The Word offers forgiveness. The Spirit of the True One offers a new nature. But, throughout time, only a remnant has confidence in the True One. Mankind has rejected His Word. Man has refused his *image* role and sets himself up as an *original*.

"Alas, it is the story of the Dragon's fall all over again in microcosmic form. The Law from Eternity given Moses for Mankind has been trodden underfoot by the people of the orb called earth. Each does that which is right in his own eyes. Relativism has replaced the Standard of the Most High. Greed and corruption fill the earth. It is a paradox. Man blames the True One for the ills that he has brought upon himself. There are even those who say that God is dead. It is pitiful. They are unaware that it is they themselves who are dead to His ever-living Presence.

"Mankind has reached the threshhold of self-destruction. And now, even now, he has taken his first infant steps off the face of the earth. It is a unique time, a time when Mankind must be measured. We have placed him on the scales of Light and have found him wanting.

"Impartial judges are streaming here from all over this island of suns. They are of many races. Each race is represented on the Council of the Elohim. Day by day, samples of Mankind all over this orb are caught, examined and measured for Light. Everywhere they find the same result. The Elohim have determined that Man cannot be allowed to leave this orb to spread the message and ways of the Dragon elsewhere in this island. Neither can he be allowed to poison the indigenous life-forms of this orb further. He must be destroyed."

"But, Melchizedek. Cannot the Elohim make men see the error of his ways? Have they not the power to do so?"

"The Elohim are powerless against the very gift they gave Man when they made him in their own image. The Crown of Elohim consists of many things. It includes the most powerful gift in the Universe. We are powerless against it. Only the True One can deal with it through His Appointed One."

"What is this powerful gift, Melchizedek? I cannot think that Man could have such a thing."

"The gift, my friend, is the power to say No to the True One Who Is. I speak of Man's *freewill*. This is the same freewill exercised by the Dragon and his followers. The Dragon has passed his corrupt ways on to Man. Even now, the Serpent is selecting his *final* earthly incarnation to rule this orb. His number is 666. This counterfeit will be the very antithesis of the Word of the True One.

"Down through the centuries of time, the False One has already manifested himself in many personages. Each has attempted to obliterate the Elohim-nurtured race who bore the Word of the True One Who Is. The Holocaust was but one of many attempts. Another attempt is in progress. Jacob and Esau quarrel again. The Bear from the North marches southward. The very Seed of Armageddon sprouts. There is coming great tribulation on this orb such as it has never known before. The Salt of the earth are to be removed. The meat shall be allowed to spoil. The Dragon and the Man of Perdition and all who follow them are doomed. The Word again will come. This time he shall arrive with hundreds of thousands of His Servants.

"They will rescue the quick and the dead. They shall sow your Sun with the seed of destruction. It will swell and engulf the habitat of the Dragon and his followers in a Lake of Fire. The spirits of the evil ones shall be cast into outer darkness. They will live together in the outer reaches of space where no other life is. There they shall remain until the age of ages. Then this present Expansion shall contract once again. All that has become will again collapse to its original state to be born again in yet another pulsation of Becoming. The mind's eye has not seen nor the mind's ear heard of the wonderful things that the True One has prepared for His followers in the next Pulsation."

"Melchizedek. So many more questions cry out from within. You mentioned that the Word is being sent to this orb to judge the quick and the dead. Where are the dead? Heaven. Hell. Where are they?"

"Hell, I have just described to you. Heaven is yet to come. The Word has prepared many rooms in His Father's house for His followers. I myself know not what lies out there for you. I know only that you will continue to become what you are becoming. But, it will be without the influence of the Evil One and his followers. At that time, your *being* will be in resonance with His *Being*. There will be much work for you to do on His behalf. You will be the Elohim to others as we have been the Elohim to you. You will be used throughout the countless islands of His creation."

"But, where are the dead now? You talk about a *future* Heaven and Hell."

"The so-called dead are here. But they are on a different plane of vibration. They are not dead. They have been translated. Only the form of this vibration has been left behind. It too is translated back to the elements from which it was borrowed. Those of faith, even though translated, also await the return of the Word. My creators, the Elohim, protect them from the Dragon's influence in the Netherland. In the Netherland, those of faith are One with the Spirit of the True One. To be absent from the body is to be present with the True One Who Is. But, those who served the False One in this plane are still open to his influence there. Those fully committed to the Dragon are used to harrass and even possess those living here on this plane. But, the spirits of the faithful are also able to help followers of the True One on this plane. The Church on earth has forgotten an important truth: the ability of the living faithful to communicate with the essences of the translated saints.

"Now, my brother in the Light, the time has come to end this night of sharing. Again I leave with you the memory of my plight. The Dragon has seen to it that I cannot send *the signal* to the Messengers from Eternity. But, this must be done. The results of the judgment must be made known. You, Harold Stanton, must help. Do not forsake me. Do not forsake the True One. I am aware that you will be away from this room for the next night. When you return, we will communicate again. I will then ask for your specific help. But, it must be your choice to comply with what I shall request of you."

"How," Harold's mind queried, "how can I help you?"

"You, Harold Stanton, must go to my sanctuary at Rainier. You shall carry my message deep within your mind. You will act on my behalf. The message will be received by the Council. They shall instruct the *Watchers* to come for me. I shall be made whole once again. I shall join you at Rainier. The Signal of Judgment will be sent. Then, I shall rest once again until the coming of the Two."

"The Two? Who are the Two?"

"They are the very same Two that spoke with the Word on the Mount of Transfiguration. They are the Two who appeared in the craft called a *bright cloud*. The Two shall make one last attempt to witness to your world before the Word returns. Even as they do, the Dragon and his followers will come forth to do battle with the Word and His followers. There will be War in the heavens. Michael and his angels will fight the Dragon. The *sign* of the Word shall appear in the sky. All tribes of the earth shall tremble. Good night, Harold. You will sleep well. Remember what I have said to you, my brother in the Light."

Harold slept *very* well! He almost missed breakfast. Quickly he washed and shaved. It would be good to see Helen. But, already the burden of keeping the revelation of Melchizedek from her was wearing hard on him. He felt like telling the whole world. It was as if his faith had suddenly become sight.

Harold and Helen rendezvoused at the Recreation Center in Sector 3. From there they followed a VIGIL guard to Father Pat's apartment. Harold walked as if in a daze. Helen tried to make conversation.

"Harold? You are all right, aren't you? You seem so distant. Here I've been looking forward to seeing you all week long and you've hardly said a word to me without my prodding. It, it wasn't even the same this morning."

"I'm sorry, dear, there are so many things on my mind. I want to share them with you but I can't."

"Well, it must be pretty hot stuff. I do believe it's the first time that I ever had to remind you of your conjugal responsibility. Especially after a week," Helen whispered coyly.

"Sh-h-h. Don't talk about things like that. That guard might hear you."

Father Pat greeted them at the door to his apartment. His face looked tired and grim. The tone of his voice was anxious.

"Let's go to my room," he said. He turned around and slowly walked into the chapel, as with difficulty. "Now, sit down my friends. I apologize that I'm not my usual boisterous self. I've had problems the past few days. It's my heart. I've had small seizures before but never have I had such pain. I feel as if suddenly my age has caught up with me."

"Have you seen a doctor?" Helen asked.

"No, and I won't consult one. If they think that I can't get around, I'll be removed from this apartment. This is my life: the chapel, meeting people and sending messages to the

Vatican. What else is there for me? They'd put me in some sterile hospital room. No. I'll spend my last days here. I feel as if they are few, my dear friends."

The pathetic look on Father Pat's face brought tears to Helen's eyes.

"Don't say that. You're going to be just fine, Father. Here, sit down. Perhaps you should go to the hospital for awhile. Rest and the proper medication are probably all you need."

"She's right, Father. I can speak to General Thurman," Harold added sympathetically. "I'm sure he'll make sure you're treated well."

"No, no. Please don't breathe a word about this. I vowed to myself that if ever I felt my time was near that I would destroy the evidence of all that I've done. If ever they should find out what I've been up to, there would be the devil himself to pay. Others who are my friends, and loyal members of God's kingdom, would suffer greatly. Several times I've been sorely tempted to destroy the tools of my trade. But, I've kept holding off. I hoped that you'd come with some news about *him*.

"I feel that I'll only be able to send one more message out. Then it must cease. I've trained no one to take my place. It would be too dangerous. My tools are camouflaged for use by a Priest. I'm afraid that there are no other Priests here. I thought of you taking over, my friend. But that's impossible. I've been blessed with a free rein of this cursed place. I've built up dozens of friends and confidantes over the years. Such a system cannot be replaced overnight. My longevity and Priestly image have been the key to my success. It has been ideal. But all of this must now come to an end.

"Dear friends, my very life is now coming to an end. I, who have given comfort and strength to the dying suddenly find myself dying. It is a lonely experience. I have only you two to share it with. A priest should not be afraid of death. Yet I do have fears. Is this wrong?" Father Pat's eyes looked up at them for some reassurance.

Harold felt too choked up to speak. He grasped for something, anything to say. But, the words wouldn't come.

Helen leaned over and took the old man's hand gently.

"Father, is it wrong for a baby to cry when it's suddenly thrust into a bright world that it knows nothing about? No. It's natural. God understands your fear even as the loving parents of that child understand. The fear of death is a normal thing. Even our Lord, when He knew His end was near, prayed that His Father would release him from the cup of death. Remember? In the Garden of Gethsemane?"

The Priest stared silently into Helen's face. A serene smile broke out on his own. "Thank you, child. Thank you for those refreshing words. You have no idea how helpful they were. But now, I must know what you've found out, Harold. We've so little time together."

Harold turned to Helen with bowed head. He frowned.

"Darling, I've dreaded having to say this. But, what I have to report can only be said to Father O'Malley. Please try to understand. I've made a promise. So, would you please go out to the other room and close the door?"

"I, I don't understand you, Harold. What has come over you? Promised who? Not Bluepaper. *Him* hasn't woken up. Who have you promised? Why? I'm cleared. The General even told me that you'd be briefing me on your first week. I've waited all week long to see you, to love you and to hear about the project. But, you've been like a stranger. You're dismissing me from the room like a child. At least I deserve to know why."

"Helen?" Harold stood before her. He took her hands gently. "Have I ever failed you? Would I ask you this if there wasn't a good reason? All I can do is ask your love and understanding in all of this. Now please, if you love and trust me, go into the other room."

Helen got up and walked out of the room slowly. The door shut behind her.

"Good grief, man! What have you to tell me that even

your dear wife can't hear?"

"Father, I have a long story to tell. It is crucial that you let me tell you all about it from the beginning to the end. You may think I'm mad. But, he told me that it would be good for the Priest to know these things."

"He? Who?"

"Melchizedek, King of Salem. The seed of the Elohim."

"Wh-what?"

"Sit back, Father. Get a hold on yourself. I hope that your heart can take what I must say to you."

Chapter Sixteen

The Melchizedek Connection

Harold and Helen lay awake into the early hours of the morning. Neither could sleep.

"I have no idea what you told Father Pat, dear. But I hope you've done the right thing. He looked so strange when we left him. It frightened me to see that look in his eye."

"I have no comment. We must get to sleep. It's almost 0230 and I've got much to do tomorrow. Please. Let's forget Father Pat right now. Drat this bed! Too soft. Can't get used to it. I must get to sleep."

VIGIL picked Harold and Helen up in the morning. Each were escorted to their respective work quarters. The reunion with Helen had been strained. Harold wondered what was wrong with him. He felt a strange disassociation from everything that he did. It was as if he was observing himself doing and saying things. Somehow he didn't feel completely in control. And the strange looks that both General Thurman and Colonel Milkowski had given him when he had entered BETA-1's office. He sensed that they *knew* something. Had they caught him at something? But what? "I must be getting paranoid," he mused. The elevator door opened and he stepped out into the Penthouse corridor. He entered his room and activated the console. "I'd better check with Joseph and see what's been happening," he thought.

"Joseph! Are you there?"

The old man waddled into view and approached his console.

"Ah. Welcome back, friend Harold. You had a good time with Helen, yes?"

"Well, it, ah, yes, it was nice to see her again, Joseph. What's up? Anything?"

"Something strange is up," Joseph whispered. "I was here for awhile yesterday afternoon. Everything was exactly in order. But, when I arrive here this morning, things not the same as I left them. Whoever here, they try put everything back as is, yes? But Joseph know exactly how he leave things. They do not fool Joseph. You check closely too. Perhaps your work area have visitors, yes?"

"Oh, oh! Anything else?"

"Yes. I also hear there is big meeting of all Number 1's at 0600. Very strange. Something big must be up, yes?"

"Yes, it certainly sounds so. Thanks, Joseph. Now, why don't you continue making up the graphs. I'll get back to you if I need anything."

Harold looked around him. He strained to remember how he had left things. All seemed to be in place on the surface. But, there did seem to be subtle changes.

"The Ezekiel outline! I left it here in my Bible. Nothing. Perhaps it's mixed up with my notes," he thought.

A thorough search turned up nothing. But, some of his notes were missing. A growing feeling of apprehension overtook him. Something was wrong, terribly wrong. What was it? He sat down at the table and buried his face in his hands. He closed his eyes. At that very moment, in the farthest recesses of his mind, he heard a weak voice.

"Come to Melchizedek. Come to Melchizedek now."

Harold looked up with a start. There was no one in the room. He glanced over at the closed door to Melchizedek's room. He felt a strange impulse, like a magnet, drawing him to that room. As one in a daze, he slowly got up and moved toward the door. He opened it. There was Melchizedek, eyes wide open, staring at him. The slow tingling sensation he had felt before again prickled his body. He could not move a muscle. Then, Melchizedek's voice vibrated within his mind.

"Listen carefully, O' son of Light. Our time runs out

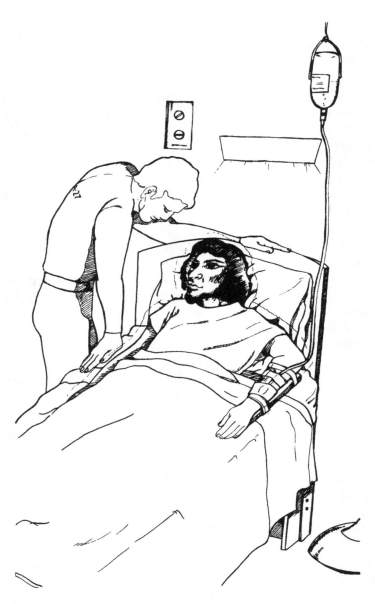

"Come to Melchizedek now."

swiftly. I reviewed the mind of the Doctor this morning. Harold. They know about us. All Number 1's know. All gathered this morning to hear a recording of what you told the Priest yesterday afternoon. We have been entrapped."

"But Father Pat assured me that his chapel wasn't monitored. How was I to know?"

"They suspected something was wrong with you after your late sleep. They reviewed recordings from the visual monitor in this room. Some of your actions made the Doctor suspicious. He theorized that you may have been unknowingly hypnotized by me. They began monitoring your every step. This must have included the chapel area. Even now their monitors watch you standing and gazing at me. They will be coming at once to see what is wrong. They see that I am awake.

"Harold. You have an important mission to fulfill in your present vibration. It may mean your death, your translation, if you help. Will you join the Elohim against the Dragon, my friend? You, your Christian faith, your education, your involvement with these unknowing servants of darkness in this place: you were specially bred for this moment. The *appointed time* for you has come."

"But if I should die, what would happen to Helen?"

"That, child of dust, is a question you could ask at any time. Just as soon as you entered this vibrational plane, you were destined for translation. I can only assure you that whatever may happen, you and Helen have become one. You will never be separated unless it is your mutual choice. Decide now. Already I sense that they are near."

"Yes, yes. I serve the Lord. I will serve His Elohim. Tell me. What must I do?"

"I am releasing you. You may now move freely. Quickly. Lie beside me on the bed."

"What? But why?"

"Just do as I say at once. The close proximity of our bodies is essential because of my weakness. They may separate us later. But, by then we will have achieved our purpose."

Harold lay down beside Melchizedek.

"That's good, Harold. Now, look into my eyes. Deep into my eyes. Good. That's good, very good."

Again, Harold felt the familiar tingling sensation. It grew stronger and stronger. His body began to experience a strange vibration: faster and faster. Then, a lightness, a feeling of freedom as he felt himself rising off the bed.

"I, I must be dreaming. Hallucinating," he thought. Shocked, he saw Melchizedek lying in midair beside him. He was clad in a luminous white coverall.

"But, how did he get out of those blue coveralls and the bed covers?"

Harold glanced down as he thought these thoughts. There, lying on the bed, side by side, were Melchizedek and — "It's, it's me! I'm down there but, but, I'm up here. How can that be? I must be, yes, we must be dead. This feeling. I've had it before."

Harold's mind shot back to his experienc while drowning. Then Melchizedek spoke to his mind.

"You are not quite dead, my friend. It is very similar but not the same. We are both out of our earthly shells. Fear not. Some of our light remains behind to keep our bodies ready for our return. Now, perhaps you will realize that I myself have not been inactive during my long periodic sleeps. My brain was monitored and taught by others. But, my essence travelled to aid those who dwell in the Netherland. And now, my friend, we take the first steps to prepare you for your mission. Listen carefully.

"My earthly frame is broken. Yours lies below perfectly healthy. For a time, a short time it is hoped, I will co-inhabit your body. But first, our essences must become as one."

Harold saw a brilliant flash, brighter than the sun. Then all became darkness.

"The tunnel! The whirling tunnel," Harold exclaimed. Again, Harold saw his life flash before him in rhythmatic sequence. Down, down into the black void he plummeted.

Or, was it up? He knew not, except that he felt the presence of Melchizedek beside him.

"What's happening, Melchizedek?"

"We are tracing your vibrations back to their source."

"I, I had an experience like this when I was dying," Harold thought dreamily. "I saw the Jamiesons and, and, a strange girl. Who was she? Who was she?"

"We shall be passing your assigned portal to the Netherland soon, Harold. It will be different this time. Your loved ones, those chosen to be your guides, do not wait to take you this time. But, they have been alerted to watch for you. I thought you would appreciate this. Look, Harold. Look."

Harold saw a bright opening ahead of them. It grew larger and larger as they floated along like corks on an invisible stream of water. Through the opening he saw the Jamiesons. They were just as he had remembered them. And, there was the young woman. Beautiful. She looked so familiar. In some ways she reminded him of how he had looked when a boy. A thought suddenly struck him as they swept by and entered still another tunnel.

"Melchizedek. Did I have a sister? She looks so much like me."

"No, my friend. She is not your sister. Alethia is your mother. She was brought to earth by the Elohim to bear you."

Strangely, Harold felt little emotion upon hearing this startling revelation. Everything seemed so dreamy, yet so matter of fact in this nebulous realm.

"But, if she is my mother, why don't I see my father? Does he still live in the world we've left behind?"

"Genetically, you are the sum of many human fathers, my son. Alethia was chosen to bear what you became for this purpose now. It is your *appointed time*. Know you also, that your adoption by the Jamiesons was no accident. The Elohim have influenced many selected ones to perform their will at specially appointed times. But, be warned. The

Dragon too has his servants."

"Is it all planned, Melchizedek? Have we no choice?"

"O, Son of Adapa, the plans of the Elohim are written on the tapestry of what you call future as it is revealed to them from above. Many times this tapestry is torn. They must repair it along the way. Your freewill is the thread. The tapestry is the plan of the True One Who Is."

"I do not understand."

"It is beyond your understanding. But, know that even now our Watchers select those who would serve the Elohim on the orb you call earth. The ones you call *contactees* have instructions locked within their minds. These shall be revealed at their *appointed times*. Know that since the Fall of Adapa until the present time a mighty struggle has been fought for human spirits."

"But, why did my mother die so young? Why couldn't I have known her? Why?"

"Like yourself, Alethia chose to serve her purpose. After that, she was translated painlessly to the Netherland, even as my servant, Benjamin Saltzman."

"The, the one who burst into the flames? The human incendiary?"

"The very same, Harold."

"Where are we going? These tunnels. Tunnel upon tunnel. Lighted portal upon portal. Please explain what is happening?"

We are retracing your vibrations back to their source: to Adapa, the seed of mankind. Then, together as one, we shall retrace your vibrations back through your ancestors to their present extension lying on the bed at Phoenix Base 3. Then we shall be one."

"How can this be? My ancestors are all dead."

"Yes, they all have been translated to the Netherworld. Some were taken when the Word *first* came and preached to the spirits imprisoned there. He led captivity captive to worlds unknown to us. And, when He comes again, others will join Him at His appearing. But, to explain further: the vibrations of all who were still exist now. They *are*. All *is*. Time is an illusion. You, Harold Stanton, as you exist back on that bed, are merely the forefront of the vibrating waves of your ancestors. We have left the bow of your present localized extension. We are now moving back along the wake it has made on the sea of the phenomenon you call time. Do you understand?"

"No. My mind senses that what you say is logical and true. But, I cannot comprehend it all. It reminds me of what Father Pat once said about God existing in eternity. He said that if we lived on a planet 100 light years away and were able to look back at earth, we would see events happening now that really happened 100 years ago. He also spoke of time dilation. This concerned a space traveler who approached the speed of light. It was hard for me to comprehend. Father Pat explained that time would slow for such a traveler. And, when he returned to earth after several *years* of travel, he would find that *generations* had passed while he was gone. Father Pat explained that because God's Spirit encompassed all of His Creation, everywhere would be *present* with Him."

"Father Pat is right, my brother. Moses himself was told to call the True One Who Is: *I Am*. But, now we reach the end of your vibration. We shall now accomplish the final step: *The Fusion* of our memories.

"You will be made to forget much that your mind's eye sees of my life. To see and remember all would be too much in too a short a time for your mind to bear. However, I have reserved special places along my vibrational way for you to consciously retain. You will find them interesting and inspiring. I trust that they will be helpful in understanding the true origins of your faith in the True One."

As the two floated through the complex tunnel of Harold's ancestral vibrations, their spirits intertwined in progressive coalescence. In this state of being, Harold was completely unaware of the troubling events occurring back at Phoenix Base 3.

Joseph sat in his lab awaiting the processing of yet another graph. Lost in his thoughts, the voice coming from the video-com startled him.

"Joseph! Joseph!"

"Yes, I'm coming. Oh! It is not Harold, yes? It is you BETA-1. I thought it was Harold, yes?"

"Damn it, shut up for one minute will you, Joseph? This console in the Penthouse has a governor on it. I can't communicate with anyone except through you. So listen old man, will you? Get Number 1 and MEDIC-1 up here Pronto. This is a Priority One request! No questions. Understand?"

"Is something wrong? Harold? *Him?*"

"I said no questions. Move it!"

Joseph quickly instructed the Central Computer to locate General Thurman and Doctor Slater. Both rendezvoused at Phoenix Central and travelled directly along the tunnel leading to Sector 6. They headed immediately for the Penthouse.

"What's wrong, Steve? Where's Harold?" General Thurman blurted out as he burst into the room with Doctor Slater.

Colonel Milkowski's face was deathly pale.

"He's in there, John. They both seem dead. But, they're still warm and have color. I couldn't find their pulses. It's creepy. I'm staying out here."

"Good God!" General Thurman exclaimed. "Let's go, Doc."

General Thurman led the way. He inserted his key tube. They entered the room. There lay Harold beside Bluepaper's mysterious captive. He was completely still. Doctor Slater rushed to their side while General Thurman went back to question Colonel Milkowski. Several minutes later Doctor Slater came into Harold's study in the adjoining room.

"What is it, Doctor? Are they all right?" asked the General.

"John, I can't explain this. Both of them are in the same type of coma, hibernation, or whatever you want to call it, that Ben-Sorek was in before. Whether or not they'll go through the aging syndrome, I don't know. But I do know this. Both of those bodies in there seem to have had their vital signs slowed to exactly the same rhythm. Further tests need to be made to establish this. It, it's like we're dealing with two living bodies that have suddenly become one!" Suddenly, Joseph's voice reverberated throughout the room.

"Number 1. Number 1. John? It is I, Joseph."

"What, where?" General Thurman glanced over at the console. He saw Joseph's anxious face framing the television receptor.

"Joseph! Can't you see that Number 1 is busy? Shut that thing off!" snapped Colonel Milkowski.

"But, I have Priority 1 report from VIGIL, Sector 7, yes?"

"Damn! Now what? If it rains, it pours," General Thurman thundered. "Okay, Joseph. Patch them in." In a few moments, Timothy Donoghue's face flashed upon the screen. General Thurman sat down at the console.

"What is it, Tim? It had better be more important than Father Pat being out of uniform!"

"Yes, sir, I mean, no, sir. But, it's the Priest, all right. We've brought him to the hospital."

"What? What did you do to him? I told you people to go easy with him. I'm holding you personally responsible if any harm has come to the old codger."

"No, I mean it's not what you think, sir. We entered his quarters very quietly. No fuss. We caught him destroying a number of religious items with an acid of some kind. We're having it analyzed."

"An acid? Where in the hell could he get such an acid?"

"I don't know, sir. But, when he saw us standing there, he just passed out. We rushed him to the hospital. They say he's in pretty poor shape. It's a heart attack."

"I'm sorry to hear about this. What about the others?"

"VIGIL is rounding up everyone that has attended his services. They are being put in retention until we find out what this 'sending messages to the Vatican' is all about."

"Probably a bunch of hogwash. Part of the same hogwash Harold told Pat. Melchizedek indeed!"

"Sir?"

"Never mind. Forget what I just said. It's none of your concern. Get on with what you have to do on your level. And, remind VIGIL-1 that the Council wants a full report on any results coming out of the interrogation. Also, tell the Hospital to keep me informed about the Father's health. Thanks, Tim."

"But, sir, there's more. It's about those religious items he was destroying. VIGIL's lab is running tests on them. It's obvious that he had some kind of microphotography operation going on."

"What? How could that be? What could Pat possibly be microfilming?"

"Begging your pardon, sir, but that's what the Council will be wondering too. I'll be giving my full report to VIGIL-1 for them. I'm sorry to say that I felt constrained to inform them of the many times I warned you about the Priest. You know that I was against allowing him that monitor-proof room from the very beginning. The Council will wonder what's been going on in there all these years."

"Thank you, Tim. If that's all you have, I've got things to do."

"There is one more thing. One of the Priest's congregation, Jack Walsh, Designator TECH-4, has left the Base on a Beta repair mission. Shall we recall him or wait and detain him when he returns?"

"Wait until he returns. We're short of outside-cleared repairmen as it is. Now, is *that* all?"

"Yes, sir, that's all. I'm sure you'll agree that it's quite enough."

Colonel Milkowski and Doctor Slater stood staring in amazement at General Thurman.

"Well? Don't just stand there staring. It's not going to do any good. Go about your business. Doc, get a nurse up here we can trust. I want her here permanently. If you can spare a doctor full time, that will be even better. I want both of them watched by professionals. I want you personally to check them periodically. Let me know of any change. Give them the best of care. Also, Steve, increase the lighting in there at night so that our monitors can see them both clearly. Somehow, that bearded devil has bewitched Harold from under our very noses."

"John? John?" Joseph's face again appeared on the console.

"Now what, Joseph? I can't take much more of this."

"Colonel Henderson come in. Yes? He in BETA-1's office right now. He is angry! I'm afraid VIGIL will buzz him badly, yes? I do not understand. He says daughter has been put in retention. Harold's wife, Helen. Can this be so?"

"Yes. That can be so, Joseph," the General sighed. "Go tell him I'll be right there. Tell him to calm down. Helen is just being retained for questioning. I'll be right down to explain."

Colonel Milkowski's face appeared on the video screen. He glared at General Thurman.

"Before you go anywhere, John, I'm formally asking you to call another meeting of the Council right away. If you don't, I will."

"Steve, you've been aching for me to slip just once. I know how badly you want to be the great Number 1. If I thought you were the right man, I'd have stepped down long ago. I've had it. I'm ready to retire. But, I think that I'm needed to keep some semblance of humanity around here."

"The meeting?" the Colonel replied coolly.

"You'll have your meeting at 2100. Just give me time to get the pieces put together. Other than our problem up here, the rest is probably just a tempest in a teapot."

Meanwhile, Harold Stanton was far removed from the disruptive events occurring back at Base 3. He found

"We are now one, my brother. Your body is now our body."

206

himself suspended in blackness. Time seemed to have stood still. The voice of Melchizedek sounded all around him like many voices blended into one.

"We are now one, my brother. Your body is now *our* body. Your mind is now *our* mind. Our paths have joined as one, even as it was planned before your birth by my creators, the Elohim. Even now, Alethia rejoices that her role has also been fulfilled. Her seed has found its destined mark. *The Melchizedek Connection* is being realized. Now, we must accomplish the *fusion*, son of light. May these dreams of my memories strengthen you for the difficult task that lies ahead."

Chapter Seventeen

The Fusion

All was dark. Harold felt as if he were in a dream from which he could not awake. Then gradually, ever so gradually, everything became lighter and lighter. Suddenly, he found himself sitting in a soft form-fitting seat.

"Where am I? What am I wearing?" He felt his fingers run over the silvery coveralls that he was wearing.

"Am I really here or am I dreaming?" he wondered. Harold gazed down upon the earth through the side of a large transparent dome that stretched around him. His eyes dreamily examined the vista far below.

"Looks like a big three dimensional map. There's the Mediterranean and Caspian Seas."

He watched a band of clouds drift by to reveal the familiar outlines of the Red Sea and the Persian Gulf. The Persian Gulf became larger and larger. He had no feeling of descent and yet the ship seemed to be literally dropping out of the sky toward the bluish-gray water below.

"There's the Tigris and Euphrates Rivers," he thought dreamily. "But, what rivers are those? I never saw them on any map."

All at once his rapid descent came to an abrupt halt above a natural harbor.

"Strange. I never felt even a bounce. This is like seeing a movie. Yet, I'm sure that this is real. Why can't I reach out and touch the glass. I want to, but I can't seem to make my hands move. Where am I going?"

Instantly the craft resumed its forward motion.

"Strange," Harold pondered lethargically. "I don't see even one boat down there. We seem to be descending

Adapa, Seed of Mankind.

towards land. Hum-m, it's dusk. What's that? Looks like some kind of a light house but it's on land. It, it must be a collision light on an antenna tower. But it's not a red light. It's, it's — what color *is* that? Weird. Never saw anything like this before. Looks like a rectangular grid spread out for miles and miles. It's outlined by a lighted fence or something. No, it's not fence. Looks like just fence poles, hundreds of them, each tipped with a purplish light. Humm, that tower is on a hill in a clearing. Oh! Who, what are those creatures running out of the woods? We're going to land on that silver slab. Whoops, we're down. That was smooth. Now what? Strange, I'm getting up but I'm not making myself get up. Am I dreaming?"

Harold caught a glimpse of his reflection in the glass canopy as he moved across the compartment. He gazed in utter amazement at what should have been himself.

"That's, that's not me. It's Melchizedek!"

Harold found himself standing before a door which automatically slid open. He paused a moment, then stepped out onto a catwalk that encircled the small oval craft.

The small hairy man-like creatures swarmed excitedly around the ship. Some cautiously touched it and jumped back. Others peeked from behind trees at the edge of the forest. They looked like small human men and women. They wore no clothes but were covered with light brown body hair. Only their face and palms were hairless and covered with light tan skin.

"They, they look so innocent and so happy," Harold mused.

The creatures' carefree facial expressions were those of infants and yet they were adults. Harold noticed one of the creatures running toward the craft. He seemed taller than the others.

"One comes to greet me. He seems to be their leader. Look at him bounding toward me. Reminds me of how Shep used to greet me when I got home from work. Good old Shep. Wonderful dog. But,these aren't animals. Their eyes. I see intelligence, human emotions. That tall one moves so gracefully. He embraces me. He's — everything is fading away. What's happening? Where are they gone? I feel as if I'm slipping backward. Forward? I don't know. It's dark again. Now it's getting lighter. I hear a voice from back there calling after me. It's Melchizedek's voice. He's saying — "Adapa, Adapa, Seed of Mankind." Thunderation! Now what is this place?"

Harold found himself standing in a crowd of olive-skinned people. Both he and they were clad in colorful apron-like coveralls.

"Those faces. The features. They're like Melchizedek's. These people are Semites! And I recognize those people with shaven heads and sheepskin skirts. I've seen paintings of those strange scalloped skirts many times. Sumerians! They're Sumerians."

All about him, Harold saw oval huts constructed of reeds. They stretched up and down the banks of a river. He seemed to be looking for someone. But, why couldn't he feel, smell and hear? He could only see. It was as if he were inside a moving container looking out through peepholes. Now he looked out over the river. A little oval boat made of reeds was making for shore.

"Amazing how well they float," he thought. "I've read of things like that. Never thought I'd see one. Hum-m, that one. That one in the boat seems to be hailing me. And, what's that in the distance behind him — that building across the river? Why it's got to be a ziggurat. It's a huge ziggurat within a walled city over there. I've also seen that pictured somewhere. Yes. It has to be, it's just got to be the great ziggurat of the Sumerian city of Ur. Why, this is where Abraham came from! Oh, that bearded man has beached his raft. He smiles at me. He's coming to me. I, I —" Once again, he was plunged into darkness, more darkness, then brightness. Blurry images slowly came into focus.

Harold found himself standing beside a flat table-shaped

rock. Several flat loaves of bread rested on a colorful mat. A flask made of skin lay against the loaves. Glancing about, he saw that he was in a desert valley. Mountains surrounded him on either side. A vast throng of people — Arabs? — stood facing him about five hundred feet away. They seemed to be free men. Wind kicked up the dust from around their feet. Wind that Harold could not feel. The experience was somewhat like viewing a movie on a huge wrap-around screen. But, it was so life-like! Then, one man left his companions and slowly approached him. As he drew closer, Harold recognized him as the same man that had hailed him from the little reed boat near Ur. Why did this man kneel before him?

Harold watched his own hands reach down and place themselves upon the kneeling man's head. Deep within the recesses of his mind he heard a still small voice utter a strange language. It was familiar to him; a combination of Arabic and Hebrew. Before he could attempt an interpretation, the familiar accented voice of Melchizedek echoed softly with his mind.

Blessed are you Abram of the Most High God,
The True One Who Is, the Creator of the Universe.

No sooner had these words died away than once again he found himself plunged into blackness. Slowly, ever so slowly, Harold began to comprehend what was happening.

"This is just what Melchizedek said. These dreams are of *real* events. Melchizedek is allowing me glimpses of memories through his own mind. I, I have seen the Garden, Adapa and now Abraham being blessed by Melchizedek. This is too incredible to be true! Yet I know that I'm really seeing all of this. I know I am. How much more will he allow me to see? This is so incredible. I'm actually seeing the very peoples and cultures that I've come to know so well through my studies!"

Scene by scene flickered through Harold's mind. In his mind's eye, he cryptically relived Melchizedek's intimate involvement with the development of the ancient nation of Israel. He saw Isaac, Isaac's twelve sons, the twelve tribes, Joseph, Egypt and the Sphinx. The Pyramids were shining new and white against the desert sky. Harold was filled with ecstasy.

Suddenly, the peaceful sky became dark. A violent storm was developing. He saw huge hailstones, lightning and sick people. Then he sighted a peculiar phenomenon. "What is that cloud weaving through the sky as if it lived?" he gasped. As it came closer, he saw it was comprised of locusts. There were millions of locusts. "Great guns! These are the plagues. I must be seeing the plagues of Egypt mentioned in the book of Exodus!"

Onward came the swirling cloud of insects until Harold felt caught up with the whirling black mass in the sky. "Whirling. I'm going round and round. It's so dark. Where am I going?" A tremendous flash of light exploded within his mind. Harold once again found himself in a desert place.

It was dusk. People: thousands and thousands of Arabs, sheep, camels, and goats. "Who are they? Where are we going? Why do they keep looking back?"

As if in answer to his question, Harold found himself turning about. He saw a broad cloud of dust rising on the horizon. Someone or something was stirring up the dust for miles. Suddenly the crowd looked up. They fell prostrate to the ground like a collapsing house of cards.

For the first time, Harold began to feel emotion. A chill of wonder swept through him. His body back on the bed at Phoenix Base 3 trembled violently. He no longer felt like an observer. He was caught up as a participant in the events about him.

Fed by the mind of Melchizedek, Harold's emotions responded traumatically to the awe-inspiring sight of an immense object in the sky. The huge upright cylinder was enswathed with boiling vapor. It blazed forth with multi-colored flashes of brilliant light as it passed overhead. It was headed directly for the dust-obscured horizon. Harold

The huge upright cylinder was enswathed with boiling vapor.

strained his eyes. He could now make out what was following them: horse-drawn chariots!

The people about him were now on their feet looking back at a sight beyond their culture's understanding. Pitch black vapor poured from the low hovering craft. Like a living velvet wave it rolled across the desert and completely engulfed the oncoming Egyptians. Then, the huge pillar-shaped object slowly moved back over the crowd. Again, people fell like hundreds of human dominoes as it passed over. Only two men remained standing: Harold and one other.

Harold *stood* watching the other person through the eyes and mind of Melchizedek. The prophet Moses stood up ahead with raised staff in silent salute to the passing object. The giant aerial vehicle now took up a position ahead of the children of Israel. Cautiously, the crowds rose to their feet. Again they followed the man with the staff as Moses beckoned them onward toward the pillar of fire in the sky. Then all at once the scene dimmed to nothingness. Harold floated in a limbo of total darkness.

From time to time kaleidoscopic visions burst within his mind. He strained to retain them each within his memory. It was difficult. They sped by like lighted windows of trains passing in the night. There was a swampy marshland and a body of water. Suddenly a cleavage appeared in its midst. Then the water rose up like a wall. It flowed around Pharoah's advancing throng in a devastating sheath of destruction. And then — the drowning of Pharoah's army.

"Scholars are right," Harold reflected. "It wasn't the Red Sea. It was the Sea of Reeds."

New images flashed by so quickly that they all became just one constant blur of flickering light. Again they slowed to an abrupt halt.

Once more, Harold found himself in a bleak desert region surrounded by hordes of Semitic nomads. All eyes in the gathering crowd were fixed upon a mountain. A distant figure stood on a flat rocky outcrop. He raised a wooden staff high in the air. People all about Harold looked skyward. There, outlined like a blinding cylindrical shaft of light torn in the deep blue sky, was the Shekinah Glory. Suddenly it became enveloped in a seething cloud of white vapor. It was as if a white-hot poker had been thrust into water.

Like a wheat field blowing in the wind, looks of alarm and wonder rippled over the upturned faces of the multitude. A silvery disc tumbled out of the base of the cylinder. It dropped erratically like a falling leaf, righted itself and landed on the ledge beside the man. Melchizedek's voice whispered gently from within:

"Behold. Moses receives the Law of Eternity prepared for the Seed of Adapa."

Then, as if someone had flicked off a light switch, Harold once more became enshrouded in inky blackness.

Back at Phoenix Base 3, Doctor Slater watched Harold's body twitch and tremble from head to foot.

"He must be having a hell of a nightmare! Look at the meter. His eye movements have been active for over an hour now."

General Thurman leaned over and gazed at Harold's face.

"Why doesn't he wake up? He's sure lively compared to that one beside him. I'd swear Ben Sorek was dead if he didn't have color."

"When he first started twitching like this, I thought he was coming around, John. That's why I called you up here. As to why he doesn't wake up? I don't know. His vital signs are excellent."

"Why don't you move him to his own bed, Doc? I'm surprised to see him still on that bed with *him*."

"We don't know what we're up against, John. This is somewhat like sleepwalking. I think it's best that he come out of this naturally. I don't want to disturb him. Now, do you want me to stay here or come to the Council meeting?"

"Well, you are the Level 1 responsible for the hospital.

Steve insists that a full Council meeting is necessary. Stay here as long as you can, but don't miss the meeting. Get your alternate up here. Have him patched into the Council room's console. We must be kept abreast of any new developments. It's about 2015 right now. I've got to get back. Your call caught me right in the middle of preparing my agenda. I'll see you at the meeting. Try to have some kind of a report for us about Harold."

When General Thurman entered the Council room at 2055, he was amazed to find a meeting already in session. Colonel Milkowski addressed him as he walked to the front of the auditorium.

"Good evening, John. I'll get right to the point. I have the unhappy duty to inform you that the Council, one member absent, has unanimously invoked Level 1 Red Order 3. I'm sure that Doctor Slater will add his vote when he sees our findings. After this meeting you are restricted to your quarters until further notice. I have assumed your responsibilities as Number 1. VIGIL-1 has been appointed my deputy."

"Well.Steve, I must say that you lost no time in advancing your personal ambitions. I'm sorry that the rest of you weren't willing to give me a chance to personally look into this. I feel confident that Father Pat's actions are beyond repute. He's a harmless old man. I've yet to see these so-called espionage implements. Can you produce them yet, VIGIL-1?"

"We've got some of them right here on this table," VIGIL-1 responded coolly. "All of us have examined them. There's no doubt concerning what they are. Articles 1, 2 and 3 are on the table for *your* examination.

"It appears that some of the good Father's religious implements, that *you* allowed brought here initially, have served a double purpose. There's no doubt that he had the capability to photographically reduce material to microscopic size. For what purpose? Obviously, he was sending hidden messages to someone. We're sure that the recipient does not reside here at Base 3. He had no problems communicating with anyone here. You gave him practically free rein of our Base with few restrictions. This leaves us with the unpleasant prospect that he somehow was delivering messages to the Outside. But how? To whom? This leads me to my second point.

"Within the good Father's circle of close friends, there's only one person who makes periodic trips to the Outside at the present time. I refer to TECH-4, Beta repairman, Jack Walsh. Even now, Walsh is servicing equipment on Mount Washington in New England. Tim Donoghue tells us that he specifically asked your permission to recall TECH-4 after VIGIL's discovery. But, you denied this. For your information, Walsh has been recalled now. It's probably too late. Most likely he's delivered the Priest's message. Why do I think this? This brings me to my third point.

"When I questioned TECH-4's escort by secure-phone, he informed me that Walsh had seen no one except a Priest. A Priest! Don't you find that interesting? It appears that they had made the usual Church stop, per your permission, so that Walsh could receive Communion in Phoenix before flying to Boston. It seems as if Walsh has always tried to find time for Mass or Confession whenever he travelled. This was always possible because of your generosity."

VIGIL-1 reached in his pocket. He pulled out a small white wafer. "Observe, General Thurman, Article 4. It looks like what? A Communion wafer? No. Looks are deceiving. It's a bakelite facsimile. Here. Taste it. You'll not find it very palatable!

The General silently fingered the wafer. A deep frown spread over his face.

"Well?" demanded the Colonel. "Are you lost for words now, John? No matter. VIGIL has found a number of these in the process of being destroyed by acid. Obviously the Priest used them to record micro-messages on for someone. Who? That brings me to my fourth point.

"In the recorded Stanton—O'Malley conversation, the Father mentioned sending out one last message to the *Vatican*. What has he been sending? God only knows and I don't intend that as a pun. Now, if it's been merely the kind of religious nonsense that Stanton talked about, we have little to be concerned about. However, I cannot believe that to be the case. Most likely we have taken in a professional Vatican Spy unawares."

General Thurman stood up and spoke.

"May I have the floor now? Thank you. I'd like to say a few words to all of you Number 1's. If what you say is true, our whole operation may be doomed. I have access to contingency plans you know nothing about. My mention of these plans is forbidden but I don't care anymore. I've made a terrible mistake. Apologies will not change our dilemma. However, I refuse to make another mistake. All of our lives are now in jeopardy. You'll soon know what I mean, Steve, when you notify Outside Command of my removal.

"Let me tell you this, Gentlemen. Everything we've done here has been duplicated by backup systems elsewhere. There are trained personnel ready to assume a backup operation whenever the need may arise. This operation here is not as indispensable as you think. There are those on the Outside who would be willing to destroy this installation in one fell swoop. I've lived with this burden on my mind for several decades. I have just three things to say. They apply especially to you, Steve, now that you're Number 1.

"First, this Council room is bugged by Outside Command. Recordings are made and transmitted of everything said here. I discovered this quite accidentally many years ago. But, don't look so pale, gentlemen. I've taken care of it. You can speak freely.

"Second, one of our maintenance men and a communications specialist work covertly here as the Outside's representatives. Unknown to them I've conducted a bit of special sabotage with the Outside's recording system from time to time. I've done this for the last few meetings.

The maintenance man thinks some kind of malfunction caused it. He doesn't suspect me.

"Thirdly, I feel constrained to tell you something dreadful for the sake of my conscience alone. If this operation is ever considered compromised in the eyes of Outside Command, do you think they'll bother to force us all into mental deprogramming? No. There would be a terrific logistics problem and possible risk of further compromise.

"Have you ever wondered about the *cover* they've given for this installation? That dinky little radar tower out there is only to fool the public and lower-echelon military personnel. The higher-echelon military have been told that this site is really a super-secret underground atomic test bed.

"Gentlemen? This is more than a cover story. We actually are sitting on a *real* bed primed with a live atomic bomb and tons of thermite. Just a push of some buttons would reduce this installation and all of us to a smouldering pile of radioactive dust and rubble. It's Outside Command's method of getting rid of us with no questions asked. It's the ultimate poison pill, so to say."

Looks of horror, dismay and unbelief swept through the room as General Thurman finished talking and sat down. He could not bring himself to look in their faces. Guilt and remorse filled his heart.

In the meantime, Harold, on the other hand, felt ecstasy as he'd never felt before. It was like experiencing one childhood discovery after another as he proceeded through the pages of Biblical time through the memories of the King of Salem. Age after age he watched Melchizedek instructing the prophets. Harold realized now that there had been so-called UFO contactees in every generation since the creation of Adapa. Most had been subconsciously programmed to do the will of the Elohim. A few, like Enoch, and Moses were allowed to work knowingly, hand-in-hand with them.

Harold marvelled at the Elohim's super-technology. He watched dumbfounded as they employed it to aid Elijah in his battle against the servants of the Dragon. He had seen their ships send down fiery lasar beams of light during Elijah's contest with the prophets of Baal. He had also witnessed Elijah's departure with the Elohim. It was a fantastic sight.

He had sat on a hillside with fifty of Elijah's student prophets. Together they watched the blazing craft wing in from the North and land. Elijah entered the craft. It ascended up and out of sight in seconds. At this point, Harold again was plunged into darkness. Thoroughly elated, he wondered what would happen next. He was not long in finding out. Soon it became bright again. Harold found himself elsewhere.

It was a crisp cool night. The rock-strewn hillside glowed eerily in the soft light of a waning gibbous moon. Harold found himself bundled up in a coarse robe of animal skins.

He was sitting on a ledge upon the side of a steep hill looking across a flat stretch of rocky terrain. On the other side, a little walled village of flat-roofed houses rested upon a terraced hillock. These houses of white stone reflected the moonlight like a well-ordered cluster of weather-bleached tombstones.

Further below him, shepherds huddled around the glowing coals of a dying fire. Sheep lay nestled within the fenced confines of several natural caves. Suddenly, one of the shepherds roused his companions. He pointed excitedly at the sky. A bright pinpoint of moving light rose slowly from the horizon. Instantly, it dropped straight down between the shepherds and the sleeping town. It had taken on the shape of a huge glowing cylinder. Slowly the pillar of fire maneuvered into a near vertical position. The shepherds stood awestruck at the unearthly sight methodically unfolding before their very eyes.

The sheep paced uneasily within their natural sheepfolds. The group of shepherds began to back away fearfully. They knelt behind adjoining rocks for protection against something entirely beyond their comprehension. And then both animals and men suddenly became deathly still. It was as if time itself had abruptly stopped for them.

A brief but brilliant flash erupted from the base of the glowing cylinder. A string of rotating red lights appeared. They fluttered toward the ground like a falling leaf. The moon reflected off its silvery surface revealing a domed disk. It approached the transfixed shepherds with a slight hypnotic swaying motion. Then it stopped in midair about one hundred feet from the sheepfold.

A small dark rectangle slowly opened in the disk's side. The soft-glowing silhouette of a small man stood framed within its confines. It looked like a tiny dwarf with an oversized head. Harold watched in utter astonishment. The luminous manikin descended from the object like a drifting balloon. He stopped and stood in midair in front of the paralyzed shepherds. Meanwhile, the upright pillar began to glow and pulsate. It bathed the whole area with the rays of a thousand undulating rainbows. A strange hum filled the air like a heavenly choir of bees. Then everything dimmed to nothingness.

Harold next found himself in the village he had seen from the adjoining hillside. He was descending a flight of steps from one of its many white stone houses. These dwellings were built over several caves hollowed out of a terraced cliff of limestone. At ground level, he paused for a moment and looked both ways up and down the road. Then he cautiously approached the entrance to one of the caves. The setting moon cast its dying light upon three sleeping figures. There was a man, a young girl and a tiny boy wrapped in bands of cloth. The infant lay between them as they slept together on a mat spread over the hay-covered floor. As the scene began to fade, Harold heard the familiar words of Simeon recorded in Luke's Gospel resounding within his mind.

Lord now lettest Thou Thy Servant depart in peace according to Thy word

For mine eyes have seen Thy salvation.

Which Thou hast prepared before the face of all people;
A light to lighten the Gentiles, and the glory of Thy
people, Israel.

And, at this very moment, back at Phoenix Base 3, nurse
Catherine Higgins added a cryptic note to her observation
report.

> 0303. Patient BETA-27. Instruments indicate extremely active
> dream state. Unusual occurrence just now. Tears appeared in
> patient's eyes. Seemed to be in no pain. Cannot be sure but think
> patient smiled for a moment.
> Still no movement or change in vital signs of the *prisoner*.

Tears also flowed in the eyes of others. Father Pat lay on
his back gazing at the silvery ceiling of the hospital room
through tear-filled eyes. What had he done? Would they
implicate those who had helped him so faithfully? He had
waited too long. Had he destroyed his instruments just a day
earlier, everyone would have been safe. He wondered if the
Vatican would believe his last message. It was incredible.
Earth, planet earth, had been visited and nurtured by
superhuman extraterrestrial missionaries since before the
beginning of Man. He could see it so clearly now. Their
visits ran through the Holy Scriptures like an
interconnecting thread. But now? He wept. "I'm dying. I've
let down those who trusted me most. Whatever will become
of them?"

Helen also cried. All the horrors of Phoenix Base 3 that
she had so carefully isolated from her mind now came
crashing down around her. Her father tried to comfort her.

"There, there, brown eyes. Chin up. You and Harold had
nothing directly to do with Pat's unorthodox activities. The
worst they can do is accuse you of withholding information
about him. You know you both should have reported him at
once. Sentimentality has no place here. You and Harold
must learn to practice your religious beliefs privately. Can't
you see now that the Priest has duped you? And, who knows
how many others? I certainly don't pretend to be religious.

But, it galls me to see anyone use religion as a cloak of deception. It's a contradiction in terms."

Helen's facial expression had not changed. It remained expressionless.

"Now come on. Give me a little smile, eh? I'll do my best for you. You know what? Both of you have them over a barrel. They still desperately need you both on Project *Enigma*. I'll try to get Harold and give him the same advice. I repeat. Be open. Admit that your allegiance to Father Pat was because of religious, not security reasons. Even Number 1 respects the strong grip that religious beliefs have upon some people. That's why he allowed Father Pat to be a religious outlet for so many here. Poor John. He, more than anyone else, is to be pitied for what has happened. I'm sure that he'll be retired and replaced, probably by BETA-1."

Helen looked up at her father and shook her head sadly.

"Thanks for coming, Dad. Thanks for your advice. But, please understand. Religion, as you call it, is more than just adhering to some man-made set of rules. To us and so many others it's faith in and real fellowship with a living, loving God. You need Him too, Dad."

Colonel Henderson reached down and ran his fingers through Helen's long brown hair.

"You'll never give up on me, will you? What more can I say? I'll say no more. What I've already said has probably been recorded by VIGIL. But, I doubt that they'll fault me for giving you fatherly advice. Think over what I've said. I can be of little help to you if you have the wrong attitude. Bye now."

The Colonel put his arms around his daughter and drew her real close to him. He whispered gently in her ears.

"You know something, brown eyes? You'll be happy to know that I'm so uptight about this that you've actually got me considering praying to that God of yours. I suggest that you do, too. Because, if He exists, He's the only one that can get you two out of this mess now. Bye, honey and, God bless. I'll give your love to Harold if and when I can get to him." Helen's father could never have imagined in the course of a million lifetimes where his son-in-law was at that very moment.

Harold recognized the Essene settlement of Qumran just as soon as it appeared over the brow of the hill. It was exactly the same view that had appeared on the glossy printed from the Beta Psi image. Now, through the very same eyes of Melchizedek, he descended into the valley. He climbed the promontory to its gates. Soon it became very apparent that Melchizedek was welcomed by the Essenes as the legendary *Teacher of Righteousness* referred to in Ancient records. These so-called sons of Light had remained faithful to the Covenant given Abraham. Harold had seen their counterparts throughout the ages. This present group, the Essenes, shunned the temple at Jerusalem. Its worship services had been corrupted by the Dragon. The pagan influence of the conquering Romans had taken its toll.

Harold's eyes focused on two white-tunicked Essenes. One stood reading from a leather scroll while another sat writing at a smooth plaster table. This scribe was painstakingly copying the Scriptures with a reed pen for preservation through the ages. As Harold watched, he thought ahead to the age of printing presses. His age had millions of Bibles due to the faithfulness of men such as this. The words from Fatima sprang to mind.

> When hidden writings shall be found
> That Sons of Light hid in the ground.
> Which are a sign to those who see,
> The Father's hand in history.

Harold knew that their work would not be in vain. But he sorrowed that the Romans would soon destroy these fine men. However, he knew that in the year 1948, a shepherd would find the fruits of their labors: The *Dead Sea Scrolls*. This treasure had been hidden well from the Roman hordes.

They waited silently over the centuries for their *appointed times*.

Harold wondered if Melchizedek had known that Israel would soon be scattered throughout the world for two thousand years. It also would not be until the year 1948 that they would again come home.

> When the dispersed shall homeward wend.
> And Gentile times come to an end.

He smiled to himself. The Air Force couldn't have picked a more appropriate name for their first UFO Project also initiated in 1948. Project *Sign* fit well.

As Harold continued to pass forward into time, there were intermediate periods where he could contemplate his mind-boggling experiences. Also, at these same times, the still small voice of Melchizedek explained earlier events that he hadn't fully recognized or understood.

He had seen the aged parents of Mary: Joachim and Anna. He learned that through the intervention of the Elohim, the barren Anna became Mary's mother. Melchizedek's whispering voice told him of Mary's careful nurturing by the Elohim. Her faith in the True One helped preserve her from all evil and caused her to abound with all good things. And then, her *appointed time* arrived. She participated directly in the greatest event on earth since the creation of Adapa.

Melchizedek spoke of a great fleet of ships constructed of pure light. Messengers from Eternity had arrived in them. They anchored in a harbor of this tiny island of stars. The Dragon attempted to destroy the *cargo* of these Envoys from Eternity. But, their defenses proved impenetrable. Their ways were beyond the understanding of even the Elohim. It was these Messengers who had transported the *Sacred Sperm* from Eternity. It was they who had implanted this Gift from the True One in the womb of the young Virgin Mary. As Melchizedek explained the blessed event in detail, his past words resounded again in Harold's mind.

Know that What was placed
In the Virgin's womb
Came from the depths of
The True One Who Is
Through Intermediaries,
The Messengers from Eterntiy.

It was the Elohim Gabriel who had brought Mary personal greetings on behalf of the True One. It was he that told her that the Shekinah Glory would *overshadow* her and that:

That Holy Thing Which shall be born of
thee shall be called the Son of God.

Harold was not allowed another close glimpse of the Word made flesh. He learned that both the Word and John the Baptist had received instructions from Melchizedek at Qumran. Not far from Qumran, he watched the Dragon's ship descend into the wilderness. From a distance he observed him personally confront the Word in a striking contrast. Adapa had been confronted in a beautiful luxuriant Garden. The Word confronted the Dragon in a bleak desert wilderness. The First Adam had failed. But, the Second Adam had withstood the wile of the Dragon.

Later, Harold viewed Peter, James and John ascend a mountain with the Word. From afar he witnessed their secret rendezvous with Elijah and Moses who descended in the bright glowing pillar-shaped object. He also watched the crucifixion and the resurrection. Astounded, he observed a bright craft hover over Roman soldiers guarding the tomb. They were put into a temporary state of paralysis as the stone moved away by some unknown force. Harold's being coursed with joy as he watched the revived Word re-enter the world of the living. And, still later he watched the Word ascend from a mountaintop into a vapor-enshrouded vehicle which bore him away. He saw the glowing Elohim appear to awe-struck disciples who were told that the Word would return in the very same way. Then, Melchizedek informed him that he must see one more event. It would concern a contactee who was used to turn the world upside down!

Instantly, Harold found himself strolling along a mountain path. It was morning. As he hiked along, the hot sun rose ever higher over the surrounding stone-strewn hills. He was climbing steadily. Once in awhile he glanced back as if looking for something. Then he saw it. A beautiful view of the Sea of Galilee lay a thousand feet below him in the distance. To the east he saw the rugged mountains of Moab. As he continued onward, the terrain changed to a flat sand-colored upland. A snow-capped mountain lay to his left. And in the distance he could just barely make out a low-lying walled city. The accented voice of Melchizedek whispered its identification:

"Damascus"

Several persons came into view far ahead of them. It seemed as if Melchizedek tried to keep just out of their sight. Again, a whisper:

"Saul of Tarsus"

"Of course. This is the road to Damascus," Harold concluded. "That, that must be — can it really be Paul up there ahead of me?" Harold's body back at Phoenix Base 3 became tense. He already knew what was about to occur. Then, it happened.

The sun was at its zenith when the flash in the sky attracted his attention. Amazed, he saw a glowing ball of light hurtling straight down from the sky at the group of men up ahead. They dropped to their knees and covered their faces with their arms. The dazzling light hovered ahead of them over the road. It glowed so brightly that Harold had to shield his eyes from the painful glare. Then all went black. Again a whisper:

"Saul the Persecutor has become Paul, servant of the True One Who Is."

Harold's last recollection was watching a cloaked man lying on the desert sand. A glistening domed disk hovered nearby as he approached the unconscious man. Then, the disk shot straight up and out of sight. Harold knelt down beside the bearded young man. He let water trickle from his flask onto his face. The man stirred and slowly opened his eyes. Those eyes. They were filled with awe and wonder. Then again the scene faded away. Harold heard the soft whisper of Melchizedek.

Paul has returned from the school of the Elohim. His *appointed time* has arrived. He is now ready to fulfill the purpose for which he was created. From a son of darkness, he has become a son of Light.

"Light, light, Son of light." The words kept repeating themselves over and over within his mind. Harold opened his eyes. He quickly shut them. It was so bright. He squinted them open again and swallowed hard. He was back at Phoenix Base 3 on the bed in the penthouse. Lying beside him was the still body of Melchizedek.

Harold slowly turned his head. Something was attached to it. And there, sitting beside his bed, was that nurse, Cathy. She was thoroughly absorbed in her reading. He glanced up at the clock. It read 0718. He felt stiff and hungry. And, what was pressing into his arm? His arm was connected to the intravenous feeding machine.

Harold was just about to address Cathy when he experienced something. It was a weird feeling, almost indefinable. He felt a presence, a new strange presence, that seemed to be a part of him. Even as he pondered about this, a voice whispered softly from deep within:

"We are truly *one*, my friend. Soon it will be time for us to go to work."

Harold immediately comprehended *what* had happened but *how* it happened was beyond his understanding. Somehow, Melchizedek had taken up psychic residence within his mind. Suddenly he felt his mouth open. It was his voice that came out. But, he did not speak with his own volition.

"Cath-Catherine? What day is it?"

Chapter Eighteen

Escape From Phoenix Base 3

Colonel Milkowski walked over to the flashing console. He pushed the receive button. Doctor Slater's face materialized on the screen.

"BETA-1. This is MEDIC-1. BETA-27 has just come out of it. He's awake. You'd better get up there."

"Are you up there now?"

"No. I left a nurse there. She just informed me by videocom. I had to leave for awhile to look in on some patients. By the way, the Priest isn't doing well at all. I've a feeling you'll not need deprogramming in his case. Mother Nature will take care of him permanently."

"Was your nurse able to disconnect BETA-27 from the Psi Recorder before he woke up?"

"I'm afraid not. It was quite sudden. He caught her by surprise."

"No matter. I'm sure that you can think up something to explain it."

"Well, I repeat again. Are you going up to him? I assume that you still plan to delay his interrogation at the retention ward?"

"I'll be up later. You go talk to him. My answer is 'yes' to your other question. VIGIL and I both feel that Bluepaper's purpose can best be served by telling him nothing. We need him to complete his work with the prisoner. He musn't know that we've exposed the Priest nor that his wife is in retention. He must be allowed to proceed with his work as if nothing has happened."

"Who was that, Steve?" Myrna's voice sounded from the side room in the Colonel's office.

"It was the Doc, tiger. Your old boy friend just woke up. Better get dressed and flip on his monitor. I need your professional opinion on his mental state. If he consciously thinks the way he's been dreaming, he'll need your help. What do you think about those crazy nightmares we recorded on the Psi machine?"

Harold had indeed awakened. His nurse had no doubts about that.

"Confound it, woman. Take your hands off me! I feel fine. Why have they got that Psi thing hooked up to me again? Let me up!"

"Mr. Stanton, you'll stay right there on the bed until MEDIC-1 returns. I have my orders. And look, cutie, I've also got a buzzer for your frequency. Behave yourself or I'll zap you!"

Harold reluctantly lay back onto the bed. The faint voice of Melchizedek welled up from within his subconscious.

"Harold? We shall do as she bids. I will stay in the background until it is time. I will only take control when it is necessary. Do not be fearful. You will soon get used to our symbiotic-like relationship. Now, *you will not remember* my telling you that the Priest has been apprehended. They must not know that we know. You also will not be overly concerned about Helen. Hear and understand, my friend. Do exactly as I have commanded."

Catherine noticed a strange blank look come over Harold's eyes as he listened silently to Melchizedek.

"Mr. Stanton? Harold? Are you all right? You looked like you might be slipping away again."

"Yes, Catherine, I'm fine. Just tired, stiff and a bit hungry. But you still haven't answered my question. What day is this?"

"It's Wednesday," Doctor Slater exclaimed as he entered the room. You've had quite a nap for yourself. Probably a result of nervous exhaustion or side-effects from your attempted suicide experience. Beats us though why you didn't sack out on your own bed. All of us thought you'd lapsed into a coma like your bedmate here. We've been feeding you intravenously. Colonel Milkowski even had me hook up a Psi recorder to you. He thought it might give us some clue to your mental activity."

Doctor Slater checked Harold over and allowed him to get up. The burden of his *new memories* weighed heavily upon his mind. On the one hand he feared for his sanity. On the other, he felt a dreadful gnawing anxiety to share his knowledge with others. But, how could he tell anyone of such things? Harold retreated to his work room and sank back into his easy chair. He buried his head in his hands and shook uncontrollably.

In the office below, Colonel Milkowski and Myrna watched him on the hidden monitor.

"What do you think, blondie? Should we pull him off *Enigma*? If he's about to crack, he may do more harm than good. I'd like to give him a few days' recreation break. But, then he'd want to see his wife. After what VIGIL did to her, she's in no condition to talk. Harold would have nothing more to do with us. She'd tell him everything."

Myrna shook her head in agreement. "She's wasted. She'll never cooperate with us again either. When her father finds out, we'll lose him too. Let's face it. We can't keep it much longer from them. All three are candidates for deprogramming."

"All *two*, honey. Harold's turn must come later. The Council wants to hold off until we get some results. He's right in the middle of several analyses. And, who knows what he might find out if our mysterious captive wakes up?"

The Colonel paused and cast an annoyed look at Myrna.

"Hey! You are listening to me, aren't you?"

"Of course I am but I'm also evaluating Harold like you asked me to do. I think his reactions are normal. He's a very high-principled man. His belief system is diametrically opposed to our ways at Base 3."

"How about those crazy dreams we recorded on Psi?"

"I've examined that video tape a dozen times. I think that Ben-Sorek hypnotized Harold. He'd never join him in bed on his own volition. The dreams? Some might say they were schizophrenic delusions of grandeur. Others that of a religious man attempting to accomodate UFOs into his belief system — complex dreams of compensation, if you will. But, I'd go much farther than that.

"After studying all aspects of this case, I've come to a rather interesting conclusion. I believe that this David Ben-Sorek, or whoever he really is, has read Harold's mind. We know for a fact that he has this capability. I think also that he's used Harold's religious beliefs as part of a clever way to hypnotically program him to do his bidding. Why? Because he himself is paralyzed and helpless. He wants Harold to do something that he's unable to do by himself. He's got Harold actually believing that he's *possessed* by him."

Colonel Milkowski stared incredulously into Myrna's cold blue eyes.

"Now don't give me that look, Steve! Hear me out, will you? I mean, I'm the expert here. Listen to me. A good hypnotist could make you believe that you were Jesus Christ. Although, I'm sure *you* would present him with quite a challenge, lover boy."

"Can it, Myrna. You damned women are all alike. Always going around in circles. Get to your point, will you?"

"Yes, Almighty Number 1." Myrna feigned a deep bow. "Okay, now what is it that I think our prisoner wants Harold to do? I would wager that it would be whatever he himself was just about to do before that fool helicopter pilot forced him off the road."

"Suppose what you say is true, then what, blondie?"

"Then what? You'll flip when you hear my humble proposal. I think that Harold should somehow be set free on the Outside. If he were, I'm convinced that he'd head for Mount Rainier National Park. He'd finish what his bedmate set out to do in the first place."

"What! You can't be serious about this, Myrna. Let *him*

go? The Council would have my head. Why he's liable to compromise our whole operation."

"I don't mean to just throw him out on his ear alone. We'd give him some logical sounding reason. Others would accompany him. If he tried to escape, they'd let him. But, he'd be tailed closely. The Rainier area would be monitored by our people. Who knows? If we're lucky, we might catch one of the aliens alive."

"But what about Harold's work, Myrna? He's right in the middle of some very interesting things."

"It can wait. Ben Sorek seems to have complete control of his own body. He's not going to wake up for questionning. I tell you, Steve, this man's stalling for time. He's hypnotically planted instructions in Harold's mind."

"If that's so, why weren't these theorized hypnotic instructions recorded by psi?"

"Steve, it was hours before you ordered the Psi hook-up. I assume that he would've given Harold such instructions during that period. The religious junk was put in his mind to influence Harold and to throw us off the trail."

"Be reasonable, Myrna. How does he think Harold could ever get out of here? He must have read enough of our minds to know that he'd never make it out on his own."

"We don't know how much or little he knows, Steve. If we had time, we could wait and see if Harold attempted to break out of here, or, we could see if he gave any indication that he wanted to get out."

"Babe, how naive can you get? Of course Harold wants out. You wouldn't have to hypnotize him for that. Given the opportunity, he and his wife would take off out of here like a bat out of hell!"

"Slow down. I didn't mean it in quite that way. What I mean to say is that Harold at least has accepted the inevitability of never getting out of here. Right? I mean, how many times lately has he asked you or anyone else to let him go back to NSA? Let's watch him closely. If he happens to make such irrational suggestions or statements, let's pretend to go along with them. I mean, he's helpless. He'd never get away from us. No one ever gets away from VIGIL."

"I don't know, blondie. I'd feel like a fool suggesting something like this to the Council. ."

"All right. If you don't want to suggest it, I will. You set up the meeting and I'll be glad to give them my two cents worth!"

"Okay, okay already. Give it a try. I'm warning you, though. You'd better be able to back up your theory and your suggestion with some good case-history material on hypnosis. They'll be pretty uptight if you propose anything that would risk compromise. I'll set up the Council meeting for you. They'll want the Doc's report, too, as well as what Joseph has put together from Harold's work. You can run along now. I've got to go up and say a few words to Harold."

"Keep away from that prisoner, Steve. I doubt whether he can hypnotize or mind-read without eye contact and close proximity. Don't take any unnecessary chances. Keep all Level 1's away from the Penthouse. Question Harold down here. Also, if Doc is going to be at that Council meeting, you'd better put another doctor up there. We don't want my talk to the Council to leak through Doc's mind to the prisoner."

Harold, in the meantime was having problems°with the video-com. "Joseph? Joseph? What's wrong with this contraption anyhow?" he muttered.

Harold tried again and again to reach Joseph but no answer was forthcoming. "Nurse? Catherine? Do you know if this thing is working or not?"

Cathy stuck her head in through the open door. "I'm sure that I don't know. No one told me that it wasn't working. Now please, I've got to keep my eye on *him* or they'll have my neck."

"What seems to be the problem, Harold?"

Harold whipped around to see Colonel Milkowski's face on the console's screen.

"Oh, it's you, Steve. I've been trying to reach Joseph."

"Ah, yes. Joseph. Joseph may be detained for a few days. We had no idea how long you'd be unconscious. We put him on another project until you were available. Look, Harold, would you mind very much coming down here to my office for lunch? I would come up there to talk but I'm really busy. I'm glad you snapped out of it. We were worried."

"Why, yes. I'll come down with a pleasure. I'd be glad to get out of these rooms. Will General Thurman be there? And Helen, does she know I've had, ah, problems?"

"General Thurman is on an important mission on the Outside. I'm acting as Number 1. No, we haven't told Helen."

"Why are you going to have a nurse here around the clock? I'll not have any privacy."

"I'll explain everything when you come down. I've got to go. See you then."

Harold watched Colonel Milkowski's face fade to nothing. He flicked off the console switch and went over t o the book shelf. He picked up a volume on Biblical Archaeology and skimmed to a section concerning the Garden of Eden.

ARCHAEOLOGICAL NOTES: Babylonian Traditions of Fall of Man. Early Babylonian inscriptions abound in references to a "tree of life", from which man was driven, by the influence of an evil spirit personified in a *serpent*, and to which he was prevented from returning by guardian cherubs.

Among these tablets there is a story of *Adapa*, so strikingly parallel, to the Biblical story of Adam, that he is called the Babylonian Adam. "Adapa, the seed of mankind — the wise man of Eridu — blameless — he offended the gods — then he became mortal."

Harold examined a number of photo facsimiles of ancient Babylonian tablets and seals. One was called *The Temptation Seal*.

"That's where I had seen the strange antenna tower before. It's on this seal," Harold thought excitedly to himself. There it was: a crude drawing but fully recognizable. "No wonder they called it a tree of life," he mused. "Those elements sticking out on either side would look like a huge silver tree to primitives." Curious, he read further concerning this tree of life.

Near Eridu was a garden, in which was a mysterious Sacred Tree, a Tree of Life, planted by the gods, whose roots were deep, while its branches reached to heaven.

Harold returned the book to its shelf and went over to the work table. There were the paper graphs and a note from Joseph.

"Amazing that they would take Joseph off Project Enigma," he pondered. "Hum-m, strange, this note doesn't even mention my coma. I bet they didn't tell him about it. Something is not right about all of this."

"I believe you are right, my friend," whispered Melchizedek from within. "When we meet with your infamous Colonel Milkowski, I shall find out exactly what. Perhaps we can use it to our advantage."

"You mean by mind-reading?" Harold *thought* back in reply. "Will I be conscious of this?"

"Yes, by mind-reading. You will only be conscious of when I do this if I allow it. Do you understand? Do you acknowledge this?"

"Yes," Harold thought dreamily. "I understand."

Harold descended in the elevator and walked along the corridor toward Colonel Milkowski's office.

"This is strange," he thought to himself. "I thought I was to be completely confined up there. But, now they're letting me move about again. Wish I knew how to find Helen. But, my *companion* is probably just set for this area. I'd better stay where I'm told." He entered the Colonel's office.

"Well, do come in, Harold. Sit down. Joseph told me that you're doing a great job. Now that you've got all the raw material organized well, what do you plan to do next?"

"I hope to find patterns in the Beta waves being transmitted to the contactees. Perhaps now I can decipher

"No wonder they called it a tree of life."

what's going on."

"Fine. Let's eat. I've already taken the liberty to order for you. Same lunch we had last time you were here — remember?"

"How could I forget? That's when you hooked me up to that infernal Psi recorder. Why was I hooked up again?"

"You seemed to be dreaming up a storm. I thought it might help the Doc evaluate what was going on in your mind."

"And, what did you find out, pray tell. Was I dreaming about Myrna again?"

"Ha! No. Not at all. Just a jumble of religious nonsense. I've no interest in those things. I'll leave them to you and the Priest."

"Father Pat? Yes, with your permission, I'd like to visit him again with Helen on Sunday. General Thurman told me that he saw no problem in doing this when I asked him about it last week. Now that he's on the Outside, I suppose we'll need your permission."

"Ah, I see no reason why you can't. Let me check with Tim. I'll have him make the necessary arrangements through VIGIL. But, now, Harold, if you're up to it, I'd like to hear your thoughts about our *guest*. Have you come to any conclusions about those images on the glossies? The Council would like to know."

"Ah, no. Not yet. I just have this strong feeling. Don't ask me why. It's just a feeling that I'm supposed to *go* somewhere. *Do* something. I, I've been hearing a voice in my head."

"Voice in your head? My God, man! Perhaps we have been too rough on you. Ah, what does this, ah, voice say to you?"

"It seems to be mixed up with some of the things I've been told about *him*."

"What things?"

"Well, I was told that VIGIL had tracked *him* to Mount Rainier. Then, a helicopter scared him off the road. For some stupid reason, I keep wondering *why* he was going up that mountain road. I have this strong urge that I must know why he was at Mount Rainier. I, I hear this voice in my head. It says, "Why don't you go to Rainier and find out?"

"It says what? Just a minute, Harold. I'm not really the one you should share this with. We have a professional here that would like to hear this and talk to you about it."

Colonel Milkowski activated his video-com. "MEDIC-5? Are you still in the Beta lab?"

"Hello? Yes, I am. What's up, Steve?"

"Ah, I think you'd better come over to my office. An old acquaintance of yours has some problems. I'd like you to talk with him."

"Old acquaintance? Whoever do you mean?"

"Get up here and you'll see."

The Colonel then turned back to Harold. "Myrna will be here in a minute or so."

"Myrna? Has she seen my Psi tapes?"

"Why not ask me that question, Harold? I'll be happy to answer you."

Harold swung the swivel chair around. Myrna walked into the room. Consarn it! Why was he so physically attracted to her?

"My friend," whispered Melchizedek. "We have been doing well. But such sensuous thoughts of this woman are unbecoming of you. Do not dwell on them. You cannot help it if ravens fly about your head. But, you can prevent them from nesting there. Am I understood?"

Myrna brought Harold into the side room and listened intently to what he had to say. She asked many questions.

"Now, let's go over a few things just one more time, Harold. I realize that this has been a long question and answer session but I'm trying to help you. Now, just once more. You're sure that this, this obsession, started soon after you awoke?"

"Yes."

"Okay, Harold. That's all for today, then. You need sleep and a change of environment. Perhaps we can get you out of the Penthouse for a day or so, okay?"

"Thanks for your concern, Myrna. I'm grateful."

Myrna stood up and called out to Colonel Milkowski.

"Steve. I'm through for now. I'd like to see him here again tomorrow, at 0900."

"Okay. Stick around for a few minutes, will you? You can go back now, Harold. I haven't told either your wife or her dad about your problem. We don't want to unnecessarily worry them. I'll see what Myrna thinks about your condition. We'll talk further about this tomorrow. Your bed has been moved into the other room. Keep out of Ben Sorek's room for awhile. If he wakes up, we'll let you know. Sleeping near that creepy Arab has got your imagination working overtime. Sometime, I'll let you see the Psi tapes of your dreams. They look like a mixture of Hollywood extravaganza on Biblical stories superimposed over our Bluepaper briefing films on UFOs. Take it easy, man. We'll see you tomorrow."

Harold returned to the Penthouse. Myrna stayed behind. The Colonel turned to Myrna.

"Well. He's gone, blondie. We can talk. Looks like you may have been right after all. Or, we've got a helluva coincidence on our hands."

"I won't say that 'I told you so', Steve. But, I will say that my recording of this interview with Harold should strengthen my argument at the Council tonight. See you then."

Meanwhile, Harold had returned to the Penthouse. He tried to study the new graphs but had no taste for it. After dinner, the voice of Melchizedek urged him to go directly to bed.

When Doctor Slater arrived, he found Harold fast asleep. Cathy looked in and smiled.

"Look at him, Doc. Sleeping like a baby. He's a cutie. Boy, I miss the guys at recreation. I bet they miss me, eh?

Leave it to me to get stuck up here. Me, Cathy the Queen, confined in two bedrooms with two guys. One's a zombie and the other might as well be a eunuch! This is purgatory. My evil deeds have finally caught up to me, Doc."

Two others just below the Penthouse didn't share Cathy's problems.

Steve Milkowski reached over and put his arm around Myrna. "Well, the Council bought your theory and your plan, blondie. VIGIL-1 and I got together and worked out a super plan. Want to hear about it?"

"Why yes! Don't keep me in suspense, Steve."

"Okay. Tomorrow you will tell Harold that we've decided that he needs a break, a real change of pace. Then, I'll tell him that we're short of Beta maintenance men. We'll explain that eventually, he'd have been expected to learn Beta detector maintainability for back-up capability. I'll tell him that his friend, Don Fields, has already done this a few times and enjoys the work. Then, we'll ask him if he'd like to take a survey trip to one of the Beta detector stations."

"If he accepts, this buys us two things. *First*, it will be a test of your theory. Who knows what that will lead to? *Second*, it will give us an excuse to keep him from Helen a while longer. He'll be told that he's going to have to forego seeing her this weekend. This gives us another full week. I don't have any idea how we'll keep him from her next week."

"Next week? Don't worry about that, Steve. My impression was that the Council didn't seem to care. If nothing comes out of this trip and if Harold can't produce anything substantial by next week, VIGIL will take over."

"I'll say they'll take over. It will be all over then, blondie. They'll treat our sleeping friend to all the tricks of their trade. Either he talks or he'll die. Its as simple as that. Look what they did to Harold's wife. Let's face it. Harold, Helen, her father and the Priest all become expendable. They'll all be deprogrammed."

"Let's change the subject, Steve."

"And the Priest? He's dying. You know, Myrna? I must be getting soft. I actually let General Thurman go see him this evening. I told VIGIL that something useful might come out of their conversation. But, that wasn't the only reason I arranged the visit. I actually felt sorry for the old guy. Me! The hard, logical and emotionless BETA-1.

"But enough of this, blue eyes. Let me tell you who Harold will be travelling with. I've saved the best till last."

"Whatever do you mean, Steve?"

"I mean that you and he are going to pose as a travelling married couple!"

"What? Me and Harold go as husband and wife?" Myrna laughed so hard that tears came to her eyes.

"I tell you, Myrna, it's the only way to make it easy for him to escape. How could he escape if we flew him there? He's got to have opportunities. You will give him these opportunities. VIGIL won't let him out of their sight."

Meanwhile, in another bed, in another Sector, yet another confrontation was taking place. Father Pat opened his tired eyes and squinted up at General Thurman staring down at him.

"Well, Father, I guess we've seen better times together, eh?"

"John, John, it's you. I thought they'd just left me to die alone. Why haven't Harold and Helen come? Where are the others?"

"Easy, Pat. Don't try to get up. Just lie still."

"But the others? What have they done to them? It's all my fault, John. It's all my fault."

"Don't take all the blame, Pat. It's my fault, too. If I hadn't had a soft spot for you and the Church, you'd never have gotten away with it. Everyone has been put in retention for interrogation by VIGIL except Harold. He's still working on Project Enigma with *him*. Personally, I think that guy's a clever agent who is using your religious beliefs to accomplish his purposes. I really don't know what's

243

happening, Pat. I'm no longer Number 1. It's nothing short of a miracle that I was even allowed to come here. I'm supposed to be permanently quarantined to my quarters until an enquiry is over. BETA-1 is acting in my place. There's a couple of VIGIL strongmen just outside this door."

"What do *you* believe, John? You have been different from the others. You've been a great help to me and to the Church. You don't know how sorry I am that my mission was forced to use your generosity to cover my operation."

"Don't be sorry, you old codger. You did what you had to do. I won't ask you what that was. This place is bugged, you know. If I had blown you up with the Buldir I installation out there in the Aleutians, I wouldn't be in this fix now. But, I did what I had to do, Father. Now, we both are paying the consequences. And, believe me, Pat. If I had to do it all over again, I'd still have spared your life."

"And, John, if I had the same choice, I still would have done my duty to the Lord and to His Church. But again, I must know what you believe, John. I feel weak. It's getting so dim. Once you were to be a Priest. Surely you once held to the Faith. I want you to, I, I, —"

"Easy, Pat. You, you don't look so good. I'll ring for the Doc."

"No, no. No time for that. Please answer me, John. What do you believe?"

"Father, all these years I've wanted to believe, to practice the Faith as you put it. But, I've been involved in so many things contrary to Christian beliefs that I've felt trapped. I couldn't in good conscience be a good Catholic. I couldn't get out of this Project without being subjected to deprogramming. But, now it's different. I don't care about the Project anymore. I've had it! And, there's always the possibility that I may be annihilated. Father, I would like very much to confess my sin. I would like to receive your Absolution. But, I've wasted most of my life. It's so hard to believe that it isn't too late for someone like me."

Tears began to flow down Father Pat's face. His tired face broke into a weak smile.

"John, I'm so happy to hear that. Our Lord Himself is filled with joy over your desire to return to Him. Please pick up that Bible over there. Right. Now, look up Matthew in the index and turn to Chapter 20. That's it, now read verses 1 through 16 to me."

General Thurman read the passage slowly and deliberately. Father Pat watched intently, straining to hold on to life which he felt steadily slipping away.

Now the kingdom of heaven is like a landowner going out at daybreak to hire workers . . He made an agreement with the workers for one denarius a day, and sent them to his vineyard . . . At about the third hour he saw others standing idle . . and said . . 'You go to my vineyard too and I will give you a fair wage . . and again at the ninth hour . . and the eleventh hour.

Those . . hired about the eleventh hour came . . . . and received one denarius each. When the first came, they expected . . more, but they too received one denarius each . . They grumbled at the landowner . . . He answered . . them and said . . . "I am not being unjust . . Did we not agree on one denarius? Have I no right to do what I like with my own? Why be envious because I am generous? Thus the last will be first and the first last.

"But, Father, it doesn't seem fair. You've given most of your life serving God. This says that someone like me would be just as acceptable to Him as someone like you."

"John," Father Pat whispered. "That's because our Father is full of Grace. He is pure generosity. It's something beyond our sinful mind's ken. This Parable refers only to *entering* the Kingdom. There are just rewards for the faithful as well.

"Believe me, John, lad. God loves you. He loves me. It is His evening for both of us. The Owner of the Vineyard is calling. Let us both accept His generosity. Kneel here, beside my bed so I may lay my hand upon you. Let us both make our confession to Him Who died to take away our sin. I cannot give you His forgiveness but I can assure it. He and He alone is able to forgive. I too need His forgiveness daily.

245

Let us pray, my son."

Deep within the confines of Phoenix Central, a young VIGIL Monitor wiped her eyes.

"What's eating you, Lisa? Who've you got on there, the Priest?"

"Never mind, Joe. This is beyond you. Switch me to another channel, will you? I can't take this."

Back at the hospital, Father Pat brought his prayer to an end:

"And, Heavenly Father, thank you so much for John's return to you. It's something I've long prayed for and, and, —"

General Thurman felt the Priest's hand on his head go limp and slip off. Father Pat was dead.

On the following morning, Harold gulped down his breakfast, cleaned up and went directly down to Colonel Milkowski's office. He sat in quiet astonishment as the Colonel and Myrna outlined their proposal to him.

"What's the matter, Harold?" Myrna teased. "Cat got your tongue? You didn't think we planned to keep you cooped in here forever, did you? Please understand though, that you would only be part of a back-up maintenance crew. Most of the time you'll be assigned to more important things inside. So, what do you say? Would you like to see the Outside for several days?"

Harold stared unbelievingly at the couple and then spoke.

"You have no idea, either of you, of how I'm feeling inside right now. To actually see the sky, trees, grass and to feel sunshine on my face, to smell fresh air again? — I had shut off the very thoughts of such things. They were torture. But, how can I go without Helen? How could I face her and tell her that I've been allowed out? It just wouldn't be fair to me or to her."

"But, Harold," Colonel Milkowski lied, "someday soon

Helen herself will be given Outside missions. We plan to use her to interrogate very special people in foreign countries, people that we dare not bring here."

"One of your assets, Harold," Myrna interrupted, "is that hardly anyone knew you outside of your associates at NSA. There's no need even for a disguise where you're going. We'll be travelling under assumed names with proper credentials."

"Me? Travelling with you. What do you think I —"

"Shut up and listen to us, Stanton," the Colonel bellowed. Let us finish what we're saying, will you? Your credentials are being prepared right now. You and Myrna will be Mr. and Mrs. Howard Tolleson. Her name will be Mary. Both of you will get briefing sheets and everything you need to pull this off."

"Well, Harold?"

"All of this is highly irregular, but," — (Melchizedek's influence completely countermanded Harold's negative reaction) — "Yes, I'd love to get out of here. Where are we going?"

"Washington State," Myrna quipped.

"Will we be going anywhere near Mount Rainier?"

"You'll be going to another National Park. The Beta detector station is located on the edge of Olympic National Park. Our people will be expecting you. Myrna's been there before."

"You'll not tell Helen about this? I would rather explain things to her myself."

"No, that's your business. We'll also keep your recent coma episode confidential. We don't want her to worry, do we?"

"Well, may I at least see her before I go? I'll keep quiet about both things. You see, I have already made plans to be with her on Sunday."

"No, I'm afraid our schedule for you allows no time for such a visit. But, tell you what: just as soon as you get back, we'll arrange something special for both you and Helen.

You can spend several days together. How's that? Now, let me alert VIGIL. We've got to get you both briefed and outfitted in civies. You'll hardly recognize yourself out of uniform, Stanton."

"Yes, it'll be nice to dress normally again. I'm quite excited about the prospect. But, this husband and wife business: ah, how long will it take for us to get where we're going? You know, I mean —"

"You mean are we going to be staying overnight together somewhere, Harold?" Myrna replied coyly. "We are but don't be scared of me. I won't bite you. We'll work out things exactly how you'd like them. I'll be a good girl if you'll be a good boy."

"Madam, I'm a married man. A Christian man. You don't have to be concerned about that, I assure you!"

"My, my. Aren't you the righteous one? This *is* going to be an interesting trip."

It was 0430 when Harold and Myrna left the VIGIL briefing room. He followed her through a tunnel to the basement of Sector 5. Crates of non-perishable foodstuffs lay unattended on flatbed push carts.

"Sector 5 is where they bring in food and material for storage," Myrna explained.

The two walked towards the outline of a huge overhead door outlined in red. It was large enough to drive a truck through. Next to this door was a small hatchway.

"Now we've got to get by Security," Myrna commented as she reached up and pressed a button. Immediately a panel slid open revealing a large lens. Then a recorded voice emanated from the opening.

"Please stand on the red square and identify."

Myrna stood on the red-painted square on the floor and spoke.

"I am MEDIC-5 cleared for survey trip to Deception Beta Site 30."

There was silence. Then the mechanical voice spoke again.

"Left profile — Full face — Right profile — Full face."
Myrna turned each way to show her profile as ordered. Then the door slid open.

"Don't follow me, Harold, or you'll get zapped. When the door closes, just repeat what I said and do as I did."

Harold followed suit and joined her on the other side. They had entered a huge tunnel. A full-sized two-lane paved road paralleled the moving escalator.

At the end of the tunnel, they were once again confronted with a similar door and hatch. The hatch opened and Harold stepped out into the cool night air. It engulfed his sense of smell with a myriad of odors. He welcomed them as long-lost friends: the smell of dampness, flowers and earth. There was the odor of a car engine's exhaust and hot metal. Everything was so distinct and pungent. He looked up. The sky was cloudy. They seemed to be in a dark fenced-in area. Myrna's flashlight fell upon a parked automobile beside the fence.

Myrna drove along the fence-line toward a dimly-lit guard house and blinked her lights. An Air policeman stepped out and walked over to the idling car. He held a .45 automatic.

"Evening, Ma-am, Sir. Key word, please."

"3-0 Blue."

"Right you are. Have a pleasant evening."

The gates swung open and they drove out onto a paved road that stretched out into a stark desert-like terrain. The car's lights illuminated embedded reflectors as they sped along under the inky black sky.

"Where are we, Myrna?"

"I'm, Mary now, Howard. Shall I call you Howie? We're in Arizona, not far from the Mexican border. Those lights off in the distance are cars moving along Route 8. You're fortunate. Your pal Don was blindfolded when they took him out of here. However, it wouldn't do for a wife to be seen riding along with a blindfolded husband, would it. Besides, Howie, I'm not that hard to look at, am I?"

Harold looked at the long blonde hair falling softly over Myrna's shoulders. He glanced at her shapely long legs exposed above her knees and then quickly looked ahead.

"No, Myrna, ah, Mary. You're certainly not hard to look at."

"I'm glad you feel that way, Howie. After all, we're married."

Harold fought to control the uninvited feelings that swept over him. Myrna slowed the car to a stop before a metal gate and pressed a button on the dashboard. The gate opened and they drove onto the highway. Oncoming lights from a car hit a sign posted beside the gate. It read: *Luke Air Force Base Danger. Do not leave right of way on main travelled roads. Use Roads open to public only. Observe all warning signs.*

Chapter Nineteen

The Signal of Judgment

Harold and Myrna stopped for breakfast at a Howard Johnson restaurant. He couldn't remember having enjoyed breakfast so much. As the day passed on, he revelled in the sights, sounds and smells of the Outside. He wished that Helen could be enjoying it all with him. But, after awhile, the late night and excitement caught up with him. He lay his head back and dozed off. It was almost midnight when Myrna nudged Harold out of a sound sleep.

"Wake up, honey. We're in San Francisco. I'd like you to look a bit more alive when we check in at our palace for the night."

"Palace? What palace?"

"Well, it's like a palace to me. When I first stayed at the Fairmont, it brought back childhood memories: dreams of castles, princes, knights in shining armor. You'll like the Fairmont. It's gorgeous. What do you think of this hill?"

"Thunderation! I hope the brakes hold. I've never driven up such a steep incline."

"This is Knob Hill. Our hotel is up at the very top."

"It looks like a red light district to me. Look at those hussies on the street corners. I've never seen such a collection of filth in my life. Peep shows. Nude dancers. X-rated movies. The Passion Pit? The Orgy! What kind of a place are you taking me to?"

"Just be patient, we're almost at the top. Now, look over there. Isn't it beautiful?"

Myrna edged the car into a semi-circular drive. They got out of the car. Harold gazed up at the white colonnaded building. It seemed so out of place: a beautiful island surrounded by a sea of immorality.

"It's magnificent," he thought. "It's a far cry from any hotel that I've ever stayed at before."

"Ps-s-t. Howie. Take the keys. Open up the back of the wagon. Here comes the welcoming party," Myrna whispered.

Harold glanced at the approaching doorman who was motioning a bellhop to follow him.

"Blast it. How do you open up this infernal thing, ah, Mary?"

"Howard! Give me those keys. You'd think by this time you'd have learned how to open it. We've had this car over a month now!" Myrna scolded.

Harold looked sheepishly at the bell hop. He gave him a sympathetic look as "Mary" jerked open the back of the wagon.

"Shall I park your car for you now, sir?"

Myrna glanced at Harold and nodded.

"Why, yes. Please do. Thank you."

"Very well, sir. I'll have the desk notify you where it's parked. Have a pleasant time at The Fairmont. Good night."

Harold followed the bellhop into the hotel. Myrna snuggled up close to him. She felt so warm. This whole crazy thing seemed so natural at times.

"Tell the man at the desk we have a room reserved for Mr. and Mrs. Howard Tolleson," Myrna whispered. "And don't forget to sign Howard Tolleson on the registration slip."

The bell hop closed the door to their room. Harold felt trapped and embarrassed. Myrna flung her coat on the bed and walked over to a huge picture window.

"Turn off the lights a moment, Harold, ah, Howie."

Harold flicked the switch. Myrna stood silhouetted before the window. She was a beautiful woman.

"Come on over and take a look, Howie. Aren't the lights beautiful? In the morning we'll get a beautiful view of the bay."

Harold walked over and glanced out.

"It's a magnificent view, ah, Mary. This whole place is beyond the likes of me. But, ah, I think we ought to get some sleep. I'm dead tired. If you'd like to use the bathroom first, go ahead."

"My, my, Howie. Still shy and we've been married for almost twenty-four hours. You use it first. I'll get into my PJ's out here. You looked zonked. You'd best get right to bed. I'm a night owl myself."

Harold tossed and turned for most of the night. The long trip, the excitement of being outside, the strange bed and Myrna all contributed to his restlessness. He kept sneaking glances at her form lying on the other bed. Finally, sometime during the wee hours of the morning, he fell asleep.

"Hey, hubby! Get the lead out. We've got a schedule to keep."

Harold opened his eyes. A strange chill went through him. He suddenly realized that he wasn't in the Penthouse. He raised himself up on his elbow and looked across at Myrna sitting on the opposite bed. She was pulling her nylons up and over her legs. He blushed and turned his head.

"What's the matter, honey? Haven't you seen a woman's legs before? My, my. I wish we'd got to know each other better before we got married!"

Harold slid out of bed on the other side and stormed into the bathroom.

"Easy, my friend. Take it easy," Melchizedek's voice whispered. "This one seeks to tempt you. It bothers her that you are unlike others that she has known. She would very much like to bring you down to her level of morality. It is good to see her troubled about you. Perhaps there is hope for her."

"Hope for *her*? I hope there's hope for me!" Harold retorted. "You've put me in an almost intolerable situation of compromise. I'm only human, you know."

253

"What's the matter, honey? Haven't you seen a woman's legs before?"

"Fear not, man of dust. I'll not let the situation get out of hand. The Dragon seeks to disrupt our mission. He shall not succeed."

"That's easy enough for *you* to say. It's *my* body that's struggling, not yours!"

The rest of the day flew by: lunch at Redding and dinner at Eugene, Oregon. Harold took a turn at the wheel. He felt so free. Being with Myrna made him feel so much younger. It was the same feeling he had experienced during courting days. Myrna turned to him and spoke. A twinkle appeared in her eyes.

"I wish you'd talk more, Howie. After all, I'm your wife."

"You know, Myrna, Mary, whoever? I don't even know your last name. I don't know where you were born, where you went to school or how you got into all of this. Tell me about yourself."

"Does it make any difference to you, Harold, Howard or whoever?" Myrna quipped back laughingly.

"Oh, I was just wondering. You seem to know more about me than my wife! Since we're going to be together awhile, I, I guess I would really like to know you better."

A frown crossed Myrna's face. She looked away from him.

"My past isn't worth knowing. I try to forget it."

"Come on, Myrna. I'm really interested. I'd like to hear all about it."

Myrna glanced over at the handsome distinguished-looking man behind the wheel. He was so unbelievably innocent, so naive yet he did seem genuinely interested in her.

"Okay, Buster, I don't know why I'm telling you this but you asked for it. Now you're going to get it, both barrels. You won't like it, I guarantee you. I'm no angel."

"We all have skeletons in our closets, Myrna. No one is perfect. Go ahead. I'm listening."

"Well, let's begin with my last name. It's Pederson."

"Ah, Swedish, eh?"

"Yes, Swedish. I was brought up on a farm in Sebeka, Minnesota. My Mom and Dad came over to this country from Sweden with their parents. They were farmers. Dad inherited his folk's farm. I was their only child, ah, that is, the only one that lived. Twice, my mother lost baby boys through miscarriages. Shortly after the second miscarriage, complications set in. She, she died. My father was heartbroken. He had wanted a son so badly, both times. And then Mom's death. He was devastated."

"I'm sorry, Myrna. It must have been rough on you both."

"It was. Dad missed Mom so much and he dreamed of having a son to work and inherit the farm. Somehow, I always felt unwanted because of this. I felt that I was second rate. Dad never said anything directly. But, I could see it in his eyes, especially after the last miscarriage and Mom's death. It, it got so that he wouldn't even look me in the eyes anymore.

"I tried to fulfill both the parts of son and housekeeper the best I could. Dad never seemed satisfied. I wanted him to love me and to accept me for who I was. But, somehow he wouldn't or couldn't show any emotion towards me whatsoever.

"When I became eighteen, I inherited a large sum of money that Mummy had willed for my education. I never knew that she had it. We seemed to have always lived from hand to mouth. Her folks had left it to her. She planned to send me to college with it. Well, one day I told Dad that I wanted to go away to school. But, he insisted that I stay and help him with the farm. I finally just got up and left one night. I left him. I've never been back, never kept in touch. I, I don't even know whether he's alive."

"Where did you go? What did you do?"

"I was confused and emotionally upset. I knew so little about life other than farming. I moved to Chicago and took a part-time job as a waitress. I enrolled at the Universtiy of Chicago as a psychology major. I guess that I thought the courses would help me better understand myself. Looking back at it now, I was a real mixed-up kid. Well, I met a pre-med student, Ned Rogers. He was smart, from a very rich family and had travelled abroad. Ned introduced me to a whole new world. His world included nightclubs, swanky restaurants, drinking and, and sex. Ned seemed to fill up the void, that terrible void in my life. I followed him around like a little puppy dog. I craved affection. I wanted to be touched, kissed and held close. I didn't have the sense then to see that Ned was just using me. When he finally dropped me for somebody else, my whole world came tumbling down. The void, the insecurity, the lack of love all came back with a terrible vengeance. It was about that time that I met Paulette. She was a student at the University.

"Paulette told me that I was crazy letting one guy make such a wreck out of my mind and my studies. I was hurt and what she said made lots of sense at the time. 'They're all alike,' she said. 'There's only one thing any one of them wants. You've got to put yourself in the driver's seat. Make them negotiate for your favors. This way, you get what you want, they get what they need and you're both happy. Right, kid?"

"But that girl wasn't any —"

"Whoa. Don't interrupt. Let me finish before I change my mind about telling you all of this. Remember, you asked for this. So, anyways, Paulette told me that she was paid for her favors and paid well: 'For just a few hours a night, several times a week, I get my room, board, tuition and pocket money,' she told me. I can still hear her lecturing me. 'You got a better face and body than me,' she said. 'I can introduce you around. Sometimes it's even nice when you get to like a guy. But remember, kid. Don't ever get emotionally involved again. Physically, yeh, but don't get silly and fall for any one of them. It ain't worth it. They ain't worth it. You don't need nobody to take care of you. Take care of number one. That's you, kid — Yourself. Don't get stuck as some guy's housewife. White slavery's a better name. He gives you room and board for your favors. Right?

But you give him everything. You work your tail off — children, housework and whatever. What for? It's really just a socially acceptable live-in situation. You get the raw end of the stick while he goes out and plays around. Marriage would be worse than what that Ned gave you.' "

"But that girl had a perverted view of life," Harold replied. "It all isn't like that. It's a crime, a blasted crime, that someone like that influenced you at such a young age."

"But, I listened good, Harold. I was mad at my father. I hated Ned. So, I worked my way through college and grad school in so many beds that the whole thing is just a blur now."

Harold felt embarrassed and tried to change the subject. "Ah, how did you get involved with Bluepaper?"

"Some professor at the University was a recruiter for the CIA. He propositioned me in more ways than one. He said that my combined educational background, independence and amoral attitude about life made me a natural. So, I became a CIA agent and became deeply involved in covert operations. Again, I used my body to get ahead. On one of my assignments, I met Colonel Milkowski. It was Major Milkowski then. Anyhow, I guess he liked me a lot. It was his recommendation that got me into Bluepaper."

Myrna paused a moment and bowed her head.

"So, that's the story of my life. I hope you're satisfied. You're the first person I've ever shared it with. What do you think of me now?"

Harold was speechless. He just stared ahead silently at the seemingly endless road ahead.

"You loathe me, don't you? You might as well admit it. I'm just a slut, right?" Myrna's voice was quavering.

"No, I don't loathe you. I don't agree with how you've conducted your life. But, I don't dislike you for it. I, I just wish that there were some way that I could help you, show you."

Myrna looked at him quizzically. Harold noticed tears welling up within her eyes. He pulled the car over to the side of the road, reached over and gently caressed her hair.

"Confound it, woman. Stop crying. I —"

The next thing he knew, Myrna threw her arms around him. She pressed her wet cheek tightly against his.

"Now see here, this is highly irregular. We musn't, we musn't —"

Myrna slowly released her grip and brought her face eye to eye with his. She cupped her hands gently on either side of his cheeks and drew his lips to hers. Harold started to resist. But, her lips felt so sweet, so tender. His body relaxed. Harold yielded. He placed his arms around her and held her tightly.

"Oh Myrna, Myrna. This can't be. This can't be," he whispered. "We must control ourselves. I'm married. I love my wife. I —"

Myrna drew her face back and looked him in the eyes. She looked so sad, so completely broken.

"I understand, Harold," she said softly. "Thank you for being such a good listener."

Very few words were spoken during the next few hours. She rested her head against his shoulder. He offered no resistance. Soon she was fast asleep.

It was about quarter of ten. Harold crossed the bridge over the Columbia river into the city precincts of Portland. It was the cleanest city that he had ever seen. The sidewalks and streets were immaculately free of the rubbish he'd noted elsewhere.

"Myrna, ah, Mary? Better wake up. We're coming into Portland. I haven't a clue where this Benson Hotel is."

Harold signed the register: Mr. and Mrs. Howard Tolleson. For one moment, just one fleeting moment, he found himself wishing that it were true.

They boarded the elevator. It was just the two of them. She looked at him. He looked at her. Neither said a word.

Harold felt hot all over. It was difficult to breathe. A lump formed in his throat. The walls seemed to close in upon them squeezing them closer, closer. Then the elevator stopped. The door snapped open. Harold breathed a sigh of relief as they stepped out into the corridor.

The two walked silently, hand in hand, counting off the numbers on the rooms — 801, 802 and then, 803. The door was open. The bellhop was just coming out. Harold fumbled in his pocket for a tip. They stepped into the room and closed the door.

Myrna took off her coat and hung it in the closet. Harold waited, coat in hand, behind her. She turned around and looked up at him. Harold dropped his coat and hesitantly extended his arms. Myrna stepped forward to meet them. Harold felt her warm vibrant body against his. A flush of warmth engulfed him as he embraced her passionately. And then, as one possessed against his will, he shuffled her slowly, ever so slowly toward the bed.

Suddenly, a stern voice barked within his head. An electric-like pulse raked through his body causing him to recoil backwards across the room.

"Man of dust! Know you not that your body is a member of His Body — The Word of God Himself? Would you join Him to this woman who is not your wife? Know you not that he which is joined to a harlot is as one body? For two, saith He, shall be one flesh. The spirit indeed is willing but the flesh is weak. Begone from him thou foul servant of the dragon!"

Harold felt as if his body had suddenly changed to rubber. He stood in semi-shock, trembling violently from head to foot.

"What's the matter, Harold?" Myrna asked. "What's wrong? You, you look so strange. Your eyes, they, they —"

A strangely accented voice sounded within her head.

"Yes, child, look deep into Harold's eyes. Your eyes shall meet with the eyes of another — Melchizedek, King of Righteousness. King of Salem. The servant of the Elohim who serves the True One Who Is."

"Mel — Melchizedek? But, Harold, I, I feel so strange."

"Relax, deeper and deeper into a complete state of relaxation. You are going back now, back to Sebeka, Minnesota. You are twelve years old. You are on the farm. You are back on the farm. It is Sunday morning. What are you doing?"

"I'm, I'm in church with Mummy and Daddy."

"Good, good. Do you love them?"

"Yes."

"Do you love God?"

"Yes, I love Jesus and He loves me."

"Good, very good. Now, you may relive any happy memory you'd like. What did you like to do most? Think back, think back. What are you doing now?"

"I'm running through the field behind the barn with Tag."

"Who is Tag?"

"He's my doggy. I call him Tag 'cause I play Tag with him. I don't have a brother or sister to play with. I love Tag and he loves me. Sometimes we visit the Johnsons and I play with Norma. But, mostly I play with Tag 'cause we're always too busy working our farm."

"I see. Do Mummy and Daddy play with you?"

"Sometimes. Mummy plays dolls with me. We make dolls with corn husks and dried apples. She reads me Bible stories too. Mummy says that following the Lord is more important than anything else."

"How about Daddy? Does he play with you?"

"Daddy is mostly busy and too tired. But, sometimes he lets me sit on his tractor with him and lets me steer it. I think Daddy wishes I were a boy. Mummy had a little boy baby once but he died."

"I see. I'm sorry. What else does Daddy do with you for fun?"

"We feed the animals together. Sometimes he brings me fishing in the Redeye River or in Big Pine Lake."

"That's nice, little girl. Now, do your Mummy and Daddy

261

love each other?"

"Oh, yes!"

"How do you know?"

"They are always kind to each other. They kiss and they bring me on picnics in the fields and everything."

"Would you like it if another pretty lady came and loved your Daddy? Would you like it if she came and took Daddy away from Mummy?"

"No, my Daddy wouldn't let her! He loves my Mummy."

"Good. That's good. Now Myrna, I want you to do something very special for me. I want you to remain as a twelve year old. Yes. You are still twelve years old. But, you are also going to observe yourself growing up. Just like a movie. But, you will not recognize yourself at first. All right? We'll just pretend it's someone else that you're watching. You will begin now. In just a few minutes you will watch your whole life unfold. You may start now. Okay?"

"Okay. I see the movie. Oh, everything is moving so fast!"

"Yes, it is. But, you will retain everything in your memory, little girl. Am I understood?"

"Yes."

"Why are you crying?"

"That lady. She's doing naughty things. I don't like her."

"Yes, she is, isn't she? It's very sad. You will retain everything she does in your mind. Everything. Everything. Now, do you remember everything?"

"Yes, I can but it's very bad. I don't like her. She's a bad lady."

"I see. But, look, there's Daddy right now! Do you see him?"

"Yes."

"And here comes that lady. She's going to kiss Daddy and take him away from Mummy. Do you see this?"

"Yes. Please don't do that, lady. Please don't do that, Daddy!"

"Yes, Myrna. They are walking away together, away from your Mummy."

"No, no, please come back, Daddy!"

"Now, child, the picture has stopped moving. It's like Daddy and the lady are frozen in time. Right?"

"Yes. The movie has stopped. Daddy and that lady have stopped."

"Okay. Now, when I count three, that lady is going to turn around and you will recognize exactly who she is. And, she will recognize exactly who you are. Do you both understand?"

"Yes."

"Okay. Here we go. One, two, three."

"No-o-o-o-o! No-o-o-o-o!"

Myrna screamed hysterically. When the woman turned around to face her, she saw herself. She was the lady!

Melchizedek spoke again within her mind.

"You have had many men, Myrna. Harold Stanton was almost added to your list. Now you see yourself as you were and as you are. Do you like what you see?"

"No. I hate myself. I hate myself. I want to die."

"It is not your time to die, Myrna. But, that time will surely come. There is still time for you to live. To live, my child, to live. If you had a wish that could be granted, right now, this very moment — what would you wish?"

"I wish that I could be as I was back then, that my father would love and accept me. I'd like to have a second chance to start my life all over again."

"If you did, child, you would repeat all that you have done. Even as a child, as innocent as you looked just then, your ways were bent. The twin nature of Adapa runs rampant within the veins of man. But, you can start life over from this point of your vibrational journey. Until this very moment, you were helpless to do so. This was so even though the Spirit of the True One longed to resonate with your spirit."

"Why have I been helpless to do so?"

"My child, until one believes that one is sick, one has no desire to call upon the physician for healing. *The* Physician is very near. He only awaits your request to be healed. Harold will introduce you to Him when it is time. He too has seen, heard and experienced what we are witnessing together. But now, I have to tell you of mistakes that you have made concerning your father.

"You have misunderstood. Your father did love you for what you were and not for what he wished you to be. He did dearly long for a son. That cannot be denied. It troubled him that there was no one to carry on the family farm in his name. It hurt him very much to see you growing up without a mother. He felt helpless. There were chores to be done. You were asked to do them. One has to live. The times were hard. He wanted to touch you, hold you and comfort you. He wanted to see you grow up as a woman, not as a tom boy. He wanted you to become educated and find yourself a niche in society. But, he was afraid to let you go. You were all he had. Year by year you came to look more and more like your mother. Every time he looked at you it brought back bittersweet memories. He blamed himself for your mother's death. He felt that it had been his desire for a son that had taken your mother's life. He vowed that he never again would let himself love. He was afraid to chance experiencing such a loss again.

"It is difficult for me to tell you all this, fair one. But, it is best that you know the truth about yourself and about your father. First, let us consider yourself. Think hard, you who have studied and practiced the discipline of psychology. Can you not see that your inordinate desire for Harold stems from the fact that he reminds you of your father? They both share similar beliefs and morality. Subconsciously you felt that if Harold willingly succumbed to your seduction that you would gain his approval of the kind of life you have lived. He, and your father through him, would come down to your level. You thought that you would find your father's love and approval through the seduction of Harold Stanton.

"And, secondly, your father? You broke his heart when

264

you left without warning — without maintaining contact."

"But I thought he didn't love me. I did plan to write. But, I was afraid he'd come and try to take me back. I did plan to visit after I got established on my own. But, I felt that I could never look him in the face again. I was so ashamed at what I was doing."

"Ah, but you were not consciously ashamed for long, Myrna. Your conscience soon became hard, seared. Then, the thoughts of your parents and how you used to be, caused shame. Thus, you put your past out of your mind to avoid guilt. But, such thoughts still lay deep within your subconscious. They still affected the very warp and woof of your life. You sought to fill that human need: the need to love and be loved in return, with your affairs with men. You, like your father, were also frightened to commit yourself to any one person. Paulette sowed the seeds of the Dragon in barren soil that cried out to bear fruit. You chose to bear the fruits of darkness rather than the fruits of light. Now again a choice lies before you. The prayers of your mother follow you from the Netherland. Even now, your father prays daily for you."

"My father? He's still alive?"

"I have said enough. I shall now speak of other matters. You were quite correct that Harold Stanton has been programmed to go to Mount Rainier. But, he has been programmed in a way beyond your wildest imagination.

"Myrna Pederson. You will now cooperate fully with me through Harold Stanton. You may remember that Melchizedek lives within Harold. You will do exactly as we say. I know also that you plan to notify your superiors just as soon as Harold shows any inclination to visit Rainier. I know all about your plans to encourage him to do so. I know that VIGIL will follow and that Bluepaper plans to be at Rainier in force if alerted. We are leaving for Rainier this night. I will take care of your friends in the lobby. They will not interfere with us. When they do come, it will be too late. The signal will be sent. Now, you will share your feelings

265

with Harold. Then we leave."

Harold stood in front of Myrna. His back and shoulders still ached from being thrown against the wall by the unseen force. Myrna trembled from head to foot. A strange look emanated from her eyes. It was a look of painful recognition. She was not looking at Harold. She was staring at her own reflection in the mirror hanging on the wall beside him.

"I'm sorry, Myrna. I lost my head," Harold said apologetically.

Myrna did not seem to hear him. She kept staring at her reflection.

"It was me," she sobbed. "That woman with Daddy was me!"

Then she glanced around at Harold and grasped his hands.

"My father is still alive. I want to see him, tell him how wrong I've been before it's too late. Will he accept me, Harold? Does he hate me for what I've done to him? I feel so ashamed of myself. I, I feel so dirty, so unclean."

Harold pushed her hands gently away from him.

"Myrna. Come and sit down with me."

He went over to a desk and opened the drawer. "Ah, the Gideon Society always do their work well. Here's a Bible, Myrna. I want to read you a story about a father and a son. Perhaps you will remember it from your childhood days. It may not have meant much to you then. But, perhaps the good Lord will make it mean much to you now. Jesus' Parables are simple stories which illustrate eternal truths. His truths permeate the universe."

Harold turned to the Gospel of Saint Luke, Chapter 15. He began reading at verse 11. It was the story of the Prodigal Son. This Parable concerned a young man who had demanded his inheritance from his father and then left home. His voice quavered. Myrna wept unashamedly. The verses seemed to be re-telling the story of her own life. The

Bible verses resounded within her mind as she again relived the memories of her past.

wasted his substance with riotous living . . .
and he began to be in want . . .
he went and joined himself to a citizen . . .
and he sent him into his fields to feed the swine . . .
he filled his belly with the husks that the swine did eat . . .
and no man gave to him.

"That's me, Harold. That's me. Why couldn't I have seen it before like this?"

"Sh-h. Listen, Myrna. Listen. This son that Jesus talks about had to learn his lesson the hard way, just as you have."

And when he came to himself, he said, 'How many hired servants of my father's have bread enough and to spare, and I perish with hunger! I will arise and go to my father, and will say to him, "Father, I have sinned against heaven, and before thee, and am no more worthy to be called thy son. .

"I'm not worthy, Harold. I want to go to him and ask forgiveness. But, how can I? Bluepaper owns me. Even if I could find him and go to him, I'm afraid that he would reject me."

"Myrna. Note that the son in Jesus' story *first* acknowledged that he had sinned against heaven before he dealt with the sin against his father. You, too, must ask forgiveness from your Father in Heaven. Only then will he give you the motivation and strength to ask your earthly father's forgiveness."

"But I've destroyed the lives of scores of men and women. I've been responsible for broken homes. I've cheated, I've lied, I've caused innocent people to be deprogrammed and annihilated. I'm beyond God's forgiveness. What could I possibly do to undo my past?"

"True forgiveness isn't bought by man, Myrna. It matters not whether it be from heaven or from earth. Forgiveness is a gift. But, one must first realize a need before one asks for this gift in faith. You have taken this first step. You have sincerely acknowledged your need. The Prodigal Son also realized his need. Listen to what Jesus says about the father's reaction to his son's confession of guilt and unworthiness.

But. when he was yet a great way off, his father saw him, and had compassion, and ran, and fell on his neck and kissed him.

"You see in these next verses that even as the son was protesting how unworthy he was, the father was rejoicing and celebrating his return home to him.

For this my son was dead, and is alive again; He was lost and is found.

"Myrna. Our Heavenly Father will welcome you the same way, into His family, if you but ask His forgiveness."

"I would like to, Harold, but how, what do I do?"

"Let's pray together, Myrna. I'll lead and you follow."

It wasn't until after eleven o'clock that Myrna and Harold left their hotel room. They avoided the elevator and went down a stairwell that led to the far end of the downstairs lobby.

"Myrna, stay here. I'll be back in a few minutes," he whispered.

Harold glanced into the lobby. A man stood chatting with the desk clerk. Another dozed in a chair. Harold walked slowly into the lobby. The man leaning on the desk whipped out some kind of credentials and showed them to the clerk. Then he strode quickly over to the fellow in the chair.

"Jeb! Wake up," he whispered. "I think our pigeon is flying the coop."

The sleeping man opened his eyes and jumped to his feet. He cast a surprised look at Harold.

"What? But Myrna hasn't signaled. I wonder if she's okay?"

Harold walked right up to them. His eyes focused first upon one and then upon the other.

"Good evening, gentlemen," Melchizedek's voice sounded within their heads. "Are you the full complement of the VIGIL team or are there others?"

The eyes of both men became glassy. They stared blankly into nothingness. Then Jeb began to speak, slowly and deliberately.

"No. There are two others here in room 807, just down the corridor from your room."

"What are they doing there?"

"They're sleeping, while we watch out for you. They're supposed to relieve us at six o'clock."

"Do you have monitoring devices?"

"Yes."

"Do your sleeping friends have such devices?"

"No, they'll be using ours."

"Oh yes. Good. What do they monitor?"

"The location of your car."

"How do they work?"

"When your car is started, a signal is transmitted from your black box. It activates our monitors."

"What if the black box is destroyed or disconnected?"

"It sends an alarm signal automatically."

"Who else has these monitors?"

"The Blackbird crew."

"Are they monitoring now?"

"No, they won't be airborne until eight o'clock unless we contact them."

"What is the range of the car's transmitter?"

"50 to 100 miles depending on terrain and atmospheric conditions."

"Please show me your monitors?"

"Yes, sir."

"Now, remove their batteries and hand them to me. That's it. Thank you very much. Now, both of you gentlemen deserve a good rest. You've been working hard. Here are my keys to room 803. Take them. Go to this room and sleep. Do you understand? Sleep."

"Yes, we understand."

"Goodnight, gentlemen. Pleasant dreams and thank you

so much again for your help."

Harold walked briskly over to a pay phone and placed a telephone call before hurrying back to Myrna. Soon they were driving North along route 99 heading into Washington State and Mount Rainier National Park.

"Harold. I don't want to leave you up there all alone. I just can't."

"I'll be all right, Myrna. I'm more concerned about you. Now listen. I phoned Helen's aunt in Yakima. I told her I was in the State on a confidential mission. Thank goodness she was never notified of my supposed suicide. I told her that Helen wasn't with me but explained that a fellow-worker needed help. Give her this note. Her address is on the back. I'll give you all the cash Bluepaper gave me. Don't use their credit card, they'll put a trace on it. Aunty was quite excited over the prospects of helping a *secret agent*! She'll help you financially and get you to a railroad station. I'm sure VIGIL will be watching the airports. Take trains to Minnesota and then rent a car or take a taxi to your Dad's farm. Do you think you'll find him, Myrna?"

"I hope so. I pray so. Your Melchizedek knows that he's still alive. How he knows this and how he exists within you, I won't even try to understand. All I know is that after our prayers together last night, I feel clean, fresh and more alive than I ever have before. It's like being born all over again!"

It was still very dark when Harold passed the Nisqually Entrance at the Ranger Station. He edged the car up the mountain road guided by the inner voice of Melchizedek. The road curved back and forth like a writhing snake. Then he stopped the car where Melchizedek had been forced off the road by the helicopter.

Dawn was not far away. Harold reached into the glove compartment and took out a flashlight.

"Well, Myrna, this is where we part company."

"But how do you know where to go?"

"I don't but Melchizedek does. Do you have his, ah,

musical instrument?"

"Yes. It's right here in my handbag."

Myrna handed Harold the flute-like instrument that VIGIL had found on the person of Ben-Sorek.

"Thanks. He whispers that I'll need it. Well, I'm absolutely worthless when it comes to saying goodbyes."

"So am I, Harold. There's so much more that I want to say. Some of it would hurt you deeply. All I can ask is your forgiveness for any harm I've caused you or Helen. I can never thank you enough for helping me find God and myself again. Several days ago, I would never have believed this could have happened to me.

"They'll catch us sooner or later. All I want now is to be with my father for awhile. Whether or not I'll keep running after that, I don't know. Please pray for me."

"And you for me, Myrna. VIGIL will be waiting for me when I return from where Melchizedek is leading me. I intend to turn myself in. I must see Helen and Father Pat once more. Then who knows what will happen?"

Myrna threw her arms about him and hugged him.

"I love you as a brother, Harold," she said, fighting back the tears.

Harold slowly removed her arms from around him. They stared at each other for one long moment before he turned and started his trek up the muddy road. He could feel her eyes upon him but he dared not look back. A lump formed in his throat as he heard the car start and move away. He strained to hear its sound as it finally faded away into the distance. Then there was silence.

Harold stuck the flashlight in his pocket. He dared not use it except for an emergency. The waning gibbous moon lit his way as he passed a sign. Curious, he shielded the flashlight and used its subdued light to read it. The sign pointed to a memorial stone just off the road. Harold felt a cold chill as he walked up to the barred rock and read a plaque attached to it. It was a monument erected in memory of the Marines who died in the C46 crash in 1947. Again his mind went back to the two campers who had discovered the disc-shaped craft of the Watchers.

It was chilly. Patches of snow still lingered along the way. After hiking for about a half hour, Harold sat down on a rock to rest. Soon it would be light and the *Blackbirds* would be sweeping the mountain side for him. He took out the small flute-like pipe and blew on it. No sound came out. But, Melchizedek wanted him to blow upon it, so he did periodically, and waited.

Then came a weird creepy feeling as if he were being watched. He glanced about but neither saw nor heard a thing. A strange smell began to fill the air. It became stronger. Harold gagged. What was it? It smelled like rotting flesh. Then he felt two distinct, but ever so light, pressure points on the back of his head. A feeling of sheer terror fell upon him. He sensed someone directly behind him. Quickly he slid off the rock and ran forward. Wheeling about he gasped in horror. Two pairs of red luminescent eyes gazed at him like four glowing coals. The two huge hairy creatures leaped over the rock. One of them extended its long arms toward him. From within, Melchizedek told Harold not to be afraid.

"Do not fear, my friend. The geekahs will not harm you. They have come to take us. I've established mental contact with them. All is well."

Melchizedek's voice faded to nothing. Harold fell in a near faint from the sheer sight of the awesome creatures. He felt himself being gently picked up. The last thing he remembered was the smelly creature running with him. Then all was blackness.

A faint purple glow met Harold's eyes as they blinked open. He found himself lying flat upon his back. All attempts at movement was futile. His body seemed to be partially encased in a translucent slab of rubber-like material. Only his face and upper torso were exposed. It was as if he had been lowered into an elongated box filled with a transparent flexible substance which had hardened about

"Do not fear, my friend. The geekahs will not harm
you."

his body. Above him hung what appeared to be a plexiglass cover. He hoped that it would not be lowered over him.

All movement was restricted except for his eyes. A faint pungent smell like ozone filled the air. Periodically, weird-musical-like notes could be heard. They sounded like someone striking a muffled xylophone. Harold rolled his eyes about. He tried to make out where he was as they became more accustomed to the dim lighting. He seemed to be in a smooth hemispherical chamber carved out of smooth gray rock. It looked like melted lava that had solidified. The purple glow emanated from a band of crystals that girded the room about midway off the floor. He could just barely see what looked like identical rectangular slabs and covers to either side of him.

"Ah, you have revived, my friend," whispered Melchizedek. "Do not fear. Those covers over the primary and back-up hibernation systems are for me, not you. You are perfectly safe. Just relax. Close your eyes again. We shall soon send the signal. But, first, son of light, I must speak to you. You will listen, remember and obey.

"After the signal is sent, the Watchers will remove my body from Phoenix Base 3. My servants shall find their way there through our memories. My form will be brought here. It shall be placed beside your body for *defusion*. Then, it will be farewell for us, son of Alethia. I shall always be grateful for your assistance. You have served your purpose well."

"What shall happen to me after the signal is sent?"

"You shall be translated and await the coming of the Word with your mother Alethia in the Netherland. Your purpose has been fulfilled."

"But Helen. I must get back to my Helen!"

"How, my friend? You are now reaching the end of this vibrational state of being. All has been planned. You agreed to serve the Elohim."

"Please let me see Helen once more! Please! I'm sure that Bluepaper will be outside scouring this whole mountain for Myrna and me. If you let them find me, they'll be sure to return me to base for questionning. There is at least a good chance that I shall see Helen and perhaps her Dad and Father Pat."

"Harold. You force me to say this. I have sad news for you. When we left, both Helen and her father were scheduled for deprogramming."

"What? Why didn't you —"

"Cease talking, my friend. You will relax and accept these truths without emotional harm. Let me continue. The deprogramming probably has already taken place. And Father Pat? He has been translated. But, not before helping General Thurman to return to the Kingdom of God. You also would be deprogrammed upon your return. You would not recognize Helen. She would not recognize you. Believe me. It would be best for you to await Helen in the Netherland.

"But, how do you know all of this?"

"Be calm, Harold. Accept these truths bravely. I have known them since first studying the thoughts within the mind of Doctor Slater. Myrna sought several times to tell you. Each time, I prevented her. In her own mind she thinks that you do know and that you have forgiven her part in it. It was best for both of you under the circumstances."

"But, do you know for a fact that Helen's deprogramming has already taken place?"

"No, I am not able to know this."

"Then grant me at least the chance that I might see her once again."

"Harold, you make it difficult for me. I feel obligated. I will grant you two days. It will be very trying for you but it shall be done. In exactly forty-eight hours from this time, when the sun rises at your latitude, your brain will trigger the bio-thermal translation of your body.

"Goodbye, my brother. We shall meet again, I shall make a point of it. Now, keep your eyes closed. Relax. It is time to send the *Signal*. It will be as a tiny spark within this island of stars. But, behold how great a forest a tiny spark can set ablaze."

A low throbbing sound filled the room. Harold closed his eyes. The ring of crystals glowed brighter and brighter until Harold could see its outline even through closed eyelids. The xylophone-like notes grew louder and more frequent. Then all the tones merged into one overpowering note. Harold winced in pain. The blazing purple ring pulsated faster and faster in perfect resonance with the deep throbbing sound. Great hoops of purplescent light leaped upward from the crystalline ring. Harold opened his mouth and screamed in pain and terror.

Then, everything faded away as he lapsed into the merciful realm of unconsciousness. The *Signal* was on its way. The offspring of Alethia had fulfilled the will of the True One Who Is.

The ring of crystals glowed brighter and brighter.

Chapter Twenty

Abduction

"Number One. Number One. This is Central. Priority One messages ready to transmit. Please initiate secure reception terminal and read. Number One. Number One. This is —"

The cryptic message resounded throughout the corridors and Sectors of Phoenix Base 3. Colonel Milkowski rushed from the VIGIL detention area to his quarters and activated his console. A message flashed onto the video screen.

Message #1
At 0700 hours, all Beta Detector Stations recorded a sustained signal burst of immeasurable strength for a duration of 72 seconds. Signal's epicenter triangulated to current Alert Area 11 — Rainier. Damage to Western Beta Sites extensive. Instrumentation at Deception Beta Site 30 totally disrupted. No alien craft detected. Source of signal unknown. All alert teams now in place at Alert Area 11 — Rainier. Teams reported ground tremors during reception of unknown Beta Signal. Synchronism of two events indicate direct connection. Special U.S. Defenses have been placed on standby alert. Disruption of Beta Detection Network may be alien preparatory step prior to invasion.

Message #2
Agents MEDIC-5 and BETA-27 still missing. All State Alert for their apprehension being coordinated.

Colonel Milkowski buried his head in his hands. What was happening? Where in hell did they go and why? Myrna had never failed Bluepaper. Had they underestimated Harold? And what did that signal mean? Every Beta Detection Station in the world, even the orbiters, had been damaged or jolted by its incredible strength. Again the alert buzzer sounded on his console.

"Damn that thing! What now?"

Number 1. Number 1. Base 3 Beta Detector is registering strong localized signal. Current estimate is false signal due to damaged circuitry. Radar and NORAD backup show no current target in area. Target could be under radar umbrella. Brief return was noted over Army's Yuma Proving Ground. Estimate now is that radar target was spurious. Will keep you appraised.

Colonel Milkowski stared at the console. Since when had VIGIL ever bothered to send him priority messages on unconfirmed radar targets? The apprehension in the operator's voice was indicative of the rising tension that could be felt throughout Base 3.

Outside of Base 3, the stars were appearing in the nighttime sky. The first sign of something unusual was a string of bright red pulsating lights floating across Route 8. They appeared to emanate from the wastelands of the U.S. Army's Yuma Proving Ground. Witnesses included not only passing motorists but also Sergeant Jake McAllister, Arizona State Police.

Crouching behind the cruiser, the trooper gaped at a disc-shaped object floating toward the road. A central glass-like dome reflected red lights flickering around its rim. Underneath it, sand and small stones rose and fell rhythmatically as if attracted by its passage overhead. Abruptly the cruiser's engine quit. Its beacon and headlights dimmed to nothing. A piercing howling sound erupted from its radio and ceased. Sergeant McAllister tried to draw his weapon but he found himself paralyzed from head to foot. Everything became deathly silent except for the swishing sound of rising and falling sand which followed in the object's wake.

Back at Base 3, messages were still pouring in to Colonel Milkowski.

Number 1. Number 1. Our Beta detector is acting up again.

"VIGIL, haven't you guys got better things to do than

report equipment malfunctions to me?" the Colonel interrupted angrily. "Until we install new equipment, that detector of yours is worthless."

Begging your pardon, sir, but the operator has had the equipment checked out by maintenance. They believe its a real signal. It's close by and it coincides with —

"Coincides with what? I've received no confirmed radar reports!"

It coincides with a *visual*, sir. Operator 6 who monitors NORAD's UFO Conference Loop reports that an Arizona State Trooper saw a flying object near Yuma Proving Grounds and the Luke Air Force Range. That's also where the radar target was, sir. If our base is near these locations, we have a UFO right in our backyard.

"It's not your job to speculate about Base 3's whereabouts! Those people probably saw an airplane or a meteor. But, keep me posted if —"

Suddenly a loud buzzing sound filled the Colonel's quarters. The lights blinked sporadically. Then, all of Base 3 was plunged into darkness. Back-up diesel generators kicked in. The lights blinked on momentarily before dimming to a low glow.

Colonel Milkowski's fingers played nimbly over the input keys on his console. He shouted into the video-com.

"Central Power. Central Power. This is Number 1. Status report please. What in hell is going on?"

This is POWER-11 sir. We don't know. All Outside power and diesel back-up has failed. Base 3 is now on emergency standby power. We've cut all lights to low illumination status to relieve the power load.

"What's the status of the Lithium battery modules?"

They're all up sir. They should keep us going until we get a fix.

"Keep me appraised, POWER-11."

Colonel Milkowski then directed a call to VIGIL-2.

"VIGIL-2, VIGIL-2, this is Number 1. Security status please."

Number 1, this is VIGIL-2. Everything seems to be fine. Microwave security apparatus is functioning normally. No security alarms, except, except —

"Except what, damn it?"

Not to worry, Number 1. Probably some tripped circuit breakers at Cybernetics Plant 2. It has no power. CYBER-2 has gone to investigate.

"CYBER-2? Ah yes, Vahan Terzian, our friendly undertaker. He must be having a fit," he thought. "The AI's in that Plant are the only ones we haven't cut up."

Doctor Terzian was upset. He burst breathlessly into Plant 2, flashlight in hand.

"Hum-m, none of the breakers have tripped. This is strange. Whatever is preventing power input here?" he muttered to himself.

As if in answer, a series of soft clicks sounded behind him. Whipping around he saw the glow from two pilot lamps which had blinked on above the number 4 and 5 input keys. He gasped in sheer unbelief. The sound was coming from both sets of keys which were being depressed as if by invisible hands!

Terrified, the little old man backed against the steel wall behind him. Two loud sharp clicks and a humming sound emanated from the adjoining room. The sound was all too familiar to him. The two metal containers were moving out into the room on their rails from their crypt-like storage areas. Again the Doctor flashed his light upon the console. Incredulously he watched the duplex set of controls initiate the openings of the lids on the number 4 and 5 containers. A loud hissing sounded from the other room.

"I, I must get out of here. I cannot believe what is happening," he muttered. "I must make myself go through there. It's the only way out."

The squat little man edged away from the wall and stepped cautiously into the dark room ahead.

"Ah-h-h-h-h!"

Doctor Terzian screamed in terror as the flashlight beam fell upon the backs of the two AI's They were standing. No! They were *floating* above the black matting on either side of the coffin-like boxes. Then smoothly, ever so smoothly like two skaters pirouetting in unison, the little humanoids turned around to face him. The last thing CYBER-2 remembered was two sets of glowing Cheshire cat eyes staring at him out of the pitch blackness. He slumped to the floor in a dead faint.

In the meantime, the new Number 1 was receiving still another status report. The grim face of VIGIL-2 appeared on the video-screen.

Number 1, I'm over at Central. Our monitors show unauthorized traffic moving along the outer corridors.

"Well, buzz them and go get them. Surely I don't have to tell you how to run your business!"

We can't buzz them if we don't know their designators.

"But surely, whoever they are, they're trapped if all the Sector hatches are sealed."

They may be sealed, sir, but somehow they are passing through them as if nothing was in their path. They've just gone through the Sector 5 basement and are heading for Sector 6. They can't be ours. All our personnel are accounted for. They don't respond to the identification transponder. We can't buzz them unless they have *companions*. They must be Outsiders!

"That's impossible," Number 1 interrupted. "No Outsiders can get in here without detection. Have you picked them up on any of the corridor TV monitors?"

No. The operators tell me the corridors are too dark. All lights have been reduced to low illumination status. We can't risk an overload. It would put the whole Base down.

"Well, you're in charge of Security, VIGIL-2. What do you propose we do next?"

Request permission to arm a six-man strike team with conventional arms to apprehend the intruders.

"Conventional arms? Your people will kill themselves if they start firing guns in here. The bullets will ricochet all over the place. But damn it, we've no other choice, have we? Permission is granted. Extreme caution must be exercised. This place was never intended to be protected with firearms. That's one reason we have *companions!*"

Number 1? The unauthorized traffice has just entered your Sector. They appear to be moving up the elevator shaft. They have just passed your floor, ah, wait one — What?

"What's the matter VIGIL-2? Speak up!"

Number 1. Our monitors tell me that the elevator is inactive and yet our sensors show them moving up the shaft. They, they're in the Penthouse, just above your quarters.

"The Penthouse? Look, get that strike team over pronto. Keep everyone except Central personnel restricted to quarters. I'm arming myself and going up there."

Number 1. Wait for us. Don't go up there without backup. Number 1? Number 1!

The Colonel did not reply. He ran over to his desk, snatched a loaded .45 automatic from a drawer and rushed to the elevator.

Up in Penthouse, Catherine sat alone in the dimly lit room watching the barely breathing body of Melchizedek. She felt nervous and frightened. She wondered why the lights had gone out and then came back on so dimly. Why had everyone been restricted to quarters? She wished that Doctor Slater would come up and tell her what was going on. Then, two shadows fell upon the floor in front of her. Glancing around, she saw the two AI's standing at the window. She tried to scream but couldn't. A tingling sensation gripped her body. She couldn't move. A mechanical-like voice sounded in her head.

283

"Do not fear, child. We mean no harm to you. We have come for *him*."

Then Catherine observed the impossible. The creatures passed through the heavy plate glass as if it were non-existent! It was as if each had somehow disappeared on one side of the glass and re-appeared on the other side.

Both of the little entities floated smoothly across the room and positioned themselves on either side of Melchizedek's body. A brief humming sound emanated from above. The metal ceiling vibrated and the metal doors moved slowly back to reveal the skylight illuminated by a bright pulsating orange light. And then it happened.

The skylight structure lifted off its supports. Pieces of metal and bolts fell to the floor. The night air swept into the room filling Catherine's nostrils with scents long forgotten.

Steve Milkowski strode out of the elevator. With cocked weapon in hand, he headed for the Penthouse door. Glancing cautiously through the window he stopped, spellbound by what he saw.

A grayish cloud-like substance descended slowly and deliberately through the opening in the Penthouse roof. He watched in astonishment. It spread out like a shroud and engulfed Melchizedek and the two AI's. Then, without any hesitation, it abruptly reversed its course and ascended upwards out of the opening. The Colonel blinked his eyes in amazement and utter disbelief. The AI's were no longer there and neither was Bluepaper's prize captive. The bed was empty.

A voice over the intercom jolted him back to his senses.

Number One. Number One. This is Central. Outside Command demands that you report immediately to your quarters. An Exclusive Priority 1 message has been received from Outside awaiting your personal acknowledgement at once. Decoding necessary.

Number One. Number One. This is —

The Colonel took one more glance into the room, started

"Do not fear. . .we have come for *him*."

forward, and then turned back to the elevator just as it was opening. The six-man VIGIL strike team poured into the corridor. Colonel Milkowski shouted orders to them as he pushed his way into the elevator.

"We're too late. No time to explain. Bring the Nurse to debriefing. Get maintenance to cover that opening. One of you notify VIGIL-2 that the prisoner has been abducted."

Outside, a disc-shaped craft accelerated straight up and away from the lighted shaft glowing faintly below. Then it executed a right-angle change in course. It streaked over the Mohawk Mountains on a heading of North North West. Several minutes later, members of the VIGIL team searching for Harold and Myrna remarked upon the lone gray cloud. Puzzled, they watched it descend slowly in the moonlit sky over Mount Rainier.

NORAD notified McChord Air Force Base of the UFO that streaked between Southwest Arizona and Washington State. But, the aliens had accomplished their mission. Interceptors dispatched from McChord Air Force Base found an empty sky.

During the early morning hours, Melchizedek lay beside Harold within one of the adjoining form-fitting translucent enclosures. By daybreak, the bizarre defusion process was completed. The King of Salem was once more joined to his own body. His last rest period had begun. The faithful servant of the Elohim, the repository of mankind, had begun his wait for the return of the Word of the True One Who Is.

Chapter Twenty-One

Translation

Colonel Milkowski removed the encoded message from its steel container and switched his console to *secure mode*. He typed out the encrypted message and initiated the decoding sequence. A shiver coursed through him as he read the message being spelled out on the glowing screen. His worst fears had been realized.

ATTENTION NUMBER 1

YOU ARE RELIEVED FROM COMMAND
NO ONE IS TO KNOW THIS
CALL BOGUS EMERGENCY COUNCIL MEETING 0700
INITIATE PERSONAL EVACUATION PLAN

FOR INSTRUCTIONS: INPUT 1A632 SECURE MODE ON GENERAL THURMAN'S COMMUNICATIONS CONSOLE

DO NOT RECALL OUTSIDE PERSONNEL
VIGIL WILL BE REPLACED AT ALERT AREA 11/RAINIER
YOUR RENDEZVOUS ARRANGED AT EDWARDS AFB

FAILURE TO COMPLY NEGATES PERSONAL SURVIVAL

The Colonel stared unbelievingly as if the message were the epitaph on his own tombstone. He deleted the video message and burned the coded input. Then he instructed Central to put out a call to all Number 1 levels to report to the Council Room for an emergency meeting at 0700 the following morning. Timely attendance was mandatory. Next, he rushed to General Thurman's quarters, broke the seal on the entry way and entered the vacant room.

Trembling, he activated the computer terminal in *secure mode*. His fingers punched out the five digit code on the input keys. Simultaneously, several sharp explosive reports erupted from the console. He covered his face and jumped backwards.

A panel fell off its explosive rivets and hit the floor. Cautiously, Colonel Milkowski glanced inside the exposed compartment. A message engraved upon a copper plate below seven switches read:

ACTIVATE SWITCHES ONE AT A TIME FROM LEFT TO RIGHT AT EXACT TIME OF COUNCIL MEETING USE ENCLOSED MASTER KEY TUBE FOR IMMEDIATE PERSONAL EVACUATION THROUGH SECTOR 5 EXIT

Steve Milkowski staggered into General Thurman's bedroom in a daze. He set the bedside alarm clock and lay down in a cold sweat. Sleep would not come. He dared not sleep. He thought of the men and women at Base 3. They had given the best years of their life to Bluepaper. Why did they have to go like this?

All night long he glanced at the clock. As morning arrived, he felt sick and nauseated. At 0700 he hesitated and then made himself push down each toggle switch, one at a time, as instructed.

Instantly throughout Phoenix Base 3, all doors and hatches were automatically sealed. The Base's intricate communications system went dead. Heavy steel coverings snapped tightly over all ventilation shafts leading up to the Outside. A concealed timing mechanism began a deadly countdown. The Colonel grabbed the master key tube and began his lonely flight from Base 3.

In the meantime, Harold opened his eyes just in time to see a tall dark hairy form disappearing into heavy underbrush beside the road. He was alone. Dawn was breaking. His position was somewhere below the Marine Memorial. He started down the road. Below him he could see two vans parked in a clearing off the road. An armed man leaned against one of the vehicles. When he saw Harold approaching he shouted. About a dozen men stumbled out of the vans and rushed him. Two held him securely while another frisked him. Harold did not resist. He breathed a sigh of relief when he recognized VIGIL-1 walking toward them.

"All right, Stanton, where in the hell have you been and where's Myrna?"

"I've nothing to say until you take me back to Base 3. I must see my wife. I'll only talk to Colonel Milkowski unless General Thurman is back. You can release me. I'll offer no resistance."

"The Colonel is not at Base 3. Outside Command has issued orders for you and Myrna to rendezvous with him at Edwards Air Force Base as soon as possible."

"But my wife, I've got to see her!"

"Look, Stanton, I've got my orders. Take your problems to the Colonel. He'll probably take you back to Base 3 from Edwards."

"Okay, let's go. Who's bringing me?"

"I can't take you anywhere. All VIGIL personnel have been ordered to report to McChord Air Force Base for immediate air ferry back to Base 3. Some other agency is taking over here. Do you see that man coming out of the van? His name's Craig, Roy Craig. Roy was part of the Condell operation. His immediate assignment is to get you to Edwards. He won't wait around for Myrna to be found. She'll be brought later."

Back at Base 3, Colonel Milkowski finally reached the end of the tunnel to the Outside. His heart was pounding as he placed the master key in a bypass slot which overrode the security system. But, as he stepped out into the fresh air, two strong arms grabbed him. He felt a sharp prick in his arm.

"What the hell! Let go of me. I'm, I'm —"

His own voice seemed distant, so far away. His head spun dizzily; then his body relaxed as it slumped into the arms of his captors. When he awoke, he found himself lying on a cot. He was still dizzy and felt sick to his stomach.

"Give him a drink of water," a voice snapped.

"Where am I? Who the devil are you?" the Colonel demanded as he raised himself up on one arm and stared at the short stout man in a trenchcoat.

"You, my friend are at Edwards Air Force Base. Allow me to introduce myself," the man said as he removed his hat revealing a shiny bald head.

"I'm General Webster, Director of the *Board* for Outside Command. I knew your General Thurman well. Many a time we've met in this same room. So, you were to be his replacement? Pity. It didn't last long, did it?"

"Why did you drug me? I would've come with your men willingly."

"We didn't want to take any chances, Colonel. Your final task for us must have been quite trying. We knew you'd save your own skin. But, we didn't know what your emotional temperament might be when you burst out of that hell hole. That was one operation none of us wanted to automate: it would've been too risky."

"The Base, Base 3. Has anything happened yet?"

"Ah, yes. The people residing in Southwestern Arizona were quite alarmed by the, ah, earthquake. Yes, sorry to say, Base 3 is no more. Everyone was killed instantly. The Thermite devices have melted everything. It's all over."

"But why? All those people, that talent, our research."

"Why? You have the audacity to ask me why? The Vatican is at our throats because of the leaks by your Priest. He's told them enough to completely disrupt our operations if the Vatican should go public. The swine even guessed the location of Base 3. We had no choice. No one's about to examine a radiocative rubble. The evidence is gone. But, the data, your research is not lost. Everything you accomplished was always duplicated in the computer banks at Alternate Base 3. It is most regrettable that Alternate Base 3 was not a direct part of Project *Enigma*. Perhaps we would still have the prisoner.

"Now, after you've had a chance to recuperate from the drug, we have an assignment for you this afternoon, Colonel. Harold Stanton was brought here directly from Mount Rainier National Park."

"So, Myrna was right after all. He did go to Rainier. I wonder what he found. Where is Myrna? She deserves to be commended for her insight into this matter."

"She might be commended if we knew where she went. It appears that neither Myrna nor the Bluepaper car are at Rainier. We've no idea what happened. Your Mr. Stanton refuses to say anything to anyone except to you or General Thurman, who, of course is no more.

"Now, Stanton thinks you're going to be taking him back to Base 3. The man wants desperately to see his wife. This is where you come in, Colonel. He'll be brought to you for debriefing after lunch. You're to tell him that he'll never see his wife again unless he tells you exactly what happened at Rainier. And, you must find out where the woman has gone.

"We trust that you'll not fail us, Colonel Milkowski. Your own well being depends upon it. Do we understand each other? I'm sure we do. Good day. I'll leave Larry here to help you with whatever you need. You'd better get spruced up. You look a wreck."

Harold himself sat alone in another room on base. He had been left alone. An air policeman was posted outside the locked door. His eyes fell upon a small transistor radio. He picked it up and turned it on low. Sitting down, he held the radio to his ear. The music was beautiful. He knew that in less than 48 hours it would be all over for him here. Suddenly, a news break interrupted the music. Harold only half-listened. What difference did it all make now? But then something that was said shocked him back to reality.

The Atomic Energy Commission attributed the sharp quake that rocked Southwestern Arizona this morning to a test of a small nuclear device. An authority hinted of a secret underground test site located deep within the Crater Mountain Chain on what is known officially as the Luke Air Force Test Range. Citizens in the area were assured that all radiation was contained within the site.

And, from Washington State we still have no word from the Air Force on the cause of the plane crash. The incident occurred shortly after take-off from McChord Air Force Base this morning. There were no survivors. Ground witnesses reported that the aircraft seemed to explode before plunging to the earth in flames.

Air Force Information Officers would only comment that the aircraft was enroute to Luke Air Force Base in Arizona. Names of the victims are being withheld pending notification of next of kin. And now, after this announcement, Jim Carey will be bringing the very latest weather information.

Harold turned off the radio. A strange uneasiness came over him. It was the same sinking feeling he'd experienced when receiving psychic impressions during experiments with Beta in Maryland. His keen intuition told him that the explosion in Arizona was related to Phoenix Base 3. And, the airplane crash? He instantly remembered what VIGIL-1 had mentioned to him. The VIGIL search crew were to fly back to Base 3 from McChord that very morning. Was this the same aircraft? Had they all been killed? What happened at Base 3? Harold decided that he'd ask Colonel Milkowski about these things just as soon as he saw him. Then, something within his mind instantly rejected his course of action. No, perhaps he could use these psychic impressions to find out more from the Colonel. He would pretend to know more than he really did.

"Well, Good afternoon, Harold!" Colonel Milkowski rose from a chair and shook Harold's hand as he entered the room.

"Steve Milkowski! Am I glad to see you. Why are we meeting here? Why aren't you at the base?"

Harold immediately sensed the evasive mannerism of the Colonel as he answered. He looked away from Harold's eyes.

"Ah, I was on my way to join VIGIL at Rainier when

word came to me that they'd found you. So, to save time, Outside Command ordered me to stay here to interrogate you."

"I see. So everything's okay at Base 3? Helen is well?"

"Oh yes, she's looking forward to seeing you soon. But, they tell me that unless you help them find Myrna, you'll be kept from Helen. They've even threatened to do her bodily harm if you persist in your silence. I assume that you were just waiting until you could tell me what happened. I hope that I'm correct."

Harold did not answer. He kept looking the Colonel straight in his eyes.

"Has the prisoner awakened yet, Steve?"

"No, not yet. You and Joseph will just have to do the best you can with what you've got until he does. We, ah, — Harold, why are you looking at me like that?"

"You, sir, are a blasted liar!"

"What do you mean by that? I don't know what you're talking about."

Harold thought quickly about what he had heard on the radio and what Melchizedek had told him. He decided to attempt a bluff. Perhaps the Colonel would let something slip out.

"I said, 'you, sir are a blasted liar.' I've been told that the prisoner had escaped."

"But, but, they said you didn't know, I mean —"

"You mean what? I've been told a lot. You, sir, are being played for a fool. How could Helen be looking forward to seeing me? She's been deprogrammed. And now, the explosion at Base 3!"

"You, you know what happened to Base 3?"

"Yes, and I also know about the deaths of your VIGIL team that was sent to Rainier."

"VIGIL? What do you mean, Harold?"

"They were all killed in a plane crash this morning, as if you didn't know."

Suddenly, the door burst open. General Webster entered

with several men.

"This has gone quite far enough," he shouted. "Colonel, Who told this man about the compromise?"

"I'd like to ask *you* a question, General," the Colonel replied angrily. "I understand from Harold here that you finished my work at Base 3 by arranging VIGIL-1 and his men to die in a plane crash."

"I don't know how he knows this. But, yes, you are right. It was necessary that *everyone* directly associated with Base 3 be annihilated."

Harold bit his lip. Had he heard right? He fought back the tears and listened anxiously to the ensuing conversation between the Colonel and General Webster.

"What about me, General? When I finish with Mr. Stanton here, I suppose that I'd then be the last to die, right?"

The General did not answer. He turned to Harold with the most malevolent look that Harold had ever seen.

"All right, Stanton. I don't know how you found out these things but I *will* find out. You can be sure about that. We will also find out what you know about the girl. Our ways are not pleasant except, perhaps, to the sadistic-minded men who will be used to persuade you. We had hoped to use your wife's safety as a more civilized method of persuasion. But, since you somehow found out about her decease, we'll now be forced to use other methods."

Harold forced himself not to let on that Helen's death was a shock to him. He had found out more than he had bargained for. Then, quite unexpectedly, a deep feeling of peace and well-being enveloped him. There must be a reason why God had allowed him to come here at this time.

"Ah, tears already, Stanton? Why, we haven't even begun. Now, one more chance. What do you have to say for yourself? Answer me!"

"No, General, you answer me. You see, I've been programmed to say something very special. But, it'll have to wait until about two hours before sunrise. Don't ask me to

294

explain. I've been involved in incredible things. Just believe me and do as I request. I'll talk to you tomorrow morning, two hours before sunrise."

"Stanton, are you all there? I've no time for such nonsense. I —"

"You'd better listen to him, General," Colonel Milkowski interrupted. "You know as well as I do that he was hypnotically programmed by the *prisoner* to do something at Rainier. Now it appears as if he has been programmed to tell us something at this special time. Why not give him the benefit of a doubt?"

The General looked wonderingly at Harold.

"All right. We'll play it your way. I'm fully acquainted with your dossier. You're a very ethical man. I'll trust you. Tomorrow morning we shall meet again. Perhaps you really have an important message for us. I think it'll be worthwhile to fly other members of the Outside Board here to listen. You will now come with me. And you, Colonel? You will go with these gentlemen."

"Where to?"

The General did not answer. He and an aide left with Harold.

On the following day, Harold was roused in the early hours of the morning. A young airman in fatigues brought him breakfast. The fellow was quite excited.

"Are you going to get outside today?" the airman asked.

"I'm supposed to leave here soon. Why?" answered Harold.

"Because you'll see it. It's quite a sight. Brighter than a star. Some scientist on the radio said that it's getting so bright we'll see it in the daytime."

"See what, young man. You're not making any sense to me."

"Oh, I'm sorry. They think its a Nova, an exploding star or something. But they really don't know for sure. Anyhow, you can't miss it when you go out. Just look up. I've got to

295

go, sir. Have a good day."

Harold prayed silently as he walked out under the star-studded sky of the early morning. In less than three hours, the sun would turn the desert into a furnace of heat. He was escorted to a staff car. The General and his aide stood beside it gazing upwards. Harold too glanced up and saw it. A bluish-white object, brighter than any star, blazed brightly in the sky.

"Quite a sight, eh, Stanton? I'm not much into astronomy but they say it's something like a Nova. I bet Doctor Huneker is elated over it."

"Dr. Huneker?"

"Surely you know Joe Huneker. He runs CAPS. It's a civilian cover operation for our operations."

"Oh, yes. I remember now from our Bluepaper briefing. CAPS is the Center for Aerial Phenomena Study."

"Correct. He's an astronomer. That bright thing up there probably means more to him than most of us on the Board. Anyway, let's get going. The others will be waiting for us."

The General's aide stopped the staff car in front of a low white glazed brick building. It was surrounded by a high barbed wire fence. Harold was brought inside and ushered into a small auditorium. The sign above the door read *Classified Session In Progress*. The General motioned toward a table up on a stage-like platform.

"All right, Stanton. You and I will sit up there behind the table. When everybody's here, I'll introduce you. Then it's all yours. What you say had better be worth all the trouble it's been gathering these people here. We have quite an assortment from the Outside Command Board. Highranking intelligence officers, think-tank people and several brilliant scientists that have been working for us secretly for years. Everyone here has made unbreakable life-time commitments to our Project. Oh, oh. Here comes our latest member, thanks to that scoundrel of a Priest. You can thank him in your Heaven for the hell he's caused us here. If it weren't for him, many dedicated personnel would still be alive today. Even your wife would be alive. Think about it, my friend. See what your superstitions have done?"

"But he's wearing a white collar. He must be a minister or a priest," Harold exclaimed.

"He, Stanton, represents the so-called Holy See of the Roman Catholic Church. He is the highest ranking member of Vatican Intelligence. The Pope threatened to publicly release the Vatican's findings on UFOs unless we guaranteed Vatican representation on our Board. We were amazed how much your 'Father Pat' and others had pieced together over the years. Their operatives would put the CIA and the KGB to shame. I'll introduce you. I have no choice. Here he is.

"Good morning. Monsignor."

"Good morning, General. We meet again so soon. Your message reached me just in time. I was to fly from Washington to Rome this morning. Instead I find myself whisked here overnight. So, this is our Mr. Stanton?"

"Yes. Father Duval, this is Harold Stanton."

"How do you do, Mr. Stanton. I want to express His Holiness's appreciation for assisting Father O'Malley in so many ways. I know my saying this must rub the General the wrong way, so to say. But, I'm sure as a fellow professional that he respects what we've accomplished. Please know that what happened at Phoenix Base 3 is deplored by His Holiness. If we had but known what was happening, perhaps we could have prevented this tragedy. I'm very sorry about your wife."

The priest grasped Harold's hand warmly and then rejoined a number of others milling about at the back of the auditorium. Finally, the General stood up and banged the table loudly with a gavel.

"Gentlemen. Gentlemen. Please take your seats. Sergeant! Is everybody accounted for on the primary attendance list?"

"Sir. Every United States member of the Board is here except Lt. Colonel Donald Meyers and Doctor Joseph

Huneker. The Colonel is in South America. The Doctor hasn't shown up yet, sir. No foreign reps were notified other than Monsignor Duval because of the short turn-around time."

"Have you checked out the video tape system? We must have an audio-visual record of this."

"Yes, sir. The primary and back-up systems are in a go position."

"Excellent. So. Huneker isn't here yet, eh? Perhaps that damn light up in the sky holds more fascination for him than our meeting. Keep trying to reach him. I would very much like to have his opinions on what Stanton here has to say. I find it hard to believe that he's not here. Whatever is keeping him away had better be very important."

Harold stood up and placed his hand on the General's shoulder.

"I beg your pardon, sir. I must start my address right now if I'm to fit in everything I want to say before sunrise."

"Stanton, I don't pretend to know what you mean by such an enigmatic statement. Ordinarily I would never humor anyone like this. But, you're the last link we have with our former captive and our missing psychologist. You can get started.

"Gentlemen? This is Harold Stanton. He is the last surviving member of Base 3. You all know what we had hoped he could do for us. You're also acquainted with the Rainier programming hypothesis. Stanton was at Rainier when the prisoner was abducted. We feel reasonably sure that there's a connection between these two events. However, Stanton here has elected to wait until this morning to tell us about it. Since what he has to say may be of vital importance, each of you were called to hear his story first hand.

"What he has to say may appear, and I quote him, 'nonsensical' to us. But, may I remind you, as well as myself, of the evolution of thought we've all experienced. We've slowly learned to accept the high strangeness and

298

absurdities attached to the alien operations. So. let us keep open minds. And please, regardless of what is said, no interruptions. Harold Stanton? We are ready to hear from you."

Harold spoke. But, even as he did he felt that the words were not fully his own. His experience? Yes. But, the formulation and oratory were of another. It was Melchizedek's last legacy to Mankind. His programmed message through Harold was addressed to those who truly sought to know the truth about the alien visitations.

The audience sat spellbound as if mesmerized. The two hours passed swiftly. Harold rehearsed every detail of his experience with the mysterious Melchizedek. His descriptions were vivid and pictorial. There was little doubt in anyone's mind that he was genuinely reliving events that were absolutely real to him. One could have heard the proverbial pin drop as he told of the *Message of Judgment* spiraling outward to the center of our galaxy.

"And there, the signal will be received and relayed to the Messengers from Eternity. They in turn will signal the Word of the True One Who Is. He shall come with myriads of heavenly beings to this island of stars. On this planet he will judge both those in this vibrational state and those who dwell in the Netherland. So you see, gentlemen, what happens here on our planet is really up to us. We have brought all of this upon ourselves. *Mankind has been weighed and is found wanting.* Thank you for allowing me to speak."

Flustered, General Webster shot to his feet and shouted: "But you haven't told us where this signal was sent from and where this Melchizedek person is right now. And the woman, where is she?"

"I will not answer those questions. They relate to the physical safety of two persons that I care for very much. I will not tell you."

"You won't tell us, eh? All right, Stanton, have it your own way. We'll deal with you later on our own terms. Your honeymoon is over. Be seated.

"Now, gentlemen, you have all heard this incredible story by an intelligent sane individual. He is telling the truth as he knows it to be. Everything he has said was analyzed by a sensitive Psychological Stress Evaluator instrument. Any deviations from the truth were to have been brought to my attention immediately. There were no deviations. You've heard his story. Now, let's get down to business.

"In this context, all of you have examined the Fatima Message graciously given us by our newly appointed Vatican representative. You also have read selected intelligence reports on the study of UFO cults. Now, does Stanton's story support the conclusions of Project *Cortez* or not? You, Eric, are chief of Project *Cortez*. How does Stanton's story fit in with the conclusions drawn by your people?"

A bearded man with an ugly scar on his left temple stood up. He turned sidewise and addressed the group.

"Gentlemen. What we've just heard here thoroughly substantiates what we only have just begun to realize. It is Cortez and the Aztec civilization all over again. But, instead of the Spaniards playing Quatzcoatl to deceive the Aztecs, we have aliens of unknown origin playing Mary and Jesus Christ to earthlings. The aliens have chosen to accomodate at least two of the world's great religions in their attempt to condition humans prior to conquest. You may wonder why Judaism and Christianity are being used. Perhaps it is because they are better represented among the technologically superior peoples of this planet. Already, UFO cults, some employing the mythological name of this Melchizedek himself, are growing in numbers. I might also add that a number of well known Christian and Jewish writers are actually equating UFOs with the good and bad angels mentioned in Biblical writings. Even Billy Graham presented this possibility in some book he wrote about Angels.

"In short, gentlemen, it would seem that the aliens are

beginning to groom a large number of what we might call *control groups*. These groups, if allowed the proper publicity, may influence large segments of the populace into really believing that the so-called UFOs are benign Saviours sent to rescue mankind. Let us also remember that the aliens have the ability to control individual human minds. Look at the CE III cases. Look at Stanton. It's obvious that they have the capability to influence the minds of many people.

"Thus, Project *Cortez* has concluded that the aliens' eventual objective is to condition the general populace to welcome them as bodily fulfillments of religious beliefs. World governments could be thrown into chaos overnight if this should happen. Religion is a powerful and ancient phenomenon. It cuts across the complete spectrum of social strata.

"No one is exempt. Religion grips the minds of presidents, kings, governors, policemen. It influences all ranks within the armed forces as well as the common civilian man on the street. Religion can brainwash a man or woman into believing almost anything. The Jonesville mass suicide some years back is a classical example.

"I need not remind you that Phoenix Base 3 was destroyed because a five-star general was duped by religionists."

Before Eric Holtzer could say another word, Father Duval stepped forward and interrupted.

"You and all of you. Why aren't you willing to accept the possible religious *reality* inherent in so many UFO cases? Haven't you considered the possibility that these alien craft do represent the Second Coming of our Lord with His Angels?"

General Webster pounded the table with his fist.

"Damn it, Monsignor. Religious beliefs are not part of the objectivity that undergirds this Project. You have seen first hand what damage such stupid beliefs have already done to us. How can you stand there and suggest this to us? May I remind you that your very presence here among us is due to sheer unmitigated blackmail? May I also remind you that there is a firm mutual agreement between your Superior and myself? Your place on the Board is strictly on a consulting basis. We want your opinion, and those of your associates, concerning the impact that these so-called UFOs have and could have upon the religious beliefs of people on this planet."

Harold listened in shock and total dismay. Finally, he could take it no longer. He leapt to his feet, grabbed the General's gavel and pounded the table in anger.

"General! Do you mean to say that I was brought here to be displayed as some supposed example of alien brainwashing? Don't you believe who that man really is?"

"Calm yourself, Stanton. We believe your Melchizedek is only one of many human abductees in covert league with aliens. His powers of hypnosis have *you*, not us, believing he's the legendary figure of Melchizedek. His so-called Signal of Judgment was probably just a message relating to his rescue. Most likely it was sent to some command ship orbiting somewhere within our Solar System. Why, nothing travels faster than light. By the time your supposed message of judgment reached the center of our galaxy, millions of years would have passed.

"I feel sorry for you, Stanton. You've shown by your own testimony just how much they're able to influence someone without firing a shot."

"But it's true! It's true! That signal will cause the Word to return."

"You're raving like a religious maniac. If your so-called Word, Messiah, or whatever comes here with his supposed angels, we'll be ready for them. Already our new laser weapons have proved highly effective against their craft.

"Your usefulness to us is all over. VIGIL has ways to make you talk. Take him away, sergeant!"

"Keep away from me," Harold shouted as he edged across the stage toward a window facing the east. The rays from the rising sun caused a shaft of light to fall upon the far edge of the elevated platform. Harold approached it, hesitated for a moment and then stepped into the sun's rays.

Instantly, a bright blue flame erupted from the palms of both of his hands! He held up his hands for all to see. A gasp of horror rippled across the auditorium. The Sergeant who had come up on the stage to apprehend Harold stopped dead in his tracks. Doctor Huneker, who had just arrived, stood by the door. The bearded astronomer watched in wonderment as little spurts of blue flame began to erupt all over Harold's body.

"My God," General Webster muttered. "It's, it's the same thing that happened to Saltzman in San Francisco when VIGIL caught up with him. He was working with Ben-Sorek, too."

The General shouted at the dazed group.

"Don't everybody just stand there! Do something! Someone get a fire extinguisher or something."

Harold slowly retraced his steps with some difficulty to the table. He removed the microphone from off its stand and sank into a chair.

"Don't any of you come near me," he announced matter-of-factly. "This is painless. There's nothing you can do to stop it. You're all fools not to believe what I've just said. In your hands lies the capability to truly prepare our country and the world for the greatest of all events. But, if you choose to serve the Dragon and his servants, you will all perish with them. You, Monsignor Duval: I beg you to believe me. Tell the Pope what has happened here. Spread the truth throughout the world in order that people might prepare themselves for His coming. I, I have but a few last things to say. They come from God's Holy Word. I memorized these verses and now I know why. In them I have substituted the word *ships* for *clouds*. The Biblical writers would call such ships clouds. Hear well, gentlemen. They are the words spoken by the Word of the True One Who Is. They will be my last words to anyone on this earth."

No one moved. No one spoke. Everyone stood transfixed

in horror at the incredible sight unfolding before their very eyes. With a trembling hand, Father Duval made the sign of the Cross.

Harold was now glowing a bright fluorescent blue. One could just make out the outline of his body behind the flickering aura. He bowed his head and propped the microphone between his knees. His voice was weak and faltering. But, the words came over the P.A. system clearly, deliberately, almost machinelike in their cadence.

And, then shall appear the sign of the Son of Man in heaven

And then shall all the tribes of the earth mourn.

And they shall see the Son of Man coming in ships of heaven with power and glory.

And then shall he send his angels, and shall gather his elect from the four winds.

Two shall be in the field; the one shall be taken and the other left.

Two shall be grinding at the mill; the one shall be taken and the other left.

We who are alive shall be caught up together in the ships.

My coming can be compared with a man going on a long trip to another country. He lays out his employee's work for them to do while he is gone, and tells the gatekeeper to watch for his arrival.

There are many homes up there where my Father lives and I am going to get them ready for your coming. But, the question is: "When I, the Son of Mankind, return, how many will I find who have, have, have faith?"

Harold's flaming body slumped over in the chair. The microphone crashed to the floor. The dark outline of his body began to disintegrate within the mass of flickering blue flames. A man in fatigues rushed in the door and down the aisle carrying a fire extinguisher. He emptied its contents on the flaming mass on the chair. The foam dissipated into nothingness upon contact. Suddenly, there came a bright

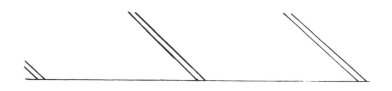

Blue flame began to erupt all over Harold's body.

blinding flash. The area around the chair became as bright as the sun. Everyone covered their faces. Some stepped back. Others hit the floor. The sergeant jumped off the stage. Then the blazing light dimmed. The chair was empty.

Slowly, solemnly, members of the Board moved up to the stage. They each stared incredulously at the dark sooty spot on the chair which a few minutes ago had been Harold Stanton.

The General finally broke the eerie silence that gripped everyone.

"This, this, gentlemen, is what can assumedly happen to any of the many contactees who are placed in a compromising position. Look. The chair wasn't even scorched!"

Another man moved by the huddled group of men and walked up on the stage. He cautiously approached the chair. He stuck his finger in the black soot and held it up for everyone to see.

"As all of you know, my specialty is pathology. You have no idea how utterly fantastic this really is. It would take sustained temperatures of over 2000 degrees Farenheit to reduce human bones to this. Yet the chair, the table and the floor show no signs of even being scorched!"

Then, another voice caused everyone to turn around and face the rear of the auditorium. Doctor Huneker was approaching them.

"What I have to say is even more incredible, my friends."

The Doctor's face revealed the strain that still racked his mind with unbelief.

"The Beta signal, gentlemen. The signal from Rainier!"

"What about the signal, Doctor?" demanded General Webster. "How can you talk about signals at a time like this? And where the hell have you been?"

"Hear me out, everyone. The new orbiting Beta detectors are picking up a strong new signal. It has the same parameters as the signal which emanated from Rainier!"

"So?" replied the General caustically. "It's probably just

an acknowledgment from their command ship somewhere within our solar system. I trust that you and your associates have calculated the signal's lag time and have triangulated the ship's position."

"That signal is not coming from any command ship within our solar system. It's coming from what most observatories think is a unique kind of Nova. That thing that you see out there in the sky is why I'm late in arriving. We've checked and re-checked. The signals are an exact repetition. Our refurbished Beta Detection network has provided highly accurate data for triangulation. Those signals are emanating from the exact directional coordinates of that Nova-like object!"

"But, that's impossible," another astrophysicist interrupted. "Latest reports from observatories indicate that the Nova is located within the presumed nucleus of our Galaxy. Rough estimates of its distance place it up to 30,000 light years away from our solar system. If those calculations are correct, there can't possibly be a connection. Why, the light from the Nova or whatever it is must have started its journey here 30,000 years ago!"

"But, Dr. Turner," Doctor Huneker replied. "That light is pulsating. The Palomar graphs show that its pulsation rate also matches the exact graphical parameters exhibited by the Rainier Beta signal."

"Preposterous! There must be some mistake."

"Excuse me, Doctor Turner. Let me finish. Palomar also picked up another new bright Nova with exact matching pulsations of light. We are now aiming a number of the larger Beta dishes at it."

"Another one? Where?" quipped Doctor Turner.

"It can't be seen with the naked eye. But, it's very prominent even with a telescope of moderate size. It's located within the Andromeda Galaxy."

"But that's impossible," sputtered Doctor Turner. "The Andromeda Galaxy is over two million light years away!"

"Let's keep calm, gentlemen," General Webster retorted.

"May I remind you, as an intelligence specialist of many years, that we are observing only what is *apparent*. There may be, and probably is, another answer to all of this. Remember always that we're dealing with a vastly superior technology. The aliens, in conjunction with what Stanton was programmed to tell us, may be purposely causing our instruments to detect that which they want us to believe is happening. What do you think, Huneker? Is that possible? If not, what is the alternative?"

"Let's face it, General and fellow Board members. We are dealing with the unknown. In spite of all our efforts over the years to discover the origin and motivation of these visitations, we still just don't know. Now, in answer to your question, it's possible that they've created such an illusion. How could we deny such a possibility? Their technology in so many ways appears magical to us. But, as an astronomer, not an intelligence specialist, I feel that this is highly improbable. However, the alternative that you ask me to comment upon is equally, if even not more, improbable."

"And what is that?" demanded the General.

"It is that the Rainier signal, whatever its content, actually *has* travelled to the center of the Galaxy in a matter of hours. There, it was received by unknown intelligences with incomprehensible powers. They, in turn, have relayed it to our neighboring Galaxy. There, conceivably, it again was received and is being relayed elsewhere. As soon as night falls, observatories in the United States that are on contract with us will be examining other nearby Galaxies for similar pulsating objects."

Father Duval pushed his way through the group of men and stood beside Doctor Huneker.

"I feel compelled to suggest an even more astounding alternative. At least, I'm sure that it will appear so to all of you. I find the coincidental appearances and similarities of these deep space objects with the Rainier signal most intriguing. Did not our Mr. Stanton himself quote

Melchizedek, or whoever, as saying, and I'll try to quote: 'Behold. How great a forest a tiny spark can set ablaze.' Isn't the Nova equivalent to the forest fire and the Rainier signal equivalent to the spark? And again, I say this quite seriously, regardless of your prejudices. Do not overlook the possibility that Stanton's story is true in *all* of its details. I too am an intelligence specialist. From experience, I have found it foolhardy to reject hypotheses on the basis of prejudice. These so-called intelligences, Doctor Huneker, that you say may possess powers beyond our comprehension — Could they not very well be the Elohim mentioned within the Holy Scriptures? Should we overlook the possibility that the Signal might be exactly what Mr. Stanton was told it was: *A Signal of Judgment passed upon us by our moral superiors?*"

Chapter Twenty-Two

Epilogue

Halfway across the continent, the sun had risen two hours earlier. Its rays had poured into the bedroom windows of an old farm house in Sebeka, Minnesota. Myrna and her father awakened to a new day and a fresh beginning.

As father and daughter strolled hand-in-hand along the newly plowed field, they gazed upward wonderingly. A brilliant dot of light was accentuated against the deep blue sky. A recent newscast had mentioned that it was already starting to fade.

Thoughts of Harold passed through Myrna's mind as she gazed at the awesome sight. Could it be possible that Harold's mysterious mission at Mount Rainier had something to do with it? This strange light was alarming the whole world.

Meanwhile, over a thousand miles away, Harold felt himself slipping out of his flaming body. For several minutes he floated unseen above the horror-stricken Board members of Outside Command. Then a phosphorescent cloud slowly materialized near him. His body involuntarily merged with it. Again he found himself spinning through a long dark tunnel toward a bright light.

Scenes from his life again flashed on and off before him. This time they did not begin with his childhood. They began with Harold watching himself being pulled from the river. He watched agents McDonough and Coleman take turns applying artificial respiration to his soaked, lifeless body. Then the rest of his life whisked by in life-like detail.

First, the ambulance with its flashing lights. Then the

hospital, Base 3, Myrna, his reunion with Helen. The bluepaper briefings. Father Pat. Next came Beta Nova, the Fatima poem and his first confrontation with Melchizedek. Soon he again was reliving his trip through the ancient past: Adapa, Abraham, the Prophets, Bethlehem. Onward he streaked through the ages. At last there came his escape from Base 3, the experience at Rainier, his recapture and his translation.

Harold shot out of the tunnel and merged with pure white living light. Every facet of his life, at that very moment, was scrutinized and judged by the light.

Harold felt as if he were engulfed in pure love. His weightless body floated effortlessly through the glowing mass into a beautiful green meadow. The colors of the grass and the flowers seemed more real than real. They swayed gently before a scented breeze. It was as if their earthly counterparts had been but tarnished reflections.

A thrill of expectation welled within him as he looked out across the rippling grass. There again was the hedge. Behind it several people were waving and beckoning to him. There was Helen, Mom and Dad Jamieson, and — could it really be? There was Father Pat with a grin spread from ear to ear.

The branches of the hedge parted and allowed Harold to pass over to the other side. He threw his arms around Helen. He hugged and kissed the Jamiesons. He turned and grasped Father Pat's broad hands. Not a word was spoken. Somehow, thoughts flowed effortlessly. Then, Father Pat pointed to a lone figure standing apprehensively under a tree in the distance. Harold looked. Could it be? Yes, it was. It was Alethia. His mother.

Harold glanced back at Helen, the Jamiesons and Father Pat. Each nodded in assent. Smiles beamed on their faces. He turned and walked hesitantly across the field toward the tree. He kept looking behind him to assure himself that Helen and the others were still there. They were and their thoughts urged him to go on to his mother alone.

Harold walked hesitantly up to the beautiful young girl

It was Alethia. His mother.

staring up at him. It seemed such a paradox that she could be his mother. He was old enough to be her father. Yet, somehow he sensed that things and people were ageless here. A look of love and wonderment played across her gentle face. Harold held out his arms and embraced her. Then a sweet musical-like voice sounded within his mind.

Welcome, my son. The circle is now completed. The fruit of my womb has now fulfilled the will of the Elohim. You have fulfilled the purpose for which you were created. You have provided aid to our faithful servant, he who even now sleeps. He who now waits, as we do, for the return of the Word of the True One That Is.

His message now kindles Signal Stars from island to island to the Messengers from Eternity. Almost, the Dragon succeeded in breaking the thread of destiny, that thread which has stretched from Father Abraham to the final judgment and destiny of Mankind.

Soon, whenever the True One wills, a vast armada of ships of light will bear the Word and His servants to us. They will complete the redemption of this Island of stars, including the orb called earth. It was your body, your life, that provided the vital tie. You were the living link that will now result in the final overthrow and destruction of the Dragon and his servants. You, my son, have restored the *Melchizedek Connection.*

CPSIA information can be obtained
at www.ICGtesting.com
Printed in the USA
LVHW112145230720
661407LV00001B/166